Praise for the n
au

Dance of Desire
"On a scale of 1-5 stars, this is definitely a 6 star book! . . . Don't miss this one!"—6 stars, *Affaire de Coeur* Magazine

My Lady's Treasure
"Filled with lively characters, a strong, suspenseful plot and a myriad of romantic scenes *My Lady's Treasure* is a powerful, poignant tale that will keep readers turning pages until the very end."—5 stars and Reviewer's Choice Award, The Road to Romance

A Knight's Vengeance
"Kean (*Dance of Desire*) delivers rich local color and sparkling romantic tension in this fast-paced medieval revenge plot."— *Publishers Weekly*

A Knight's Reward
"Ms. Kean has done it again with her talent to capture the reader's attention with all the elements of a must-read. The opening pages are filled with a wonderful tension that sets the stage for a great story."—Fresh Fiction

A Knight's Temptation
"…an entertaining medieval romance brimming with sass, action, adventure, and lots of sexual chemistry."—*Booklist*

A Knight's Persuasion
"…stirring adventure, superb characters, and enticing heroes. Ms. Kean continues to snag the reader with her fast-paced tales of heroic knights."—4-1/2 stars, *Affaire de Coeur* Magazine

Also by Catherine Kean

A Knight to Remember (Novella)
Bound by His Kiss (Novella)
Dance of Desire
My Lady's Treasure
One Knight Under the Mistletoe (Novella)

Knight's Series Novels:
A Knight's Vengeance (Book 1)
A Knight's Reward (Book 2)
A Knight's Temptation (Book 3)
A Knight's Persuasion (Book 4)

A Knight's Seduction

Seduction

Knight's Series Book 5

By

Catherine Kean

For Cynthia,
I hope you enjoy
Tye and Claire's adventure.
Warmest wishes,
Catherine Kean

A Knight's Seduction © 2015 Catherine Kean

Cover design by Kim Killion, The Killion Group

ISBN-13: 978-1514600726
ISBN-10: 1514600722

Also available in eBook.

Catherine Kean
P.O. Box 917624
Longwood, FL 32791-7624
www.catherinekean.com

Dedication

This book is dedicated to all of the readers who contacted me to ask when Tye's story would be published. I cannot tell you how much your kind emails and messages meant to me. It's very humbling—and thrilling—to know that other people love my characters as much as I do.

Many thanks also to my beautiful sister, Amanda Caux, for the insightful comments on an early draft of this novel; to Caroline Phipps and Teresa Elliott Brown, for the fantastic critiques and wonderful friendship; and to Alicia Clarke and Cheryl Duhaime, dear friends who have been with me from the very first draft of my very first Knight's Series book. In so many ways, you've all enriched my life. Thank you.

Chapter One

Branton Keep, Moydenshire, England
Summer, 1214

T ye raised his head at the *creak* of the dungeon's main
door. In his dark cell at the far end of the prison, he
pushed up from the dirt floor where he'd sat dozing, his
legs stretched out in front of him, his back against the moldy stone
wall.

Tye rose with an awkward lurch. Grimacing, he
maneuvered his splinted right leg until he stood upright, ignoring
the *clank* of the chains locked around his wrists and bare ankles.
How he loathed the fetters that secured him to the wall and kept
him trapped and isolated—just as the great lord Geoffrey de
Lanceau, ruler of Branton Keep and all of Moydenshire, wanted.

Standing now, his weight on his good leg, Tye rolled his
taut shoulder muscles and flexed his fingers, a ritual before every
battle. Anticipation rushed like potent wine through his veins. Was
he about to face de Lanceau, his father?

He smirked. He hoped so.

He'd waited too damned long to stand face to face again
with his sire. Since he'd been taken prisoner in the battle at
Waddesford Keep and chained in this cell, he'd lost count of the
days. His only measure of them passing had been the healing of his
leg; the bone had been cracked but not fully broken, his sire's men
had decided after examining it.

From the morning Tye had been captured, however, he'd
seen his father only once. Tye had refused to cooperate when
interrogated. When the only way left to get answers out of him had

been physical punishment, his sire had ordered Tye taken back to his cell. De Lanceau had walked away and hadn't returned.

He would be back, though. This was his castle, his dungeon, and Tye wasn't a common thief or petty criminal like the others in the cells. Tye knew his value as a prisoner; he had information de Lanceau needed. His lordship might not believe in torturing captives, but from all Tye knew of him, he also wasn't a man to neglect his duties—or give up before he got what he wanted.

Do as you will, Father. I am not afraid of you. A cruel laugh burned in Tye's throat. *You, though, should be afraid of me.*

Alone in his cell, Tye had imagined how the meeting might play out, how he'd answer—or not—his sire's inevitable questions, how he'd make the encounter wholly unpleasant for the man who'd made Tye's own life a living hell.

Tye shook with the force of his rage. Years ago, his mother had told him how she'd been de Lanceau's lover, and how de Lanceau had cruelly rejected her and her claim that Tye was his bastard. Tye was twenty years old, and still, his father refused to acknowledge him—and likely never would.

Tye was *naught* to de Lanceau.

Tye clenched his jaw, for of all the questions he planned to ask his sire, he wanted one answered in particular: why, in a crucial moment of their last battle, de Lanceau had reached out a hand and tried to save him from falling from Waddesford Keep's battlements. *Why* had his lordship bothered, if he didn't believe Tye was his own flesh and blood?

The offer of rescue must have been a trick—and Tye meant to get de Lanceau to confess just that. What delicious irony 'twould be, to wrest an admission of deception from the lord who was praised throughout England for upholding truth and honor.

The man Tye intended to kill.

Today, if he got the chance.

An echoing *thud* marked the closing of the dungeon door.

Tye stood very still, his head tilted to better catch the sounds reaching his cell. Voices carried: two men speaking.

Was one of them de Lanceau? Tye's hands balled into fists. The manacles dug into the sore flesh on his wrists.

Footsteps sounded on the hard-packed floor. At first, he couldn't discern what the men were saying, but as they walked into the center of the dungeon, their words became distinct.

"—you certain he will be well guarded, milord?"

Tye recognized the speaker: one of the regular guards, a gray-haired man with a cropped beard. There were always three men-at-arms on duty inside the dungeon, although one had been sent home a short while ago because of a bad bellyache; his replacement would arrive soon. That meant only one guard stood by the main door, which would only benefit Tye if he got free of his chains.

He must find a way.

He'd kill his father, overpower the guards, and then escape.

"Believe me, I understand the importance of keeping the prisoner secured, especially with such unrest in King John's lands. 'Tis why I came at night. I also brought four mercenaries. They will help guard him during the journey."

Tye frowned. That voice wasn't his sire's; 'twas deeper in pitch. The visitor's manner of speaking was also more refined, as if he spent his days among wealthy noblemen in the London courts. Tye fought bitter disappointment and wondered who the prisoner was that they were discussing.

"Aye," the dungeon guard said, "but—"

"He will not escape. Certainly not once he is delivered to the King."

The footfalls stopped. "I still think you should wait for Lord de Lanceau. I can send a messenger to the castle at Wode. Lord Brackendale, the father of his lordship's wife, Lady Elizabeth, has taken gravely ill, and they have gone to visit. These arrangements for the prisoner are not normal—"

"True, they are not, because of the man in question. The information he holds is of great interest to the crown. King John did not want anyone to know the prisoner was being moved. He feared word might leak to his friends and they would try to free him before I got here."

A troubled sigh echoed. "I understand, but de Lanceau's orders—"

"Surely de Lanceau would not refuse a request from the King?" Impatience tinged the stranger's voice. "As you saw, the writ is signed and sealed by one of King John's closest advisors."

"I... Of course, you are right."

The footfalls resumed.

Torchlight brightened the area in front of Tye's cell, vanquishing the shadows. *The visitor had been sent for him.* Eyes watering, he squinted in the sudden light that washed into his prison.

Fingering aside his grimy hair, he studied the two men: the older guard, holding the torch and wearing a chain mail hauberk over his shirt and hose; and the tall, broad-shouldered man garbed in a brown fur cloak. The sumptuous garment swept to the top of his brown leather boots. As he grabbed hold of one of the floor-to-ceiling bars and looked in, a large ring on his hand glinted. The gold had been crafted into a skull with green gems for eyes. Tye had seen that kind of ring before, designed to hold poison.

Tye met the stranger's stare. Drawing on the hatred pulsing in his blood, Tye narrowed his eyes to a glare.

The man didn't look away. His lips tilted in a thin smile. "This is the man rumored to be de Lanceau's bastard?"

"Aye," the guard said.

"You are certain?"

"I am." Reaching to the key ring at his belt, the guard added, "Mayhap you should summon your mercenaries to help restrain him."

The stranger chortled. "I can handle this one."

Really? Tye wanted to laugh. This stranger was a fat-headed fool. All the better for a chance at escape.

"How will you keep him under control? You have manacles?"

"I do." The stranger reached inside his cloak, as though to draw the cuffs out.

The guard nodded, and the handful of keys clinked in his hand. "Henry is also standing guard at the doorway. If by chance Tye should get past us, Henry knows what to do."

"Let us get on with it, then."

The guard unlocked the cell door.

Mentally blocking out the pain of his mending leg, Tye dropped to an awkward fighting stance. He might be chained, but he sure as hell wasn't helpless. The tournaments he'd entered while growing up in France—some fair, many not—had taught him how to defend himself in close combat. His scars proved how often he'd fought for his life, and how often the spectators had cheered his name as champion.

The door swung open, and the guard shoved the key ring back onto his belt. At the same moment, the stranger drew his hand from his cloak and eased his fingers into his sleeve. As he withdrew his hand, torchlight flickered on metal—a thin knife that settled in his grip as if it belonged there.

A chill skittered through Tye. He recognized the look on the man's face; he'd faced it many times in battle. The stranger intended to kill.

Seeing the dagger, the guard's eyes widened. "What—?" He dropped the torch and grabbed for the sword at his left hip.

Lunging, the stranger slammed the dagger into the older man's neck, unprotected by his hauberk.

Tye recoiled in shock.

"Inside," the stranger said, shoving the guard into the cell. The wounded man choked and clutched at his injury. Blood oozed between his fingers.

"Henry!" the guard gurgled.

"Who are you?" Tye growled at the stranger. Was he an assassin? The man had said he'd been sent by King John, but de Lanceau could have paid this lout to murder Tye. The dungeon guard had to die, too, so it looked like Tye had tried to escape but failed.

"Ha—" the guard cried.

The dagger slashed again. The guard stumbled, hit the wall near Tye, and fell, groaning. The stranger delivered a swift kick, slamming the older man's head into the wall. He collapsed, dead.

The stranger snatched the torch from the ground, shoved it into an iron bracket on the wall inside the cell, and faced Tye.

"Who are you?" Tye demanded.

"Braden," the man said in a low voice. "Your mother sent me."

"My *mother?*" Wariness became a shrill, warning hum in Tye's head. "She is imprisoned—"

"Veronique Desjardin is your mother, is she not?"

That fact wasn't a secret; many folk in Moydenshire knew it. "She is."

"We must hurry. Later, all will be explained. Now, do as I tell you." Braden grabbed the keys from the dead guard and stepped toward Tye.

Tye didn't relax his fighting stance. "Why should I believe you?"

Braden's brows rose. "Why would you not? I am here to help you escape."

Tye braced his back against the wall, readying to strike out. "How do I know you will not unchain me and then try to cut my throat?"

A grin curved Braden's mouth; he obviously hadn't missed Tye's emphasis on the word try. "Veronique said you would doubt me. She said to tell you this: she promised at the end of the battle at Waddesford Keep that your fight with de Lanceau was not over. With my help, you will get your chance to slay your sire. 'Tis what you want, aye?"

"Oy!" called a voice from a short distance away: the guard named Henry. "What is going on back there?"

Braden tossed the keys to Tye then grabbed the chain attached to Tye's right arm and shook it, causing a clanking sound.

Squinting at the keys in the shifting torchlight, Tye cursed. Every key looked the same. He shoved one into the lock of the manacles on his left wrist. The chain clanked again, pulling on his arm. "Hellfire! Stop pulling—"

"Hurry," Braden muttered. "Quit fighting, Tye," he shouted over his shoulder, his voice booming. "'Twill make matters worse for you."

"He is resisting?" Henry sounded young and nervous.

Tye shoved a second key into the lock. A third. Then Braden's palm hit the side of his face—a smack that would be heard throughout the prison.

"Bastard!" Tye shook his head to clear his vision.

"Find the damned key," Braden bit out.

"I will get reinforcements," Henry shouted.

"Nay!" Braden commanded. "Come to the cell—"

"I have my orders," Henry said, followed by the sound of brisk footsteps. He was heading for the short flight of stairs to the main dungeon door.

Braden hissed through his teeth. "If he shouts the alarm... I will try to stop him." He raced out of the cell. "Henry!"

Grabbing another key, Tye pushed it into the lock. He would *not* lose this chance to escape. He would *not*—

With a faint rasp, the key slid all the way in. He turned it, and the lock clicked. The manacle sprang open.

As he freed his right wrist, he heard the dungeon door crash open, felt a draft sweep over his ankles. Bending at the waist, cursing the awkwardness enforced by the splint, he focused on unlocking the rest of his chains.

Still holding the ring of keys, he hobbled out of his cell. He forced his stiff limbs to move faster, savored the feel of lethargic muscles fully flexing and stretching. He craved air that was free of the dank taint of the dungeon—the smell of *freedom*.

"Oy! Give me the keys," a toothless man said from his nearby cell.

"Give them to me," another begged, thrusting his grubby hands through the bars.

Slowing, Tye shoved the keys into the nearest man's hands. Tye grinned, imagining his sire's fury when he learned that not only had Tye escaped, but so had all of the other criminals. De Lanceau would waste days trying to recapture the prisoners.

Ignoring the excited cries from the cells behind him, Tye limped on. Two burly men in leather armor had entered through the doorway, dragging Henry backward between them. The guard's blond head drooped to his chest. His arms dangled, as though he was barely conscious, and blood oozed from a gash at his temple. A third person, slender and wearing a hooded black cloak, held a knife at his throat.

"Good boy," a woman murmured. "Keep quiet, now, if you want to live."

Tye's heart kicked. Hard. He knew that voice.

The woman glanced his way. He caught a glimpse of pale

skin, the curve of a crimson red mouth, before his attention was claimed by Braden, walking through the doorway with a cloak draped over his arm. After a quick study of the darkness outside, Braden shut the wooden panel behind him.

Her left arm held close to her body, the woman reached up her right hand and drew back her hood, revealing long red hair tied at her nape. Despite her weeks in prison and de Lanceau's hatred of her, she'd still found a way to get the henna she used to dye her tresses. Remarkable. A wry smile tugged at Tye's mouth. Then again, he should hardly be surprised; she'd always been resourceful, especially when it came to outwitting de Lanceau.

"Mother." Tye hobbled toward her.

"Tye."

"How is your arm? 'Twas broken when I last saw you."

"'Tis healing well. At least 'twas my left one and not my right." Her features seemed haggard, and not just because of her injury or age. While imprisoned, she'd undoubtedly been deprived of the expensive herbal creams she liked to slather upon her skin to keep herself looking young. But in her amber eyes, he saw the same need that burned as hot as fire in his own soul: a desire to destroy de Lanceau.

"Veronique, we must hurry," Braden urged.

"I know, Love." She gestured to the mercenaries, who shoved Henry back against the stone wall. Sweat and blood ran down his face. He appeared dazed and about eighteen years old—if that. His blue eyes fixed on Tye. As Henry's stare sharpened, anger contorted his features.

"Did he shout the alarm?" Tye asked Braden.

"Nay. The mercenaries stopped him before he could cry out."

"Good."

"Still, we need to get away from here, as soon as we can."

"Agreed." Tye hobbled to his mother. She met him partway, her strides still ripe with the sensuality that drew men to her like flies to sticky jam. Those lovers clearly included Braden; the man's gaze drifted over her with undisguised lust.

"Are you all right?" she asked, embracing Tye with her good arm. She smelled of night air and musty wool.

"I am. You?" he said against her hair.

"Better now that I have found you."

Tye's arms tightened around her. He'd missed her, too. Shame gnawed at him as well. He shouldn't have heeded the voice in his mind that, in his days alone in his cell, had whispered she'd abandoned him, left him to rot, because he'd failed her: He hadn't managed to kill his sire in the battle at Waddesford Keep.

Had de Lanceau realized that such cruel thoughts would haunt Tye? Had he known that in isolation, Tye's conscience would turn against him and fester until it drove him near mad?

The *bastard*.

As his mother drew out of Tye's arms, questions swarmed in his mind: how she'd gotten free, how she'd managed to get a missive from the King that would fool de Lanceau's guards; how she'd met Braden. Now, though, was not the time for such matters. "Braden is right," Tye said. "We should leave."

"We will. There is but one last detail to take care of." Her right hand tightening on her dagger, she faced Henry.

"You…will not…get away," the lad ground out.

Veronique tittered. "*You* will stop us?"

"'Tis…my duty…to Lord de Lanceau." The fingers of his right arm, pinned by one of the mercenaries, curled, as though he longed to draw his sword, still belted at his waist.

"Driven by honor," Veronique mocked. "Sorry, but you are going to die."

Uncertainty flickered in Henry's eyes. His head wobbled as she halted in front of him, but he bravely held her stare.

"First, I shall cut off your bollocks. Then your manhood."

"W-what?' Henry choked.

"Mother." Tye couldn't hold back a shudder.

"'Twill be a slow, painful death. How shocked de Lanceau will be when he finds you." She smiled at the lad, who'd turned white with horror. Her attention slid greedily down the young man's heaving chest to his groin, hidden by his chain-mail tunic.

"Nay!" he spluttered. "Please. I am…betrothed."

"You will not be of much use to your future bride, will you?"

The lad whimpered.

Veronique laughed. "Is your betrothed pretty? Does she love you? Does her body weep for your touch?"

Tye had seen enough of his mother's cruelty to know he didn't want to watch her mutilate this man—especially when they needed to get away. *"Mother."*

"I will be quick."

"Nay!" Henry cried, struggling against his captors.

"Veronique," Braden snapped.

"Hold," Tye said, crossing to his mother's side. When she arched her brows in irritation, he said, "I need a weapon. I will take his sword."

Pinned by the mercenaries, Henry glowered as Tye unfastened the belt buckle and whipped away the blade nestled in its leather scabbard. Straightening, Tye held Henry's gaze, a deliberate taunt. The lad spat in his face. Tye smothered a smile— he'd secretly hoped for such a reaction—wiped the slick mess from his cheek, then slammed his fist into Henry's jaw. The lad went limp.

"Now, we leave," Tye said, buckling on the belt.

Veronique frowned at Henry, collapsed in the mercenaries' grasp. "You struck him on purpose."

That's right. I did.

"You did not want me having my way with him."

Right again. I want to escape. Naught will stop me—especially not your perversions.

"He spat in my face. I could not ignore that insult. Now he cannot betray us. Not until he wakes," Tye said. "By then, we will be long gone."

With a disappointed huff, Veronique motioned to the mercenaries. They dropped Henry to the floor and strode to Braden.

"We will discuss your meddling later, Tye," his mother muttered.

"Among other matters." Tye flicked his gaze toward Braden. If Tye was going to trust the man, he needed to know exactly who he was and how he'd contribute to de Lanceau's downfall.

Veronique walked ahead of Tye toward the others

gathered by the doorway. As he followed, a metallic rasp came from behind him: the sound of a dagger being drawn.

Henry, you damned fool.

Tye spun to see the lad climbing to his feet, holding a knife. He must have pulled the weapon from inside his boot. Henry staggered forward, barely able to stand upright. Fresh blood trailed into the drying mess on his face.

Why hadn't Henry stayed down on the ground? He couldn't win this fight. Did he want to be slain?

"I will...stop you. For...his lordship."

"You will die," Tye warned. If the lad had any wits about him, he'd quit his foolhardy attempt to be a hero.

Determination gleamed in the young man's eyes. The challenge, unmistakably direct, hummed in Tye's blood, honing his anger to one focus: to kill. His hands flexed, readying for the fight.

Veronique giggled. "I will have my chance to cut you, after all."

Henry lunged at Tye, raising the knife. "*Whoreson*! On...my honor..."

Tye whipped the sword from its scabbard. With a lethal growl, he brought the blade arcing down, severing Henry's neck. The headless body toppled to the ground.

"Well done." Veronique gloated. "Now, I will just—"

"We must leave, Mother. *Now.*" Several other prisoners had escaped their cells and, with jovial cheers, were unlocking the doors of other captives; if they ran for the dungeon door, Tye's escape would be delayed.

"Tye is right." Braden thrust the cloak at Tye. "Put this on. Act as though you are my prisoner until we get through the main gates."

Ignoring his mother's scowl, Tye sheathed his weapon, donned the cloak then headed out into the darkness behind Braden, escorted by the mercenaries with their swords pointed at him. The dirt of the bailey was rough and cool against his bare feet, but he didn't care. He'd be wearing leather boots again soon enough. Drawing in a deep breath of the summer night air, he caught the scent of horses waiting nearby.

While Tye walked, he rolled his shoulders, easing the

curious tension that had settled there. He'd slain many men in his lifetime, more than one of them named Henry. Few of the deaths haunted him.

Tonight's killing wouldn't haunt him, either.

Chapter Two

The great keep at Wode, Moydenshire, England
January, 1215

"Mother Mary!" With an irritated huff, Lady Claire Sevalliere lifted the lid of her wooden linen chest and shoved at the garments tumbling out. The chest *had* to shut. Otherwise she wouldn't be able to travel when the men-at-arms who were to ride as her escort arrived at her chamber later that morning.

Today, she was leaving this grand fortress where she'd lived for the past five years. By the day's end, she'd arrive at her new home: the castle of her widowed sixty-five-year-old Aunt Malvina.

Claire had only met the extremely pious lady, the sister of Claire's deceased father, twice. Yet, they'd exchanged letters in the years since Claire's parents had been killed in an accident on a muddy road one stormy spring afternoon.

That tragedy had left Claire and her younger sister, Johanna, orphaned. By the King's command, Johanna had gone to live with a nobleman and his wife who'd been close friends of the Sevallieres. Claire had been made a ward of Lord and Lady Brackendale, relatives of Moydenshire's famous lord Geoffrey de Lanceau.

In response to a recent letter from Claire, Aunt Malvina had been kind enough to offer her a place to live—a relief when a more recent tragedy had made the stone walls of Wode feel as though they were closing in upon Claire.

At nineteen years of age, she was ready to begin anew; to

devote herself to the quiet life of a maiden who'd never marry, for her heart belonged now and evermore to Lord Henry Ridgeway, whom she'd loved and lost.

Fighting a pang of sadness, Claire buried her hands into the gleaming silk gowns, gauzy linen chemises, and embroidered leather shoes. Strands of curly blond hair tumbled over her face as she reshuffled the top garments then pressed down hard.

"You are losing that battle."

Claire smiled. Straightening, she faced her chamber doorway. Her dearest friend, Lady Mary Westbrook, stood there, her arms folded over the bodice of her moss green gown. Mary was trying to hide a grin behind her hand, but her brown eyes danced with mirth.

"Which clothes do I leave behind? I sold all of the gowns I could part with. I donated the money to the nearby abbey, remember?" Claire looked back at the garments and fought an uncomfortable knot settling in her throat. She'd accumulated many lovely things since arriving at Wode. The Brackendales treated all of their wards as if they were their daughters. The flowing, pale blue wool gown with silver floral embroidery at the neckline, sleeves, and hem that she was wearing today had been a gift last winter. Lord Brackendale had died a few weeks ago, and all that Claire owned had become even more precious because of her fond memories of him.

She would just have to make the linen chest close. 'Twas the only answer. She set her hands atop the contents and pressed down again. "Holy." *Push*. "Blessed." *Push*. "Mother of God!" *Push*.

"Claire, you must stop swearing. If you curse like that in front of your aunt, she will faint from the horror."

Guilt wove through Claire. "You are right. I shall remind myself every day to watch my tongue."

"Good."

In the midst of shifting the garments again, Claire paused. "Mary—"

"I am just trying to give you sound advice, as a loyal friend should."

"Please do not worry. I do not plan to cause my aunt any trouble. In fact, I want to live a very quiet, solitary existence."

Mary rolled her eyes, as though a quiet, solitary existence was so unlikely for Claire, 'twas not worth considering. "If you say so."

"I do."

"Fine." Mary sniffled. She sounded close to tears.

Claire struggled against the tug on her heart and repositioned a pair of leather shoes wedged in the far corner of the chest. She'd never imagined leaving would be this difficult.

She heard the whisper of Mary's gown, glimpsed her wiping her eyes with the back of her hand. Claire couldn't bear to acknowledge her best friend's tears, because then she'd be crying, too.

Part of her insisted she was a witless fool to leave Wode. How would she manage without Mary's friendship? How would she rein in her love of freedom to become as strictly pious as her aunt? This huge change, though, must surely be a good one. A life devoted to prayer and chastity would truly honor the young man who would have been her husband, if he hadn't been killed while fulfilling his duty for Lord de Lanceau. Henry had died while trying to stop a dangerous prisoner from escaping his lordship's dungeon. No other man she'd met—or would ever meet—could compare to her memories of her brave, beloved Henry.

"I am sorry. I do not mean to cry," Mary said quietly. "I know this move is what you want."

Claire straightened up from the linen chest. "'Tis what I must do."

"So you have said. I only ask this because you are like a sister to me, and I want you to be happy...but are you certain?" Mary wiped her eyes again. "Are you *really* sure this new life is what Henry would want for you? You only met him on a few occasions. Forgive me, but 'tis hardly enough to get to know a man."

Claire grinned as her first memory of Henry filled her mind. How vividly she saw sunshine brushing his blond, shoulder-length hair and lighting his blue eyes. "Oh, Mary, I will never forget that feast when he and I first met. Henry was so gallant that day, the way he apologized for bumping into me in the crowded bailey. He bowed, rose with my hand gently clasped in his, and smiled as though I was the most beautiful lady in all the land."

"You *are* beautiful, Claire," Mary said, envy in her voice. "You must know that, by the number of suitors you have turned away since Henry's death."

"Goodness, Mary, but you are far prettier than I."

"Nay, I am not—"

"Besides," Claire said, fighting the blush creeping into her cheeks, "physical beauty is not as important to me as what lies in a man's heart. Although, Henry wasn't just handsome, he had a beautiful soul, too."

"I believe you are right. The day you walked together in Wode's gardens? He acted like a knight from a romantic *chanson*."

"And his letters," Claire said wistfully. "Those I could never leave behind."

"Do you remember how we shrieked aloud when we read his words, over and over?"

Claire giggled. "And then, there was the day he returned to Wode to speak with Lord Brackendale. Somehow, I knew Henry would ask me to marry him. Seeing him dismount from his horse in the bailey made my pulse flutter like a caged bird. The tender kiss he placed upon my cheek, I shall cherish always."

A delighted sigh rushed from Mary. "That kiss sealed your love forever."

"It did." Claire's fingers drifted to the middle of her left cheekbone where his lips had brushed her skin. The intimacy had been quick, light, but just for her. No kiss could ever compare to it. Since she'd never been kissed by a man before that moment, and would never be kissed again, she'd treasure it as the most perfect of kisses.

"One day," Mary murmured, "I hope to have such a kiss."

"You will. I am certain of it."

Excitement gleamed in Mary's eyes. "I will write to you as soon as it happens. I will tell you all about it in great detail. That would not be forbidden by your aunt, would it? I hope not."

So do I, my dearest friend. Trying not to let doubt back into her mind, Claire shut the linen chest. No garments were poking out.

"Thank goodness," she said, wiping her hands on her skirts. "Now—"

Shouting outside drew Claire's gaze to the wooden shutters at her window. She'd closed them earlier, because of the morning breeze. Judging by the raised voices, something extraordinary was taking place in the bailey.

With Mary at her side, Claire hurried to throw the shutters wide.

Frigid air buffeted Claire. She hadn't remembered the sky being such a dense pewter gray color earlier, but then, she'd been focused on packing her belongings.

Snowflakes swirled in through the iron grille across the window, as more urgent shouts carried up from the bailey.

"What is happening?" Mary asked.

"I am not sure." Leaning farther into the embrasure, Claire peered out. Men, yelling to one another, were running along the snow-dusted battlements, their weapons raised.

"Will it be safe to travel to your aunt's castle? The roads might become covered with snow, and then the wheels of the cart—"

"Mary."

"But—"

"Please," Claire said desperately. "Hush!"

The voices outside were distorted by an icy gust of wind. Then, clear and distinct, came a man's cry. "Attack! Attack! The keep is under attack!"

Spurring his horse to a gallop, his sword drawn, Tye raced down the snowy road toward Wode's gatehouse, a score of hired mercenaries close behind him. Today, as Tye had learned from studying the keep's routines over the past several weeks, the fortress was expecting deliveries from the village alewife and fishmonger. Judging by the lowered drawbridge and raised portcullis, the castle guards hadn't anticipated an assault on this freezing, wintry morning.

Just as he'd planned.

Today, at *last*, he would take what he deserved.

He'd spent the past months moving from nearby town to

nearby town, never in one place for very long—as his mother and Braden had done, and as King John had advised. Last summer, after receiving Veronique's missive sent during the battle at Waddesford Keep, the King had secretly agreed to help her and Tye in any way possible, in exchange for information on de Lanceau's activities in Moydenshire. If the clandestine agreement were discovered, however, the King would vehemently deny all knowledge of it and would claim a conspiracy within his London court.

King John was well aware of de Lanceau's attempts to unite his peers against the crown with a Great Charter. While the sovereign didn't dare arrest a lord as wealthy and well-connected as de Lanceau, he planned to use every bit of useful information to undermine de Lanceau's efforts.

While Tye's leg had healed, and while he'd watched and listened for the King, he'd toiled for shop owners, farmers, blacksmiths, and carpenters, trading his work for food and a place to sleep.

That life, though, had ended.

Today, he'd seize his destiny.

Today, after months of studying Wode's daily routines, eavesdropping in taverns, and delaying his attack until the ideal opportunity, his wait was over.

Frantic cries from Wode's battlements reached him. The sentries had seen him and his mercenaries and sounded the alarm; yet, he'd be across the drawbridge before the men could lower the portcullis.

As he neared the towering fortress, falling snow clung to his hair and his cloak trimmed with fur; water from melting flakes slipped down the back of his neck and under his chain mail hauberk. Snowflakes landed on his face, but he relished each icy, tingling kiss. He savored the muffled crunch of snow beneath his horse's hooves, for he felt *alive*—more than at any other moment in his life.

An arrow hissed past Tye's head. He spied the archer on the wall walk above, heard a mercenary behind him slow his horse and prime his crossbow. Tye had ordered the mercenaries to only kill when necessary. Killing bred hatred and resentment, and to maintain control of Wode, he needed to win the folk's loyalty. The archer would soon be wounded, though, unable to fight like several of his colleagues.

An agonized cry rent the air, accompanied by a splash as a guard fell from the battlements into the ice-skimmed moat. Tye's mercenaries were earning every coin they'd been paid.

His horse's hooves thudded on the drawbridge, and then he passed under the teeth of the portcullis and into the shadows of the gatehouse. The hoof beats of the mercenaries' mounts thundered close behind. He tightened his grip on his sword, his palm warm inside his black leather glove. Wode, the castle that had been ruled by the de Lanceau family since the reign of King William the Conqueror, would soon be *his*. 'Twas an insult his sire wouldn't be able to ignore, especially when Tye's rule of the keep was swiftly approved by King John.

As of today, Tye would be called 'lord,' a title that recognized the noble blood in his veins. A title, also, that brought respect. Using Wode as his base, Tye would conquer castle after castle, while he anticipated the moment he confronted his father in battle. In a triumphant fight, Tye would slay his sire. All of Moydenshire would bow to his control.

No one would stop him.

Especially his sire.

Tye looked to the bailey opening directly ahead. Wode's men-at-arms, slipping on the snow-covered ground, scrambled to block his entry. Some of them were old enough to be his grandfather.

"Do not let them pass!" bellowed a stocky, white-haired warrior, likely the captain of the guard. "Defend this keep, as Lord Brackendale would have expected of you."

Lord Brackendale. Tye's lip curled in a sneer. The old man's death had caused a stirring of grief among the folk of Moydenshire. His passing had also left the castle without a ruling lord. De Lanceau undoubtedly intended to replace Brackendale with one of his loyal lackeys, but he hadn't done so yet, likely because he hadn't wanted to offend his lady wife and mother-in-law, who were both very upset by the death. The lack of leadership had worked to Tye's advantage, especially when unrest had taken de Lanceau and his armies away to other parts of the county—leaving Wode ill-prepared for an assault.

Tye slowed his mount, using his horse's last steps within the shelter of the gatehouse to assess the opposition. The snowfall was thickening. Still, he counted a dozen men-at-arms approaching and more on the battlements, ready to bring him down.

Let them try. My attack will not fail.

Ahead, a black-haired archer stepped forward, raised his bow, and fired at Tye. Tye dodged the arrow, heard it whistle past before it clattered against the stonework behind him. Expression grim, the man nocked another arrow, but before he could shoot, leather creaked behind Tye, immediately followed by the *hiss* of an arrow. The archer reeled backward, the arrow launched by a mercenary buried in his shoulder. Blood streaming down his armor, the archer collapsed against one of his colleagues. With angry cries, the other guards edged forward, swords raised.

"Yield," Tye yelled.

"You will not pass," the captain of the guard shouted.

"Yield or *die*."

The white-haired man scowled. "*You* will die this day."

Tye held the man's gaze through the swirling snow. He heard the mercenaries, who'd slowed their horses to match his, rallying behind him; the odors of worn leather and wet metal carried on the wind.

"Attack!" the captain of the guard bellowed. As he rushed forward, weapon glinting, Tye's horse flailed its head and stepped backward. Instead of reining the spooked animal in, Tye slid off its back and raised his sword.

Shouting battle cries, the mercenaries spurred their mounts into the bailey.

"Stop them!" the captain of the guard yelled as the riders cantered past. Men-at-arms ran after the mercenaries.

The older man's sword collided with Tye's. Twice. Three times. Teeth bared, the captain of the guard rallied another strike, while several other men spread out in a wide circle to entrap Tye. With a guttural cry, Tye brought his blade whipping down to cut the captain's lower leg. He screamed, hobbled, blood staining the snow.

With angry roars, the men-at-arms surrounded Tye.

Air rushing between his teeth, he met strike after strike of the warriors' swords. The fight became a blur as he spun, lashed out, and dodged blows. Blood from wounded men dotted the front of Tye's armor and spattered on the snow. A handful of mercenaries, some on horses and others on foot, crowded in around him. They worked alongside him to quell the resistance as quickly as possible.

With a brutal slash of his sword, Tye thwarted a final assault from one of the wounded swordsmen. As the man fell sideways into the snow, groaning, Tye signaled to five of the mercenaries. "Come." As arranged earlier, the men fell in alongside him. Leaving the rest of his forces to conquer the bailey, Tye headed for the forebuilding that led up into the keep's great hall.

Shouts and the crash of swords snapped his attention to the far side of the bailey, where light from the stables and kitchens tinged the snow pale yellow. Huddled in the kitchen doorway, servants watched, terrified, as mercenaries battled more men-at-arms. Archers on the battlements continued to fire down arrows, even as their numbers dwindled. A man priming a crossbow on the battlement screamed. An arrow had pierced his right arm; he careened sideways and disappeared from view.

Tye focused again on the forebuilding, less than ten paces away. Over the metallic *clang* of a nearby swordfight, he caught running footfalls.

"Milord!" cried a mercenary behind him.

Tye whirled to confront whoever neared. Through the falling snow, he recognized his mother, garbed in her black cloak trimmed with fur. Strands of red hair poked from the edges of her hood. Braden, in his thick fur cloak, hurried along beside her, his bloodied sword at the ready.

As they reached Tye's side, the mercenaries turned and watched the bailey, keeping a lookout for enemy assailants.

"The gatehouse is under our control. Our men will lower the portcullis and raise the drawbridge shortly." Veronique's eyes were bright from the pleasure of the fight. Fresh blood glistened on the dagger in her gloved hand.

"The castle is expecting deliveries this morning," Tye said.

"Tell the men to turn away anyone who approaches. They are to say there is sickness in the castle."

"Very well," Veronique said.

"What of the postern gate?" Tye asked. This doorway in the castle's outer wall, built to enable folk to escape in the event of a surprise attack, couldn't be left unguarded.

"'Tis secured," Braden said.

"No one escaped?"

Veronique shook her head. "As you ordered, mercenaries are standing sentry on both sides of the postern. No one can get in or leave by that door."

"Good." Tye grinned. All was going just as he'd planned.

You will loathe hearing of my victory today, Father. You will hate to the very depths of your soul that I am ruler of this keep—and I will bask in your hatred!

Another of the men-at-arms in the bailey fell to a mercenary's blade, and Tye's grin widened. What he would give to see his father's face when he received news of the conquest. De Lanceau would blame himself for leaving Wode vulnerable, for the opportunity he'd overlooked that Tye had seized. His sire's guilt and regret would be akin to strings looped through Tye's hand; he'd tug, tangle, and manipulate them, without mercy, without a glimmer of forgiveness, before in a glorious final fight, he ran his father through.

A chunk of melting snow slipped from the edge of Tye's cloak and settled against his neck: an icy chill against his skin. A reminder that while his victory was nigh assured, 'twas not complete. His attention shifted to the keep, its stone rendered dull gray by the overcast sky. With a harsh cry, he summoned the mercenaries to follow him.

"We will speak later, Mother."

"We will." Her triumphant laughter followed him as he threw open the door to the forebuilding. "Wode is yours at last, as you deserve."

Chapter Three

Do you think Lady Brackendale is aware of the attack?" Mary's voice was barely a whisper in the torch lit corridor.

"I hope so," Claire answered as they raced toward the solar. There was a very good chance, though, that she was oblivious. Since Lord Brackendale's death, her ladyship had become withdrawn and despondent. She'd taken to sleeping late into the morning and breaking her fast in her chamber. Her ladyship might still be asleep. All the more reason for Claire and Mary to *hurry*.

"If the attackers managed to defeat the men outside…" Mary said.

"I know." Claire dreaded running headlong into wild-eyed, murderous ruffians inside the castle—although there was a very good chance of that, too. Most of the castle's warriors had recently been summoned to ride alongside de Lanceau. Her sense of dread deepened, for it couldn't be a coincidence that the assault had happened when the keep's defenses were at their lowest in years.

Ahead, the iron-bound wooden doors to the solar were closed. As she'd feared, it seemed that her ladyship was unaware of the danger.

Claire rapped on the right door. "Milady!"

Muffled voices came from within.

"Milady!" Claire knocked again. "We must speak with you."

The door opened on a waft of warm air. Sarah, Lady Brackendale's lady-in-waiting, stood in the doorway, her auburn hair braided as usual into a tidy coil around her head. She frowned as she curtsied. "Good morning, Lady Sevalliere. Lady Westbrook. 'Tis early and her ladyship—"

"'Tis urgent." Claire brushed past Sarah. Lady Brackendale, still wearing her white linen night rail, was sitting in bed, propped up against a mound of pillows with the blankets tucked around her waist. Her gray hair hung loosely about her shoulders. A tray rested on her lap, and she held a piece of buttered bread.

"Claire? Whatever is the matter? You look dreadfully pale—"

"The castle is under attack," Claire blurted. At her side, Mary nodded.

The fire in the hearth popped, and Claire jumped, her nerves wound as tightly as a spool of yarn. Lady Brackendale exchanged a glance with Sarah, still standing in the open doorway, then set down the bread and patted her lips with a linen napkin. "Are you certain, Claire?"

"Aye!"

"My dear, we know you are blessed with a vivid imagination. I well remember that story you wrote, the romantic adventure involving a wounded knight—"

"But—"

Her ladyship thrust up a wrinkled hand laden with rings. "The captain of the guard was planning to run extra drills this week."

Claire shook her head. "We heard cries of alarm from the bailey. The clash of weapons, too. The assault is happening right now." She hurried past the bed and threw open the shutters at the window. "Listen!"

A snowy gust of wind brought with it the cacophony of battle. Simultaneously, from the corridor, came the sound of people approaching at a run. Murderous ruffians?

Claire closed the shutters and spun from the window. Three men-at-arms appeared in the doorway, breathing hard. The first two men halted just outside, nodded in greeting to Lady Brackendale, then turned their backs and stood watch in the corridor, their swords at the ready. The third man, Sutton, one of the keep's finest swordsmen and husband to a kitchen maid, stumbled to a halt inside the solar, his hand pressed to his side. Blood coated his broadsword. Blood also glistened on his fingers. As Sutton shifted his stance, grimacing, and the edge of his woolen mantle drew back, Claire saw broken, bloodied links of chain mail.

"Sutton." Lady Brackendale pushed away her tray. "What happened?"

He attempted an awkward bow, but tensed on a groan of pain. "We are…under assault, milady."

"God above! Claire, I should never have doubted you. Sarah, fetch my robe. Help me rise. Sutton, tell me all that has transpired."

"Mercenaries. A swift, brutal assault." His face twisted on another spasm of pain.

Claire's gaze fell to the rectangular wooden stool pushed against the wall, but before she could fetch it for Sutton, he waved her away. "Thank you, milady, but I will not rest. Not until the battle is over."

Sutton wasn't fit to return to battle. If he went anyway, and the situation in the bailey was as dire as she believed, he might not live to see this chamber again. He was a proud warrior, though—as were all of Lord Brackendale's men. Sutton had said he'd rather die honorably in battle than in his sleep; his heart was as brave and noble as Henry's had been.

Tears threatened, but Claire blinked them away. Later, she could weep; now, she needed to help Lady Brackendale.

Her ladyship stepped to the floor. Sutton averted his gaze while she slipped on the embroidered white robe Sarah offered. "How many attackers?" Lady Brackendale asked.

"Twenty. Mayhap more."

"Do they have a leader?"

"A dark-haired man. Skilled fighter. Not a lord from one of the local estates. I have never seen his face before today."

"I see." Concern etched her ladyship's features. "The gatehouse?"

"Overrun"

"The postern?"

"Captured. Our men are fighting hard—"

"—but we are losing."

25

His expression grave, Sutton nodded.

Lady Brackendale sighed. "How long do we have?"

"Not long, I fear."

Claire's stomach clenched. Her instincts had been right. The awful knot inside her warned that she hadn't seen the worst of the day yet. Sarah looked frightened and lost. Mary, standing close to Sarah, was as pale as the bed linens.

Her ladyship's trembling hand tightened on the front of the robe. As though she'd reached an important decision, she nodded once. "We must ready ourselves, then, to meet our conquerors."

"Oh, God." Mary wilted onto the wooden stool, her white-knuckled hands clasped in her lap.

Sutton gestured to the men outside the solar. "These warriors will protect your chamber, milady. They will not leave their posts."

Lady Brackendale laughed, a brittle sound. "How thoughtful, Sutton. You know as well as I, however, that two guards will not stop our attackers from breaking into this room."

A ruddy flush darkened the older man's cheekbones. "At least they will slow down and injure the whoresons—I mean, the ruffians, milady."

"They will. Go, now. Do what must be done." She bestowed upon him a sad smile. "And thank you."

Sutton nodded, turned on his heel, and strode away.

Lady Brackendale ordered Sarah to shut the door. The chamber fell silent except for the crackle of the fire. Her mouth forming a grim line, her ladyship motioned to the dark gray wool gown and linen chemise draped over a chair. Sarah hurried to fetch the garments.

"My beloved Arthur," the older woman said softly. She stared at the fire, as if she saw more than burning logs. "As he drew his final breaths in this very room, he warned me Wode might be attacked once he was dead. His fear of an attack and of what could happen to me tormented him."

Claire moved to her ladyship's side. "Did he say who might dare such an assault?"

"He did not give names. However, he knew the strategic

value of this castle. As you may be aware, this keep has been ruled by Lord de Lanceau's family for almost one-hundred-and-fifty years and rightfully belongs to him."

"I did not realize that," Claire said.

"Arthur was appointed lord here by de Lanceau. 'Twas an agreement made between the two men years ago after a fierce battle between them. They were once sworn enemies. Difficult to believe, but 'twas before de Lanceau was married to Arthur's daughter, Elizabeth."

Claire had met de Lanceau, a handsome, authoritative, but also kind man who adored his beautiful wife, several times in the years she'd lived at Wode.

"Arthur loved his daughter very much. He also loved this castle and its hard-working folk. How he hated to think that enemies might seize power here."

"I am sorry, milady." Claire fought rising helplessness. "What can we do? Can we get a message to Lord de Lanceau?"

"Not with the gatehouse and postern captured."

"There must be something we can do," Claire insisted.

"De Lanceau keeps close watch on his lands and will know, quickly enough, of the assault. He will bring his army and crush the conquerors." Her ladyship's eyes glittered with unshed tears. Her gaze shifted to Sarah, who waited with the garments, but then she caught both of Claire's hands and held them tight. "Take Mary and go to your chamber. Lock the door. Push the table against it and stay inside until I tell you 'tis safe to come out."

Claire gasped. "We cannot leave you to face the ruffians alone."

"I agree," Mary said, standing now at Claire's side.

"I am pleased you feel that way. I am an old woman, though, who has experienced a great deal in her lifetime. You two have lived very…innocent lives. I will do all I can to protect you."

"Milady—"

"When the attackers reach this level," the older woman cut in sharply, "they will first claim the solar. If I can negotiate with them to keep you safe, I will." Her voice wavered. "Arthur would expect such of me."

"Surely 'twould be safer for us to remain together?" Claire

said.

"You will do as I have told you." Her ladyship pointed to the doorway. "Go now. *Go!*"

Claire jumped, for Lady Brackendale had never spoken to her in that way before. Today was far from usual, though, and if her ladyship was even half as worried about facing their attackers as Claire was…

Claire curtsied then grabbed Mary's hand. Together they raced back to Claire's chamber. Once inside, they bolted the door and pushed the heavy oak trestle table against it, as her ladyship had instructed.

"Are we going to be all right?" Mary asked, her eyes enormous.

"We are."

"What if the ruffians plan to slaughter us all?"

"'Twould be very foolish of them," Claire answered, trying to sound calm and clear-headed, despite the panic buzzing in her mind like a trapped fly. "I doubt the conquerors would want hordes of angry friends and relatives of the deceased rushing to the castle to demand vengeance. Moreover, there would be no one left to cook the meals, or wash the floors, or care for the horses, or otherwise maintain Wode."

"There are worse things than dying." Mary's voice shrilled. "The ruffians might batter down the door, take us prisoner, and then…" Her words faded on a moan.

"Mary." Setting her hands upon her friend's shoulders, Claire waited until Mary blinked and met her gaze. "You and I will be fine. We must be as brave as Lady Brackendale. We are not helpless, after all."

Mary looked confused.

"We have blockaded the door. If need be, we have plenty of things in this chamber to use to defend ourselves."

"We do?"

Claire glanced at the hearth. The blaze that had warmed her chamber through the night had burned down, and fresh logs hadn't been added because the servants had expected her to be leaving for her aunt's castle.

Catching Mary's hand, she pulled her friend to the

fireplace and threw on more logs. She and Mary were going to be in this chamber for a while and might as well be comfortable. Then she pulled the fireplace poker from among the implements made of iron. Jabbing it in the air a few times, Claire said, "Perfect."

"*That* is going to save us?"

"If I poke a man in the right place," Claire said with a wink, "he will come no nearer."

"Oh, I see. You will aim for *that* part of him, then?"

They way Mary spoke 'that part,' she sounded as though Claire was going to do something drastic and...wicked. Claire flushed, for she had heard rumors about one place on a man that was especially sensitive to pain. She'd seen proof last spring, when a kitchen maid wielding a cast iron pot had marched into the bailey, shrieked at one of the stable hands, and then slammed the pot between his legs. The man's high-pitched screams had brought half of the castle servants running to his side, and he'd walked strangely for days afterward. Yet, Claire would rather not have to wound a man there if she could thwart him another way.

With a shrug and stab of the implement, Claire said, "If I threaten to stick an attacker in the eye, he will back away."

"The eye." Mary tsked. "I thought you meant..." Her face reddened. "Well, *you* know."

"I do." Claire's flush intensified. "'Tis a last resort, though, to poke him in his male parts." Truth be told, the thought of poking a man in his dangly bits made her want to throw up, but she should have no such qualms. If left with no other choice, she must do what had to be done to protect herself and Mary.

Claire picked up a bit of kindling, a branch sturdy enough to deliver a sound wallop or even knock an attacker senseless. "Take this." She pushed the kindling into Mary's hands.

"I have never used such a weapon before."

"Neither have I, but—"

Somewhere in the distance, women screamed.

Mary wailed. She scrambled to turn the branch and hold it like a sword.

"Those screams came from the great hall," Claire said. The fire iron wobbled in her grasp. Mercy! Her heart was going to pound its way out of her ribcage.

"Those poor women sound terrified. Do you think they are being taken captive? What if...?" Mary swallowed loudly. "Will the ruffians come to get Lady Brackendale and then...us?"

Claire tightened her grip on the fireplace poker. "Whatever is about to happen, we will be ready."

Chapter Four

"How *dare* you think to lay your filthy hands upon me!" Tye glared down at Lady Brackendale. The crackling fury of her words still hung in the air, as palpable as if she'd struck him hard across the cheek. She eyed him as if he were a wayward boy who deserved a whipping—a mistake she'd quickly regret, if she wasn't careful.

He'd already subdued her guards and searched the chamber. The auburn-haired lady-in-waiting stood weeping by the doorway with a mercenary standing guard over her. All that remained was to search her ladyship for weapons or costly jewels hidden beneath her gown. If the old woman had jewels up her skirts, she might try to bribe one of the mercenaries to help her escape or get a message out of the keep; Tye would not risk her ruining his carefully-laid plans.

Tye slowly tightened his grip on his gloves, clasped in his left hand. At the soft *creak* of leather, she swallowed hard, her wrinkled throat moving. "'Twill be far easier if you cooperate," he warned. "Refuse me, and there will be consequences, not just for you, but others within these walls."

The lady-in-waiting moaned.

Her ladyship, however, glowered all the more fiercely. "I want assurances from you, especially for the two wards within my care."

"Assurances? I think not."

Her eyes flashed. "You are willing to invite the wrath of the King, then? I promise you, my wards—"

"Enough." Tye signaled to two of the three mercenaries behind her ladyship. They caught her arms, holding her still as he dropped to a crouch, set down his gloves, and lifted the hem of her gown.

She squirmed and kicked him in the leg. "Stop, you disgusting, unprincipled—"

His hand locked around her left ankle. "Kick me again, your ladyship, and I will bind your hands and feet. You will stay bound until I decide to free you, which might be days from now."

Her ladyship snorted. Yet, finally, she stood still. He ran his hands up and down her legs, then dropped her skirts and patted down her arms and her bodice. She glared at him throughout the search, but he ignored her. Finally, he took her hands in his and slipped the rings off her fingers; he slid them into the leather bag at his hip, along with his gloves. The money raised from selling the jewels would help pay his hired men.

"Take her ladyship and her maidservant to the great hall."

"My wards," Lady Brackendale said. "I must know they will be safe."

"As I told you earlier: no assurances."

Fear touched her gaze. "Now you listen—"

"Take them," Tye snapped. Lady Brackendale had delayed him long enough, and there was still much to accomplish. The mercenaries pulled her ladyship toward the doorway, heedless of her shouts and struggles.

After a last quick search of the solar, Tye strode into the passageway, the remaining mercenary following him. They continued searching the rooms on the upper level of the keep.

His keep.

Four chambers down, he caught up with the mercenary, who'd come upon a locked door.

"Whoever is inside will not open the door, milord."

"Did you warn them we will break it down?"

"I did." The mercenary grinned, baring his crooked teeth. "A woman inside answered. She told me to stay out, or she would take drastic measures."

Tye whistled and shook his head. Either the woman was extremely brave or completely witless. By now, everyone in the keep would know of the siege. She must realize that she and any others in the chamber had no hope of avoiding capture.

Of the three rooms he'd investigated so far, one was a place for ladies to retire and chat, with a large hearth and unfinished embroidery and wooden games resting on the side tables. The second room appeared to be made up for unexpected guests. The third, judging by the silk gown draped on the chair near the bed, was the chamber of a young lady, likely one of the wards her ladyship had mentioned.

Was she behind the door he faced now? The other young woman might be in there with her.

One way to find out.

He hammered on the door. "Open up."

Startled gasps sounded from inside the chamber.

"Leave us be!" came a sharp retort, slightly muffled by the panel.

The corner of Tye's mouth ticked up. The voice was without doubt a young woman's, and it had a rather pleasing lilt. Whoever she was, she clearly hoped that he'd move on to easier conquests.

Whoever she was, she'd sorely underestimated him.

"Last chance," Tye commanded. "Obey, or I will knock down this door."

"I obey Lady Brackendale's orders," the woman replied with admirable defiance. "The door remains closed until she tells me to open it."

The hell it does. Tye signaled to the mercenary, who kicked the door. Then, Tye hefted his booted foot and slammed it into the door. Again and again they attacked until, with a loud *crack*, one of the wooden slats split.

"Oh, nay!" a woman wailed from within—a different female to the one Tye had heard moments ago.

"Stay calm!" said the woman who'd defied him.

A heady swirl of anticipation raced through Tye, for the willful young lady intrigued him. He looked forward to setting eyes upon her, to staring her down until she blushed nervously and averted her gaze and thereby yielded to him. To further prove he was in control now of everything and every*one* at Wode, he might even haul her into his arms and steal a lusty kiss from her. His loins heated at the thought.

Another well-aimed kick, and the split in the door widened. The mercenary shoved his left hand inside, found the key in the lock, and turned it. The lock mechanism clicked. The door was now open, but through the gaping hole, Tye saw a sturdy trestle table blocked the doorway.

On his signal, he and the mercenary both slammed their shoulders against the door. It jostled, but didn't move inward.

"Damned table," the mercenary said, rolling his shoulder.

"Again," Tye ordered. This time, the door jarred inward a fraction.

With a triumphant growl, Tye pressed his palms flat to the door and shoved. The mercenary also pushed. A grating noise came from inside. The panel slowly moved as the table was pushed back across the planks.

A woman wailed. "'Tis the end of us."

"Do not say that," the lady of the dulcet voice said, although her words sounded unsteady.

Enough of a gap had formed at the door's edge. Tye pushed through, swung his legs over the table, and landed on the other side, his sword poised for attack. His dramatic entrance clearly made an impression, for the wide-eyed damsels before him—one slender and blond, the other curvaceous and dark-haired—shrieked and stumbled back.

"Well, well," he murmured. They both wielded weapons. The brunette, though, was clutching a large stick, and seemed more likely to collapse in a teary heap than do any real damage.

The blonde holding the fireplace poker, however...

"Stay back," she ordered.

So *she* was Lady Defiant. She would indeed jump into a fight and deliver wounds, if he believed the fierceness of her tone and the blaze of her blue eyes. Wisps of wavy hair had come loose from her braid and fanned out around her face. He grinned, for she reminded him of a fluffy kitten, hissing at him, threatening him with her tiny claws.

"I warn you," she said, "if you do not turn around and leave—"

"You will skewer me?"

A strangled sound of both shock and distress broke from

her lips that were full and pink and just right for kissing. Aye, he liked the idea of stealing a kiss from her before he left this chamber. Still grinning, he winked at her, and her posture stiffened, indicating she didn't like his flirtation.

Good. The more uncomfortable he made her, the faster she'd surrender.

Hearing the mercenary move in to guard the doorway, Tye deliberately let the silence lag. He stole a quick glance at the rest of the room, searching for signs that any others—knights, ladies, or even children—might be hiding in the chamber. The room was sparsely furnished. Apart from the table, the only large pieces of furniture were a linen chest and an oak framed bed. 'Twas unlikely anyone was hiding under the low bed or in the chest, but not impossible.

His gaze returned to Lady Defiant. Her throat moved with a swallow, but she didn't lower the fire iron. He continued to hold her stare, refusing to give her even a moment of reprieve. Once he'd thoroughly unsettled her, she'd be more likely to put down the implement and save them all a scuffle. It would end, after all, with her as one of his hostages. He didn't want to hurt one so lovely if he didn't have to; she might be worth a sizable ransom, and would be more valuable to him unharmed.

She shifted the angle of the fireplace poker, a nervous reaction. His gaze narrowed. Indulging in the curiosity nagging at his better judgment, he dropped his gaze, and it skimmed over her, slowly, so slowly, from her crown of flaxen hair to her neck, to the shadowed dip between her breasts that disappeared into her fitted, embroidered bodice. He'd tasted, teased, and touched many women's breasts in his years, and even though hers were covered by silk, he knew they were perfect: round, full, heavy enough to spill with delicious softness into his cupped hands. The thought sent a sweet, sharp ache through his loins, for he yearned to see those beautiful breasts uncovered—not that she'd ever yield that pleasure to him. Not willingly. Not today.

He savored one last, thorough, appreciative ogling, before his attention dipped lower, to her flat belly, and then to the fullness of the gown swirling about her ankles.

She wasn't just a fighter, this one, but a beauty.

His beauty, if he so chose.

He fought the hardening of his groin, even as his attention returned to her exquisite breasts. Her breathing quickened. Her bosom rose and fell with enticing frequency.

"Please," she said. "Leave us alone."

Her voice sounded very different from before. He had offended her, he guessed, in his roguish appreciation of her beauty. That meant his plan to unsettle her was working.

"Leave?" Tye smiled. "We only just met." He savored the dismay in her eyes. "Tell me, is there anyone else in this room except for you two ladies?"

Her chin edged up a notch. "Why should we tell you? You are an enemy of Wode."

"Not exactly."

"Nay? Then why have you attacked this keep? Who are you, and what is it that you want?"

"Be careful," the brunette said, nudging her friend in warning.

The blonde spared her companion the barest glance. Then, as though collecting her resolve, she pushed her shoulders further back. When she'd spoken, her voice was firm and steady once again. The questions, combined with her unwavering stare, might have persuaded Tye that she was fully in control of her anxiety and prepared to attack him.

Indeed, with her holding the fire iron straight out toward him, he might have heeded the wariness skating at the base of his skull. A hostage could inflict a good deal of harm with such an implement, except that it was wobbling. If she didn't take care, she might drop the end on her foot.

"You ask a great many questions, Kitten," Tye said.

Her gaze sharpened on the word kitten. "You have not answered even one."

Laughing, he flicked his hand, motioning the mercenary into the chamber. The man strode forward and began to search the room, starting with the bed. The brunette gasped and huddled further behind the blonde.

"At least tell us your intentions toward us!" the blonde said.

"Mmm." Tye took several steps toward them. If he herded them back against the far wall, there was less chance of them dashing for the doorway.

As he expected, the women took a hasty step back. The fire iron wobbled a little more. Ignoring the blonde's insistent stare—a foolish dare to lock gazes with her again—Tye looked along the length of metal to her bare arm. What he could see of it, anyway, exposed by the drape of her wide sleeve. He noted a delicate wrist, as fine-boned as the fingers clasping the implement's handle. Her skin appeared to be smooth and soft; the skin of a spoiled woman who'd been handed countless privileges because of her noble birth, not because she'd toiled, or suffered, or fought with passion and conviction to earn them. Hers was the kind of life he'd been deprived, because of his sire's rejection; 'twas the kind that deep in the pit of his soul, he envied.

The ever-present bitterness flickered inside him, and as he met her gaze at last, his jaw hardened.

"I asked your intentions," she choked out.

"I heard you. Do as I say and you will not be harmed."

A *thump* carried from the other side of the chamber: the lid of the linen chest falling shut. "Milord," the mercenary said. "There are no others 'ere. Only the women."

"Good." Tye let the word roll upon his tongue and infused it with roguish menace. "No witnesses, then. No brave heroes to rush to the rescue, if matters get…complicated."

"Oh, God, " the brunette whispered, sounding as if she expected to be run through and left for dead within the next moment.

The blonde's face was paler than before. "Swear that you will not harm us."

Astonishment jolted through him. She, the one at a disadvantage, was making demands of him? He clearly wasn't unsettling her as much as he'd thought. That wasn't just annoying, but wholly intriguing.

Hellfire, but now wasn't the time to indulge his fascination with this woman, who was entirely too bold. *He* was the one in control of this situation, not her. "You dare to make demands of me, milady? Do not. I might consider that proof you will not cooperate with me and my men."

The brunette loosed a frightened moan. "Now you have done it, Cl—"

"With respect," the blonde hastily said, "I did not refuse to cooperate. I merely wanted your promise—"

"—of safety. I know. 'Tis a promise I shall not give, because what occurs today in this chamber depends entirely upon *you*."

The tiniest of sounds—a stifled groan, mayhap—drew his attention down the slender slope of her nose to her lips. His interest stirred again, intense and undeniable. He wanted a *taste* of her. Would she be sweet and ripe, like a forbidden fruit? His lust flared anew. At the very least, kissing her might shut up her bold chatter.

As though sensing his wayward thoughts, her lush lips pressed together. "I warn you, I will not stand by and let you hurt us. I *will* use this fireplace poker to defend Mary and myself."

He chuckled; he simply couldn't help it.

Indignation made her eyes even brighter and bluer. "Why are you laughing?"

"Defend yourself and Mary? You can barely hold that fire iron steady."

"Steady enough to—"

"Put it *down*," he said, very firmly.

The blonde trembled, but she didn't obey him. He had to admire her fortitude. Most gently-raised young women would have fainted at his feet long before now.

"I will not relinquish the fire iron," she said, her voice low but steady. "Be warned, I know how to wound a man."

"Really."

She nodded solemnly. "I know exactly where to aim. That place where it *really* hurts."

Behind her, Mary turned scarlet. He was growing more intrigued by the moment.

With a practiced tilt of his wrist, he aimed his sword at Lady Defiant's throat. There were too many steps between them for his weapon to touch her, but a swift lunge would resolve that. "I ordered you to put down the fireplace poker. Do it. Or—"

A loud clatter. The one called Mary had dropped the stick.

"Do as he says," Mary squeaked. "Quickly!"

"Listen to her," Tye said. "My patience grows thin, and I have been more than courteous."

"Courteous?" The blond looked aghast. "You attacked Wode. You broke into my chamber and—"

"Courteous," he repeated. "I do not have to *ask* you to obey me. I do not have to wait for you to comply." His gaze raked most thoroughly down the length of her body. "I can simply take what I want from you, Kitten."

Chapter Five

I can simply take what I want from you.

The man's silkily spoken words, combined with the unwavering challenge of his sword, made Claire's breath catch in her throat. He'd intended to frighten her. He'd succeeded.

Without the faintest hint of conscience, he'd sworn he could get what he wanted from her, without needing her permission. That meant by brute force. A ghastly thought.

Was that his plan? To take? And what, exactly, would he take from her?

Would Mary also fall prey to his depravity?

The chamber had fallen silent, as though Mary and the mercenary waited, too, to see what Claire would do next. Unshed tears burned her eyes. Fighting the tears and the shaking of her legs was taking tremendous willpower. Doubt shrieked inside her, telling her she'd already lost this fight, that he was so much stronger than she was, and that if she were wise, she'd put down the fireplace poker and not provoke him further. He might be merciful, if she surrendered.

Might.

The rogue continued to stare her down, no trace of kindness or concession in his steel-gray eyes. Not that he seemed a man to ever concede. His was the face of a man who'd fought all of his life—and likely *for* his life. His dark brown hair, pulled back from his face and tied with a strip of leather, added to the severity of his features, for it made his cheekbones look more pronounced, his sun-bronzed face chiseled and angular. His nose was slightly crooked, suggesting it had been broken at least once. His squared chin drew focus to his broad, sensual lips.

The man before her wasn't beautiful, not in the way refined, golden-haired Henry had been pleasing to the eye. There was an untamed handsomeness, though, to the rogue's features. Her fiancé had been akin to a polished river stone; this man was a rock broken from a sea-battered crag, with rough edges and a wildness that made his expression ruthless and hard.

His features, for some reason, reminded her of another man: Geoffrey de Lanceau. Yet, 'twas surely a mistake to draw a comparison between this thug and the powerful, respected lord.

The rogue's gaze sharpened. His thick, black eyelashes dropped a fraction, and that slight action made her pulse leap. His stare was like a solid weight pressing into her, commanding her without words or physical contact but in a manner that pierced deep inside her and was thus, somehow, even more powerful.

Claire could never let him see how terrified she was. If she revealed how much he affected her, she'd give him an advantage, and so far, she'd managed to hold her ground. Indeed, she *mustn't* yield, and not just because of her concern for Mary. The way the rogue looked at her, as though he wanted to shove her into a corner and run his big, strong hands all over her naked flesh, was akin to a promise. As soon as he took away the fire iron, she'd belong to him.

Most frightening of all, however, was the tangle of feelings within herself that she couldn't quite explain. She was just so *aware* of him physically. The skin across her bosom tingled. Her whole body felt unnaturally restless.

And in that moment, she knew she wouldn't yield—no matter how afraid she was. She fought the doubts still taunting her, fought them with a strength pulled straight from her soul. Her relationship with Henry, however brief, had taught her much, above all, the importance of honor. Surrendering now would be the easiest choice. Fighting for herself and Mary was terrifying, but also *right*. Her fingers tightened on the fireplace poker and, with the rightness of her decision settling inside her, she edged her chin higher.

"That is your final answer, then," he said. "You will not put down the fire iron."

"I will not."

"I warned you what would happen." He took a measured step toward her.

She fought a sickening surge of light-headedness.

From behind her came a gurgled moan: Mary. She didn't sound at all well. A shifting of air brushed Claire, accompanied by the rustling of cloth, and then a *thud*.

"Mary?" Claire said.

No reply.

The thug's focus shifted to the floor behind her.

"W-what happened to Mary?" Claire demanded.

"She fainted." The rogue smiled.

How dare he enjoy poor Mary's predicament!

The urge to glance at Mary, to see if she was all right, burned within Claire, but she didn't dare take her attention from the rogue.

"You are cruel to smile," Claire said sharply. "She could be hurt because of that fall, thanks to you." Anger, fueled by her fear and tension, swirled inside her with the crackling energy of a thunderstorm. She raised the implement a fraction higher, wishing her tired arms were steadier.

He took another step toward her. He moved with sleek efficiency, like a trained hunter. A predator who was pursuing *her*. He was close enough now that he could slash her arm with the sword—a sure way to make her drop the fireplace poker. An awful coldness settled in her belly.

"Stay back," she said, trembling.

He stepped forward again, too swiftly for her to move away, and his hand captured the end of the fire iron. The strength of his hold sent a brutal tremor racing through her.

Triumph now softened his roguish smile.

Refusing to heed the panic welling inside her, she wrenched the implement sideways.

His grip tightened. "You should have let go." He jerked his arm, an elegant, calculated movement. She winced, for pain shot up through her hand into her arm. Her fingers instinctively loosened. The implement, torn from her grasp, flew through the air, hit the wall beside her, and landed with a *clank* on the floorboards.

Before she could flex her fingers, cold metal pressed into the valley between her breasts. The point of the thug's sword pressed against her skin, right at the dip of her bodice. With the slightest nudge forward, he'd draw blood.

Her heart pounding, Claire stood very still. Was he going to take whatever 'twas he'd threatened earlier? Or had he decided to kill her?

Her thoughts shifted to Henry, who had died by a sword wielded by a murderous prisoner. Had Henry been afraid in his final moments of life? Nay. He'd died a hero. He'd been lauded at his burial for his tremendous courage by Lord de Lanceau himself. If she was meant to perish at this rogue's hand in the coming moments, she, too, must show such strength, in honor of Henry.

Clinging to that thought, she said shakily, "Go on, then."

"Go on?" the rogue murmured.

"Do whatever evil deed 'tis you intend. If you have any mercy, you will do it quickly."

His eyes lit with admiration. Then, as though he suppressed the flare of emotion, his mouth set into a hard line. Drawing the sword away from her flesh a fraction, he said, "Move. Toward the wall."

What was going to happen once she'd reached the wall? Claire's mind raced, each possibility more frightening than the last, but she obeyed him, turning slightly and then stepping backward. Her shoes made a shuffling sound on the planks. He moved with her, his strides bold, light glinting on his sword.

Claire looked past him at Mary, who still lay on the floor, her eyes closed. The mercenary stood guard over her.

"Please," Claire said. "Mary—"

"She will be all right."

Shivering, Claire pressed back against the stone wall. "How do you know? You have not even checked her for injuries… Or does it not matter to you whether she lives or dies?"

His brittle laugh skated along her nerves. "She is not going to die."

The tiniest burst of hope warmed Claire. He sounded so certain. Mayhap his intentions didn't involve killing her and Mary. "Why do you say that?" she dared to ask.

"I have seen enough wounded in my days to know that she will be fine."

The sword again touched Claire's skin. Her momentary flare of hope faltered, for while his words were encouraging, he'd given no assurances as to their fate. If she kept him talking, though, she might learn more. "Mary should have woken by now, should she not? She might have hit her head when she fell. Her injuries could be of the kind that do not cause visible bleeding, and that are only apparent later."

Holding her stare, the rogue flicked his hand at the mercenary. With a scowl of reluctance, the burly man dropped to his knees beside Mary, set down his sword, slid off his right glove, and pressed his dirty, scarred fingers to Mary's neck. Then, he lifted Mary's head and checked the side of her face that had lain against the planks.

The mercenary grunted. "She looks fine to me. No bruises. Unlikely she hit her head."

"Good." The rogue's attention didn't shift from Claire. "Now, search her."

Claire gasped. "W-what?"

"Mary might have a weapon hidden in her garments. Say, a small lady's dagger bound to her thigh."

"Nay!"

"'Twould not be the first time a lady had a knife hidden up her skirts."

True, but how did he know that? He didn't seem like a man who'd be familiar with what went on within the noble elite. He could have gotten his knowledge by some other means, of course, such as seducing a lady and in the midst of heated passion, finding the knife. *That* Claire would believe. Her skin tingled, an uncomfortable betrayal of just how vividly she could imagine him undertaking a seduction.

Still, Mary didn't even own a dagger. She'd lost the one Lady Brackendale had given her and hadn't replaced it. At Wode, her safety had never been in question. Until now.

A lusty grin curved the mercenary's mouth as he slowly ran his hands up Mary's limp arms.

"She doesn't have a weapon," Claire insisted. "I swear."

"I might believe you," the rogue said, "if I hadn't seen her brandishing a stick."

Revulsion coiled up inside Claire, for the mercenary's palms were sliding toward Mary's shoulders. Soon, his grubby hands would be heading to her bosom. Such violation shouldn't be allowed, although she *had* heard of ladies concealing daggers between their breasts. "Tell him to stop. Please."

"I will not."

"But Mary—"

"He will finish his search. 'Tis the surest way to confirm you are not lying to me."

Claire swallowed the awful taste in her mouth. "He must not touch... 'Tis wrong, his hands on her—"

As though sensing Claire's thoughts, the rogue glanced over his shoulder. "Do more than search her for weapons," he told the mercenary, "and your pay is forfeit."

The lout paused, his splayed hands on Mary's upper chest, his fingers shockingly close to her bosom. Frowning, he muttered under his breath, skimmed the sides of his hands down between her breasts, and moved on to her belly and lower back.

"The stick was my idea," Claire said. "I gave it to Mary and told her to wield it."

The rogue chuckled. "That, I believe."

"We had to defend ourselves! We did not know what would befall us in the attack." Claire focused all of her desperation into her gaze. "We still do not know. Nor do we know *who* has dared this assault."

"*I* dared."

"Who, exactly, are you?"

"You can call me Tye."

"Tye," she repeated, committing it to memory. "No surname?"

"Just Tye."

How unusual, that he didn't wish to share his last name. There must be a reason. She didn't want to appear too curious. "I have never heard the name Tye before."

Anger sparked in his eyes. Had he thought himself more renowned? Had he expected her to know who he was and respond with a shocked cry? Mayhap the arrogant rogue had even expected her to swoon. "My name is one that you, and all of Moydenshire, will soon know very well."

"Why? What is—?" The mercenary's moving hands claimed Claire's attention. He was now at the hem of Mary's gown. Fine wool bunched beneath his fingers, revealing the embroidered edge of Mary's cream-colored linen chemise and her calf, covered in silk hose. Claire shuddered as he yanked up both garments and shoved his hand up along her leg. "Oh, Mary." Claire's dear friend would collapse in horror if she learned such a highly improper inspection had taken place while she was rendered senseless.

"Remember what I told you," Tye growled to the lout.

"Aye," the mercenary said sourly, his tone suggesting he was bitterly disappointed that he couldn't enjoy a grope under Mary's skirts. After a brisk sweep with his hand, he yanked her clothing back down and then skimmed a finger inside both of her shoes. His search complete, he picked up his sword and rose. "No weapons."

"As I told you," Claire said.

The mercenary snorted, a disparaging sound, and Claire's hands curled into fists. How she wanted to smack his ugly face.

Wry laughter snapped her attention back to Tye. "Easy, Kitten."

"Stop calling me that!"

"Why? It suits you."

"I am *not* a cat."

"What should I call you, then? You have not told me your given name, even though I told you mine."

Claire hesitated. She'd rather he didn't know who she was. However, she disliked even more the way he said kitten, infusing the word with unwelcome affection. The endearment seemed to slide around on his tongue and end on a sensual purr, a shocking way to speak such an innocent word. Of course, a rogue like him could probably make the word 'buttercup' sound sinful. "Claire," she said. "That is my name and what you should call me."

"Claire," he echoed. "A lovely name. Yet, I still prefer Kitten."

"As far as I am aware, I do not have four paws, pointed

teeth, or whiskers," she answered tartly. "Or a tail."

Of all things, his smile broadened. "No tail? How unfortunate. Yet, you are reckless and impulsive, just like a young cat."

"Now you are being ridiculous."

Tye's eyes glinted. "In a moment, you are going to hiss at me."

"Hiss? What makes you say that?"

Tye summoned the mercenary to his side. Once the thug had drawn near, Tye said, "Keep your sword trained on her."

"My pleasure." The mercenary shifted the point of his weapon to hover at her neck.

Steel rasped as Tye slid his sword back into its sheath. His hands, sun-bronzed and callused, were now unencumbered.

Oh, mercy. "You cannot mean to—"

"I do." Tye winked. "'Tis your turn to be searched, and I shall do it myself."

Tye reached down and caught Claire's right hand. Her skin was smooth, soft, and had not a single rough patch, as he'd expected for a cosseted young lady. Her fingers were still tightly fisted, a small measure of defiance, but he patiently worked them open, refusing to let her deny the pressure of his hand, and then slid his fingers through hers. With her firmly in his grip, he pulled her arm out at her side, so that her sleeve draped like an angel's wing. He felt his way up her arm, pressing and squeezing.

She trembled while he worked. His attention was on her arm, but he felt her gaze on his face, a stare of silent challenge. He'd expected her to protest his search, but to his surprise, she'd said not a word. She must have decided the easiest and fastest way to deal with the unpleasantness would be to endure.

Despite her silence, anger and fear defined the closeness between them. He couldn't blame her for being afraid—he'd anticipated such a reaction from a maiden who'd never been touched by a man, especially one as thoroughly, unapologetically experienced as he was.

What he hadn't expected, though, was the way she'd make him feel. Touching her, even through the fabric of her gown, was akin to a form of torture. Her flesh was supple, her garment's luxurious cloth as soft as a woman's bare thighs. As if that were not torment enough, she smelled luscious—like honey and milk blended together. He wanted to draw in a long breath and savor her. As his hand traveled to her shoulder, stray strands of her glossy blond hair brushed the backs of his fingers. Pure, unfettered lust rippled through him.

He sensed the narrowing of her eyes, the question forming in her mind. Refusing to meet her stare, he lowered her arm, freed his fingers, and moved to her other shoulder. Fine wool whispered under his fingertips.

She cleared her throat. "Once you have searched me, and found for yourself that I do *not* have any weapons, what will happen to me? And what of Mary?"

His fingers trailed over the embroidered hem of her sleeve and her wrist. He thought of delaying his answer, at least until he'd finished with her. If he told her that her life wasn't in danger, she might do something rash. The threat of death was an effective means of control. Yet, she was still trembling, and as much as he wanted her to obey him, he saw no sense in keeping her such a heightened state of fear.

Finally meeting her gaze, he said, "You will be my hostages."

"Hostages." Relief softened the word. "You are not going to kill us, then."

"I see no reason to kill you."

"Well. That is good news."

Tye fought a grin; instead, he scowled, with enough menace to ensure she continued to comply. Setting both of his hands on her shoulders and moving them inward toward her bosom, he said, "Of course, if you disobey me, or try to escape, I may change my mind."

Her ribcage expanded beneath his palms as she drew in a sharp breath. Her posture tautened, as if she expected his hands, sliding down through her cleavage, to slow their inspection, spread wide, and close over her plump, round breasts.

God's teeth, 'twas exactly what he wanted to do. She'd mold perfectly into his hands, and when his thumbs grazed her nipples, she'd sigh, mayhap even moan, and her eyelids would flutter...

"Is Lady Brackendale safe? Is she also a hostage?"

Tye snapped his focus back to his task. Annoyance swept through him. He shouldn't be so easily distracted by a fetching pair of breasts, especially those of a lady who was likely a virgin and who'd never bare her body for anyone but her wedded husband. "She is," he said.

"As your hostages, what will be expected of us?"

"That will depend."

"On what?"

He shot her a frosty look. "How well you listen to what my men and I tell you."

A frown furrowed her brow. "And?"

"Your value as a hostage."

"You mean, whether I am from a wealthy family or not? If I am, will you demand an extortionate ransom?

"You ask a lot of questions, Kitten."

"If you were in my position, would you not want to know what is going to happen? 'Twould be foolish *not* to ask."

He shrugged. "True."

"You said you weren't going to kill us," she went on, as if her questions required explanation, "but there are countless other things, some quite awful, that could befall us—"

"Also true." Tye dropped to his knees before her.

"Oh! Goodness. W-what—"

"Hold still." Their gazes locked as his hand slid under the hem of her gown. "'Twill go faster."

"Nay! I...I do not have a knife. I swear!" she said, sounding panicked. Another warble of protest broke from her, but he pushed aside the layers of garments to reach her leg. Like Mary, she wore silk hose beneath her gown.

Tye swept his hand up her calf. Even her clothes smelled like milk and honey. His jaw clenched, tightly enough to cause him pain. Good. Pain was familiar. Pain he could tolerate. The torment Claire caused him? That might drive him to do something very,

very unwise.

He'd just lifted her skirts higher to bare her right knee—a shapely knee at that—when a cry broke from behind him.

The mercenary grunted. "The other lady's awake."

"So I heard."

"Claire!" Mary gasped.

Tye concentrated on Claire's slender legs, his palms gliding upward. The sooner he finished his search, the better.

"Mary, do not worry. I am all right," Claire said with more calm in her voice than he'd expected, for she was quivering beneath his touch. *The way she'd quiver if you caressed her, coaxing her to spread her thighs for you*, his wicked mind pointed out. He forced aside the tantalizing thought.

"His hand," Mary said. "'Tis inside your gown."

"Aye, but—"

"On your leg!"

How easy 'twould be to touch that secret part of her, that naughty voice in his head taunted. *She'd never let you touch her there otherwise. You are so far beneath her noble rank, you are naught to her.*

The pain in Tye's jaw intensified. A muscle jumped in his cheek as his fingers slid higher, wanting to touch more of her. Wanting...

The furious swish of wool came from behind him. Mary had scrambled to her feet. With one last sweep of his hand down Claire's left leg, he dropped her gown and pushed to standing. He nodded to the mercenary to lower the sword from Claire's throat.

Tye pointed at Mary. "Move to the wall. Beside Claire."

Her bosom rising and falling on quickened breaths, Mary glared at him. Yet, she did as he'd commanded. When she reached Claire, she threw her arms around her friend and they embraced. Mary sniffled as though she might dissolve into tears.

Tye ignored a tingle of remorse, gestured for the mercenary to stand guard at the chamber door, and then strode toward the linen chest. He sensed Claire's gaze upon his back, but resisted the urge to turn and meet her stare. He still hadn't finished in this chamber, and there was the rest of the castle to secure. In no way was a woman going to stand in the way of his victory.

"What a miserable ordeal you went through," Mary

whispered. "How dare that ruffian feel around inside your skirts."

"I am fine," Claire whispered back. "He thought I might have a hidden dagger, 'tis all."

"He did not hurt you? Nor the other thug?"

"Nay."

"I am glad." Mary sighed, the sound laden with guilt. "I am sorry for fainting. I did not mean to."

"I know," Claire soothed.

Tye halted in front of the linen chest and lifted the lid. A waft of Claire's scent drifted up to him, and he fought the hot lick of desire in his loins.

"What happened while I was oblivious?" Mary asked. "Did they search me in that awful way, too?"

"I am afraid so—"

"How completely *awful*! Who searched me? Was it... *him?*"

Tye felt both of the women's stares boring into him. Refusing to acknowledge their scrutiny, he turned the heavy chest sideways and dumped out the contents. Silks, linens, shoes, and other items poured onto the floorboards.

A pile of folded papers, bound with a silk ribbon, skidded to a stop near the toe of his boot. Love letters? A lady as beautiful as Claire no doubt had suitors, even a betrothed. He fought a ridiculous, unwanted stirring of jealousy and bent to pick up the bundle.

"Stop!" she shrieked. Hurried footfalls came up behind him.

The papers firmly in his hand, Tye faced Claire, standing a few paces away. She looked torn between scratching his eyes out and succumbing to tears.

"How dare you? Those are my belongings."

"Everything in this castle belongs to me now."

She sucked in a furious breath, drawing herself up taller. "Not true."

"Claire." He fully expected her to retreat. Grown men had fled when he'd used that tone of voice.

Brave little kitten, she stood her ground. "Only the lord of a castle can claim all within belongs to him," she said. "*You* are—"

"—Wode's new lord. As of today."

"You have not proven your right to rule here. Not to me. As far as I know, not to Lady Brackendale or anyone else within this fortress. Therefore, what you have done here in my chamber is a *violation*."

He laughed. "You should know by now that I have no shame. Or must I prove it to you again? Mayhap in an even more direct manner? I am more than willing to do so, milady."

Chapter Six

C laire clenched and unclenched her hands and struggled not to lunge at Tye. What arrogance! What boldness. Never had she met a man who dared speak to her in such a shocking, disrespectful manner. And to treat her treasured things as though they were his to do with as he wished?

Unforgivable.

"Claire," Tye said, his tone a warning.

She glowered at him. Aye, she feared him, and even now, her heart jumped in her chest like a frightened frog. However, when it came to Henry's letters, Tye had pushed her too far.

The insolent curve of Tye's mouth mocked every hope she'd ever had of keeping her missives from Henry hidden from him. Seeing that precious bundle in his hand made her want to scream. They were *her* letters, filled with sweet words and heartfelt confidences written for her alone.

True, she had secretly shared Henry's letters with Mary. After he'd been killed, Claire had lain on her bed, read them over and over, and trailed her finger over the neat lines of ink, while remembering his face the last time he'd seen him—and, of course, his kiss. She and Mary, huddled beside her, had both wept, and some of Claire's tears had fallen on the parchment to blur the ink. The rogue before her, though, didn't need to know what Henry had written, or to see the proof of her anguish in the random ink smudges.

Tye might have declared himself lord, but that did *not* give him the right. Lord Brackendale, who'd had the right, would never have taken such a liberty, out of respect for her.

The fury accompanying that thought convinced her to

step forward and stretch out her hand. "I would like my letters."

Tye didn't move. "No doubt you would."

She drew a breath shaking with rage. "Those letters are private and personal. They were written by my betrothed, who died a few months ago."

"Ah. I am sorry to hear—"

"What he wrote is of *no* use to you."

"I do not know that yet."

"I assure you—"

"Your plea is quite convincing, Kitten. However, since I hardly know you, I would be foolish to trust you. I will find out for myself whether there is information of value or not."

"What can you possibly hope to learn from my letters?" she demanded.

His cloak stirred as he nudged the heap of her belongings with the toe of his boot. "Who knows what I might discover? Secrets about this castle and the people living here. Secrets about you."

"I have no secrets."

He chuckled, a rough, earthy sound. "Everyone has them, Kitten, although not everyone is willing to admit to them."

His booted foot moved again. Garments shifted. Shoes tumbled. His sly gaze slid to her, before he shoved the letters into the leather bag at his hip and picked up another packet of missives that had emerged: letters from Johanna. Lying beside them was Claire's dagger, still in its leather sheath.

He held up the knife. "You do have a dagger, after all."

"Not bound to my leg," Claire bit out. "As I told you."

Laughing, he pocketed the knife. Then he bent and snatched up her bag of jewelry, just visible beneath her favorite dandelion-yellow gown. He picked up a leather-bound journal, found its pages were blank, and dropped it back to the planks.

A frustrated groan burned her throat, rising in volume as he kicked aside an inlaid box in order to see what lay underneath. "Do you have to treat my belongings in that way?"

"I must be sure you do not have any more weapons among your finery."

"Or jewels," she said tartly.

"Or jewels," he agreed. "What about coins? Do you have a bag of those as well?"

Claire refused to answer. She did have a small bag of silver, but she was certainly not going to help him steal it.

Her reluctance didn't seem to bother Tye. He nudged several folded chemises, clinging together, to reveal another leather-bound journal, the one in which she'd penned her tale of the knight that Lady Brackendale had so enjoyed. There were other adventures in there too, that she'd written with Mary in a quiet corner of the garden, with no one about to hear them giggle and squeal with delight: silly, romantic stories about lonely maidens being rescued by gallant heroes and falling in love. She and Mary had spent two days writing one scene about a hero and heroine kissing, inspired by her wonderful kiss from Henry. Even as she desperately prayed that Tye wouldn't be interested in the journal, he leaned over and picked it up.

A moan broke from her, the sound echoed by Mary. "Please," Claire said.

"You do not want me to look at this book?" Tye's eyes gleamed. "Why not?"

If she told him what was in the journal, 'twould only make him more intrigued. Fighting the flush racing over her skin, she merely shrugged.

"What is in these pages, Claire?" Tye's thumb brushed the strip of leather tied in a loose knot that kept the cover closed. "Did you write personal musings in these pages? Did you share thoughts and dreams you never thought anyone else would see?"

Her blush deepened.

"Did you reveal secret desires?" His words trailed off on a seductive hiss.

She fought the shiver trailing like a forbidden caress down her spine. 'Twas not fair that his voice should wreak such havoc upon her. In truth, her writings weren't that scandalous, but she'd rather he didn't read her stories, especially the one about kissing. The act of kissing was, after all, two people sharing a pure, glorious, ever-after love. He would only mock her for what she'd written.

She folded her arms and met his stare with one of silent

mutiny.

He chuckled. "My, my, Kitten, you make me even more curious. I look forward to settling back with a goblet of wine and reading—"

"Enough!" Claire snapped.

"—every page."

"Oh, God," Mary croaked. Her eyes bulged, as if she might choke on her dismay.

Never before had Claire felt so vulnerable. The urge to plead with Tye, to beg him not to read what she'd penned, welled inside her. Yet, 'twas exactly what he wanted: for her to grovel. She would rather eat every page of her journal than give him that satisfaction.

As she discreetly dried her sweaty hands on her skirts, she heard several people approaching. The mercenary at the doorway moved out into the corridor, his sword raised.

Claire met Mary's gaze. Judging by Mary's expression, she was clearly hoping for a dramatic rescue, but Claire refused to indulge in even the briefest flare of excitement. From all she'd seen, Tye's assault had been too quick and too complete for Wode's men-at-arms to have had a chance of winning the battle.

The mercenary returned, followed by three more rough-looking thugs. Their cloaks and chain mail armor were stained with blood. Fighting the pain of loss—heaven only knew how many of Wode's loyal fighters had perished in the battle—Claire looked back at her garments scattered on the floor.

"Milord," a mercenary said.

Tye swept past Claire. His earthy scent, of leather and horse and crisp morning air, teased her, and she fought the unwelcome temptation to watch him walk away, his strides full of command. Instead, she knelt and began to gather up her belongings. Mary dropped down beside her to help.

"What news do you bring?" Tye asked, his voice seeming to fill every part of the room.

"The bailey is secure," a mercenary answered

"Good."

"There are wounded prisoners, milord. You asked us to summon you—"

"I did."

Claire sensed Tye's gaze upon her. Ignoring him, she pulled the inlaid box over beside the silk gown she'd folded.

She continued to fold as Tye strode up behind her and halted. She knew 'twas him. She *felt* him, his presence brazen and demanding. He stood just to her left, watching her every move.

Mary, her eyes wide with apprehension, followed Claire's lead and continued to straighten the items before her.

A defiant smile tilted Claire's lips. Tye might *expect* her to look up and acknowledge him, but she wouldn't obey. He didn't control her will. He didn't deserve her respect, and he'd *never* have it.

As she straightened back on her heels, adding the chemise to the folded pile, the warning *creak* of leather sounded beside her. Before she could scoot away, his fingers closed under her chin and tipped it up.

She tried to pull free, but his fingers tightened—not enough to hurt, but enough to hold her still.

"We will speak again later, Kitten." Tye's gaze skimmed her upturned face and then settled on her mouth.

Claire swallowed against the pressure of his fingers. His ravenous stare warmed her, made her lips burn and tingle, as though he'd bent and crushed his mouth to hers. He stared down at her as if he meant to claim her. To make her *his*.

Never.

Her heart belonged to Henry. It always would.

Claire wrenched from Tye's grasp. "I see no reason for us to talk ever again."

He laughed softly, clearly amused by her defiance. "We *will* speak again. Of that, you can be certain."

As soon as the men quit the chamber, relief sluiced through Claire, allowing her tense shoulders to lower. Mayhap now the knot in her stomach would ease a bit.

"That was the worst experience of my entire life!" Mary collapsed on her back on the floor, her gown tangled around her legs. Her plump arm covered her face.

"'Twas indeed awful." Claire rose from the neat pile of belongings in front of her, her legs unsteady. "It could have been much worse, though."

"We could have been beaten senseless," Mary said, not lifting her arm, "and left to bleed all over the floor."

Claire shivered. "Aye."

"Or brutally ravished." Mary's words were a strangled whisper.

"Aye."

"Or both." Mary moaned like a dying hound.

"True," Claire agreed, determined to stay calm. "But none of those terrible things happened. That, surely, is a reason to be thankful."

A disbelieving snort broke from Mary. Claire stooped, gathered her tidy pile of items, and put them into the linen chest, along with the garments Mary had folded. Pausing a moment, her hands braced on the sides of the open chest, she closed her eyes and prayed for fortitude and a clear, rational mind to help her think through their situation.

She must be as brave as Lady Brackendale. Succumbing to hopelessness and tears would not help matters—although Claire had learned in the days after Henry's killing that she often felt much better after a good cry.

Straightening, she looked at her chamber door, battered but serviceable once again. Before leaving, Tye had ordered one of the mercenaries who'd arrived from the bailey to find some wood and hammer it across the broken slats. The thug had completed the task and then had slammed the door shut, to stand guard along with one of his colleagues.

Claire caught the sound of the men conversing now and again, although she couldn't make out what they said. Disappointing, for she longed to know how Lady Brackendale and the others fared, but at least she and Mary had a measure of privacy now. With the door repaired, the men outside couldn't peer in. Nor could they easily hear what was being discussed— which hopefully would work in their favor.

"I cannot believe you think there is any reason to be

thankful." Mary sniffled. "We are prisoners. We have no idea what will happen to us. Truth be told, I am worried beyond measure. Oh, Claire, I cannot stop thinking about Lady Brackendale. I hope she is being treated well."

"I do, too." Concern for the older woman weighed upon Claire. Lord Brackendale's recent death, followed by the conquest of the castle, could be overwhelming for her ladyship in her fragile emotional state. Claire would be sure to ask Tye about Lady Brackendale when she next saw him, which was likely to be soon, if she was to believe the promise in his parting words.

The thought of facing him again was most unpleasant. 'Twould mean experiencing his hard, keen gaze upon her. 'Twould mean fighting the unsettling, breath-snatching pull of masculinity surrounding him like an additional layer of armor. Yet, she must speak with him again. The rogue might not heed a word of what she said, but she'd do her best to make him attend to her ladyship's wellbeing.

Mary's arm over her face lifted a fraction. "Do you think Lady Brackendale is all right? I mean… Do you think she was ravished?"

Claire mentally pushed aside the possibility. "I would hope that the attackers extended the same respect to her as they did to us—if not *more* respect, considering her position."

Mary peered up at Claire. "Respect? Claire, that…that thug took your letters and journal. He knew they were important to you and also highly personal."

Ugh. As if she needed a reminder. "He did," Claire agreed. "They will not be of much use to him, though, if he cannot read."

Mary pushed up to sitting. "Considering he is a lowborn ruffian, 'tis more than likely that he *cannot* read. I certainly do not know any thugs who can understand written words."

Claire stifled a smile. She'd never imagined Mary was so knowledgeable about thugs.

"Whether Tye can read or not, though, is another matter," Mary continued, her tone anxious. "We were speaking of respect and his lack of it. He had his hand up your gown!"

"I know, Mary, but—"

"He touched your legs! And the way he stared at you, as if

he wanted to devour you…"

A blush heated Claire's face. To try and hide her reaction, she plucked an imaginary loose thread from her sleeve. She needed no reminders of what had taken place. Hidden by her gown, her legs still tingled from Tye's touch that had felt more like a reverent exploration than a rough search. She'd never forget the heat of his hands upon her, or the strong, unforgivable yearning that had stirred within her at his caress. "What happened earlier is behind me—*us*—now. We should concentrate upon what lies ahead."

"W-what do you mean?"

Claire crossed to Mary and gently pulled her to her feet. Struggling to piece together the frayed thoughts racing through her mind, Claire squeezed her friend's hand. "You and I need to stay alert, to listen, and to watch with great care. We must remember the smallest details of all that takes place during this occupation. Such information will be important."

"To Lord de Lanceau?" Mary asked, swiping at her bottom eyelashes.

"Aye. As Lady Brackendale said, he will soon know of the takeover here and will launch a rescue."

Mary's gaze brightened with hope. "You are right. He will."

A smile tugged at Claire's lips. "Of course I am right."

Mary giggled. "Well, most of the time."

"*When* have I—?"

"The stable, two winters past. Remember?"

Oh, mercy. Claire did indeed remember. "All right, so I *was* wrong about the young lord waiting there for your kiss."

"Very wrong." Mary frowned. "That situation could have been extremely mortifying, if I hadn't recognized the man standing in the shadows as Sutton."

"Aye. Well." Claire cleared her throat. "That incident aside, we need to focus on the here and now. We might be captives, but we are also first-hand witnesses to—"

"Chroniclers," Mary said.

"Aye!" Excitement fluttered inside Claire like a handful of butterflies. "Oh, Mary. What a wonderful idea!" She hurried to her linen chest and dug down in the contents. With a grin, she pulled out the blank journal Tye had looked at earlier and discarded, along with a drawstring bag containing quills and ink.

"I was saving this tome for my musings on my first weeks with Aunt Malvina."

"Your aunt will still be expecting you today." Mary said, her eyes widening. "When you do not arrive, will she not be worried?"

Claire shook her head. "This snowfall will have affected much of Moydenshire. She told me in her last letter not to leave Wode if the weather was foul. She will suspect I was sensible and stayed behind until a better day for traveling."

"I see." Mary gnawed her lip. "Well, if you are willing, I say 'tis a worthy sacrifice, to use this journal for our account of Tye's conquest."

"I can always buy another journal."

Smiling, Mary nodded.

Motioning for her friend to follow, Claire headed to the trestle table and set down the book and bag. She opened the tome, the binding creaking slightly, the pungent scent of cured parchment rising to her.

"How shall we begin?" Mary sounded a little breathless. "Should we start from the moment we heard the shouts?"

Claire drew the pot of ink and a quill from the bag. She carefully opened the ink, making sure not to spill any. Dipping the quill into the black liquid, she said, "How about: 'Twas a snowy morning—'"

"A *cold* and snowy morning," Mary corrected, leaning closer.

"Very well." The nib of the quill scratched across the parchment. *'Twas a cold and snowy morning that fateful day at the great keep of Wode...*

Chapter Seven

P ulling off her leather gloves, Veronique strolled into the empty solar. She studied the rumpled bed, the food left on the tray, the oak table opposite the bed that was set with small pots, combs, hair pins and jeweled hair ornaments. The furnishings in the chamber were simple but of fine quality and suited to a wealthy older lady who enjoyed her comforts.

A hard smile curved Veronique's crimson-painted lips as she crossed to the table, tossed down her gloves and dagger, and trailed her fingers over the collection of luxuries there, dragging them out of the organized arrangement that had suggested each item had a special place. Pins tumbled to the floorboards; she left them where they fell. She swept a silver comb onto the planks where it landed with a clatter.

Her hand lifted, hovered, and picked up a brown earthenware pot.

"What have we here?" she murmured, removing the lid and taking a whiff of the lavender-scented cream inside. She dipped in a gnarled finger, scooped some cream out, and rubbed it on the back of her hand. The cosmetic was a nice, smooth consistency. Excellent quality. It had likely had cost her ladyship— or more likely Lord Brackendale—a small fortune in coins. Her smile broadening, Veronique put the lid back on the pot. Slipping her hand inside her cloak, she shoved the pot into the leather bag at her hip, along with two gold hair combs studded with gemstones.

Picking up a silver hair piece inlaid with pearls, she tapped it against her palm and walked farther into the room. The spacious chamber was well kept. 'Twas the kind of large, comfortable room

Veronique liked. Indeed, that she bloody well *deserved*.

Her hand closed around the hair piece. The delicate tines bent under the pressure, but instead of relenting, she crushed even tighter. If circumstances had been different, she would have enjoyed a lavish chamber like this and all of the privileges due a rich lady day after day, year after year. Aye, her life would have been very different if that *bastard* Geoffrey de Lanceau hadn't cast her aside in favor of Lord Brackendale's young daughter, who had quickly become Geoffrey's wedded wife.

'Twould have been different again if Geoffrey hadn't refused to accept that the boy Veronique had birthed was his child.

Tye *was* Geoffrey's son; she hadn't lain with any other man during the weeks that she'd gotten with child. Geoffrey had only himself to blame for the inevitable battle ahead; he deserved to die a painful death for the way he'd spurned her and her babe.

What a wondrous day that would be: the day Geoffrey died, killed by the son he'd forsaken twenty years ago.

Laughter bubbled within Veronique and filled the silence of the chamber. Pride burned in her breast, for at last—*at last*—Tye was taking the role she'd envisioned for him since the day he'd burst from her womb. It had taken long years of teaching, guiding, manipulating, but all of it had finally coalesced into one sole purpose: to destroy de Lanceau.

Tye *would* destroy him.

Opening her hand, Veronique looked at the crushed ornament, too damaged now to be worthy of repair. Geoffrey would soon be damaged, destroyed. That it would happen at Wode was even more fitting. Geoffrey had been born in the castle—in this very room. He'd fought years ago to reclaim Wode and his family's honor, as part of his plan to avenge his father who had died condemned as a traitor. And here, in the fortress that had been home for so many lords of his revered Norman bloodline, he would *die*.

Her lips twisted, and then she flung the jewel against the wall. As the *clink* of metal faded, rumbled voices from the corridor reached her. She'd seen the battered chamber door farther down the passageway, and among the voices, she recognized Tye's. He had a talent for breaking down doors—and for swiftly quelling any opposition—as the occupants of that room had no doubt discovered.

Veronique trailed her hand over the end of the wide rope bed, the pale blue silk coverlet soft beneath her palm. When Tye assumed the role of bold warrior, he could be formidable. Exceptionally so. His handsome face turned hard, and his gaze became knife sharp, piercing.

At times, she was a little afraid of him. She'd never admit that to him, though. Why should she? She had no reason to fear her son. He'd never harm her; she'd kept too good a hold over his emotions for him to ever dream of turning against her.

Judging by the frightened murmurs following Tye's raised voice, the women in the chamber were obeying him. And so they should. They were now his subjects, for him to do with as he pleased. A bawdy giggle tickled Veronique's throat. With his healthy sexual appetites, they would please him, all right.

She sensed movement near the solar door, spun, and grabbed for her knife, but then Braden strode in, his sword at the ready. How she loved the unapologetic arrogance in his walk; it had appealed to her on a raw, sexual level from their very first meeting.

When he saw her, he grinned and lowered his weapon. "Love."

She smiled back. "All is well in the great hall?"

"'Tis secured, just as we planned. I came to see if I was needed up here."

Needed. Her womb pulsed, a throb of anticipation. She always needed him, and had done since the day she'd first laid eyes upon him.

Braden strode past her, his gaze sharpening as he scrutinized the chamber. She knew that look. He'd once studied her with such thoroughness. She'd been a prisoner then, chained by her wrists and ankles to a dungeon wall, captive to his stare and harsh words. A slick fire began to burn between her thighs.

How clearly she remembered when he'd entered the dungeon of the castle ruled by Dominic de Terre, de Lanceau's closest friend and most loyal knight. She'd been imprisoned soon after the defeat at Waddesford Keep. De Lanceau had put her in

Dominic's care so that she and Tye would be in separate secure locations—what little good that had done.

When Braden had stepped into dungeon, she'd felt his presence like a hot hand sliding over her body. Introduced as an interrogator who reported to the King, he'd walked into her dank, solitary cell to question her and slammed the door; she'd shivered inside with wicked desire. She'd challenged his quelling stare, fought his inquiries with her wits and feminine wiles, and in the coming days, had found his weaknesses: loneliness and failed ambition.

As the days of interrogation had worn on, she'd secretly tried to convince him of the advantages he'd gain by helping her and Tye, especially when Tye would soon rule all of Moydenshire. "You could be a lord," she'd coaxed, keeping her tone hushed. "A *rich* lord. A man with an estate, a castle, and a title worthy of great respect."

"Beware," he'd growled. "I do not tolerate lies."

"Lies?" She'd scoffed. "I do not lie. All that I mentioned could easily be yours." She'd paused for a significant moment, letting her words settle before she went in for the final verbal thrust. "'Tis clear to me that you are an intelligent and skilled man. Surely you aspire to be more than an interrogator? Surely you *deserve* more?"

He'd scowled, told her to stop trying to deceive him, and continued with his questioning. The next morning, his face an emotionless mask, Braden had arrived with a covered wagon, four armed men, and a signed missive, and hauled her in chains from her cell.

"King's orders," Braden had told Dominic, who'd been angry enough to smash a hole through the dungeon wall with his bare hands. "I am to take her to London. The King has questions about information she provided during my interrogation. On those matters, she will answer to King John himself."

Dominic had fiercely protested her being taken away, but no lord could overrule a summons from the crown. Some distance from the castle gates, however, the wagon and riders had been set upon by mercenaries, and the men who'd accompanied Braden had been killed—just as he'd arranged.

After liberating Veronique from her chains, Braden had explained that the escape was part of King John's secret agreement with her; the days of interrogation she'd endured were a necessary ruse, to ensure Dominic wouldn't try to stop Braden when he took her from the dungeon. In exchange for her freedom, she'd relay information on de Lanceau to the King. Moreover, Braden was to be her personal protector. She'd agreed to the terms and then seduced him in a passionate coupling that had sealed their arrangement. That night, before word of the killing of Braden's entourage had spread throughout Moydenshire, they'd successfully freed Tye from de Lanceau's dungeon.

How she'd grown to appreciate Braden. While he obeyed his King, he also saw that with the political instability caused by King John's ever-increasing taxes, his confiscation of castles and lands throughout England, and his war with the French King, there were opportunities for ambitious men. He wanted to rule a fortress; he looked forward to becoming king of his own court and enjoying the rich future she'd offered him.

She adored his self-centered ruthlessness, almost as much as she loved his naked body on top of her, pounding into her...

Braden approached the solar window and drew open the shutters to look out. Her body tingling with desire, Veronique crossed to the door and shoved it closed.

Braden glanced at her. He was clearly trying to appear surprised. Yet, she knew him too well to mistake the glint in his eyes for astonishment. That fiery look was pure lust.

Veronique indulged in a bawdy giggle. Hips swaying, she strolled toward him.

Braden closed the shutters and met her halfway. "Why were you laughing?" He slid his arm around her waist. The scent of him—a blend of worn leather, fresh air, and pungent sweat—accosted her senses, rousing visions of their nude limbs entwined, thrusting together. Her womb fluttered greedily.

Smiling up into his face, she said, "I am imagining Geoffrey's rage when he learns Wode has been captured. He will be especially furious when he hears the name of the new lord."

Braden chuckled. "'Tis the only reason?"

She nibbled his jaw. "Nay." Braden always tasted so good:

salty and spicy, like danger and excitement.

As her hands prowled under his cloak, he said softly, "Should we not find Tye?"

"We will. In a moment."

Braden's heated gaze settled on her mouth. "Tye does have the situation under control."

"He does."

"The fortress *is* taken."

"'Tis." She found the hem of Braden's tunic, and then her hands slid underneath, to the bulge of his sex constrained by his snug-fitting woolen hose. Her hands closed over his manhood, and she was rewarded by his sharp inhalation and shudder.

"Veronique—"

"We will be quick. No one will miss us."

"Mmm," he growled, a sound of definite interest. He shuddered again as she stroked his swollen flesh.

"After all, 'tis up to Tye to lead this day," she coaxed with her words and fingers. "'Tis his moment of glory. We do not want to take any of the victory from him."

"True." Braden clenched his teeth against her continued torment.

"And, we have a bed. A *real* bed, not a smelly, lumpy pallet."

With his free hand, Braden unbuckled his sword belt and tossed it on the bed, leaving the weapon close enough for him to grab it if needed. His arm around her tightened. As her hands slid up to his chest to unfasten the pin securing his cloak, he drew her lower body more fully against his.

Veronique's lips parted on a groan of desire. She'd fornicated in many places, but to couple in this solar where Geoffrey had been born, in this castle that he held so very sacred... How he would loathe such a deed. All the more reason to do it. Heady excitement made her limbs go weak.

Still in Braden's grasp, she turned and edged backward, until her legs hit the wooden bed frame. With a low growl, he released his hold on her, just long enough for her to push away his cloak. The instant the garment fell from his shoulders, he caught her to him, pulled her flush against his hips, and slammed his mouth against hers.

His tongue lashed in a rough, hungry, possessive kiss. She kissed back. A harsh pant broke from her as she bit and kissed and suckled his wet mouth. Her thighs quivered. Her free hand moved, sliding between their bodies, delving through layers of fabric so she could yank up her skirts and take his hardness into her.

"Wench," Braden said against her mouth.

She laughed softly. She'd never liked the word 'wench.' It sounded common; unremarkable. But the way Braden's voice hoarsened, roughened, when he spoke it, made it sound like an endearment.

"Aye," she breathed back. "I am *your* wench." She ravished his mouth in another heated kiss, while she pulled him down onto the mattress. The ropes squeaked as they landed together on the bed. After shoving aside her hand still between their bodies, he slid his fingers into her clothing. He was still wearing his gloves. She wanted—*needed*—to feel his bare skin against hers.

Then the cold leather of his glove slid over her hot, slick flesh, and she gasped, arching her back, blinded by the pleasure. A moan wrenched from her. Oh, but it felt good—

Braden's gloved finger flicked over her most sensitive nub. Her head spun with the exquisite sensation. "More," she panted. She wanted a lot more—

Voices broke into her groggy, pleasure-hazed mind. Men were outside the chamber. One of the voices was Tye's.

She hissed an oath. He had better not interrupt. Not now.

As her body tensed for another delicious throb of pleasure, Braden swore and shoved up to sitting. He pulled his hand from her just as the solar door crashed inward.

Tye raced in, two mercenaries at his heels, their weapons drawn.

Pushing up on her elbows, Veronique glowered at her son. Tye abruptly halted, eyes narrowing. With a sniff of disdain, Veronique sat up, tugged her garments back into place, and rose along with her lover.

"Mother. Braden."

Braden adjusted his clothes and stooped to pick up his

cloak. "I will go to the hall," he said, snatching his sword belt from the bed. "I will check all is in order." After a curt nod to Tye, he left the chamber.

"Tye," Veronique said, enough bite in her tone to let him know she hadn't appreciated the interruption. He must have seen that the door was shut. He could have at least knocked. She glared at the leering mercenaries on either side of him, and their smiles vanished. Their gazes dropped to the floorboards.

Frowning, Tye lowered his sword. "Now I know why the doors were closed. I had deliberately left them open."

Veronique indulged in a brittle laugh. "You thought servants might have escaped from the hall and taken to hiding in here?"

He sheathed his blade. "'Twas a possibility."

She scowled at him. Damned, wretched nuisance of a son. "Was it?"

Tye laughed as if she'd jested. "Of course. This castle *is* under siege."

"*Was*," she corrected. "You won the battle. The keep is under your control. There is no doubt."

"I am glad you have faith in me, Mother." His words were pleasant enough, but there was an edge to his voice. She didn't deserve such disrespect, not after all she'd sacrificed in her life to bring him to this long-awaited victory.

A thin smile settled on her lips. Mayhap he needed a reminder of just how much he owed her, how far he'd come in his twenty years because of all *she*'d done to make him the warrior he was today. Within the next day or two, she'd find a suitable, unforgettable way to make that reminder very clear. Her blood heated anew at the thought of such a challenge.

For now, though, she'd let him savor his victory. He needed the glorious taste of triumph to realize how much he liked it; once he'd tasted the all-encompassing power of a noble lord, he wouldn't want to relinquish it, and *that* would keep him firmly at her side until the day he slew his sire.

Walking past her, Tye went to the table and drew a leather-bound book from his cloak. He didn't throw it onto the table top, but set it down with great care—unusual, for him. His attention shifted to the items scattered across the floor. "I see you inspected the solar."

"I did." She smoothed her cloak sleeve. "If we are to help you keep your control here, we must be familiar with all of the rooms."

Tye snorted and drew a stack of letters, bound with ribbon, out of his cloak. He set the bundle atop the book.

Curiosity drew her to the table. "What have you there?"

"Naught that concerns you."

Her fingers itched to untie the shimmering ribbon and glance through the missives. "Did you take these items from one of the castle folk?"

"From a young lady. She is in the chamber down the hall."

Veronique leaned her hip against the edge of the table. "A pretty young lady?"

"Very pretty."

She smirked. "Who knows what scandalous secrets you might have discovered about her?"

He grinned. "My thoughts exactly."

"Well, then…" Veronique reached for the letters.

His hand closed on hers in a firm grip. His bronzed fingers looked so strong and capable holding her gnarled, bent ones.

Anger flared that he'd dared to stop her. Veronique inhaled a slow, calming breath and told herself she must let him win this day; later, she would bring him to heel.

"This evening, we can enjoy what we have taken. Now, there is still work to be done." Tye gestured to the mercenaries near the doorway. "Mother, take these men and go and find Braden. Search the rest of the upper level. Make sure no one is hiding in the far stairwells or on the rear battlements."

"Surely you have men checking the battlements already?" Veronique groused. The thought of going back outside into the cold made her bones ache.

"I do. Yet, until we have counted prisoners and the dead, I cannot consider my takeover complete. And, Mother," he smiled that wide, captivating smile that always warmed her heart just a little, "I know you are as eager to celebrate our victory as I am."

Chapter Eight

Tye loped down the enclosed stairs of the forebuilding and out into the bailey. The snow was falling less heavily now. Flakes swirled in the breeze swooping in over the battlements and down into the bailey where the white ground was darkened by churned up dirt, bloodstains, and fallen weapons that needed to be collected and counted.

Mercenaries guarded the gatehouse. The portcullis was in place and the drawbridge up, as Tye had ordered. More of his armed men walked the battlements, while others tended to prisoners herded together by the dungeon, some with their hands bound. No corpses lay on the ground as a stark reminder of the takeover; they had been removed. The bailey held a sense of controlled calm.

Tye halted halfway across the open space and drew in a satisfied breath. Intense pride rushed through him. All had gone remarkably well. Wode, and all within its walls, belonged to him now. He thought of the willful lady he'd encountered earlier and indulged in a wolfish grin. She'd been an unexpected surprise, but one he intended to enjoy.

Boots crunching on snow caught his attention. He turned to face a mercenary with greasy brown hair and an unkempt beard, walking over from the dungeon. "Three dead, milord," the man said, "including one of our own."

Tye nodded. Losing any man was regrettable, but the mercenaries had known before the siege that grave injury or death were possible. "All is in order with the prisoners?"

The mercenary scowled. "Most of them are refusing to cooperate. They will retaliate at the first opportunity, I am certain.

If you would allow us to beat them or use our knives on them—"

"As I told you before, 'tis not how I want things done." Holding the man's challenging stare, Tye added, "I want a list of the prisoners' names. If neither you nor your men can make the list, get a captive to do it. At least one of them will be able to read and write."

"How are we to persuade a prisoner to write the list?"

Tye smiled coldly. "You will find a way. After all, I have paid you very well to handle such matters."

Sounds of a struggle drew Tye's focus to the men by the dungeon. One of Wode's warriors, bloodied and wounded, resisted his two captors. "Start with him," Tye said.

The mercenary snorted. "That one will not help us."

Oh, but he will. Drawing his sword, Tye strode to the prisoners. Shoving several aside, he pointed the weapon at the chest of the man who still fought the mercenaries pinning his arms, despite the sheen of sweat on his ashen face and the blood oozing from his broken chain mail.

"You," Tye said.

"Go to hell," the man seethed.

"Been there and back. Now, you will—"

"I *will*? Or what? You will kill me?" Hostility blazed in the warrior's eyes.

"Keep struggling and you will kill yourself." Tye pushed his blade into the center of the man's chain-mail-covered torso. "What is your name?"

The man pressed his lips together, refusing to answer.

Tye's gaze slid over the mutinous faces of the captives until he reached a blond lad, cradling his right arm, who stood near the dungeon entrance. He looked no more than fourteen years old and was likely the son of one of the castle's men-at-arms.

When Tye's attention returned to the warrior, concern shone in the man's eyes. Ah. He suspected that Tye would use his sword on the injured lad. Tye had no intention of doing so, but the warrior need not know that.

"If you will not help me," Tye warned quietly, "I will find another who will."

"No one here will help you," the man ground out.

A shout echoed from across the bailey: a woman's cry. Shocked murmurs rippled through the prisoners, and the mercenaries crowded in, jostling the captives, weapons aimed to keep the prisoners secured.

Tye stole a glance. His mother strode toward him, Braden at her side. Stumbling along in front of them was a brown-haired boy of no more than eight or nine years, his hands bound in front of him. Blood glistened on his brow, and his cloak and the legs of his hose were wet and bloodstained.

The warrior swore under his breath.

"Do you know that boy?" Tye asked.

His expression one of dismay, the man nodded.

"Move," Veronique snapped, walloping the boy across the back of the head. He yelped and staggered, almost pitching forward into the dirty snow.

The warrior struggled anew, ignoring the press of Tye's sword, but failed to throw off the mercenaries.

"Tell me what I want to know," Tye said, "and the boy will be safe."

Wariness shadowed the older warrior's eyes.

As Veronique neared, she grabbed the youth by the back of his cloak and hauled him against her. Her dagger glinted, a bright flash against the side of his neck; she forced his head back against her body. The boy's terrified gaze fixed on the warrior, and the boy moaned.

"Kneel," Veronique sneered.

The lad obeyed, his movements awkward. Once he was kneeling, she grabbed a gloved handful of his hair and pulled hard.

"Another captive, I see." Tye turned so he could address both her and the warrior.

"I found him hiding behind some cart wheels propped against a wall." Veronique glowered down into the boy's face. "He was using a slingshot to fire stones at the mercenaries guarding the postern. He was trying to injure them and then escape out the door."

"Well done, Mother."

Her red-lipped smile broadened, turned cruel. "He will serve as an example for any others planning to try and escape."

Shoving the tip of the knife against the lad's skin, she yanked his neck back further, baring the stretched column of his throat.

Tye suppressed the urge to flinch. During rough questioning by de Lanceau's men, he'd had his head wrenched back at a similar angle, and 'twas not pleasant. However, judging by the warrior's rising tension, the boy meant a lot to him; the lad's predicament was the extra persuasion Tye needed.

"Be still now. There's a good boy," Veronique cooed to her captive. "When I cut you—"

"Nay," the lad gurgled.

"Please," the warrior rasped.

"Hold, Mother."

Frowning, Veronique stilled. The boy drew in panicked breaths, his chest lifting and falling in a merciless rhythm.

"Why must I wait?" Veronique snapped.

"Please," the warrior said hoarsely. "He is my grandson. Witt is but nine years old."

Holding the older man's fraught gaze, Tye remained silent, waiting. The other captives glanced at one another, clearly uneasy.

The rebellion drained from the older man's posture. His shoulders slumped, and he suddenly seemed weary. "My name is Sutton."

"You will do what I command, Sutton?" Tye asked.

The warrior nodded once. "If you spare Witt, I will."

Tye lowered his sword and stepped away. "A wise decision." He signaled to the mercenaries to relinquish their hold on the warrior. To his parent, he said, "Release the boy."

A furious growl broke from Veronique. "Tye—"

"Do as I say."

She muttered words he didn't hear, but lifted her knife away from the lad's flesh. The boy dashed to his grandfather and wrapped his arms around his waist. Tears glistened on the lad's face.

Wincing with the pain of his injuries, Sutton curved his broad arm around the boy. "What have you done with Lady Brackendale? Is she safe? What of the other ladies?"

"They are all well."

Through gritted teeth, the warrior said, "What do you

want of me?"

"To start, I expect a list of all of the prisoners' names."

"Why do you want such a list?"

Tye didn't have to explain himself to this captive, but the reply was quick to land on his tongue. "Wode is my keep now. Every man on that list will owe loyalty to me."

"Not by my reckoning," the warrior muttered. "When de Lanceau finds out about this siege—"

De Lanceau. At the mention of his sire's name, Tye tightened his hold on his sword's leather-wrapped grip. "I care not about de Lanceau. I want the list. You will start it now."

"Someone is coming!" Mary whispered.

Crouched by the hearth in her chamber, Claire frantically glanced at the drying ink on the open pages of the journal. She and Mary had just finished writing two detailed pages on their perceptions of Tye. Mary had been especially helpful at finding the right words to describe how menacing and thoroughly despicable he'd been.

"Hurry, Claire! Hide the journal." With a nervous cry, Mary snatched up the ink bottle and quill and shoved them into the linen chest.

Claire scrambled to her feet, searching for a good hiding place. *The bed.* She dashed for the headboard, stooped, and slid the book onto the narrow ledge where the headboard joined onto the bed frame. Thankfully the journal fit into that slim space between the bed and the wall.

"Well done." Mary said, just as the door opened.

Two mercenaries—big, burly men—stepped inside. "You are to come with us," one announced, his voice akin to the snarl of an angry dog.

Mary hurried to Claire's side. Linking her fingers through Mary's, Claire asked, "Why? What do you want with us?"

"We do not question his lordship's orders," the other thug said. "We just obey."

Claire's throat tightened, as if she'd swallowed the hard,

rough pit of a plum. For what reason had Tye requested to see them? Yet, he didn't need any reason, not if he viewed himself as the ruling conqueror of Wode.

"Very well," Claire said, giving Mary's hand a reassuring squeeze. She didn't want to see Tye, but by leaving the chamber, she and Mary would gain further insights on the state of the castle after the siege that they could write about in the journal.

With one mercenary walking in front of them and one trailing behind, she and Mary were escorted down to the great hall. The vast, cavernous chamber was almost silent. Never had Claire heard the heart of the castle where most of the servants ate, conversed, and slept, so quiet, especially when she counted more than forty people within its walls: frightened servants, watchful mercenaries, and a resolute Lady Brackendale.

Even the fire in the huge stone hearth seemed to burn without its normal hissing and popping. The blaze had burned lower than usual, no doubt because the maidservants in charge of maintaining the fire had not been allowed to tend to it. The women sat crowded together at tables on the opposite side of the hall, weeping or staring down at their hands.

As soon as she reached the dried rushes and herbs covering the floor, Claire hurried past the lead mercenary to Lady Brackendale, seated at a bench at a table nearby. Mary stumbled along beside her.

"Oy! You," the thug behind Claire shouted, but she ignored him.

Sarah was sitting opposite Lady Brackendale, a dog huddled by her feet. The trestle tables were normally where the servants sat and ate. However, the table on the raised dais reserved for the nobility was blocked by three mercenaries with drawn swords. The men stood along the edge of the dais, clearly keeping a lookout for any hints of rebellion from their hostages.

Freeing her hand from Mary's, Claire sank down on the bench beside her ladyship. In the afternoon sunshine streaming in from the hall's overhead windows, the older woman looked wan, her age-spotted hands clenched together atop the table. Her fingers no longer glittered with rings; the costly jewels had obviously been confiscated. Yet, despite the indignities she'd no doubt faced, she sat with regal poise, her gown draping neatly over the bench, not the slightest slouch in her posture.

"Milady." Claire touched her ladyship's arm. "Are you all right?"

"As well as can be expected." Lady Brackendale's lips formed a taut smile. "'Tis good to see you."

Claire smiled back. "And you."

The mercenary reached Claire's side and glared down at her. "I did not give you permission to sit here."

"You are right," she said quickly. "You did not permit me, but surely there is no harm done? I promise we will not cause trouble."

The thug, about to grab hold of her arm, hesitated.

"Leave her be," Lady Brackendale commanded.

"Please." Claire forced a soothing tone. "'Twill be easier for you to keep watch on us if we ladies sit together."

As if to show her agreement, Mary settled on the bench beside Claire and huddled close.

The mercenary sneered, then stepped away, his hand falling to his side. "Fine. Stay for now. His lordship will be here soon enough."

The thought of seeing Tye again made Claire light-headed and uncomfortably warm all over. The way he'd lingered in her thoughts, every moment since he'd broken into her chamber, was shocking and most unwelcome.

"You are well?" Lady Brackendale asked, her earnest gaze shifting from Claire to Mary. "You have not been mistreated?"

"Nay," Claire said.

"Good. Sarah and I also have been treated reasonably well. So far, at least."

Mary leaned forward. "Claire, you must tell her ladyship how brave you were. Why, when that knave Tye—"

"Tye?" her ladyship cut in. "What is his surname?"

"I do not know," Claire said. "He would not tell me."

"He is the dark-haired one? The leader?"

Claire nodded.

"At least you found out his given name. Well done. How did you manage that?"

Frowning, Mary asked, "Aye, how *did* you manage that, Claire? You must have done so before he—"

"Aye, before he issued his threats," Claire cut in, hoping Mary would realize the importance of not divulging all that had taken place upstairs. Her ladyship didn't need any more to worry about. She was under enough strain. "His words earlier were intended to frighten us and make us obey. He did not intend to harm us."

Mary wrinkled her nose in clear disagreement.

Her ladyship's mouth dropped open in astonishment. "Why would you think he had no intention of harming you?"

Because of the gentleness of his touch when he searched me. Because he'd had plenty of opportunity to inflict harm if he so wished, and he hadn't. And because of the way he looked at me, as though I was fascinating, and beautiful, and...prized.

She was still struggling for a suitable reply when Lady Brackendale's gaze sharpened. "Claire?"

Betraying warmth crept into Claire's face. She fought it, hoping desperately to find an answer that would satisfy her ladyship. "His hired thugs would no doubt argue he had reason to hurt both me and Mary when he broke into my chamber. We had, after all, refused to open the door. We did threaten him with a fire poker and a stick. However, Tye chose not to hurt us."

Her ladyship frowned. "He was likely too busy finishing the siege."

"True, but—"

"Did he take your jewels? Your coins?"

"Aye," Claire said.

"He will use them to pay his hired men," her ladyship said, "and to buy loyalty here at Wode."

"He will try to bribe the servants? To turn them against you?" Mary shuddered.

"'Twill not work," Claire insisted. "Your servants adore you. They are loyal to you. They swore fealty to his lordship—"

"Who is dead." A trace of defeat shadowed Lady Brackendale's gaze. "Most of the servants are steadfast, but I have no doubt some can be bought for the right price."

A strained silence settled around the table. Her ladyship

looked tired. The shock of the day was finally taking its toll.

Claire tried to find something else to discuss, a subject that wouldn't add to the despair settling like a dusty blanket. They might be captives, but they also had knowledge of the keep and the people who lived within it. There must be a way to thwart Tye's plans. They just had to stay strong and figure out what to do.

"When this Tye arrives, I will tell him exactly what I think of him and all he has done," her ladyship said. "Why, he deserves—"

A door boomed shut, the sound rising from the stairwell leading up from the bailey. Lady Brackendale stiffened, and her clenched hands tightened, turning her knuckles white. At the opposite side of the table, Sarah shivered.

Booted footsteps echoed on the forebuilding's stairs. Silence fell across the hall.

He was coming. Claire recognized the low rumble of his voice. Other people were walking with him and would soon enter the hall.

The hairs on her arms prickled. A sudden tightness formed in the middle of her chest, making each breath uncomfortable. Bracing her elbows on the table, she pressed her fisted hands between her ribs, against her bodice, to try and lessen the discomfort.

The mercenaries on the dais looked at the opening to the stairwell.

Claire resisted the urge to glance there too. Still, she knew the moment Tye stepped into the hall. Awareness skittered through her, making her acutely aware of the unyielding oak beneath her elbows, the coolness of the wood against her skin, and the scent of beeswax rising from the table.

Mary scooted even closer to Claire.

He is just a man, Claire told herself. *Not a king or a god. Just a flesh and blood man, and a criminal at that.*

Never must he know how much he intrigued her. She held her head high and stared straight ahead, at the table of maidservants who were gazing wide-eyed in his direction.

He strode to the edge of the dais, coming into her view at last. Sunshine skimmed over his wind-tousled hair, broad shoulders, and the folds of his cloak, rendering him in a wash of gold. As he shoved back the edge of his cloak and set his gloved hand on the hilt of his sword, the light played down his strong, muscular legs.

Mother Mary, but he was magnificent. Just a man—and a criminal—but the most beautifully formed male she had ever seen.

"At last," Lady Brackendale muttered. "Now I will have some answers."

"Please, beware," Claire whispered. "'Tis a dangerous situation, and you…" *are old and frail.* "I do not want to see you come to harm."

Her ladyship's lips parted, as though she would reply, but then two more people walked into view: a slim, red-haired woman in a long cloak, holding a dagger; and a tall warrior holding a broadsword. They appeared to know each other well, judging by the seductive smile the ruby-lipped woman bestowed upon the man. The pair halted a short distance from Tye and studied the hostages, their stares hard and piercing. The woman looked especially ruthless.

"Who are those two?" Mary whispered behind her hand.

"Hush," Claire whispered back, hoping not to attract the cruel-looking woman's notice.

"I cannot bear this day," Mary said softly.

At the dais, Tye spoke quietly to the three mercenaries, who grinned. Then he stepped onto the raised platform and walked along behind the massive table, the hollow echo of his steps carrying through the hall. He stopped at the imposing, carved oak chair pushed against the table, where the lord of the castle would sit, then drew out the chair and moved in front of it. Looking down across the room, his gaze seeming to travel over every face staring back at him, he pulled off his gloves and dropped them on the tabletop.

Bracing his hands flat on the table, Tye leaned forward, like a displeased lord about to lecture his serfs. Strands of dark brown hair, loosened from the strip of leather at his nape, slid along the fur collar of his cloak and accented the hard line of his jaw.

Lady Brackendale huffed. "Look at him."

"I am," Claire said. He was handsome, frightening, and compelling; she couldn't tear her gaze away.

Tye's stare settled on Claire. The corner of his mouth lifted in a smirk that reminded her of every word and touch that had passed between them earlier. A wild heat raced through her, straight to the tips of her toes. She instinctively dropped her gaze to the tabletop.

Regret clamored inside her. *You should not have been the first one to look away. Hold his stare and do not break it. He will see that you are not meek and helpless, but strong and proud, as both Henry and Lord Brackendale would have wanted of you.*

She forced her chin up and glanced back at the dais. Tye's attention was no longer on her, but Lady Brackendale. The bench beneath Claire wobbled as her ladyship, shaking with anger, rose to standing.

"I demand an explanation for today's outrageous attack," she said, her tone sharp enough to chip stone.

"That is why you were brought here," Tye answered coolly.

"Explain, then."

A terse smile curved his lips. "Soon."

"Soon? Ha! I vow you have no reasonable explanation," Lady Brackendale said. "Whoever you are, you have *no* right to stand on that dais."

Anxious mutters rippled through the hall. Claire swallowed hard as the two mercenaries hovering near the table strode toward her ladyship.

"You are not a lord, *Tye!*" Lady Brackendale clawed at the thugs who grabbed her arms. "You are a greedy, lowborn, selfish ruffian who—"

"I am a lord," Tye said, his voice ruthlessly calm. "As of this day, I rule this fortress."

"Never!" Lady Brackendale struggled. The mercenaries had trapped her arms and were trying to force her to sit back down. Claire winced at their rough treatment. At the very least, their punishing hands would leave nasty bruises on her ladyship's skin.

Claire leapt to her feet. "Please." She met Tye's stare.

"Lady Brackendale will be injured. 'Twill not help matters."

"She should sit down and be quiet," Tye growled. "So should you."

Claire knotted her hands together. How she wanted to remain standing, to show loyalty to her ladyship and prove to those around that she wasn't afraid to confront the conquerors, especially Tye. Yet, as his stare lit with an unpredictable glint, her shaking legs collapsed, and she sat.

"You have no right to give orders in this keep!" Lady Brackendale finally sat, pinned by the imprisoning hold of the mercenaries, her eyes blazing, and the neckline of her gown askew. "Do not listen to him, any of you! He speaks lies."

A dark flicker crossed Tye's features. "Do I lie? I assure you, my blood is as noble as yours. Some of it, anyway." He motioned for the thugs to release her ladyship and move away. They obeyed, but remained close enough to restrain her again if needed.

"You are of noble lineage, you say?" Lady Brackendale challenged. "To what esteemed family do you belong?"

"The one that has ruled this castle for almost one-hundred-and-fifty years."

Her ladyship made a choking sound. "You cannot mean—"

"My sire is Geoffrey de Lanceau."

"*What?*" Lady Brackendale gasped.

A stunned cry broke from Claire. This man was Lord de Lanceau's *son?* Impossible. Surely. She'd met his lordship's charming heir before. His name was Edouard.

Yet, there *was* a striking resemblance between Tye and his lordship. Did that mean Tye was de Lanceau's *illegitimate* son? If so, Tye wouldn't be the first bastard sired by a wealthy lord.

"What you claim is a lie!" Her ladyship's voice shook.

"'Tis the truth," the red-haired woman said with a smug smile. Her fingers shifted on her knife in a manner that turned Claire's innards as cold as ice.

Her ladyship glowered. "I know Lord de Lanceau and his wife, Elizabeth. They do have a son, but his name is Edouard."

"Edouard is my half-brother." Tye's mouth flattened. "I

am a bastard, the son de Lanceau wishes had never been born. This"—he gestured to the red-haired woman—"is my mother, Veronique Desjardin."

Lady Brackendale's gaze slid over Veronique, and then she sniffed loudly, a noise of intense disdain. "Lord de Lanceau would never—"

"Betray his lovely wife? Spill his seed into someone other than the mother of his children?" Mockery dripped from Veronique's every word. "Do you really believe he would refuse other women who spread their thighs for him?"

Mercy. Did Veronique have no shame? To speak of a highly respected lord in such a way wasn't just ill-advised, but unforgivable.

A flush reddened her ladyship's cheekbones. "You speak in a most vulgar manner."

Veronique laughed. "I only say what we all know to be true. His lordship is no different in his lusty desires from any other man—except that through his cloth empire, he has distinguished himself by becoming one of the richest and most powerful noblemen in England."

Tense silence stretched across the hall. Shock registered on the faces of the servants who bore witness to the conversation.

"If I understand you correctly," her ladyship said carefully, "you are one of the women who, as you put it, 'spread their thighs' for his lordship? Tye is the result of that joining?"

"That is correct," Tye said.

Veronique smiled. "I satisfied Geoffrey's *every* need the night Tye was conceived."

"I see." Lady Brackendale's face had turned ashen. She looked about to be physically ill. "Furthermore, if I understand you correctly, his lordship betrayed his wife, whom he is said to love very much, to lie with you?"

Veronique's gloating smile faded. Rage tightened her features.

Tye answered for her. "Veronique was my father's lover many years ago, before he met Lady Elizabeth. He took the lady to be his wedded wife."

"Ah." Her ladyship's expression brightened with relief.

"So, if I understand you correctly, Veronique... You did not satisfy his lordship's *every* need, after all?"

Claire smothered a startled giggle.

"Oh, my," Mary whispered.

"*Bitch!*" Veronique shrieked. The man beside her scowled. She strode toward her ladyship, glee in the overly bright gleam of her amber eyes. "Just you wait."

The air turned thick with danger. Claire lunged to her feet again, fear pounding in her veins. "Please," she cried to Veronique. "None of us wants more bloodshed."

Veronique didn't acknowledge Claire or slow her strides. Her cloak snapped about her legs, the noise ominous in the ugly silence.

Sweat dampened Claire's palms. *Why* had her ladyship spoken so boldly? Had she *intended* to come to harm? Had she deliberately provoked Veronique to prove the brutality of the conquerors? If so, that plan bore grave risk. *Deadly* risk.

Her teeth bared in a malicious smile, Veronique neared their table. Her posture rigid, head raised high, her ladyship waited, as though resolved to accept whatever unpleasantness would occur next.

Just steps from her ladyship, the red-haired woman raised her knife.

Claire's panicked gaze flew to Tye, who stood silent and watchful on the dais. In the dim lighting, the angles of his face were defined by shadow, his expression unreadable. Why was he not stopping his mother? Was he going to let her stab Lady Brackendale? Desperation flared until Claire could barely breathe past the pressure crushing her ribs.

"Stop her!" Claire shouted at Tye. "If Lady Brackendale is harmed, you will win the loathing of every person at this keep."

Tye's gaze pinned her where she stood. "Is that so?"

Claire fought the panic trying to overwhelm her. Now was *not* the moment to stay silent. She must save her ladyship. "Aye."

Tye straightened, his hands lifting from the table. His carefully controlled movements reminded her of an angry cat readying to attack.

Halting behind Lady Brackendale, Veronique shoved the

dagger against her ladyship's neck. Steel glinted against pale, wrinkled skin. One slight move, even the barest flinch, and Veronique's dagger would draw blood.

"Please!" Claire cried. Her stomach lurched. Oh, mercy, she was going to vomit, right here, in front of everyone.

Worst of all, in front of *him*.

As she fought the mortifying urge to retch, Tye crooked a finger at her. "Come here."

Chapter Nine

Across the distance that separated them, Tye watched Claire's eyes widen with shock and trepidation. Her lips parted on a sharp inhalation that proved she hadn't expected him to challenge her in such a manner.

She should have. She was akin to a spoiled kitten who'd just indulged in a whole lot of reckless mewling—and who'd suddenly come face to face with a battle-scarred tom. Her claws were no match for a seasoned cat who could quell an adversary with one strike.

This was *his* hall now, with everyone in it beholden to him. Claire, of all people, should have yielded to his authority by now. The fact that she hadn't... Fury growled in Tye's gut. He admired Claire's defiance, but no way in hellfire was he going to lose this clash of wits and words to a woman, especially in front of so many witnesses.

This was one battle he was going to win.

By whatever means necessary.

Still standing at the table, Claire nervously wrung her hands, but didn't immediately obey his order. His simmering anger heightened; with the thrill of the morning's victory still burning in his blood, he acknowledged the growing fire of lust.

He could be patient a bit longer, but if she pushed him too far, she left him no choice but to do what he must to subdue her. He'd use any weapon within his grasp. That included desire.

"Come here, Claire. *Now.*"

"Oh, Claire," Mary whispered, grabbing her sleeve.

Lady Brackendale's hand, clasping the edge of the table, fluttered, a sign of distress, but she obviously didn't dare speak or move with the knife at her neck. Her eyes, though, shone with concern.

"'Twill be all right," Claire said, patting Mary's shoulder. She smoothed her hands down the front of her gown and started toward the dais.

Tye watched her approach, never taking his gaze from her. God above, but she moved with such lithe grace, almost gliding over the rush-covered floor. Sunlight shimmered on her wavy hair, turning the tresses to silken gold. The light skimmed lower, highlighting the pleasing curves of her breasts and hips.

She was beautiful. Elegant. A lady of perfect noble breeding.

A woman who deserved the attention of a far more worthy man—not a bastard-born murderer like him.

The thought struck him like a fist. He managed to quell the instinctive urge to flinch. Hell, he wouldn't apologize for who or what he was. His bloodlines might not be as pure as hers, but he was a son of Geoffrey de Lanceau. More importantly, Tye was a lord now. He could have any woman he wanted, whether she was a lady or not. *Especially* if she was a lady.

Claire halted in a stream of sunlight below the dais and looked up at him. The movement caused a glossy coil of hair to tumble back over her shoulder. He followed the slither of blond silk, let his gaze travel to the curve of her elbow, and then along her slender arm to her hands, clasped tightly in front of her. Then, slowly, his gaze trailed up the front of her gown, while he enjoyed again the lush swells and provocative shadows of her figure outlined by her gown. Finally, his stare locked with hers.

Claire pressed her lips together, an obvious attempt to control her anxiety. He fought a smile, recognizing pride and stubbornness in the set of her mouth. She was a worthy opponent. One he would enjoy bringing to submission.

He flattened his hands once again to the tabletop and leaned forward, coming closer to her eye level. From his viewpoint, he could see partway down the front of her bodice, to her shadowy cleavage between the uppermost swell of her breasts—a sight more tantalizing than he'd ever imagined.

He caught the enticing milk-and-honey scent of her and

wanted to breathe deeper, to indulge. There would be time for that, and so much more, later.

He could hardly wait.

She quivered slightly under his perusal, but didn't glance away.

"You speak very boldly for one in your position, Kitten." Despite his rage, he kept his voice low, ensuring his exact words would not reach the others watching them. There was power in keeping the witnesses wondering what was being said, in fueling the fear and suspense practically humming in the air.

Her fingers twitched. "I was only trying to help."

He laughed, the sound rough to his own ears. "By threatening a mutiny among the servants?"

"By speaking the truth," Claire said firmly. "Her ladyship is well liked here. Her loyal subjects—"

"Are mine now. By right of conquest, they will be loyal to me, whether they like it or not. So will you."

Anger lit her blue eyes. He heard her silent retort as clearly as if she'd spoken it: *Will I, you bastard?*

"I will not tolerate rebellion or disloyalty in this hall, especially when 'tis voiced in front of a room full of other people."

He half expected her to yield on a blurted apology, or to give voice to a flood of anguished words that would prove he'd won this clash of wills. Yet, despite her wary expression, he saw no sign of surrender. "I had to speak up," she said fiercely. "I could not stay silent. Someone had to help Lady Brackendale, before she got her throat cut."

"Her ladyship is old enough to look out for herself." His lip curled into a sneer. "With her years of wisdom, she should also know when to keep her mouth shut."

Claire's gaze darted away, as though his words had struck her conscience. "That may be so. However, she is unwell. She has been since Lord Brackendale's death."

"She is a fool to provoke me and my mother."

"Your mother." Claire's lips parted on a shaky breath. "You could have stopped her, but even now, Veronique has a dagger pressed to her ladyship's neck and is threatening her life."

He looked at Lady Brackendale, held hostage to the knife

blade. His gaze met his mother's, burning with triumphant fury, and he smiled before his attention again settled on Claire. "Lady Brackendale must take responsibility for what she said. 'Tis only just."

Her eyes flaring in desperation, Claire shook her head. "Hurting her will accomplish naught."

True. Harming Lady Brackendale, even if his parent did the cutting, was probably the worst tactical move at this moment, especially with tensions running high and with so many onlookers. Sensing Claire wavering, though, torn between her loyalty to her ladyship and yielding to his demands, was too delicious to let go— especially with all gazes in the hall upon them.

"What choice to I have?" he asked. "I will not ignore her insult to my mother. Lady Brackendale will be made to understand that I am the one in power here."

"Please—"

"Please?" The heady taste of victory flooded his mouth. He loomed even closer to her. "What, exactly, are you saying, Kitten?"

"I am saying…" She gnawed her bottom lip.

"Do you wish to bargain for her ladyship's safety?"

"W-would you allow it?"

"That depends." His fingers curled, his fingertips pressing against the hard oak table. "Your offer would have to be worthy of the offense her ladyship has caused. There is also the matter of your own bold words."

Staring down at her exquisite face, he could think of one offer he'd readily accept—a bargain his loins craved with ruthless intensity. She would have to offer herself willingly, though. He had enough skill with the fairer sex to ensure that even though she was likely a maiden, she'd be thoroughly pleasured in his taking of her.

He shifted his weight to ease the inconvenient, pressing tightness of his hose.

"I…have naught to bargain."

He laughed softly. "Not true, Kitten."

"You took my jewels and coins along with my journal and letters. You have no use for any of my other possessions. What, then—?"

"Surely you can think of at least *one* thing that would please me?"

Claire stared at him, as though searching for the answer in his features. "You cannot mean—"

"What, Kitten?"

She blushed and crossed her arms over her bosom.

"I cannot read your mind," he coaxed.

"And I cannot read yours!" she hissed, her face turning a darker shade of red.

Claire clearly didn't want to admit to the dangerous truth filling her thoughts. She was going to keep at this war of wits, to try and sidestep the verbal snare into which she'd walked so neatly. Well, this time, he wasn't going to let her get away.

He leaned even closer to her, the folds of his cloak pooling on the table top. He was almost close enough to reach down and touch her, to run his fingers down the dewy plane of her cheek if he so wished.

Softly, he murmured, "If what you are thinking involves my mouth moving upon yours…"

She made a strangled sound.

"You would be right."

"A kiss," she choked out. Her gaze riveted to his lips. Her expression registered both revulsion and fascination. "You would bargain for my kiss?"

"Aye. To begin."

"To *begin*? W-what happens after the kiss?" She was breathing more quickly now, like a cornered rabbit caught in a hawk's sight.

"I would touch you."

She nibbled her bottom lip with her teeth again. He imagined the taste of her lush, rose-red lips beneath his, and how she'd gasp with stunned pleasure when he slid his tongue into her mouth, gently at first, and then more deeply, fiercely, each slick stroke intended to thrill and seduce her.

"Where…would you touch me?"

"Wherever I wanted."

Her mouth parted on a little moan.

"I would not just touch you with my hands," he added,

"but with my lips and tongue." His voice became a lusty growl. God's bones, but he wanted to start *right now*, regardless of where they were, or who was watching. "I would learn every bit of you, every womanly curve, dip, and hollow."

"Mother Mary!" Claire squeaked.

"And then…"

"Then?" Her lashes fluttered. She looked as if she might succumb to a faint.

"Then," he said, drawing out the last note for a poignant moment. "If what you are imagining is shocking, inappropriate, and unquestionably sinful…then 'tis exactly what would happen."

Her hand flew to her throat. Her fingers curled against her neck like the wilting petals of a flower. "Nay!"

"Aye," he rumbled.

"You say such things to shock me!"

He laughed huskily. "I say such things because I mean them—"

"Tye," his mother called, shattering the sensual web that had ensnared him. "How long must I wait?"

He slowly straightened. At the trestle table, his mother still held Lady Brackendale captive at knifepoint.

"I understand your impatience, Mother," Tye said, aware of Claire's anxious gaze upon him. "You have every right to want retribution, for her ladyship was disrespectful. She deserves to be punished."

"I am glad you agree." Veronique yanked her ladyship's head back even more. Horrified whispers rippled through the servants, and several lurched to their feet, as if to intervene.

"However," Tye said, "I have decided, in honor of my victory, to be lenient."

Claire gasped.

Veronique choked. "*What?*"

"This one time, I will allow Lady Brackendale to go unharmed. She spoke rashly. In future, such foolishness from her or anyone else at this keep will be met with swift punishment."

Spitting a foul curse, Veronique let go of the older woman and drew away the knife.

He met his mother's furious stare before looking at her

ladyship. "Lady Brackendale has lost the privilege to be in this hall. Mother, take the two mercenaries behind you. You and Braden will escort her ladyship to the guest chamber opposite the solar. She will remain there, under guard, until I say otherwise."

Lady Brackendale's disdainful smile sent rage whipping through Tye.

"Get her out of my sight," he muttered. The hired men pulled her ladyship from the bench and, with Veronique and Braden close behind, they propelled her up the staircase to the castle's upper level and disappeared from view.

Tye's attention returned to Claire, still standing below the dais. She seemed relieved, but also wary.

"Thank you for not harming Lady Brackendale."

"Do not be so quick to thank me, Kitten." Hunger for her still burned within him. The need taunted him, filled him with a chafing sense of frustration.

As though attuned to his volatile emotions, she said quickly, "You and I did not make any bargain. Y-you spoke of your...desires, but we did not agree—"

"True, we did not. Not on the matter of Lady Brackendale. Yet, I have still to pass judgment on your insolence."

Her face paled. "I know I spoke rashly—"

"You did. You will also leave my hall. Like Lady Brackendale, you will remain locked in your chamber until I say otherwise." He motioned to two mercenaries standing below the dais. As the men caught hold of her arms, he said, "Once you are alone in your chamber, I suggest you think on what we discussed. You and I will speak again very soon."

Chapter Ten

S tanding at the front edge of the dais, Tye gazed out across the great hall. *His* hall. At last.

A short while ago, he'd sent the servants back to their duties; he'd assured them they wouldn't come to harm as long as they obeyed him and his men. He'd recognized anger and resentment in the folk, especially after Lady Brackendale had been escorted from the hall, and had forewarned them that his mercenaries would crush any attempts at uprising; those who rebelled would be punished.

As the crowd had left, he'd ordered several women to help tend to the injured in the dungeon. Since his wounds had been treated when he was a prisoner in his father's dungeon, he would show the same mercy to the warriors at Wode. Hopefully such generosity would help the castle folk look upon him more favorably.

Soon, a mercenary would arrive in the hall with a list of the wounded prisoners. Tye also awaited an accounting of the weapons recovered after the siege. For now, though, he had naught more pressing to do than wait.

As he smiled, savoring the heady glow of accomplishment, the *thump* of logs on glazed tiles drew his attention to the maidservants kneeling before the hearth, setting in fresh wood to rekindle the blaze. They glanced nervously at him before returning to their work. He ignored their furtive whispers. As the days passed, they and all the others would grow used to his presence. Once King John officially approved Tye's position, the whispers would diminish. Even more so when Tye slew his sire and claimed all of Moydenshire. Excitement rippled through him, for his long-awaited victory over his father would come soon. Very soon.

He walked along the dais, studying the hall that appeared to be well kept. The rushes on the floor were reasonably clean; the high, animal-horn-covered windows weren't cracked or broken; and the walls were decorated with colorful tapestries that were free of dust. 'Twas a hall its lord would be proud of. And he was.

He circled the end of the table and walked down the back, halting at the chair reserved for the lord of the castle. Drawing the chair out, he eased down into it. His fingers curled over the armrests, worn smooth over the years. How many men of de Lanceau bloodlines had sat in this chair before him? The aged oak creaked while he shifted his weight, swung his legs up onto the table, and crossed them at the ankles.

'Twas strange to look down from this privileged position into the rest of the room, when all of his life, he'd been unworthy of setting foot on the dais.

Even in the lord's chair, though, 'twas a damned *drafty* view.

He was glad he'd kept his cloak on, for now that the most pressing demands of the day were over, the hall seemed cold. Glancing back at the hearth, he saw the fire was burning well; the maidservants were readying to leave.

The fire in Claire's chamber would have burned out by now. Had there been one in the room Lady Brackendale now occupied? He couldn't remember. While he'd be quite happy to let her ladyship freeze her sharp tongue off, he was, regrettably, responsible for her wellbeing.

As the women turned away from the fire, he called to them. "I want the fires tended in the rest of the keep," he said. "Also, tell the servants in the kitchen I want hot food and drink served as soon as possible."

"Aye, milord," the women answered.

They hurried into the stairwell. More servants appeared, carrying linen cloths and steaming buckets of water to clean the trestle tables. They glanced at him and then quickly set to work.

Moments later, his mother descended the stairs from the landing, Braden at her side.

"All is in order?" Tye asked.

"Lady Brackendale is secured in the chamber, as you ordered," his mother said.

She was gloating. Tye raised his eyebrows, a silent request for further information.

"Her ladyship has a few bruises. Hardly noticeable." Thrusting a gnarled finger at him, his mother said, "If you stop me from cutting a prisoner one more time, I will wallop you about the head."

Tye laughed. "You have not walloped me in years."

Reaching the hall floor, Veronique strolled toward him. "You deserved far more wallops than you got."

"Of that I have no doubt." He grinned. "I am too big now for you to bend over your knee."

"Do not tempt me. I might just surprise you."

Braden chortled. "Beware, Love. Your son is a grown man. He might just surprise *you*."

"He had best *not* surprise me."

Tye couldn't resist a teasing chuckle. "Do you not like surprises, Mother? Or do you not trust what I might do?"

He'd spoken in jest. Still, her gaze bored into him—long enough that disquiet stirred within him, an unwelcome sensation that reminded him of every time he'd failed to meet her expectations.

Her mouth flattened into a hard line, and she unfastened her cloak. "I do not expect surprises from my own flesh and blood. Tye knows his efforts should be spent on more important matters."

In her crisp tone, he heard a reminder of why they'd captured this castle: to destroy his sire and take control of the de Lanceau empire. 'Twas what they both wanted, what they'd patiently worked toward, and what was easily within their grasp now.

Tye's mischievous smile faded. His mother was right to chastise him; she, after all, had always fought for what was best for him. She'd protected him, raised him, when his father, if given the chance, would have killed them both. Tye dipped his head to her in a brisk nod, and she smiled coolly.

She slipped off her cloak, tossed it onto the table on the

dais and then smoothed her hands over the gown clinging to her slender curves. Braden's hungry stare skimmed over her, and she smiled at him, so suggestively, Tye had no doubt that they'd soon be finishing what he'd interrupted when he'd stormed into the solar earlier.

"By the way," his mother said, "Braden and I will be staying in the large chamber in the north tower. The solar, of course, is yours."

They'd agreed days ago that he'd occupy Wode's solar, but she obviously wanted to exert some control over the day's arrangements. "Fine," he said.

"Good. Now, we must celebrate your victory this day." Veronique frowned at the table. "No wine? No ale?"

Aware of the toiling servants listening to the conversation, Tye said, "I have ordered food and drink. 'Twill arrive soon."

Veronique scowled. "The servants owe you their loyalty. If you ordered food and wine, they should have been brought immediately. You cannot ignore this slight. Those working in the kitchen should be hauled out into the bailey and soundly whipped."

"Mother—"

"I can see to the whippings for you, Tye," Braden said, sounding eager for a reason to inflict pain. No wonder he and Tye's mother got along so well.

"I am certain what I ordered will be here shortly." Tye caught the gaze of one of the servants, who was clever enough to understand the silent command in his stare. She dropped her cloth and hurried into the stairwell.

Veronique watched the woman go and then once again faced Tye. "Before I forget, there is another matter we must discuss."

"What matter is that?"

"The lady who challenged you."

"Claire." Tye's body responded with a ravenous ache that rekindled the fire in his groin. Soon, he'd go and check on her. He must be sure the servants had tended to the fires, after all.

"Claire, is it? I did not realize you two were so well acquainted."

His mother always had to pry. Unwilling to divulge more about Claire than he had to, he said, "We are not well acquainted. I barely know her."

"She is the pretty one you discovered while searching the upstairs chambers?"

He nodded.

"I am surprised you let her get away with such disrespect earlier, especially with all of those servants bearing witness."

"I could have crushed her at any time, Mother, if I had so wished."

"Yet, you did not. I am disappointed."

Disappointed. Tye hated that word coming from her lips when she spoke of him.

Smothering an irritated growl, Tye slowly pushed back in the chair and lowered his feet to the floor. He wouldn't apologize for the way he'd handled the situation in the hall. His mother might have preferred a gruesome spilling of blood, but bloodshed would not win him respect among the castle folk.

His mother's laughter pierced his thoughts. "You have no more to say on the matter?"

He deliberately held his mother's mocking stare. "I will have other opportunities to quell Claire's boldness, if need be."

"Mmm. I saw how intently you spoke to her—and how you looked at her."

"How, exactly, was that?"

"As though you wanted to throw her down on the table, shove up her gown, and take her."

Exactly right. A roguish grin tilted his lips. "How well you know me."

"You *are* my one and only son." She smiled. "You are also a man of lusty appetites, whether the woman be a maiden, a courtesan, or a widow. I am surprised you did not ravish the lady during your first meeting."

"In the midst of a takeover? 'Twould have been more than foolish."

She glanced coyly at Braden, who chuckled, and then back at Tye. "Well, now that the siege is over and this castle is yours, you can do whatever you want with her. *Whenever* you want. As *often* as you want."

On that, they were in agreement. Just thinking of Claire sent a hot shiver rippling through him. "Lady Sevalliere is quite lovely, even if she—"

"—is trouble," Veronique interrupted. "Lovely or not, whether you lust after her or not, she is a challenge to your rule here. One we would be wise to eliminate."

Tye was all too aware of the way his mother dealt with people she viewed as problematic. Her dagger had sliced more throats than he could count on two hands, and those were the killings of which he knew. "Mother—"

"She cannot be allowed to oppose you in that way again."

"I can handle Claire." He shot his mother a warning glare.

"I have no doubt you can and will *handle* her. Your clever hands have fondled half the women in England."

Tye clenched his jaw. He might have needs, but he wasn't *that* loose with his affections. He didn't couple with just any wench. He met a sour glance from the woman scrubbing a nearby table; she doubtless hated the thought of him touching well-bred, innocent Claire. Spurred by a sting of annoyance, he smirked at her. She flushed bright red and scrubbed as though her life depended upon it.

Veronique's painted lips parted, as if she intended to say more, but a muffled *bang* carried from the forebuilding. A moment later, the mercenary Tye had been expecting appeared.

At bloody last.

Tye rose, the legs of the chair scraping across the floor.

The man, sporting a purplish bruise on his brow, halted and bowed. Clumps of ice fell from the hem of his cloak.

"The prisoners are taken care of?" Tye asked.

"Aye, milord. I have the list you requested, written by Sutton."

Tye strode along the back of the table. "You can review the list with me on the way to the dungeon. I wish to check on the prisoners myself." Ignoring his mother's outraged cry, he said to her, "I regret having to leave, but I do have duties to attend. I will join you in celebrating our victory as soon as I can."

With the mercenary close behind, Tye crossed the hall and

headed down to the bailey. When he burst through the forebuilding door, he blew out a sharp breath, immensely glad to be out in the fresh air.

As Tye took a quick assessment of the bailey, a dark shape caught his attention: a furry black object squeezed behind a barrel near the stables. He might not have noticed it, but for the feathered fletching of an arrow jutting out from behind the barrel at an odd angle. The object didn't move, though, and judging by its size and shape, was likely no more than a discarded garment.

"Milord?" the mercenary asked.

"Tell me about the list," Tye said, motioning to the dungeon. Whatever was behind the barrel would have to wait.

Tye is the most disagreeable, irritating, arrogant man I have ever met. I vow he has no knowledge of honor or gallantry—very surprising in this era of chivalry—and have reached such a conclusion not just because he boldly claimed this keep for his own. Truth be told, I am still shocked by the outrageous bargain he proposed in the great hall, one that involved him kissing me, touching me, and even more that I am too mortified to remember and, if I dare to ponder further, will cause me to swoon.

What kind of man believes he has a right to such intimacies, especially with a lady he hardly knows? My thoughts refuse to stop mulling this question, even though I would never yield to such a ridiculous agreement.

I know that kissing is a most wonderful, special intimacy between a man and woman who love each other and who will spend the rest of their lives together. I know exactly how kisses should be from the one Henry and I shared. A kiss simply cannot be enjoyed with a conquering rogue.

If Tye believes he can kiss me, he is very much mistaken. I am, and will always be, devoted to my beloved, departed Henry.

Setting down the quill, Claire read over what she'd written and gave a satisfied nod. She'd covered most of what she'd intended to say. She tucked the quill and ink back into the bag and stowed them back in her linen chest.

Then she set the journal down by the hearth so the ink would fully dry. The fire had burned down to embers, and the mercenaries had taken away the implements so she had no way to stir up the blaze, but hopefully there would still be enough heat. If only she hadn't wasted so much time deliberating before setting quill to parchment; however, that couldn't be helped now.

Aware of a chill settling in, Claire strode the length of her chamber, rubbing her arms with her hands. She felt a bit warmer, although the coldness wasn't just in the air; it was deep inside her, an icy knot of uncertainty as to what would happen to her next.

Tye's words rumbled again in her mind. *If what you are thinking involves my mouth moving upon yours... you would be right.*

Choking down a little cry, she spun on her heel, her gown swirling at her ankles, and paced back across her chamber.

I would touch you. . . I would learn every bit of you, every womanly curve, dip, and hollow.

He should *not* be able to torment her when he was nowhere near. Yet, his words simply would not leave her be.

Worry gnawed its way into Claire's thoughts. What was happening in the hall now? Was Lady Brackendale all right? And what of Mary?

Claire sighed, for it seemed an eternity since the guards had brought her back to her room, shoved her inside, and locked the door, without any wood for the fire or even something to drink. If only she could speak to Tye, ask him outright his intentions, not just for the folk living at the keep, but for her.

She had no prior experience to guide her with a man such as him: a rogue governed by fierce passions and dark secrets. That he would desire her was both terrifying and—God help her—thrilling.

She scowled at her idiocy. "*Not* thrilling. Not, not, *not!*"

Crouching by the hearth, she inspected the ink. It seemed dry, but she would wait a little longer, just to be sure, before hiding the journal again.

Just as she rose to standing, voices sounded outside her door. Gasping, she snatched up the journal, slammed it closed, and dashed for the bed.

She'd only just tucked the journal away and straightened, when the door opened.

Tye strode through the doorway.

Chapter Eleven

laire's pulse jumped as Tye's gaze fixed on her standing near the bed. Memories of their previous conversation crowded into her mind, and dread wove through her. Had he come to finalize the bargain he'd so brazenly proposed?

Tye walked several steps into her chamber and then halted. His lips formed a thin line, as though he assessed whether she was going to cooperate or challenge him again.

Claire's legs suddenly felt unsteady. She was *not* going to collapse in front of him. 'Twould only prove how much he unsettled her, and her pride simply refused to bolster his arrogance. Maintaining eye contact with him, she walked to the hearth and stopped at the edge of the glazed tiles, glad of the heat that began to warm the right side of her skirts.

Turning slightly, Tye beckoned to someone in the corridor. A young girl hurried in, carrying a tray. Claire caught the fragrant scents of mutton stew and freshly baked grain bread as the girl set the food on the trestle table, then waited with her eyes downcast.

"Bring the rest," Tye said, "as well as more firewood."

The girl curtsied and dashed out. After nodding to his men on guard outside, Tye shut the door.

He had shut them in together.

Just the two of them.

Claire had never been alone with a man before. Not a flesh and blood one, anyway—as opposed to the gallant heroes who had filled her daydreams and romantic imaginings. She'd always had Mary to chaperone visits with Henry, to avoid any impropriety—not that Claire had expected any from her most honorable suitor—and also thwart any attempts by those who thrived on castle gossip to stir up a scandal.

Tye obviously didn't care about propriety or the potential to create a scandal that would quickly reach the servants' ears. Shame tugged at Claire, mocking her for all of the instances she'd been so careful to protect her good name and maidenly virtue. All had been for naught.

Swiftly following that shame, though, was indignation. If she'd had a choice, she wouldn't have allowed Tye into her room. Yet, she did *not* have a choice; she was a prisoner. A hostage to be ransomed or used to further his ambitions.

When he did not speak, just stood watching her, Claire crossed her arms. With luck, by standing with her arms folded, he wouldn't see how much she was shaking.

Tye's gaze dropped to her arms, then rose again to her face. His mouth eased into a lop-sided grin.

She could bear the awkward silence no longer. "Why do you smile?"

"Because I want to."

"*Why* did you want to?" Had he noticed her trembling? If so, she was going to have to find a better way to conceal her unease.

Tye shrugged. "Better to smile than to scowl, aye? Or should I be scowling? Were you up to mischief, Kitten, while you were all alone?"

Mischief. That could describe her recent entry in the journal. Surely, though, what she'd written was more aptly described as first-hand information on an important historical event. Therefore, *not* mischief. "I did naught of consequence," she answered, proud that her voice didn't catch and betray her lie. Remembering that he'd found her standing by the bed, she added, "I took the opportunity to rest."

His brows rose. If she made him suspicious, he might order a search of her chamber. He might find the journal behind her bed.

"How could I get up to mischief?" she said hotly. "You took my letters, as well as the journal that I might have read or written in to help me pass the day."

An emotion she couldn't name flickered in his eyes. "So I did."

"There." She nodded briskly. "You have the truth." As the words left her mouth, she cringed inwardly. Why had she said that? She was going to get herself into trouble if she didn't steer the conversation onto safer ground. As his stare sharpened, she asked, "How is Lady Brackendale? I have been worried about her."

"She is resting and comfortable."

"Is she all right? When she was forced from the hall—"

"She is well."

A sigh of relief broke from Claire. "I am glad. And Mary?"

"In her chamber. She is well, also." Tye's smile broadened, revealing his even, white teeth. "However, I expect she is probably fretting that I drugged her stew."

Claire's attention shifted to her tray of food. Tainted food was a possibility. What better way to keep an enemy castle under control than to taint the fare with drugging herbs? Leveling him a cool stare, she asked, "Did you drug the stew?"

He rolled his eyes. "Of course not. I did not go near the kitchens this day."

"One of your men could have done it, or even...your mother."

"My mother was seeing to other matters. Trust me, Claire. If I wanted you subdued, there are other ways of accomplishing that."

What a hideous thought. A curious part of her wanted to ask what ways he meant, but in truth, she didn't want to know.

He motioned to the food. "Why not eat while 'tis warm?"

"Thank you, but I am not hungry—" Her belly loosed a loud gurgle and she instinctively pressed her hands over her stomach.

Tye chuckled.

"All right. I am hungry. But—" *Even if the food isn't tainted, I could not eat one bite with you in the room, watching my every move.*

"I should not have mentioned drugging the food." Tye headed to the table, his long strides consuming the short distance. "Here. I will prove to you that the food is not corrupted."

"Really, you do not need—"

"Oh, but I do." He picked up the wooden-handled spoon—the one and only utensil. 'Twas dwarfed in his callused, sun-bronzed hand. He held the implement up for her to see and then picked up the earthenware bowl of stew. Cupping it in the palm of his left hand, he dipped in the spoon and lifted it to reveal a mounded heap of vegetables coated with thick brown gravy.

Her mouth watered. The cook made a good stew, always richly flavored with wine and dried herbs grown in the castle garden. How Claire longed for a taste.

A mischievous glint in his eyes, Tye raised the spoon and opened his mouth. The stew slid between his teeth, a smear of gravy glistening on his bottom lip. He closed his lips around the spoon and pulled it out, slowly, tiny bit by tiny bit, while his eyes closed in an expression of extreme delight.

"Mmm," he said, the appreciative sound deep and rumbling. "Delicious."

The muscles in his jaw shifted while he chewed. She wanted to look away; *should* look away. Somehow, she couldn't. She could only stare helplessly at his full, well-formed lips as they moved; his eyes were still closed, his thick lashes brushing against his skin. At last, he swallowed, and his eyelids opened, his gaze intense and gloating.

Again, he held up the spoon.

"Fine." Her voice emerged oddly strained and breathless. "You have proved your point. Thank you for—"

"I am not done yet."

"You wish to eat more stew?"

He laughed softly, as though eating was far from his intent. Then, holding the spoon like a lit candle, he brought it to his mouth again. His tongue flicked out to glide over the bowl of the spoon, as if to lick away every last drop of gravy.

Mercy. Did he do that after every spoonful of stew he ate, or were his dramatics intended to torment her? His tongue slid in a slow, slick exploration, while he watched her watching him.

She tried to remain impassive, but what he was doing was both thoroughly revolting and completely mesmerizing. How curious, that a strange, tingling heat had kindled in her lower belly.

His glistening tongue curled over the spoon with such sinful decadence, as though 'twere not a spoon at all but something else entirely... What, though, she had no idea, and that flustered her all the more.

"Enough," she said, trying to ignore the distressing sensations he'd evoked.

"I am upsetting you?" Tye gave the spoon another slow, lusty lick. Judging by his expression, the spoon now tasted just as good as when it had held stew.

"That spoon is more than clean," she said tartly. "And now 'tis covered with your spittle."

Tye winked. "What a shame."

"I hope there is wine in that mug on the tray. I shall use some to cleanse the spoon."

He chuckled, a sound of wry amusement, and then set the utensil down on the table. It settled with a soft *clunk*. "There is indeed wine."

"Thank goodness."

"Although if I were to kiss you, you would have my spittle on your mouth."

If I were to kiss you. Claire's whole body froze, numbed by the thought of his mouth pressing to hers. How did he know that while she was alone, her mind left with naught to do but worry and wander, her thoughts had, indeed, drifted to Tye drawing her into his arms and kissing her? Of all treacheries, her body had ached for just that to happen—even though she knew his kiss could never compare to Henry's.

There was only one way she'd determine for certain, though, that Tye's kiss couldn't compare.

Oh, God, what was she thinking?

She faced the fire, her heart beating wildly. *If I were to kiss you, you would have my spittle on your mouth*, her mind taunted. "Do not speak of such matters," she said. Her voice sounded meek, and she cleared her throat before she glanced at him.

Tye hadn't moved from the table. "Why should I not speak the truth?"

"You spoke of kissing." Claire raised her right hand and pressed it above the hearth, as casually as possible; she needed the solid weight of the stone for support. "*Us*...kissing."

"Aye."

Her fingers curled against the rough stone. "Kissing is not a matter to take lightly," she said, trying to sound stern.

"I agree."

He didn't appear to be mocking her. Indeed, he seemed to be taking their discussion quite seriously.

"Kissing also takes place between men and women who care about each other. Who have a romantic attachment to one another."

"Usually," he agreed. "But not always."

How dare he look so roguishly attractive, so dangerously appealing, when she was struggling to be rational and prove him wrong. Did *he* know all there was to know about kissing? Unlikely. However, he undoubtedly knew a lot more than she did.

Niggling curiosity welled inside of her, a longing to know just how many women he had kissed. Were the women he kissed beautiful? Did he kiss like the heroes in the *chansons* she and Mary had pored over? Were his kisses so passionate and skillful that the woman in his arms nearly melted with delight?

Stop it, Claire! Such curiosity is unwise.

Claire watched the smoke rising from the fire. How she hated the feeling that Tye was silently laughing at her. Her life had been so much less complicated before he broke through her chamber door.

Leaning his hip against the table, his broad arms now crossed over his garments in a masculine echo of her posture, he said, "You have gone silent, Kitten. Does that mean you agree with me?"

She struggled to remember exactly what he'd said.

"You said men and women who kiss have a romantic interest in one another," he reminded her. "I said 'tis usually true, but not always."

His smoldering stare pinned her where she stood. She felt that keen look as intensely as if he'd touched her. A maelstrom of fluttery sensations arose within her, ones that were entirely new to her and that she couldn't control. Beneath her sheer linen chemise, the skin across her bosom turned hot, itchy. She wanted to slip her fingers under her gown and smooth the irritated skin, but she didn't dare.

She didn't want to agree with him about kissing. His gaze warned her, on a very primitive level, that he was determined to win their battle of words.

"Well." She waved her hand in a dismissive gesture. "It does not really matter what I believe about kissing, does it?"

"Why not?"

"You and I are never going to kiss."

He laughed. The brazen sound taunted her. "Never?"

"Never."

"Why not? Are you afraid of my kiss, Kitten?"

"N-nay." *Liar*, her conscience screamed. *In truth, you are terrified, because you crave his kiss. More than you ever wanted kisses from Henry. How very, very wicked.*

With a lazy elegance she wouldn't have thought possible for a man of his size and strength, he straightened away from the table. Purpose, now, glinted in his eyes.

"I am *not* afraid," she repeated firmly. "I have kissed a man before. The kiss was *perfect*, and for that reason, I do not desire any more. Ever."

Tye laughed again, the sound rougher this time. He had interpreted her words as a challenge. Why would he have done so? She'd merely stated the truth.

He drew near, his arms at his sides, his hands lightly fisted.

Claire instinctively stepped backward, and her heel bumped the side wall of the hearth. Her body pressed to the stone, drawing upon its solid support. Strands of her hair caught in the stonework as her gaze flew to the door. No chance of dashing past him. Even if she did reach the doorway, the guards outside would stop her from escaping.

What was she going to do?

She must keep him talking. Distract him from the wholly dangerous, tricky subject of kissing.

"N-now that we have that matter settled," she said quickly, "there is another I wish you would explain."

He hesitated a few steps away. Firelight gleamed on the hilt of his dagger at his hip. Her nervous gaze slid up the front of his tunic, the cloth clinging to the broad muscles of his chest, to meet his gaze. He smiled, as though he knew exactly what she was going to ask. "What is that, Kitten?"

"I cannot help wondering why, if you are Lord de Lanceau's illegitimate son, you waited until this snowy January day to decide to challenge him." Tye's expression shadowed with wariness, but she forged on. "Why did you not speak with him years ago? Why not try to settle your differences long before now?"

"I did confront my sire, months ago, at Waddesford Keep. Yet, the situation did not unfold as my mother and I had anticipated."

"Waddesford Keep," Claire said. "I remember hearing of a battle there."

"A battle in which I had hoped to finally win my sire's acknowledgment that I am his son—not just a man he wanted slain."

"He wanted you *killed?*"

Fury heated Tye's eyes. "He wanted me dead from the day I was born. I have spent most of my life eluding his spies."

She couldn't imagine such a life. "Mercy! Whatever the circumstances of your birth—"

"—a man like de Lanceau would accept his responsibilities? Oh, aye, he wants people to believe he is a man of honor, a man who *cares* for his subjects and his family, but he is not. Not when it comes to me and my mother. He has wanted her dead, too, for many years. I am very glad he never succeeded in killing her."

Claire shuddered at the bitterness in Tye's voice.

The fire snapped, shot up sparks, as he said, "My mother told me of the day years ago that she took me to a meadow. I was but a small boy then. She had arranged a meeting with my father, to present me to him. My mother believed 'twas the right thing to do. Even though my sire had cast her aside, she had loved him deeply, and out of respect for him, felt he deserved to know about me."

"What happened?" Claire asked softly.

"My sire arrived with a small army. He refused to believe I

was his child. He demanded proof of my parentage, which, of course, my mother could not provide. Not to his satisfaction, anyway. Still, de Lanceau wanted my mother to hand me over to him. She refused. She told me she feared I would be slaughtered."

"De Lanceau would have ordered the murder of a *child?*" Claire shook her head. "He is said to adore children, especially his own. I cannot believe it."

"Believe it," Tye growled. "My mother ran from the field with me in her arms. She saved my life. She remained on the run, traveling from town to town, doing whatever she had to do in order to buy food, all the while trying not to be captured and killed. For our safety, she fled to France, where I grew up. There, my father and his men couldn't reach me as easily. When I was old enough to hold a sword, Mother made me start training to become a warrior. She said I had to know how to defend myself, to fight in even the most cutthroat battles, because one day, I would again stand face to face with my sire. I grew strong. I entered tournaments to win money for food and lodgings. I became a man, and I became even more determined to fight my father to the death and claim what I had been denied."

"When did you return to England?" Claire asked, appalled but fascinated. Tye's tale was akin to one of the heroic *chansons* she so enjoyed.

"I returned to these lands months ago. I knew I was strong enough to challenge my father and win. Mother agreed. We settled at Waddesford Keep, working on a plot to overthrow my sire, but regrettably, thanks to my wretched half-brother Edouard, our plans went awry. Mother and I were wounded and captured. Luckily, with the help of Braden, my mother's lover, we both managed to escape."

The anguish and bitterness in Tye's tale was hard to witness. Was there any truth in what he'd told her? Could de Lanceau have treated him so foully and still want him dead?

"During your imprisonment," Claire said cautiously, "you must have seen your sire. Did you not have a chance to speak to him?"

"When he interrogated me, you mean?" Tye snorted, the sound filled with derision.

"That was surely not the only time you saw him."

A terse smile touched Tye's lips. "When I refused to answer his questions, he walked out and did not return. No doubt he had hoped I would die alone and forgotten in my cell at Branton Keep, but…"

Branton Keep. The castle where Henry had been slain. A sharp ache pierced through Claire. Was it possible Tye had been a prisoner there when Henry had been on duty in the dungeon? Could Tye give her any new insights into her beloved's last moments?

She'd memorized every detail of what she'd been told about the prisoner escape and Henry's murder. The information Lord Brackendale had relayed to her in the privacy of the solar, though, his large hands holding hers and his voice softened by fatherly concern, had been sparse, no more than the barest sketch of what had happened to Henry. His lordship had tried to spare her feelings—a kindness that had been wasted, for she'd cried for days. Tears burned Claire's eyes now, for she wanted to know all, to understand the true nature of the circumstances that had taken her betrothed from her. She *had* to know all.

A touch on her arm made her jump. Tye had closed the distance between them. How had she not been aware of him moving closer? He must have moved without making a sound.

Tye was close. *Too* close.

She was shockingly aware of every aspect of his nearness. He filled the space in front of her, a solid wall of tall, strong, imposing man. Warmth from his body teased her, coaxed her with the possibility of reaching out and touching him, of feeling the heat of his body though his tunic. What wickedness, that no one else would ever know about that touch except the two of them. And for that reason, she wanted it all the more—even though she *shouldn't*.

With each quickened breath, she inhaled his scent, the smell of leather strongest, the hint of soap less intense, and most tantalizing of all, the earthy masculine essence that was uniquely his. Her head swam with both anxiety and anticipation.

"Tye—"

His finger pressed to her lips, silencing her. "No more

questions. I am finished talking about me." His hungry gaze settled on her mouth.

He wanted to resume their discussion about kissing.

With a sideways jerk of her head, she dislodged his finger. Still, though, she felt the weight of his skin pressing to hers. "W-what you want, I—"

"What I want, I take. If you learned naught else about me, you must have understood I am that kind of man."

"You are going to kiss me," she whispered.

"Aye."

"Even if I am not willing?"

"Aye."

"Even if I have already had the perfect kiss?"

"*Especially* if you believe that."

His face was barely a breath from hers. She pressed back against the hard stone, expecting the brutal and unrelenting crush of his mouth. Instead, the tip of his nose brushed hers in a gentle, teasing caress. Loose strands of his hair tickled her face, while his breath skimmed over her cheek.

"I could be wrong," he murmured, sending tingles racing across her skin, "but I thought you might be willing."

His hands settled at her waist. His hold, light but firm, sent sweet fire racing through her veins. Oh, but she mustn't let him kiss her. If he knew she wanted his kiss, there was no telling how far the intimacies might go.

Her mind whirled, desperately trying to think of a way to stop him. Tilting her chin up, she asked, "Why would you think—?"

His mouth covered hers. His soft, warm lips brushed against hers with the lightest of touches. Her body answered instantly. The heat within her leaped, soared. She suddenly felt hot, weightless, as if she'd been caught up in a blinding beam of sunlight.

She hadn't realized she'd closed her eyes until she heard his husky laugh.

Her eyelids fluttered open. The air in her lungs expelled on a sigh.

He grinned. "Well? Was that as good as your perfect

kiss?"

"Nay," she managed breathlessly. A lie. A necessary falsehood. She had to get away, for the kiss had been wonderful. So astonishingly marvelous, in fact, she wanted another, but she was *not* going to swoon in this rogue's arms.

If she made him angry, he'd release her and step away. Wouldn't he?

"Nay," Tye repeated. His eyes narrowed.

He didn't look at all deterred. Indeed, he appeared even more determined to prove her wrong.

Oh, God—

Without warning, Tye's mouth came down on hers. Before, his lips had invited. This time, they mercilessly tempted. His mouth plundered, following hers as she tried to turn her face away.

With a rough growl, his hands rose to capture her face. Without breaking their kiss, his thumbs settled under her chin. He held her firm and kissed her with relentless skill. This wasn't just a kiss; it was a promise that she would never, ever forget this moment.

A tremor of uncertainty rippled through her. She tried to summon a protest, but a thrilling friction had spread from where their lips met. The exquisite fire rushed like a greedy flame through her torso to her womb, making her whole being come alive with yearning. The force of his kiss pushed her head back against the stonework. With his body crowding hers, she was helpless to stop his onslaught.

And, of all shameful imaginings, she didn't want to. Never had she felt so incredibly *alive.*

She couldn't move. She couldn't think. She could barely draw a breath. Tye consumed her whole focus with the shocking sensation of his lips claiming hers.

Claire gasped, starved for air. Starved for him.

He lifted his mouth from hers, allowed her the barest chance to inhale, before his lips ravaged hers again, the kisses faster, fiercer.

Too much.

A moan welled inside her. As she yielded to his seduction,

as her lips opened and kissed him back, his tongue slid inside to glide against hers.

Pleasure.

Her legs buckled. Still kissing him, she sensed her body slowly sliding down the wall, her hair and gown snagging on the stone. His broad arm slid around her waist, catching her, hauling her back up, keeping their mouths locked in a frantic, wet dance as he pulled her forward against his hard, muscled—

A knock rattled the chamber door. "Milord," a mercenary called from outside.

Claire blinked, startled in Tye's arms.

Tye lifted his mouth from hers. "What?" he bellowed. As the door slowly opened, he let her go and spun away, leaving her to find her footing. A sudden sense of loss, of having something extraordinary wrested from her, tore through Claire. Sagging back against the wall, she dragged in a breath, tried to clear her muzzy mind.

The maidservant who had delivered the food earlier peered around the doorway. "I have the water you ordered, for her ladyship to wash," she said, clearly afraid to move farther into the chamber.

"Leave it on the table," Tye said, striding to the doorway.

Concern etched the girl's features as she glanced at Claire and then hurried inside.

The lingering bliss within Claire vanished, and she raised an unsteady hand to her lips. She had kissed the conqueror who had led the takeover of Wode. He'd made his intentions clear, and even knowing what was going to happen, she hadn't screamed for help, or struggled, or rammed her knee into that place that supposedly hurt men so much. Instead, she'd let him do as he'd wanted.

And she'd loved it. Even now, she wanted him to kiss her again. Those kisses had felt so beautiful and *right*...which only proved just how cleverly the rogue had seduced her. A skilled master at wooing women, he'd known just what to do to make her surrender to him.

Her eyes stinging, she whirled and stared at the fire. How had she let that kiss happen? Why hadn't she found the strength within her to fight him? Her weakness was a betrayal, especially of Henry.

"There are others behind me," the maidservant was saying. "They have firewood."

"Good," Tye answered. "Send them in."

A chestnut-haired woman knelt beside Claire and added more wood to the blaze. A younger girl dropped down beside her to stack extra logs on the tiles. "Are you all right, milady?" the woman asked quietly. "We were worried."

"I am fine," Claire said. "Thank you."

As the servants finished with the fire, Claire mentally crushed all lingering thoughts of Tye's kisses. She was a fool to focus on the pleasure he'd shown her; he was the enemy. Her anger kindling anew, she recalled Tye and the mercenary forcing their way into her chamber, the confrontation with him in the hall, and poor Lady Brackendale being hauled away. *Those* were the moments for her to keep in the forefront of her mind.

Once the servants had left, Claire faced Tye. His gaze clashed with hers, and again she felt his lips pressed to hers, his hands on her waist, his breath on her skin. Traitorous excitement soared within her, but she stiffened her spine.

Tye's mouth curved in a knowing grin. His expression suggested he knew exactly how she felt: torn by guilt, but also desire. Had he planned to bring her to such torment? Mayhap his goal all along had been to make her want him.

Resentment prompted her to ask him. Yet, just as she was about to speak, Tye strode out. The door closed behind him with an uncompromising *click*.

Chapter Twelve

T ye strode past the mercenaries guarding Claire's chamber. Smoke wisped from the wall torches and filled the passageway with murky shadows; the acrid haze stung his eyes, but he welcomed the discomfort, for his whole body was wound tight with pent up tension…and unfulfilled desire.

Moments ago, he'd kissed Claire because he'd wanted to—and just because he could. He knew how to pleasure a woman with his lips and tongue, how to bring her to such an exquisite state of lustful craving, she'd whimper, moan, gasp, and plead for him not to stop. When haughty little Claire had pretended to be indifferent to him, had insisted they'd never kiss, had claimed to have already experienced the perfect kiss, his masculine pride had roared within him like a beast answering a challenger's cry.

At first, he'd kissed her as a sheltered, highborn lady like Claire would expect of a suitor: with reserve and gentleness. He'd witnessed such kisses in the past, on the few occasions he'd visited noble courts, usually as a guest of his mother and her lover at the time. A small, foolish part of Tye had wanted to show Claire that while he wasn't her equal, and never would be, he understood her expectations and what it meant to be chivalrous.

When she'd said his kiss wasn't comparable to her perfect one, though… *That* had obliterated his desire to be gallant. The familiar driving need to vanquish, to excel, had risen within him, and he'd drawn upon his years of skill to give her a kiss she'd never forget.

He'd kissed her the way he'd seduce a courtesan or an experienced widow who knew the sensual games played out between men and women in the bedchamber—and Claire had bloomed in his embrace. She'd answered his sensual assault with an astounding passion he'd never expected.

Even now, he still felt her lithe body arching against him, her soft hair brushing his wrist, her eager sighs against his mouth. He'd aimed to remain in control, to kiss her until she yielded, eyes glazed, to whatever pleasure he offered next. Yet, when she'd kissed him back, his manhood had hardened with a hunger stronger and more urgent than any he'd experienced in a long time.

He was still rock hard. *Bloody hell.*

Halting in front of the doors to the solar, Tye dragged his fingers through his hair. What was wrong with him? A maiden's kiss shouldn't have aroused him this much.

He shoved open one of the solar doors. A few moments alone would help him regain control of his groin and clear his mind—

His mother, kneeling in front of a square of cloth laid out on the planks, looked up at him. "Tye."

"What are you doing in here?" He slammed the door behind him, with enough force to warn her he wasn't in the mood for verbal sparring.

Her fingers tightened on the cloth bag she held. "What is the matter with you?"

"Naught that concerns you." He strode past her to the trestle table, where a servant had left a jug of red wine. He poured himself a goblet full and downed a large mouthful.

His mother's gaze hadn't left him. Her assessing stare traveled over him, and he glared at her, while glad that his tunic concealed the most pressing reason for his foul temper. His mother thrived on sexual gratification, but in no way was he talking sex with her right now, especially when he was so damned starved for it.

"You look like a tomcat that got his paw stuck in a door," she said with a sultry laugh.

Tye downed more wine, letting the piquant liquid swirl in his mouth before swallowing. "If you say so."

"I do." Her laughter grated on his frayed nerves. "Order one of the maidservants to pleasure you. There are plenty about. They cannot deny you. Spend your lust and you will feel much better."

Was that supposed to be good, motherly advice? Tye forced the wine down before he would choke on it. "There are more urgent matters right now."

"More important than you enjoying your rights as lord of this castle? More important than establishing your authority here? I do not think so."

With a *thud*, he set down his goblet. Hands on his hips, he glowered at her, still down on her knees on the planks. "You never did tell me what you are doing in *my* chamber. On the floor."

Her ruby red lips curved into a smile of disdain. "Do not worry. I have not forgotten that the solar is yours. Once I am finished here, I will join Braden in the tower room we are using."

Tye gestured to the bag she was shifting in her fingers; the contents rattled. "I am guessing, then, that you are here because of what is in that bag?"

She nodded. "I wanted to test my new rune stones."

"Rune stones?"

"For fortune telling. I bought them a few sennights ago, to help me see how the future was going to unfold. Specifically, *your* future."

Tye fought an impatient sigh. "Mother—"

"I needed *some* way to find the answers. My set of finger bones would have worked, but as you know, those were stolen from me at Waddesford Keep."

He remembered those finger bones. Ghastly things. They'd been cut from the hands of French prisoners and given to his mother as a gift from a smitten suitor. She'd cured the bones, kept them in a bag among her most prized possessions, and claimed that casting them had given her insight into the days ahead. The bones hadn't helped them triumph at Waddesford Keep and, truth be told, he'd been relieved when they'd disappeared. Now she was placing her faith in rune stones?

"Actions, not foolish stones, are going to see us win in the days ahead."

She lifted one perfectly shaped eyebrow. Stones spilled onto the swatch of cloth. "I believe there is great power in this chamber. Your father was born in this room."

Tye shrugged and drank more wine.

Annoyance tightened the set of her shoulders. "You do not care? 'Tis even more fitting that you will slay your sire at this keep. The circle of destiny will be complete."

His mother sounded so certain, if not a bit addled in the head. As Tye raised the vessel to his lips again, his gaze shifted to the items on the cloth. "What in hellfire—?"

Studying the blanket, his mother's right hand hovered, as though she assessed the pattern of strewn objects before her.

"Are those *teeth*?" Tye stepped closer, leaned down, and picked up one of the small bits of white bone, unable to tamp down a jolt of revulsion. The one in his hand was a back tooth, with a blackened patch of old, dried blood underneath. "Judging by the size, this belonged to a child." His stomach rebelled. "I hope you did not cut this out of the gums of some poor little French boy."

"Of course not," his parent said. "They are your infant teeth."

"Mine?" Tye laughed, the sound empty of any humor. Before he could caution the words, he demanded, "Did they fall out on their own, or did you wrest them from my mouth?" Surely he would have remembered that kind of pain, but then again, his mother was devious. She could have accomplished that particular goal in numerous ways if she'd wanted: drugging herbs, a swift blow to the head...

"You have to ask?" Shock widened her eyes. She blinked, as though fighting a rush of tears. "I would never hurt you like that."

Tye steeled himself against a tug of remorse. His mother was a damned good actress; he almost believed her. Yet, in his heart, he knew she *would* hurt him if it served her purpose. 'Twas a foul thing to acknowledge about one's parent, but he'd witnessed the depths of her cruelty many times over the years. Still, he perceived no guile when it came to the teeth. "Why bother to keep my teeth?"

"I did not save them all, only a few. I thought they might come in useful. Indeed, they have."

"Useful," Tye echoed. "In what way?"

"They help guide the stones." Her expression turned intense and focused as she leaned closer to the blanket. A thoughtful sigh parted her lips.

Another object that had tumbled closer to the blanket's edge caught his attention: a chunk of amber, containing a bee, locked forever in its resin prison. A glimmer of memory scratched the back of his mind. He picked up the amber, entranced by both the beauty and the grimness of the memento. "This was mine, too."

"Mmm," his mother murmured.

"Someone gave it to me," Tye said. "I cannot remember who."

"Nor I," his mother said briskly. "Not that it matters."

Turning the smooth object in his palm, he asked, "Why do you have this amber? Did I tire of it and no longer want it? Or—"

"I took it away. You were too attached to it. You were distracted, when you needed to concentrate on other matters."

His fingers closed around the amber, the resin cool against the roughness of his palm that bore permanent calluses from wielding weapons. Anger crawled along the edges of his nerves. By her own admission, she'd taken away yet another possession that had been important to him, because she'd wanted to control his focus. What else had his mother kept from him that he might never know had happened or existed, because he'd been too young to remember?

His mother pushed back on her knees with a grunt and the *pop* of joints. "Do not think too long about that silly amber. 'Tis not important."

"You are right. Still, I will keep it."

"Why?" Mockery tainted her features. "'Tis a trinket. 'Tis of no use to a lord."

"I like it. 'Tis reason enough for me to keep it." Rising, he turned and set the amber atop the journal and letters he'd taken from Claire.

His mother cursed under her breath. Stones clattered. He glanced back to see her raking her fingers across the cloth, gathering up the items to put them away.

"Did you find out what you wanted to know?" he asked.

"The stones were unclear. I found it hard to concentrate. Next time, the path will be clearer."

"If you say so."

"I do." She folded the cloth, tucked it into the bag, and then drew the bag closed. When she pushed up from the floor, he took her arm and helped her to her feet. "Now." She patted his arm. "Go find yourself a wench. Several, if you wish. The bed is big enough."

He grinned, but didn't answer as she strolled out of the chamber. As the door shut behind her, he sighed. He hungered for only one woman, and she was not going to willingly lie with him any time soon.

The memory of Claire standing in her chamber, eyes sparking with both desire and fury, roused a fresh stirring of lust within him. He could go to her now, toss her down on her bed, and slake the heat in his loins. She couldn't stop him. She might hate him for the way he made her yearn for his touch, but he could bring her pleasure.

Did he dare?

Was he a fool *not* to dare?

He downed the last of his wine and strode for the door.

Chapter Thirteen

C laire woke with a start. Her sluggish mind acknowledged her chamber was still as black as ink, as it had been when she'd blown out her candle to go to sleep. That meant 'twas still night. As her senses sharpened, she realized someone was standing beside the bed, holding a burning taper.

Tye.

Her eyes flew wide. Lying on her back under a mound of blankets to keep out the nighttime chill, she stared up at him, his face cast in pale gold and murky shadow by the flickering candle. The light, although weak, revealed he was still dressed in the garments he'd worn earlier.

What did he want?

"Do not scream," Tye said quietly. "Agreed?"

She pushed up to sitting, hugging the blankets to her bosom. Her mind raced with explanations of why he was in her chamber. Every new reason was more unsettling than the last.

Was she wise not to scream? Even if she did, Tye might have told his men not to heed cries coming from her room.

Just because he wanted her to remain quiet, though, didn't mean he intended her any harm.

Praying she wasn't being completely foolish, Claire nodded.

Stepping away from the bed, he gestured to the chamber door. "Come."

She was to leave with him. Was he taking her to another part of the keep, away from his men?

"Now?" she asked.

"Now."

"'Tis the middle of the night."

"Aye."

"I am not dressed."

His mouth flattened, and in that subtle shifting of his expression, she saw the weariness in his features. "Wrap yourself in a blanket. You will understand why soon enough."

Her fingers pressed deeper into the warm bedding. She didn't want to go with him. Kissing him that afternoon had proven that when it came to him, she had few defenses. If he kissed her again with the possessive hunger and devastating finesse he'd used before, he might shatter all the defenses she had left.

"Disobey me," Tye warned, "and Lady Brackendale will suffer."

He sounded so frightening, she didn't dare to disobey. She pulled back the covers.

Tye's gaze dropped to her breasts, her nipples round beads beneath the linen. She blushed, even as heat smoldered in his eyes. A muscle ticked in his jaw before he turned his back to her.

"Come now."

"I…should put on a gown."

Halfway to the door, Tye shook his head. "A blanket will do."

"But—"

"*Now*," he snarled.

At the same moment, a woman's shrill cry carried in through the open doorway. The sound set Claire's teeth chattering, for 'twas Lady Brackendale's voice.

Claire scrambled out of the bed and pulled a blanket from among the bed linens. The thin, scratchy cloth wrapped easily around her body. She shivered, for the floorboards felt like sheets of ice beneath her bare feet.

"What has happened?" she asked. "Is her ladyship all right?"

Without answering, Tye strode out. She followed, almost bumping into one of the guards outside. The lout scowled at her, and she hurried on after Tye.

He halted at Lady Brackendale's chamber and knocked

three times. The door opened, revealing a mercenary whose grim expression was rendered even more frightening by a scar disfiguring his top and bottom lips.

"Lady Sevalliere is here to help," Tye said.

The mercenary stepped aside, allowing Claire into the room. Candles burned on the nearest table, casting a hazy glow. Lady Brackendale sat on the edge of the narrow bed, a blanket draped around her shoulders, staring at the fire opposite. Her hands were clasped in her lap, her posture rigid with defiance. Yet, her focus seemed to be somewhere other than the present.

"Did she have a nightmare?" Claire asked quietly. Lady Brackendale had suffered from them since her husband's death. The day's events had been enough to give any occupant of the castle night terrors.

"The second time she disturbed me with her screams," Tye said from the doorway, "I vowed I would either shut her up or kill her. Her lady-in-waiting was no help; she broke down in tears, so I sent her away. That is why you are here."

Claire nodded, even as she felt his gaze upon her back. With the blanket draped around her, little of her body was exposed to his view, apart from her bare lower legs and feet, but her stomach still fluttered wildly, as if she stood before him naked. How shocking, and mortifying, and yet, of all shameful sensations, how incredibly thrilling, to think that a rogue like him would stare at her in that way.

Beware of the danger he poses to you and all you hold dear. Think not of yourself, Claire, but of helping Lady Brackendale.

Curling her hands tighter into the blanket, Claire forced calmness into her expression and glanced back at Tye. "Her ladyship will not bother you again."

"Be sure she does not." He spun on his heel and walked away. The mercenary followed and once outside, shut the door, leaving Claire alone with her ladyship.

"Lady Brackendale," Claire said gently, crossing to the bed. She sat and took hold of her ladyship's wrinkled hands. The older woman drew in a ragged breath, but did not stir from staring blankly at the fire.

"Lady Brackendale," Claire said again, running her hand

down the woman's loosened hair trailing down the blanket. "Are you all right?"

The older woman blinked and then met Claire's gaze. Recognition softened her ladyship's features.

"Claire," she whispered.

"Did you have a nasty dream?"

The older woman nodded and then looked at the chamber door. A violent shudder ran through her. "As I woke, a mercenary came storming into the room, shouting at me. He warned me not to scream again. He threatened…" She shuddered again. "Never mind. He did not hurt me, and you are here now. 'Tis a great comfort."

"I will not leave you," Claire promised, gently pressing her ladyship's hands. "I will stay with you until dawn."

"Thank you." The older woman shook her head. "Having you here… 'Tis a kindness I did not expect of our captors."

"Nor I," Claire admitted. Yet, before she could ponder the puzzling kindness further, her ladyship drew her hands free and reached up to catch the blanket slipping from her frail shoulder. Ugly bruises marred Lady Brackendale's forearm.

"Mercy!" Claire gasped. "Did you get those bruises when you were taken from the hall?"

"Aye." Easing her age-spotted fingers under the blanket, her ladyship pulled down the neckline of her nightgown to reveal another purplish-red bruise near her collarbone. The injury would not be visible when her ladyship was dressed, but every movement, every brush of cloth against that tender skin, would cause her pain.

Angry tears burned Claire's eyes. "How horrible! Who—?"

"Veronique," Lady Brackendale said. "She wanted to hurt me, and she did, using the hilt of her knife. I am surprised she did not break any bones."

"I am sorry," Claire said. "The way she hurt you… 'Tis unforgiveable."

The older woman smiled wanly. "I am still alive."

"Did she hit you anywhere else?"

"Nay." Lady Brackendale's expression sobered. "And you? Are you all right? After that rogue summoned you to the dais, I feared you might suffer grave punishment."

Claire fought a hot-cold tremor. "He did not like my challenging him, and told me so quite bluntly. However, I left the hall without being harmed." Indeed, his impassioned kisses earlier in her chamber had been far more of a punishment; he'd roused within her an astonishing craving that still hadn't gone away.

"I am very relieved you were unscathed." Her ladyship was silent a long moment, her thumb and index fingers worrying the fringed edge of the blanket. "You must be careful of him, Claire."

"I know."

Lady Brackendale studied Claire's face. "Whether Tye is de Lanceau's bastard or not, whether Tye can persuade King John to grant him a legitimate claim to this fortress and its lands or not, are matters beyond our control. They will be resolved soon enough. However, Tye is a ruthless, intelligent, and determined man. He is the kind of man who, when he sees something he wants, will take it."

Tye had said as much himself. A flush warmed Claire's face, for she knew where this discussion was leading. "Milady—"

"'Tis plain to see that he wants you."

"It does not matter," Claire said, a bit too quickly. "He shall never have me."

"Can you really be so sure?" Her ladyship sighed, the sound fraught with concern. "Tye is no fool. He may treat you kindly at first, as he woos you and wins your trust. Like all men lusting after riches and power, though, he knows the best way to secure his rule here is to marry and have heirs."

"Marry! Have heirs." Claire twisted the front of her blanket tightly to her breast. "That has naught to do with me."

"You are not married or betrothed. Even better for him, you are an orphan."

"Regardless—"

"He will not have to make many inquiries to learn that you come from a distinguished bloodline. You are, sweet Claire, perfectly suited to his needs."

"I have no wish to marry him!"

"He will not care what you want, only how he will achieve

his ambitions."

This discussion was becoming more and more unsettling. "Milady," Claire pleaded.

"I know 'tis upsetting to hear, but you must fully understand the situation. Tye has, regrettably, taken Wode at a time when the King is struggling to maintain his hold over England. As you may have heard, Lord de Lanceau and many of his allies resent the heavy taxes and fines the crown has imposed in recent years, among other grievances. Before he died, Arthur told me that de Lanceau is organizing an important document, a Great Charter that will put restrictions on King John's powers. The King is aware of this document and, of course, strongly opposes it."

"I see." Claire had never heard of the Great Charter before, but having met de Lanceau, she could see him pursuing such a course if he believed 'twas necessary and just.

"Lord de Lanceau's actions pose a significant threat to the King. If King John believes Tye will be loyal to him, and will further the ambitions of the crown, he very well may grant Wode to him."

"Surely not! This castle has belonged to Lord de Lanceau's family for many years."

"*Especially* for that reason." Her ladyship's gaze shadowed with unease. "What better way to insult Lord de Lanceau, to demonstrate the King's superior power, than to grant all rights to the estate to someone else? Not just anyone, of course, but the illegitimate son his lordship has never accepted?"

Claire gnawed her lip. The situation sounded quite dire, but surely more so for her ladyship, who would be forced from her home, than Claire. "If I understand what you've told me, milady, the King can cede Wode to Tye if he so desires. Tye does not need to marry and have heirs to have a claim to the castle. So, therefore, he has no reason to pursue me."

A wan smile touched Lady Brackendale's lips. "'Twould bolster Tye's petition to the King to say you are carrying his babe—especially if he can claim you lay with him willingly."

Shame poked at Claire, mocking her for finding pleasure in kissing Tye. Obviously, his kisses were intended to wear down her resistance to him until she surrendered her innocence; he wouldn't have to force her, she'd eagerly give him what he wanted. How he must be gloating, for she'd hardly resisted at all.

Unable to sit still any longer, Claire rose from the bed and hurried over to the fire. Closing her eyes against the bright light of the flames, she fought to find logic in her world that was spinning beyond her grasp. "'Surely, milady, what you have said cannot come to be? Tye told us he is a bastard. He is not the first born son of a married lord and lady. By the laws of England, because he is illegitimate, he cannot inherit."

Lady Brackendale laughed, the sound harsh. "If King John wishes to grant Tye this castle and a bride, he will find a means to do so. In the past, the King has used bribes, imprisonments, coercion, and even sanctioned murders to get his way."

"*Mercy*," Claire rasped, her eyes flying open. What dangerous words. Yet, they showed how deeply Lady Brackendale trusted her, that she'd share such sentiments.

"Think about it, Claire," her ladyship said softly. "If given the choice to award Wode to Tye, a rogue the King believes he can control, or de Lanceau, a man he knows is his enemy, whom do you think will get the castle?"

Without doubt, Tye would.

Her ladyship rose and moved to Claire's side. "I know 'tis a lot to consider."

"'Tis indeed." Claire hated how her voice wavered.

"We can only pray that de Lanceau's men arrive soon, and that they will crush Tye and his thugs before the King has had the opportunity to grant Wode to Tye. Better yet, Tye will be killed in the fight, and you will not have to worry."

Claire's innards clenched. While she had no desire to wed Tye, she didn't want him to die, not from gruesome wounds inflicted in battle. She wouldn't wish that kind of death upon anyone. "I do not want any more deaths at Wode. Besides, surely de Lanceau will spare his son's life, even if he is illegitimate."

"We will see," Lady Brackendale murmured. She didn't sound convinced.

Claire struggled to contain the emotions still roiling inside her. "For now, I will do all that I can to avoid Tye. The less I am around him, the less chance he has to…to…"

"Seduce you," her ladyship finished.

Seduce. Claire fought a moan. Even the hissing, snakelike sound of the word implied temptation.

The logs on the blaze shifted, stirring up red sparks. Claire jumped, and her ladyship clucked her tongue and touched Claire's blanket-covered arm.

"I am sorry to have unsettled you, although what I told you needed to be said."

Torn by the sadness and regret in Lady Brackendale's voice, Claire held her ladyship's gaze. The older woman looked tired and fragile in the flickering firelight. "You have made me see my situation here in a much clearer way," Claire said. "For that, I am grateful."

Lady Brackendale smiled. "You have always been courageous, most of all in the difficult weeks since Henry was killed. I admire your strength of will. 'Twill see you well through the coming days."

"Thank you, milady, but—"

"—which is why I hope you will stay strong and not succumb to despair. All is not lost here. Not yet."

Confusion sifted through Claire. "Forgive me, milady, but the way you explained Tye's ambitions…"

"True." Lady Brackendale huddled deeper into her blanket and her tone hushed to just above a whisper. "However, as I passed the afternoon alone, watching the shadows shift on the wall, I remembered something Arthur once told me. An important detail he had warned me to keep to myself, unless there was a dire need to share the information." Hope glimmered in her ladyship's eyes.

"What detail?" Claire asked, intrigued.

"In the lower level of the keep are several rooms used for storage. Do you know the ones I mean?"

"Aye. One holds wine and ale. Another, weapons—"

"Exactly. There is a secret door built into the back wall of the chamber used for wine storage. 'Tis part of a hidden passageway that leads to a door in the castle's outer wall."

"I have heard of secret passageways inside keeps," Claire said. Mary would burst with excitement when she heard of such a passageway at Wode. She'd want to explore it and record the experience in the journal.

"There are several other secret doors inside the castle, but I cannot remember where they are. My memory... 'Tis not as it used to be." Grimacing, her ladyship shrugged. "In terms of the passageway in the wine room, the outside door has long become overgrown with vines and ivy. That should not pose a problem. Lord de Lanceau grew up in this keep. He will know where to find the doorway and may use it when liberating the fortress."

Claire grinned, her excitement growing by the moment. "We can use the doorway to escape."

"Not unless we can get down to the lower level. 'Tis impossible right now with our chambers being guarded day and night. Also, there is the matter of getting through the door at the other end. The foliage outside will need cutting back before the door will open."

"I could try, or we could send one of the maidservants—"

"And have her get all the way to the other end, only to find herself trapped? I cannot imagine the danger if she failed and Tye—or his cruel mother—found her. Such failure would also guarantee that Tye would seal off the passageway so that de Lanceau could not use it."

All good points. "'Twill take some considering, then, to come up with a sound plan," Claire said. "We must do what we can to help. We certainly cannot just sit by and wait for his lordship to rescue us."

"I agree." Lady Brackendale's eyes gleamed. "We can, at the very least, ensure the doorway in the wine room is unlocked."

"Unlocked?" Claire repeated.

"The key is under a loose flagstone by the rear wall."

"I see. Well, I shall try to think of a way to get down to that room."

"You will need a convincing reason. Otherwise, Tye will be suspicious.'

Claire suddenly felt chilled despite the blanket and the heat of the blaze. She'd never been a good liar. She did *not* want to know what her punishment would be for deceiving Tye. "'Tis not an easy task," she finally said, her words competing with the crackle of the fire.

"Not easy at all," her ladyship agreed with a weary sigh.

Tye lay on his back in the solar, his arms folded behind his head on the feather pillow, the bedding drawn up to his bare chest. Light from the hearth opposite cast shifting shadows on the chamber walls.

Earlier, two maidservants had put fresh linens and clean blankets on the bed, working quickly so they could finish and leave. Leaning in the doorway, he'd watched them tuck and fold, while two leering mercenaries stood guard close to the bed. While for the most part Tye trusted the thugs he'd employed, he had wanted to be sure the women didn't steal any of his belongings or trick the men who, triumphant after the successful siege, were itching to spend their enthusiasm between the thighs of a pretty wench or two.

On Tye's final walk of the bailey before retiring for the night, he'd seen one mercenary in a shadowed corner, his hands cradling the breasts of a woman pressed up against the wall, his right leg nudged between her thighs. Her eager moans had followed Tye as he'd walked into the forebuilding. He'd clenched his fists, fought the potent stirring of his blood, for so easily, he'd imagined himself caressing the lush fullness of Claire's breasts, coaxing those same hungry sounds from her lips.

Desire shuddered through him. Tye groaned, rubbed his brow with the heel of his palm, and tried to shove all thoughts of Claire from his mind. Aye, he wanted sex, but he needed sleep more. He'd gotten little rest in the days leading up to the attack, and his limbs ached from the day's exertions in battle, especially his formerly fractured leg, which had healed well enough, but still pained him on cold or damp nights. He needed all of his wits about him on the morrow, for there were sure to be new challenges ahead—including those posed by a bright-eyed, willowy blonde.

Tye shut his eyes, sucked in a slow, purposeful breath, and then released it. It had been months since he'd slept in such clean, soft bedding. The rope bed with its thick feather mattress was a luxury he'd only experienced in his dalliances with rich widows or wealthy courtesans; most nights, he'd slept on a straw pallet on the floor, with a single blanket to ward off the night chill. Now, each time he inhaled, the sweet scent of sun-dried linens filled his nostrils. The mattress cradled his body. The fire's hiss and crackle lulled.

Yet, sleep refused to come. Because of *her*.

"Hellfire," he growled, his eyes opening. He flung an arm wide. It thudded down on the mattress, the sound surprisingly loud. A startled rustling noise came from the hearth.

Guilt coursed through him as he drew back the bedding, rose, pulled on his woolen robe draped at the end of the bed, and walked to the fireside. Ignoring the draft skimming across the floorboards, he squatted beside the wooden screen he'd propped at one end of the hearth. Behind it was a low-sided box, lined with a blanket. A black and white cat lay huddled inside, ears flattened, its golden eyes fixed warily on Tye.

When he'd investigated the arrow jutting out from behind the barrel in the bailey, he'd found the cat. The unfortunate creature had taken an arrow in one of its back legs. One look at the animal and Tye knew he couldn't leave it to die. Ignoring the feline's yowling and clawing, he'd pulled it out from its hiding place. With a mercenary holding the animal still, Tye had removed the arrow, washed the wound with wine, applied salve, and then tied on a bandage.

"Easy now," Tye murmured. He stretched out his hand toward the cat. The feline wasn't wild, for its coat was thick and glossy and 'twas obviously well fed. Earlier it had let him stroke its back and scratch it under the chin, its eyes closing in pleasure. It had also snatched bits of cooked chicken from his fingers.

The feline hissed and struggled to rise, but its bandaged back leg hindered its ability to move. With a pleased smile, Tye noted the bandage wasn't bloodstained. A good sign. With luck, the wound would heal quickly.

He scratched the cat's fuzzy head. The feline tolerated the attention, its posture still wary. With luck, though, its disquiet would soon ease. Tye said gently, "I will bother you no more. Rest, my friend. I will see you in the morning."

The feline made no sound, just flopped back onto its bed. Eyes glinting in the firelight, it watched Tye walk to the table and the waiting jug of wine.

He downed a mouthful of the piquant red, savoring the burn that ran down to his gut. His mother would think him stupid for rescuing the cat, but he'd felt compelled to do what he could, if only as a tribute to the black and white kitten he'd found in a back alley in Rouen when he was a boy. For a few months, that cat had been his best friend.

His beloved pet had vanished one day, and his mother had refused to let him have another. "Pets are a distraction. You cannot become attached," she'd groused, silencing his tearful protest with a stinging slap across his face. "You have more important matters to think about."

He drank more wine, even as the pain of losing that pet years ago brushed his heart again. Scowling, he forced the anguish aside. He wasn't a lonely boy any longer; he was a grown man with a destiny. He couldn't change his past, but he could make his life now what he wanted.

His gaze strayed to the solar doors. Claire was only a short walk away. Would she understand how much he'd missed that kitten that had followed him like a dog and slept at his side every night? Somehow, he knew she would.

Claire. The heat in his groin roused anew, and his hand tightened on the stem of the silver goblet. He longed to kiss her again, to feel her quiver in his arms, to drown in her scent. She was far more than he'd ever deserve, but still, he wanted her for his own.

He forced himself to turn away from the door. As his gaze slid over the table, he stilled, caught by the stack of letters and the journal he'd taken from her chamber.

What better way to learn how to charm her, tempt her, seduce her, than by finding out all he could about her? Those pages held her secrets; they held the way to win her heart, if he dared to try.

Since he couldn't sleep, he might as well make good use of the night.

Chapter Fourteen

"W ake up."

The man's voice intruded into Claire's sleepy mind. Her eyes still shut, she sighed, her thoughts chasing a fading dream. She'd been hurrying through a crowded market, following Henry who was walking ahead. Somehow, he'd been unaware she was behind him. She'd frantically called to him, tried to catch up to him…

"Claire, wake up."

She groaned, for her eyelids were too heavy to open. Lady Brackendale hadn't been able to fall sleep for a long while, and Claire had refused to let herself drift off until her ladyship was slumbering. It seemed only moments ago that Claire had gone to sleep.

Sunlight suddenly glowed beyond Claire's eyelids. Someone had opened the shutters at a nearby window. As Claire stirred, her eyes opening at last, she realized she was still sitting in the high-backed chair she'd drawn up next to the bed so she could talk to her ladyship while the older woman kept warm under the blankets.

A floorboard squeaked close by, and then someone lifted a length of hair from Claire's shoulder. *Him.* Tye came into view beside her, garbed in a dark green wool tunic, hose, and black leather boots. His gaze slid from the hair trapped in his fingers to the blanket curled around her, and then lower. She looked down, to see that a corner of the blanket had fallen to her waist while she slept, exposing her left breast barely covered by her chemise. Because of the crisp breeze blowing in from outside, her nipple had become as round as a berry under the thin fabric.

She snatched up the blanket and pushed it into place across her other shoulder, concealing all but her neck.

Tye chuckled and released her hair.

Beside Claire, Lady Brackendale stirred, her tousled head lifting from the pillow. She peered blearily at Tye.

"Good morning, milady. Did you sleep well?" Tye asked.

The older woman snorted, a sound of disgust.

"I will take that as agreement." Tye's attention returned to Claire. "There is food waiting in your chamber for you to break your fast. A maidservant is also bringing water for you to wash."

"Thank you," Claire said, her mouth dry from sleep.

"I will escort you back to your room."

"Must you?" The thought of spending another day all alone and a prisoner made her cringe inwardly.

Tye's brows rose. "What is wrong with your chamber?"

The dangerous note in his voice made her uneasy. In truth she had no right to complain; she'd rather be locked in her room than in the dungeon. Still, holding tightly to the blanket, she said, "Surely you will not confine us to our chambers every day that you are lord here."

"Lady Brackendale is to be confined until I say otherwise, as I said in the hall." His eyes narrowed. "I am a man of my word."

A man of his word. That was a matter of debate, yet as he spoke, Claire's thoughts slid back to the discussion she'd had with Lady Brackendale last night. Keeping their voices hushed, they'd plotted ways for Claire to get down to the storage rooms. The plan they'd devised was risky and more likely to fail than succeed, but she'd do all she could to make it work. First, though, she had to be able to walk freely about the keep.

"Indeed, you did insist on her ladyship's imprisonment," Claire said, "because you were demonstrating to all those in the great hall that you were the one in power. However, there is no longer any doubt that you are the ruler here. You and your men have full control of Wode. There is no way any of us can escape."

"I am glad you understand that," Tye said with a tight smile.

"Since we know we cannot flee the castle," Claire added,

"we pose no threat to you. I am certain I speak for Mary and her ladyship when I say I would enjoy eating with them in the great hall, and walking in the gardens, and sitting by the hall fire in the evenings, instead of being shut away in my chamber. Such activities might also help to ease her ladyship's nightmares."

Tye shook his head. "'Tis not—"

"If naught else, will you grant us a short walk outside in the fresh air? Surely 'tis not too much to ask?"

"Beware, Kitten. You sound as though you are setting demands."

"Not demands." She lowered her gaze and softened her tone so she wouldn't appear confrontational. "Requests."

"*Requests* will only be granted if I wish to grant them."

She fought the stirring of resentment. "Of course—"

"And if I see there is some...benefit...to me."

Claire tensed. She had no doubt as to the kind of benefit he meant.

A gasp came from Lady Brackendale, now sitting up in bed, her blanket drawn up around her. "How *dare* you make such a suggestion?"

Tye's hand settled on Claire's shoulder. As she drew in unsteady breaths, his strong, bronzed fingers slid along the fold of the blanket bunched up near her chin, a light but controlling touch. One swift yank of the fabric, and he could bare her breast again, and there was naught she could to do stop him.

"Oh, I dare," he murmured. "Why should I not?"

"She is an innocent young lady, who deserves the attentions of a man *far* better than you," Lady Brackendale bit out, in a tone to make a grown man cower.

Tye's face, caught in a wash of sunlight, hardened into a mask of fury. His hand slid from Claire and balled into a fist. "I am well aware of who and what I am—and who and what she is. I have learned a great deal about her since we first met, now that I have read some of her letters."

"Mercy," Claire choked out. "Did you read my missives to Henry?" They'd been returned to her after being discovered in Henry's belongings, and she'd tucked them in with the letters she'd received from him.

"So far, I have read a few from your sister." Tye smiled again. "Tonight, I will read more. And then, there is your journal…"

She could only imagine what he'd think of her then, of the mockery he'd make of her tale about kissing.

Through a haze of embarrassment, she heard her ladyship say, "Do not fret, Claire. A thug like him cannot read. He is just saying he can to torment you."

"I *can* read," Tye said.

Lady Brackendale laughed. "You? Really? Who taught you such a skill?"

"A woman I knew in France." Smirking, he added, "Shall I fetch one of Claire's letters and read it aloud? I will try to find a good one."

Claire winced.

"Heavens, nay." Her ladyship huffed. "I can quite imagine what those letters might say."

"You?" Tye grinned. "Really?"

The older woman's expression soured. "If you have any respect for Claire, you will return those private letters to her. And, you will stay away from her. *Far* away."

"You are in no position to tell me what to do, Lady Brackendale." Glowering, he stepped away. "Claire, your visit here is finished."

"But—"

"Again, you contradict me, Claire? 'Tis clear you do not respect me, either."

The rage in Tye's voice silenced the rest of what Claire wanted to say. He was right. She *didn't* respect him. She doubted she ever would.

As though attuned to her mutinous thoughts, he caught her arm and pulled her to her feet. "Think on that," he said, "before you dare to make any more requests."

Sitting in the round wooden bathing tub positioned by the hearth, Veronique scrubbed her bare arm. Soap lathered on her glistening skin and on the linen washcloth in her hand, while the heady scent of roses wafted from the bathwater that was already growing cold, despite the nearby fire.

Sighing, she turned her attention to her other arm.

"You are frowning, Love," Braden said from the bed across the chamber in the north tower. He lay beneath the blankets, one broad arm folded behind his head as he watched her bathe. The gemstone eyes of the skull ring on his right hand glinted in the light cast by the fire and the morning sunshine filtering in through cracks in the shutters covering the window.

Veronique pouted. "There is a draft from the window. Also, the water is no longer hot."

He chuckled. "Not because of the servants' lack of effort. They hurried up and down the stairs with their buckets as though they were being whipped."

Wrinkling her nose, Veronique said, "I wanted to whip them, the way some of them glared at me."

"I know you did. You showed remarkable restraint."

He lingered on the word restraint, and she smiled. "So I did. Just like last eve."

They'd fornicated on the bed, on the trestle table, on the floor... She'd made him work hard to pleasure her, but she had no doubt he'd enjoyed every moment of their noisy, exquisite, satisfying couplings.

Thinking of the way he'd thrust into her, dominated her, his manhood so hard and thick and impatient, brought a flush skittering over her skin. Her nipples hardened.

"Love?" he purred, levering up onto his elbows. The blankets slipped from his upper body to reveal more of his well-muscled chest sprinkled with dark hairs. She'd crawled atop that stunning body of his last night, suckled and teased and caressed him until he was sweating, panting, and swearing he could endure no more.

"Mmm?" she finally answered, concentrating on washing her hand. The soap slipped over her skin, bubbled between her fingers, dropped with a whisper onto the hazy surface of the water. She was acutely aware of every sound and sensation as her body stirred in lusty anticipation...

Catherine Kean

The bedding rustled, but she didn't look at him. 'Twould ruin all. She'd ignore him until he came to her, as he would. As she expected.

His footfalls thudded on the planks, and then he lowered to his knees beside the tub. He caught hold of her face and forced her to meet his gaze. Heat blazed in his eyes.

"Do not ignore me, Wench," he growled.

Heat throbbed between her legs. How she loved when his passion roughened. "Give me a reason, then, to give you my full attention."

"I will." His voice hardened. "First, though, you will tell me when I will receive my due."

The tips of his fingers dug into her jaw. He wasn't hurting her, but clearly expected her immediate reply. She pulled free of his hold, the submerged half of her hair stirring in the water, and said calmly, "You know what must happen first. Tye must kill his sire."

"Then I will be awarded a castle of my own," Braden said.

"Of course. We have discussed this many times before." Tsking, she stroked his cheek with her wet, dripping hand. "You must be patient."

"I have been, for a long while already," he grumbled.

"I know." She forced a soothing tone, even as she silently scorned his impatience. The lure of ruling a keep of his own had kept Braden under her control for months; she must keep him eager for that reward, at least until Tye's victory. "I promise, you will get your castle very soon."

"I do not want just any keep. I want a large, profitable estate. I want a fortress as fine as Wode."

She bit down on her tongue. *Greedy bastard.*

"I am entitled to such a rich reward. You cannot deny it."

Can I not? Rage welled within her as she raised her left knee to scrub it.

"I risked my life more than once for you and Tye," Braden added while she lathered her skin. "Without me, you would never have been able to conquer Wode."

Greedy and also bloody arrogant, her mind amended. Yet, in truth, she'd known that ages ago. She'd found his arrogance highly

138

compelling, especially when she'd recognized his ambition was as great as her own.

With effort, she tamped down her anger. Too much could still be lost, despite Tye's takeover of Wode. For now, Tye needed Braden. So did she. When she'd used her rune stones last night, they'd revealed that to her.

Over the slosh of water, she said, "You are right. We would never have succeeded without you."

"I will have my fine keep, then."

She met his stare again. "When de Lanceau is dead, you will have your pick of his estates. Does that please you?"

Braden's eyes lit with anticipation. "Tye will agree to that arrangement?"

"I will ensure that he does."

"I will hold you to that promise, Love."

She paused, her soapy hand on her raised right knee. Surely, Braden hadn't threatened her. He well knew she wouldn't tolerate that kind of boldness, even from him.

His callused fingers slid along her jaw, as if to soothe the rage he sensed churning within her. "When I am lord," he murmured, "I will not just attend my own desires, but also yours."

"How so?" she asked, unable to quell a flutter of delight.

His fingers glided, caressed. "You will stand by my side as lady of my castle. You will have a title, privilege, all that you have ever wanted: gowns of the finest silk; glittering jewels; servants to attend to your every wish, no matter how small."

Ah. Mayhap he was not such a damned fool after all. "Will you truly give me such luxuries?"

Smiling, he leaned forward and pressed his lips to hers. "I will."

She sighed into his mouth, for his kisses were as seductive as his words had been. His lips demanded, claimed, and she leaned toward him, taking all that he offered.

Drawing back, he whispered, "I love you."

She froze, her breath jammed like a lump of stone in her throat. He *loved* her? Many of her lovers through the years had said those very same words, but they were acknowledgment of infatuation, naught more. She wasn't the kind of woman men loved.

Braden was jesting; he had to be. Tittering, she said, "Of course you—"

"I do."

"You—?"

"Love you," he repeated, his expression solemn. "You know 'tis true, aye?"

Astonishment and pleasure rippled through her, weaving their way into her heart that had shattered, shriveled, and died after Geoffrey de Lanceau's rejection. Loving and losing de Lanceau had hurt beyond measure; she'd vowed never to love again. She would not allow such vulnerability, for that weakness had almost destroyed her. Instead, she'd manipulate, use, *take* what she wanted and needed from men, but never offer her heart.

With Braden's admission of love, though, part of her swiftly answered; part of her acknowledged that, of all unexpected and unwanted occurrences, she just might love him, too.

She dropped the washcloth; her mind reeling with shock, she watched the linen slowly submerge beneath the cloudy water. How had she allowed herself to fall in love? When had she become so weak?

"You seem surprised," Braden said with a wry laugh.

Veronique swallowed, grappling with emotions she couldn't control. *Hellfire.* She didn't like being unsettled. "I—"

"We are well matched, you and I. Together, we will be truly formidable. We will be the subject of many *chansons* sung with both awe and fear throughout England."

What a tantalizing prospect. However—

"Do you not want to stand at my side, Love? To be my wife?"

His wife. He wanted to marry her. Suspicion crowded into her stunned mind. Did he really care for her, or did he want to wed her in order to have more influence over Tye? Braden was a clever, cunning man who craved power. She might just be part of a devious plot—

He sighed. Clenching both hands on the side of the tub, he rose, bringing his splendid, aroused nakedness into her full view.

Unable to tear her gaze from his impressive manhood so close to her face, she moistened her lips. "Braden—"

"My love is true, Veronique." He reached down into the tub, hauled her to her feet, and lifted her into his arms.

Water dripped from her wet hair and body onto the planks. In the cool chamber air, goose bumps rose on her flesh. "What are you—?"

"I will prove that I love you," he growled against her mouth. "Over and over and over again, until you agree to marry me."

A lusty cackle broke from her. "You can try."

"Oh, I will." He strode to the bed, dropped her onto the mattress, and crawled on top of her, parting her legs with his knees.

Her hair a tangled, sopping mass beneath her on the sheets, she squinted up at him. "You are far too brazen. I do *not* love you. I will *never*—"

"Never?" His face taut with desire, he plunged into her, then stopped, holding perfectly still, making her gasp, squirm, and moan in frustration. As she cursed and dug her fingernails into his bulging arms, his lips drew back in a rough laugh. "You should know better than to challenge me. I aim to win."

Chapter Fifteen

L ooking out her window at the cloudless afternoon sky, Claire startled when brisk raps sounded on her chamber door. She hesitated, her fingers curling on the stone window sill, while she decided whether or not to acknowledge the knocks. Tye was likely outside her door, and she was too tired after a mostly sleepless night for another confrontation with him. Moreover, she still didn't understand how he made her feel the way she did: unsettled; hot and prickly all over; and eager for another kiss. 'Twas utterly shameful that she should feel such things—

Her chamber door opened.

Claire gasped, for she hadn't yet answered. Thankfully she hadn't been in the midst of changing garments or writing in the journal. Turning from the window, she clasped her hands together in front of her.

Tye strode through the doorway, his mantle drifting at the calves of his knee-high boots that bore wet stains. His hair, tied back as usual with a thin strip of leather, appeared windblown.

She tried to cling to her outrage, but the sight of him so undeniably handsome brought a rush of admiration weaving through her. He didn't look like a lowborn thug; he resembled a lord who ruled a vast, prosperous estate. A man who, as he'd told her before, took what he wanted and did as he pleased. That obviously included walking without permission into ladies' private chambers.

"Good afternoon, milady."

Even his voice affected her. She quivered inside, as if she were a harp string that he'd plucked with his fingers. "Good afternoon," she said, her tone cool yet polite.

"You were enjoying the sun, I see. 'Tis warmer outside than earlier today."

"Good." That meant the snow would melt and de Lanceau would be able to move in his army and oust Tye and his mercenaries. Once again, she'd have her freedoms and at last, she'd be able to travel to her aunt's and start her new life.

"You seem pleased," Tye noted.

Claire managed a careless shrug; she certainly wasn't going to share her thoughts with him. "I do not like the cold."

"Nor do I, truth be told. I much prefer the milder spring days. When the trees are in blossom and the fields are green again, the days somehow hold so much more—"

"Promise," she finished for him.

"Exactly."

They both smiled. A companionable silence settled.

Mercy, but she shouldn't feel at ease around him. They might both enjoy the beauty of spring, but she was his prisoner. She drew upon the outrage that had simmered within her moments ago and said, "I am guessing you have a reason for walking into my chamber without waiting for my permission to enter? A reason that has naught to do with the weather?"

The mirth faded from his eyes. "You guess correctly. Did I offend you, entering as I did?"

"'Tis an accepted courtesy that a man waits for a lady's acknowledgment before entering her private room. She might be dressing, or bathing, or…otherwise indisposed."

"What if you did not hear me for some reason, such as a loud noise outside? Should I have continued to knock? Or should I have realized that you were indisposed?"

A fair question. Tye didn't appear to be teasing her; he seemed genuinely intrigued by the nuances of chivalry. "Normally, you would wait outside and keep knocking until you got acknowledgement from me. If I didn't answer, you would come back later. Of course, if I were gravely ill, and under the effects of a healing potion, I might not hear your knock and therefore would not be able to reply. In that instance—my being ill—'twould be all right to enter my chamber without waiting for permission."

"'Tis good to know," Tye said.

"Our current situation, however, is a little different than usual," she conceded. "While I may be a lady, I am also a hostage. The rules of propriety are undoubtedly different."

He grinned. "Undoubtedly."

His roguish grin softened his features. She fought the unwelcome flutter of her belly. "Now that I have explained—"

"—in such an insightful manner," Tye cut in, "I owe you an explanation. First, though, forgive me for not waiting for your response earlier. I will remember to be more gallant in the future. As gallant, that is, as a rogue like myself can possibly be."

Was Tye teasing her now? She couldn't be sure.

"My true purpose in coming to see you," he went on, "was to ask if you would like a walk."

"A walk?" Excitement raced through her. 'Twould be wonderful to enjoy some fresh air. Also, 'twould give her a chance to see how the rest of the castle folk were faring. "'Tis a most pleasant and welcome idea, milord."

Astonishment glowed in his eyes. "You called me 'milord.'"

"I did"

"It pleases me."

She'd only done so to pacify him. Still, Claire fought a ridiculous tingle of delight. "We are both pleased then, because I am very glad you offered a walk."

"At last something I have done pleases you."

Longing threaded through his words. It suggested that her respect mattered to him, even though he championed himself and his ambitions above all else.

Discomfort trailed through her, and she averted her gaze, not quite knowing what to say next.

The silence lagged. She became intensely aware of his gaze as it traveled over her, from the squared neckline of her fitted emerald green wool gown to the hem decorated with a graceful pattern of flowers embroidered in silver thread, to match the embroidery at the ends of her sleeves. She'd laced on brown leather shoes with pointed toes, and when he saw them peeking out at her hemline, his mouth twitched and he dragged a hand over his mouth as though to hide a smile.

Claire set her hands on her hips. "What?"

He chuckled.

"Is my gown so amusing? I had thought it modest and well suited to a day alone in captivity."

"What you are wearing is quite lovely." His tone became a husky growl that conveyed his full appreciation of the perfectly fitting garment that had been designed by a tailor who'd traveled from London, and who had also made gowns for Lady Brackendale and Mary. "However,"—Tye gestured to her shoes—"two steps outside, and those dainty bits of leather will be ruined."

"I will put on my boots. If I had known about the walk, I would have been sure to don them earlier."

Despite the hint of frost in her tone, Tye's roguish smile didn't waver. "I am certain you would have, milady."

For some reason, because of his smile, she was having trouble concentrating on what she must do. "'Tis still cold out, so I will also fetch my cloak."

"A wise idea."

"And my warmest gloves."

"Mayhap a hat, also?" He shook his head. "I cannot remember ever being so involved in a woman's dressing."

Claire walked to her linen chest, opened the lid, and reached inside. "That is because you are usually busy with a woman's *un*dressing."

As soon as the words left her mouth, she stilled. *Holy Mother Mary.* Had she really said that aloud? She should have stopped herself.

Tye's laughter echoed. "Kitten, you know me so well."

Oh, God. She'd never, ever intended to be so coy or speak so bluntly. The folded garments before her became a colorful blur, and she squeezed her eyes shut and prayed for fortitude and wisdom. "I barely know you at all, milord. I do not know why I said those words."

Opening her eyes again, she searched for her favorite fur-lined gloves. She didn't dare look at Tye—couldn't look at him—while she continued to wrestle with her embarrassment.

"I am not certain either why you said what you did," he

murmured, his voice akin to a purr. "Although, I can guess."

Anxiety clutched at her. "Do not trouble yourself—"

"Were you thinking about me undressing one of my lovers?" His voice lowered to a seductive whisper. "My palms skimming over her gown. My fingers unfastening the ties down the side, one by one. My hands, drawing up her soft linen chemise—"

"Cease." Claire fought the traitorous heat tingling over her skin, snatched up her gloves, and slammed the lid of her linen chest. "I was not thinking such sinful thoughts."

Tye's blazing gaze captured hers. "Mayhap, then, you were imagining—"

"I was *not*—"

"—me undressing you?"

Her mouth fell open on a gasp.

"Seducing you?"

"Goodness!" Claire whispered.

"*Taking* you?"

Oh, dear God! She would have dropped the gloves but managed to catch herself and bring her focus back to the conversation, disastrous though it might be.

"In your mind, you saw my palms skimming over your gown," Tye rasped. "My fingers, unfastening the ties—"

"Nay."

"—while my hands drew up the fine linen of your—"

"Enough!" She shook with a mortifying rush of need and forbidden longing. She must stop his taunting, as quickly as possible.

Lady Brackendale had been right to warn her last night; Claire mustn't, for an instant, forget the truth of who Tye was. "Never would I imagine such a bawdy encounter between us," she managed to say.

He winked, a gesture that told her he knew she was lying. "You were imagining other scandalous occurrences, then?"

She tamped down a frustrated cry. "How *did* our conversation get twisted onto such a path?"

"*I* wasn't the one who spoke of undressing."

"I am sorry. I will not speak of it again."

"Mayhap I will."

146

She threw up her hands. He wasn't going to relent. He was going to make her squirm, until...what? She fell to her knees in front of him and begged him to kiss her, touch her, undress her as he'd described, because she longed for his attention? How appalling, that she wasn't completely horrified by the notion.

His smug smile hinted that he could read the emotions warring inside her, even though she'd never intended for them to be laid bare for his scrutiny.

With clumsy fingers, Claire put on her cloak. Then she shoved her hands into the gloves, stretching each hand wide to ensure the leather was correctly settled on her fingers.

Every silent moment was torture. He didn't move closer, didn't try to touch her, but watched her with his familiar, predatory stare.

"I will not bother with a hat," she said, "so I am ready for my walk."

"Not quite," he murmured.

He was going to kiss her again! He was going to demand it, in return for releasing her from her chamber.

She couldn't allow that physical contact; one devastating kiss, and she'd be lost—

"Your boots." He motioned to the floor beside her linen chest, where her knee-high leather boots waited.

"Oh. Thank you." Claire snatched up her boots, sat on the edge of her bed, and removed her shoes.

"'Twas a curious look on your face," Tye said, sounding amused. "What did you expect me to say just then?"

Claire held aside the thick folds of her cloak and gown so she could see her left foot and then shoved it into her boot. "'Tis not important."

"Allow me to judge that for myself."

Now he seemed annoyed. The last thing she wanted was to make him angry; he might change his mind about the walk, and she wanted it so very much. Tugging on the right boot, she said, "I thought you were going to set conditions on my leaving the chamber. Thankfully, I was wrong."

"Conditions? Such as a kiss?"

"A-aye." Her boots on, she rose, smoothing her cloak and

gown back into place. Despite the calmness she'd managed to convey in her movements, her heart leapt and fluttered like a wounded sparrow. Her lips tingled, her flesh remembering how passionately he'd ravaged her mouth before, and knowing that he could easily do so again.

Finally meeting Tye's stare, she found him smiling. Her breath hovered, suspended, as his hungry gaze settled on her mouth. "This day is not over yet, Kitten."

She adjusted her gloves again to busy her hands. Was he planning to kiss her outside, mayhap in front of a bailey full of witnesses? What an unnerving thought. "True, the day is not over," she said, "but that does not mean we will kiss."

He looked ready to disagree with her. Instead, he spun on his heel and strode for the doorway. "If you want a walk, you will come now."

Claire hurried after him.

He yanked the door open and gestured for her to go first. As she swept past, he said, "A warning, Claire. Try to escape me on this walk, and you will not like the consequences. Understand?"

"Aye."

His strides brisk, Tye took her down the smoky corridor to the landing and the steps leading down into the great hall. As she descended the stairs, she quickly glanced about the large chamber spread out before her, hoping to see that the celebrating conquerors had indulged in too much food and drink the night before, and thus wouldn't be as effective today at maintaining their hold on the keep. However, the room appeared to be maintained to its usual standard, the tables and benches scrubbed and a generous fire burning in the massive hearth. Dogs dozed on the hearth tiles. At the lord's table on the raised dais, a maidservant spread out a fresh linen tablecloth. Apart from the armed men standing near the entrance to the forebuilding, keeping watch on the stairwell that led down to the bailey, the room looked as it did every other day she'd lived at Wode.

Tye nodded to the guards as he strode into the shadows of the forebuilding, Claire close behind. Torch smoke and a damp mustiness enveloped her as she descended the stairs, and then she was through the lower door and outside, into the brilliant sunshine.

Claire couldn't resist a smile.

A wry chuckle snapped her gaze to Tye waiting several paces away.

"Why are you staring at me?"

"I have never seen you smile like that before," he said.

"'Tis such a glorious afternoon." Unable to stop the rush of excitement, she added, "A day this lovely must have wondrous things ahead."

"A rescue, you mean?"

'Twas indeed what she was thinking. She didn't bother to answer, merely smoothed hair away from her face. Tye didn't seem to care. He gestured across the bailey, and she walked in the direction he'd indicated, across melting snow that had been trodden into whitish slush.

Ahead, the kitchen doors were wide open and the scents of freshly baked bread and roasting meat wafted on the breeze. Maidservants were returning from the chicken coops with baskets of eggs, while outside the stables, young lads groomed horses, the animals' coats gleaming in the sunshine. All appeared as it normally did, she noted with a shiver, except for the mercenaries on the battlements who were watching all that went on in the bailey below. More hired thugs guarded the gatehouse and entrance to the dungeons. She mustn't forget to record those details in the journal.

Tye took her to the keep's garden. A waist-high mortared stone wall with a wrought iron gate separated the garden from the rest of the bailey. Lifting the latch, he pushed the gate open. He motioned her inside.

Snow still spread like a downy white blanket over the raised beds where the cook grew vegetables and herbs. Bare-limbed apple, plum, and pear trees stretched toward the sky. As she walked farther into the garden, a large clump of snow dropped from a tree limb and landed with a loud *thump*, making her jump.

The same instant, someone else yelped in shock. Claire saw a woman, frantically sweeping snow off her head, stumbling out of the shadows of a tree. Some of the snow had obviously gone down the back of her neck, for she squirmed and wriggled in an odd little dance.

"Mary," Claire cried.

Her friend spun, her gloved hand still clutching the back of her cloak. "Claire?" Mary waved and ran toward her, but her strides slowed when she spied Tye, who'd shut the gate and was leaning against the wall, arms crossed, watching them.

"'Tis good to see you," Claire called.

"And you." Mary's cautious gaze slid to Tye again. "All is well? You have not come to any harm?"

An indignant snort broke from Tye.

Claire closed the distance between her and Mary and drew her friend into a tight hug. As she inhaled her dear friend's familiar scent of soap and floral water, tears pricked her eyes. "I am much better now that I have seen you."

Drawing back to arm's length, Mary smiled. "I know what you mean. Spending all day alone in my chamber has been awful."

"A torment," Claire agreed. "How are you? Are you well otherwise, apart from perishing from boredom?"

"I am. What of Lady Brackendale?"

"I saw her last night. She is well enough." Sliding her arm though Mary's, Claire drew her toward the snow-covered vegetable beds.

"Tye is watching us so intently," Mary said with a shudder.

"I know. I refuse to let him ruin this walk, though, and most especially, my visit with you. Ignore him."

"I will do my best."

"'Tis what the courageous heroines in our stories would do."

Mary giggled. "True."

Snow collected on the hem of Claire's cloak as she walked, crossing into a line of prints left by a bird. She paused next to rows of stakes that had been used last spring to support the green beans.

"Do you think any of what Tye told us in the hall is true?" Mary asked quietly. "Do you think he really is the illegitimate son of Lord de Lanceau?"

Claire leaned down and picked up a twig that had fallen on the snow. "I have been pondering that myself. I honestly do not know."

"He does look like his lordship, and he does have a similar, authoritative manner," Mary said. "Many noble lords have spawned bastards, in and out of wedlock, so 'tis possible."

"If Lord de Lanceau lay with Tye's mother." Claire snapped off a bit of twig. "We have both met Veronique. While I do not know his lordship well…"

"What would he have seen in her, you mean, to want to take her to his bed?"

"Exactly."

"'Twas many years ago," Mary said. "She may have been quite different back then."

"No doubt just as selfish and ambitious, though," Claire said under her breath.

"Aye, well, I suggest we find a safer subject to discuss," Mary said, sounding nervous. "She is approaching the gate."

Claire welcomed a flare of mischief. "Well, then. With both of them watching, we must give them a good performance."

"W-whatever do you mean? If you are thinking of trying to escape—"

"Not today. We are too closely watched."

Understanding brightened Mary's features. "Like our heroines, though, we will be seeking the perfect opportunity."

"We will." Claire bent, scooped up a handful of snow, and patted it into a ball. "In the meantime…" She hurled the snowball at a spindly bush, and a startled robin darted from its branches and up into the trees.

"Did that bird offend you, or was it the bush?" Mary asked.

"That bush," Claire answered with a grin, "is Tye."

Mary chuckled, before worry shadowed her gaze. "Are you sure 'tis wise to pretend such a thing? If he should realize—"

"Courage, Mary." Claire molded another snowball and threw it. Snow flew into the air in a white cloud, and she giggled. How good it felt to be silly and to laugh.

"Suddenly, Tye is no longer as comely as he was before." Mary scooped up some snow. "In fact, he looks rather scraggly."

"Nor is he as bossy and loud."

"Take that," Mary said, her snowball slamming into the

bush.

Another from Claire quickly followed. "Ha!"

Claire bent to gather more snow; a mound of icy wetness slapped against her head.

"My hand slipped." Mary's eyes sparkled.

"Mine is going to slip now," Claire warned. She tossed snow in Mary's face.

Moments later, the air was flying with clumps of white.

"Look at them." Veronique's mouth twisted with disdain. "They act like naughty children."

Watching Claire and Mary frolic in the snow, Tye smiled. "They are not causing any harm." He'd always thought Claire beautiful, but with her tangled hair gleaming like the purest gold in the sunlight and her face lit with joy, she was more exquisite than he'd ever seen her.

"Those two are prisoners. Ladies stripped of all noble rights and privileges. *Hostages* to be bartered for what we desire." Veronique's perfectly shaped brows lifted. "Have you forgotten?"

"Not at all. There are ways, though, of getting what we want." His voice lowered. "What *I* want."

"Willingly, you mean, rather than by force or coercion?"

"Aye," he said quietly. Claire had collapsed on her knees in the snow. As he watched, she fell onto her back to stare up at the endless blue sky. With a dramatic flutter of her hand, Mary fell down beside her. Both were breathing hard.

His mother stared at him, her gaze unyielding. "*Not* by force? What foolishness do you speak?"

Foolishness? Anger flared to life within Tye. He barely resisted the urge to snarl at her. "I speak what I know to be true."

"Next you will be telling me your *heart* is telling you to act so."

He chuckled, the sound devoid of mirth. "I lost my heart ages ago. You made sure of that."

"I did, and rightly so. No warrior of any merit relies on his emotions. He depends on his wits, fighting skills, and, when necessary, cold-blooded deceit."

"Claire is hardly an opponent in the tournament lists or on the battlefield, Mother."

"She is still an adversary."

Shaking his head, he muttered, "Do not worry. I know very well how at odds she and I are in a great many matters."

"I should hope so." Veronique brushed a crease from her cloak sleeve. "'Tis the way it must be if we are to win this final battle against your sire and then seize all that was his. Our victory is what is important. I hardly need to remind you, do I?"

The sharpness of her words made Tye curl his gloved fingers against the rough stone. "Mother—"

"I would hate to think you held notions of any kind of lasting attachment to Claire. You do know better."

How just like his mother to remind him of the reality of his position, to ensure he knew that a pure-blooded, cultured young woman like Claire was worthy of a far greater man than he could ever be.

For all that he had done in his life, Claire did deserve better.

Tye's attention once again on the two women who were climbing to their feet, he said, "I need no reminders. Your efforts would be better spent elsewhere."

Veronique frowned, causing a crease to form in the layer of fine powder dusting her brow. "Elsewhere?"

"Braden was to give me a full accounting of the weapons in the keep's armory by this morning. He has not yet presented me with his list."

Coyness glinted in his mother's eyes, a look that told Tye exactly what had delayed Braden. "He *has* been very busy—"

"I expect that list by sundown." When she gasped in outrage, Tye held her stare, refusing to back down. "Will you go and remind him, or must I?"

A choking rush of fury whipped through Veronique. What bloody nerve! What rudeness from her own son.

She swallowed the unpleasant burn of anger, even as her gaze warred with Tye's. He didn't flinch, didn't glance away, or give the slightest indication that he was going to relent, not even when the breeze whipped hair into his eyes. In this battle of wills, they were an even match.

Pride, fierce and bittersweet, dimmed the acidic burn of her fury, before she forced herself to break his stare and look down at the mottled stone wall between them. Better that she was the one to yield. Better that she let him believe he was in full control, having all within the keep at his command, even her. If his own mother didn't respect him as lord, no one else would, and without doubt, their confrontation was being witnessed by not only the two ladies, but others going about their work in the bailey. She had to play her part, no matter how much it galled her.

After a moment had passed—long enough for Tye to believe she'd acknowledged him as the victor—she raised her gaze. She'd wrestled the anger into submission, but still, she suffered an uncomfortable tightness in her chest. Lodged like a jagged rock against her breastbone, 'twas a sensation she'd rarely experienced, but, each time, it had been caused by Tye. Each time, it had happened after he'd dismissed her advice as though her opinions held no weight.

She was his mother. He *owed* her, more than he could ever hope to repay.

"Well?" Tye demanded.

Some of the pressure in her chest eased, for she enjoyed knowing she'd kept him waiting for a reply. "I will find Braden and ask about the list."

"Good."

"There is one other matter," she said crisply.

"Aye?"

"*Aye*. Next time we speak, you will not use such a foul tone with me. I will *not* be spoken to in that way."

Tye studied her and then the ladies who were now walking arm in arm in the garden.

"Well?" Veronique mimicked the tone he'd used when speaking to her moments ago and glared at him as she had when he was a boy, when she expected immediate compliance.

"Fine."

Not "Yes, Mother." Not "I am sorry for being rude, Mother." Merely a curt and dismissive "Fine."

Veronique fought a fresh surge of anguish. She strangled the emotion, killing it with the rage she'd nurtured for years and years and that she'd learned to draw upon at the slightest provocation.

Rage had kept her alive after Geoffrey had cast her aside and taken Elizabeth Brackendale to be his wife. Rage had sustained her through childbirth and raising Tye on her own in France, and rage would continue to sustain her, even after Tye slew his sire and Geoffrey was finally dead.

Rage, too, would give her the cunning she needed to ensure Tye did as she expected of him.

Refusing to meet her son's stare again, refusing to say goodbye, she turned and started across the bailey. As she left the shadows of the fruit trees and entered full sunlight, she smiled, for she sensed Tye wrestling with surprise, guilt, and anger over the way she'd walked away without the courtesy of a single parting word.

She hoped he fought with his conscience for the rest of the day.

Her thoughts slipped back to the way he'd looked a short while ago, when he'd watched Claire. Before he'd gathered his composure, she'd caught an expression on his face she'd never seen before. Admiration? Respect? Affection, even?

Anguish welled again, but Veronique smashed it back down. No lady was going to stand in the way of Tye's destiny, most certainly not a pretty virgin.

Veronique's smile broadened. The day promised to be interesting indeed.

Chapter Sixteen

C laire walked beside Mary, following the raised stone wall
of the herb beds peeking through the snow. In hushed
tones, Claire said, "Remember to nod and smile as
though I am telling you an amusing story."

"All right." Mary managed a grin. "Are you going to tell
me terrible news?"

"Nay."

"Thank goodness, because if that were so—"

"Listen, now," Claire said, more sharply than she'd
intended. "I am sorry. I do not mean to be impatient, but I do not
know how much longer we have until Tye separates us again."

In the sunlight filtering down through the fruit trees, Mary
looked troubled, but she dipped her head and smiled. "Go on."

"I may need your help. 'Twill depend whether I can get to
the storage chambers myself or not."

"The chambers beneath the keep?"

"Aye. Last night, Lady Brackendale was having
nightmares, and Tye took me to her chamber to calm her. She told
me of a secret passageway in the room that holds the wine and ale.
'Tis a way into the castle that de Lanceau will know from when he
lived here as a child. I must somehow get to the cellars and unlock
the door, so all is ready when his lordship arrives with his army to
confront Tye."

Mary frowned. "That sounds dangerous. If Tye finds out,
or even worse, his mother... The way she treated Lady
Brackendale in the hall—"

"I know," Claire said, "but it may be the only way to free
us all. 'Tis a risk the strong-willed damsels in our stories would

take, if they were in our predicament."

Mary laughed softly. "Thank goodness for strong-willed damsels."

"Will you help me?"

"Of course. Whatever you need me to do, I shall do." Her smile didn't completely hide her grimace. "I shall be utterly terrified, my stomach twisted in knots, my knees banging together like broken shutters, but I shall think of our defiant damsels and do my best. And I promise not to faint this time. Not unless you need me to."

Claire squeezed Mary's arm. "Thank you. Now, help me think of a good reason to visit the cellars. One that Tye and his men will believe."

"Hmm." A pair of jays, flitting through the overhead boughs, suddenly swooped down over the garden beds ahead of them. "I suppose 'tis not enough to claim that Tye's conquest of Wode has driven you to drink?"

Claire shook her head.

"Or that his kiss left such a foul taste in your mouth, you needed to rinse it out with a strong liqueur?"

Heat spread across Claire's face. "Actually, when he kissed me—"

Mary came to an abrupt stop. "He *did* kiss you! I knew it. I just *knew*, from the way he has been staring at you."

Claire caught both of Mary's hands in hers. "Listen—"

"Did he force you? Did he try to take more than a kiss? Did he...*ravish* you? If he has dishonored you—"

"He has not." Claire heard the crunch of approaching footfalls. "In truth, he has been far more chivalrous than I ever expected."

Mary gaped. Questions glimmered in her eyes. She was clearly bursting to ask just *how* chivalrous Tye had been, to glean all of the tiniest details, but he'd drawn near.

With his nearness came a swift flare of longing and forbidden desire. Trying to keep control of her unruly emotions, Claire kept her expression cool and glanced in his direction, acknowledging him but not saying a word.

"'Tis enough of a walk for today," he said.

"Tomorrow, then?" Claire dared to ask.

"We will see."

"Thank you, though, for today," Mary said. "'Twas a delightful surprise."

For an instant the wariness left his features. He smiled, a flash of his even, white teeth, and warmth lit his gray eyes. He could seduce a woman with that smile. Caught in the full force of that roguish charm, Mary blushed scarlet.

Claire fought a sudden, unexpected sting of jealousy. How stupid to feel at all jealous. Tye meant naught to her, *was* naught to her. Once de Lanceau regained control of Wode, she'd never see Tye again.

"I am glad you enjoyed the walk." He gestured toward the gate. "Now, you will return to the keep."

A protest welled within Claire, for she'd much rather linger in the garden. Making a fuss now, though, might mean she'd be denied more walks. If she was confined to her chamber, there was no chance whatsoever of her finding a way down to the cellars and completing what needed to be done. She couldn't ruin that chance; Lady Brackendale was depending upon her.

Claire nodded her assent, took Mary's arm again, and started for the gate. Tye followed a few steps behind. Claire sensed his gaze upon her back.

Were you thinking about me undressing one of my lovers? My palms skimming over her gown. My fingers unfastening the ties down the side, one by one. My hands, drawing up her soft linen chemise—

"Claire?" Mary whispered. "Are you all right?"

Claire found she'd reached the gate. Her face hot, she lifted the latch and pushed through, pulling Mary along with her. In no way was Claire going to discuss the sinful thoughts taunting her. Certainly not with Tye in earshot.

The bailey ahead was more crowded than earlier in the day. Servants were hauling buckets of water from the well to take to the kitchens. A group of maidservants scrubbing clothes in steaming wooden tubs looked at Claire and Mary, but swiftly returned their attention to their tasks, as though afraid the mercenaries on guard might think they were not doing their chores.

A boy hurried from the kitchen doorway. His hair a tangled mess, his expression grim, he lugged a bucket wreathed in steam. He stared straight ahead to where he seemed to be going: the dungeon.

Mary tugged on Claire's sleeve. "That boy. 'Tis Witt, Sutton's grandson."

Claire slowed and faced Tye. Clearly not expecting her to stop so suddenly, he almost barreled straight into her, before he halted, frowning.

"Milord, how is Sutton faring?" Claire asked.

"Not well. He has a fever."

"Oh, the poor man," Mary whispered.

"You must help him," Claire said. "He cannot die."

Tye's eyes narrowed. "He is a prisoner, injured in battle. Some prisoners perish. 'Tis the way of things."

Claire sucked in a sharp breath. He sounded so heartless, as though Sutton's fate was not his concern. From all she'd discovered about Tye, he didn't seem as cruel in his dealings with the castle folk as his mother seemed to be. "That may be one opinion on the matter," she said evenly. "However, since you have declared yourself lord of this keep, every man, woman, and child here is now your responsibility, including wounded prisoners."

"True, and I have not neglected the captives or my responsibility to Sutton. His wounds are being tended. His wife helps care for him, and Witt is at his bedside every day."

"Are you saying no more can be done for Sutton? That he is receiving all of the care that his fever and wounds require?"

"Claire—"

"They are fair questions, *my lord.*"

Menace sparked in his eyes. "They are also very *bold* questions, Kitten. Mayhap you need a firm reminder that you, also, are a prisoner. *My* prisoner." His gaze slid slowly down the front of her cloak.

"We should return to our chambers," Mary said, pulling on Claire's sleeve again.

"In a moment." They were discussing the wellbeing of an honored warrior who had devoted years of his life to defending Wode. Her anxieties must not overrule such an important conversation. "May we see Sutton?"

"Why?"

"He is a good man. A friend."

Tye's expression darkened with suspicion.

"A visit from us might lift his spirits," Claire insisted. "He may be worried about us. It might help him to see we are all right."

"In his fevered state, I doubt he will recognize you. Moreover, do you really wish to see his injuries? They are not pleasant."

Ignoring the whining protest of her belly, Claire said, "Let us see him."

Tye's gaze slid from her to a point beyond her shoulder. Someone or something else had claimed his attention.

"You will not visit Sutton today," Tye said, summoning a mercenary who was standing nearby. "Take these women to the great hall. They may eat the midday meal there. If they give you any trouble, secure them in their chambers." His gaze settled again on Claire. "If they give you any trouble, I want to be informed as soon as possible."

Wode's great hall echoed with the bawdy laughter and loud voices of mercenaries enjoying their meal. Maidservants wove between the tables, delivering jugs of ale and wine along with platters of bread and cheese. Dogs, waiting for stray bits of food, hovered near the benches where the men sat. Half of the tables were occupied, and the mercenary walking behind Claire and Mary ordered them over to a vacant table near the opposite wall. 'Twas a relief, to be separated from the raucous thugs, but the table was a fair distance from any way out of the hall.

"I will be watching you," the mercenary said. He cast a warning glare at Claire, then Mary, before heading to a table close by, dropping down on the bench, dragging over a platter of food, and stuffing a slice of bread into his mouth.

Mary sighed as she settled on the bench opposite Claire. "That walk was far too short."

Claire managed a smile. "At least we are getting to see

each other."

"True." Mary's eyes shone. "Now I also know you were kissed. By *him*, no less."

Claire pulled off her gloves, taking her time, for she didn't want to speak in front of the serving girl who was approaching their table. The girl slid a wooden board of sliced cheese and bread in front of them. A second maidservant set down a jug of wine and two mugs, dipped into a quick curtsy, and then rushed away.

Her arms resting on the table, Mary leaned forward. "No one else is near enough to hear now. So, what was it like?"

"Well—"

"Was it a disgusting, wet, slimy ordeal you forced yourself to endure? Or was it as wonderful as we wrote in our stories?"

'Twas even more wonderful than we described. Truth be told, 'twas even better than Henry's perfect kiss. Claire fought the urge to giggle.

"Were his lips soft and gentle? Or were they rough with passion, hot with the villainous desire burning through him?"

Oh, God. "Mary—"

"If you deny me the details, Claire, I will be most upset."

"I was not intending to deny you," Claire insisted, reaching for a slice of bread and a wedge of cheese.

"I am glad to hear it." Mary arched her brows. "Well?"

Claire bit off some bread and slowly chewed. "His kisses were—"

"Kiss*es*. He kissed you more than once, then?"

Claire finished what was in her mouth. "Aye."

"Let me guess. He pinned you against the wall so you were helpless to resist, then ravished your mouth. Once he'd kissed you to within a breath of fainting, he promised more wickedness if you did not bow down to him."

A bite of cheese lodged halfway down Claire's throat. She coughed, choked, and fumbled for the wine jug. With an impatient huff, Mary poured some of the crimson liquid into a mug and pushed it into Claire's hands.

Claire downed some of the wine. The strong red made her eyes water.

"Well?" Mary demanded, biting into a piece of cheese. "Was I right?"

Blinking hard, Claire cleared the teary blur from her vision. Then, she took another sip. "He was a bit demanding in his attentions," she said. "However, I cannot say that ravished is quite the right word to describe what he did to my lips."

"Abused them?"

"Nay."

"Conquered them?"

Claire frowned. "Not really."

"What then? *Wooed* them?"

Shrugging, Claire said, "Wooed is the best word you have suggested so far."

Mary blinked like a startled owl. "Goodness."

"For a warrior of his ilk, I would say he has shown rather chivalrous restraint."

Two loud heartbeats thudded in Claire's ears, before Mary frowned. "Forgive me, but I find that very hard to believe, especially of a thug who has ruthlessly claimed Wode and who has likely been conquering women as well as castles all of his life."

"I, too, find it hard to believe. And yet…" Claire shook her head, pulled some bread off the thick slice in her hand, and put the morsel in her mouth.

"Aye?"

Claire swallowed. "At times, I sense he is struggling with himself. 'Tis as if he is waging some kind of private inner war. I sense he…wants more from his life than he currently has, something that is beyond his reach." Distracted by a burst of raucous laughter from a table of mercenaries, she looked away. "I sound ridiculous."

"Not *entirely* ridiculous."

Claire chuckled. "Why, thank you."

Mary laughed and poured herself some wine. "From what you have said, it seems as though you believe Tye has a conscience."

"Mayhap he does."

Mary thoughtfully sipped her drink. "Beware of thinking kindly of him, Claire. He does not feel guilty for capturing this keep and naming himself lord. Nor is he losing any sleep over the good men who were injured in the siege. You saw how he dismissed your questions about Sutton."

"True. He does seem convinced he is owed the privilege of being ruler here." Claire put another bit of bread into her mouth and chewed. "Yet, when he and I are alone—"

"Alone?" Mary went still, her hand clenching her goblet. "What else have you not told me?"

"By alone, I mean that he has come to my chamber to speak to me or, as happened this afternoon, to escort me to the gardens. In those moments, for the briefest time, I see a different man than what he is with his mercenaries. Acting as lord, he is commanding, distant, and cold. When he is with me, there is a warmth in his gaze, a lightness in his voice, even a humor in his words that I find charming. I cannot help wondering if that is the true man."

"Mother Mary. From your lips, he sounds almost heroic."

Shrill whistling and chortling erupted from the farthest table of mercenaries. They were teasing one of the maidservants, pulling on her waist-length braid to try and draw her into the lap of a burly thug, and Claire shuddered. "I would not go so far as to say heroic. Intriguing, for certain."

"You are chronicling all of these musings, I trust, in the journal?"

"I am. I write whenever I know Tye is busy and not likely to walk in on me. 'Tis safest for all of us if he does not know about the journal."

"I agree." Mary's gaze fell to her hands as she broke apart another chunk of cheese. "I dare not imagine what would happen if Veronique found it."

Misgiving crawled through Claire. She rolled her shoulders, forcing the disquiet away. "I refuse to think about that happening. We must focus on other, more urgent matters."

Mary nodded solemnly, clearly understanding Claire's reference to the secret door in the storage room below. Claire stole a glance at the shadowed entrance to the small chamber adjoining the hall, which was used by the servants during feasts and other special occasions to pour out jugs of wine and ale; the doorway to the stairwell leading down to the lower level was in that chamber.

Challenging growls drew Claire's attention to two

mongrels fighting over a chunk of bread. Before the disagreement worsened, Witt, who was seated at the nearest table, snatched a crust off a platter and tossed the bread to the dogs. The larger animal jumped up and snatched the crust from the air and the mongrels went separate ways to devour their findings.

His head downcast, Witt returned to his meal. He was seated beside a plump, gray-haired serving woman who put her arm around his shoulder and gave him an affectionate squeeze. Her mouth moved as she spoke close to his ear, likely words of comfort.

A painful tightness closed around Claire's heart. She hated to involve Witt in her plan, but he might be the one person who could make it succeed.

Pretending to smooth a wayward strand of her hair, Mary glanced over her shoulder. She spied Witt and then looked back at Claire. Softly, Mary said, "You are going to ask Witt to help us?"

"Aye." Claire selected another piece of cheese. "With luck, he and I can slip away together and go to the storage room."

"Wine is often used to cleanse wounds," Mary said. "If you are questioned at any point, you can say the wine is needed to treat Sutton."

"Good thinking." Claire smiled and then added, "Our plan will not work, however, without you. I need you to provide a distraction."

Mary paled. Then, clearly rallying her courage, she nodded. "What kind of distraction?"

"You are good at fainting."

"I will do my best to outdo my faint in your chamber."

"Perfect." Claire studied the noisy table of mercenaries. The men's teasing interest in the maidservant had become bolder, but she was thwarting them; she swatted away a leering thug who'd tried to kiss her on the mouth. "There are more than enough bawdy and groping men among Tye's lackeys," Claire said. "With the right persuasion, you could encourage at least one of them to mistreat you in a manner worthy of a dramatic swoon."

Mary's eyes lit with excitement. Then her face crumpled with concern.

Claire readied words of encouragement, just in case Mary

needed more convincing. Without Mary, the plan was certain to fail. However, before Claire could speak, Veronique strolled out of the forebuilding, pushing back the hood of her cloak to reveal her austere, beautiful features. Her red hair gleamed.

A ripple of misgiving spread through Claire. She willed herself to stay calm and focused.

"You look unsettled. Who just entered the hall?" Mary asked.

"Veronique." Claire forced a smile. "No need to worry. She cannot know what we were discussing."

The older woman paused at the bottom of the stairs leading up to the second level. Her head tilted, and her gaze traveled over the folk at the tables until she found Claire. As their gazes locked, a freezing jolt raced through Claire, a sensation akin to plunging into an ice-covered river.

A taunting smile curved Veronique's lips. She lifted her hand, smoothed the front of her cloak, and then started up the stairs, her languid strides suggesting she had no reason to hurry. Claire sensed though that the older woman's carefree manner was an illusion. Veronique had a very definite place she meant to go and a very deliberate purpose in mind.

Claire fought a rush of foreboding. Whatever Veronique was going to do, it didn't bode well for anyone at Wode.

Especially Claire.

Veronique closed the door of Claire's chamber and leaned back against the panel. The mercenaries outside—ugly, stupid louts—would warn her if Claire was returning to her room. If they failed to tell her... Well, they'd been told what mutilations, inflicted on particular male parts, they would endure.

Eyes narrowing, Veronique studied the chamber. The room smelled of fresh air mingled with another essence. Not the perfume of roses, as she preferred. Not violets or lavender, either. The elusive scent reminded her of honey and was both alluring and sweet—a bit like the annoying young woman herself.

Afternoon sunshine washed in from the window, the

shutters open to let in the day. Light played over the unpainted stone walls, the floorboards coated in fine dust, the bed that had been neatly made, either by Claire's own hand or the servant who, judging by the blaze in the hearth, had delivered more firewood earlier and also set fresh pitchers of water and wine on the trestle table.

Veronique walked to the bed. The grass green silk coverlet was embroidered with gold flowers. So pretty. So *pathetic* for such a costly, sumptuous fabric to be wasted on a bed covering for a woman who wasn't even the lady of the keep. Her lips curling into a sneer, Veronique dug her fingers into the bedding and yanked, sending the matching pillows flying onto the floor. The honeyed scent rose from the bed sheets, and her mouth flattened in disgust.

How she longed to draw the dagger hidden inside her sleeve, plunge it into the bed, and slash and destroy. That destruction, though, would be too obvious and too easily blamed upon her.

What she needed to accomplish now must be done with discretion, for when at last Tye was recognized by the King as the rightful ruler of Wode, Tye's loyalty would be to her, his parent, as it should be—not the blue-eyed beauty who lived in this chamber.

"You will never have Tye's heart, Claire," Veronique muttered. "I will make very sure of that."

Dropping the coverlet, Veronique strode to the linen chest. She threw up the lid and examined the contents. What she sought might be here, or might take more careful searching of the room before she uncovered it. Either way, she *would* find it—an object that, when presented to Tye, would cause Claire's utter mortification. What a deliciously satisfying instance that would be, to see Claire brought to her knees by embarrassment.

Veronique eased aside the layers of clothing, shoes, and other items. She frowned and dropped the lid of the chest. What she sought wasn't inside. The items were personal, but not of an emotionally-charged nature.

Tapping her chin, Veronique studied the chamber again, for there *must* be something here. She moved down the room, studying the walls for broken mortar, the planks for any loose boards that might conceal a secret cavity beneath. She'd coupled with more than a few lords who kept their riches tucked under the floorboards.

Reaching the bedside again, she set her hands on her hips. Cursing under her breath, she tugged the bedding back into place then skirted the foot of the bed to pick up the pillows.

As she stooped, her gaze fell upon the edge of the bed frame. A thin lip ran along the frame's edge, a wide enough area to form a narrow shelf. Her mouth curved into a knowing smile as she tossed the pillows on the coverlet and moved to the head of the bed. She reached between the bed frame and the wall, and her fingers brushed smooth leather.

She pulled the object out into the light. 'Twas a book, the first quarter of its pages filled with lines of black ink. The letters were neatly formed and executed with a distinctly feminine flair.

"Well, now." Veronique opened to the early pages, the pungent scent of cured parchment rising to her nostrils while she read a few lines:

Tye broke into my chamber with his head held high, his strides unwavering, not the slightest trace of humility or remorse in his demeanor. He acted as though he had every right to claim Wode, but that cannot be, for this castle rightfully belongs to Lord de Lanceau. How, then, can Tye believe what he does?

I am cold inside with fear. I am terribly afraid, more so than I have ever been in my life, and not just for myself, but for Lady Brackendale, Mary, and all those I care about.

A gritty laugh welled in Veronique's throat. How perfect. Yet, there might be sections that were even more revealing. She fingered pages aside and paused near the middle of the entries.

I cannot explain the sensations Tye roused within me. When he took me in his arms, kissed me with such skill and boldness, I was caught up in a wild and powerful storm. A great tempest of confusion, longing, and wonder swirled up inside me. I was frightened, and yet, my heart still soars when I think of that moment. I am ashamed of the way I feel, but I need more. Want more.

"Of course you want more." Veronique turned to another page. "He has seduced more women than you can possibly imagine."

I do not know how Tye really feels about me. Yet, his kiss was both demanding and surprisingly gentle. That confuses me all the more. How can such a bitter, ruthless rogue also be tender, especially toward a woman who is no more to him than a prisoner?

Forsooth, there are moments when it seems as if the steel around his heart, armor forged of hatred and ambition, falls away. In those moments, I wonder if I see the real Tye, a man who is far more than he seems at first.

Veronique's jaw hardened.

A man with a compassionate soul.

"Nay. *Nay!*" Veronique slammed the tome closed. Tye was *not* compassionate. She'd raised him not to be, because his destiny was to destroy his sire.

Veronique glared at the journal. She should take it to Tye right now. She'd mock Claire's words and praise his skills of seduction—with Claire there to witness all. What marvelous fun.

Veronique turned toward the chamber door. As she did so, another, even more tantalizing idea took shape in her thoughts. She trembled with excitement and the anticipation of a truly evil plan.

Laughing softly, she tucked the book back behind the bed and then strolled to the door. A few arrangements to make, and then, Claire would no longer be a threat.

Claire wouldn't want to see Tye ever again.

Chapter Seventeen

T ye had just pulled open the door to the forebuilding when a shout sounded from the battlements. "Milord!"

The cry, carrying across the bailey, sounded urgent. Fine hairs prickled at the back of Tye's neck. An immediate hush fell—as though everyone within earshot had paused to hear what was happening.

He turned to look up at the wall walk near the gatehouse, where the cry had originated. A mercenary with a crossbow waved his arm high in the air, determined to have Tye's attention.

"What is it?" Tye yelled.

"A rider," the mercenary called back. "He is approaching the gatehouse."

Tye's gloved hands closed into fists. Had his father learned of Tye's capture of Wode? He hadn't expected to face his sire just yet, but 'twas still possible de Lanceau could be arriving with an army in tow...

Tye ran across the slushy ground and headed for the gatehouse. Braden met Tye halfway.

"One man?" Tye asked as Braden fell into step beside him.

"Aye. According to the mercenaries, there are no others following him. There are no armies in sight, either, from any direction."

Tye frowned. "He could be a messenger, then. Mayhap he was sent by my sire."

"Or he could have no connection to your father at all."

"We must find out the man's purpose here, above all, if he is a spy."

169

"What are your orders?" Braden asked.

"Tell him what we arranged previously: that Lady Brackendale is ill and that there is a deadly sickness running through the castle. This means no one is allowed in or out."

Braden nodded and veered toward the outer stairs up to the battlements.

"Wait," Tye called.

The older warrior hesitated and glanced back.

"I will question the man myself."

Wariness crept into Braden's expression. "Is that wise? If the rider was hired by your father to confirm you are here—"

"You will be close by, to signal the mercenaries to wound him. We will take him prisoner."

A ruthless smile curved Braden's mouth. "Agreed."

Shoving strands of windblown hair from his face, Tye headed to the shadows of the gatehouse, his gaze on the rider now visible through the wood and iron slats of the portcullis. Tye stood watching as the young man with shoulder-length, light brown hair neared and halted his mount on the bank opposite, where the drawbridge, when lowered, would rest upon the ground.

Lather clung to the gray horse's coat, indicating the rider had traveled some distance. Tye's jaw hardened. If his father had sent this lackey, he would have ordered him to reach Wode as soon as possible.

"Good day," the man called up to the men on the battlements. Then, clearly aware of Tye, his attention shifted to the portcullis. He squinted as though fighting the afternoon sunlight to try and better see who stood in the darkness behind the barrier.

"Good day," Tye called back. The man's shoulders were broad beneath his brown wool cloak. He wore a chain mail hauberk under his outer garment and a sword belted at his waist. He could be a knight, although he didn't appear to be wearing spurs.

"All is well?" the rider asked. The horse snorted and sidestepped several paces, obviously sensing his master's unease. "'Tis not usual to find the drawbridge up."

"You visit often, then?" Tye asked, deliberately avoiding a direct answer to the man's query.

"Often enough that I should not be asked such a question." The rider's frown deepened. "Who are you? I do not recognize your voice."

"I am new," Tye said easily. "I was hired from the village, along with a number of others, when Lord de Lanceau ordered his men-at-arms from Wode to ride with him, not several days ago."

The young man considered the reply and then nodded.

"You will forgive me," Tye added, "if I do not know who you are, or why you are here."

"My name is Delwyn," the rider said. "Delwyn de Lysonne. I am here for Lady Claire Sevalliere."

Claire. An unpleasant tightness clenched Tye's gut. She'd said her betrothed was dead, killed months ago. Was this lad an eager suitor, hoping to win her love? Hoping to claim her for his wife? He appeared of the right social rank, the right age, for that to be so. "What do you want with Claire?"

Tye's words emerged as a growl, and Delwyn leaned back in his saddle, clearly surprised by the vehemence. "I have a letter for her, from her sister, Johanna. Were you not told to expect letters to be delivered?"

"Nay."

"He is lying," Braden muttered, walking up behind Tye.

Tye eyed the older warrior. "Claire does have a sister who sends letters. I have seen them myself." *Read a few of them, too.*

Braden shrugged. "Let him talk a little longer, then." He looked impatient, though, to give the order to have the man injured.

Returning his attention to the rider, Tye said, "The letter is your only purpose for visiting?"

"What other reason would there be?"

Braden hissed a breath.

What other reason, indeed, you bastard.

"Forgive me yet again," Tye said, forcing calmness into his voice. The rage had risen so easily, but this was not a moment to make reckless mistakes. "I do not mean to offend, but we received word of cutthroats and thieves preying on folk within several leagues of Wode. We were ordered to be extra cautious of visitors at the gates."

"'Tis wise to be wary, especially in these uncertain times," Delwyn said. "Yet, even if I was a cutthroat or a thief—and I am not—I am one man, hardly a threat. If you have doubts about my honorable character, Claire will vouch for me."

"There is also another matter." 'Twas time to be rid of this annoying lout. "Sickness has swept through Wode. Lady Brackendale and many others are ill, and as of yet, 'tis not known how the illness is spread."

The young man's face paled. "Claire? Is she—?"

"She is well," Tye said. "Yet, until the sickness has run its course or a cure is found, no one is allowed in or out of the castle."

"I see. But—"

"Those are my orders."

Concern flickered across Delwyn's features. He adjusted his grip on his horse's reins, his gloved hands opening and closing in a gesture of frustration. "What can I do to help? Do you need food? Healing herbs? I can ask my lord—"

"There is naught to be done for now," Tye said. "We have all we need."

"I will pray for a swift recovery for all who are ill, as well as a cure to be quickly found."

A hard smile touched Tye's mouth. "I thank you. Now, if you will kindly allow us to return to—"

"The letter," Delwyn said. Relaxing his hold on his horse's reins, he drew open his cloak and pulled a rolled missive from his belt. A yellow wax seal gleamed against the whitish parchment.

"Refuse it," Braden ground out.

"'Twill make him even more suspicious," Tye answered quietly. "Also, there might be information in that letter, word on de Lanceau's whereabouts that we would be wise to know."

"Mayhap." Braden scowled. "But—"

"Tell the men to lower the drawbridge."

"*Tye.*"

"Do it." Tye held the older man's glare. "He will hand the letter to me through the portcullis. Then, he will leave."

Swearing under his breath, Braden strode away to deliver the order.

Stepping forward, Tye set his gloved hand on a horizontal slat of the portcullis and met Delwyn's stare. "I will take the missive for Claire. The drawbridge is being lowered now, so you can ride across and hand me the letter. The portcullis will remain in place."

"Agreed." Relief softened Delwyn's features.

With the squeak and groan of iron workings, the drawbridge lowered over the moat. A gritty *thud* echoed, the sound of the platform settling on the snow-covered dirt.

The hooves of Delwyn's mount clattered on the planks as he rode the horse forward. He halted next to the portcullis. Leaning down, he pushed the missive through the slats. The parchment rasped against the barrier, and then it was through and in Tye's hand.

He met Delwyn's gaze, a silent confirmation that their exchange was complete. The young man nodded. Then his eyes narrowed, and he studied Tye's face before he eased away and straightened in his saddle.

"Give my regards to Claire," Delwyn said. "Tell her we will see her soon."

Tye waited until Delwyn had ridden halfway down the road that led to and from Wode. Tapping the still-sealed missive against his open palm, and convinced the lad was well out of earshot, Tye turned to Braden, still standing in the shadows. "I want you to follow him for a day or two."

A sly grin widened Braden's mouth. "I will be glad to."

"I want to know where he goes next, what he does, whom he meets. We need to know for certain if he is reporting back to my sire."

"I will saddle my horse and be on my way."

"Also, make some discreet inquiries in the local villages. Find out what you can about my father's whereabouts. Beware, though. If my sire knows that you helped me and my mother escape imprisonment last summer, you will be a wanted man."

Braden snorted and rested his hand on the hilt of his

sword. "I have eluded him so far. Moreover, I can fight better than most knights. I am not worried."

"Very well. Report back to me as soon as you have news."

"Agreed." The older man's expression turned smug. "Truth be told, I am glad of a reason to quit the keep for a while."

"Why is that?"

"I gave your mother something to think about this morning. My being away…" Determination and mischief gleamed in Braden's eyes. "With luck, my absence will encourage her to give me an answer."

"Answer?" Judging by the red bite marks and scratches on Braden's neck, Tye almost didn't want to know the nature of what had been discussed. If it concerned the plans for Wode in any way, though, he wanted to know all of the details.

Braden merely grinned and strode for the stables.

Chapter Eighteen

Three brisk raps on her chamber door brought Claire straightening up from her linen chest, where she'd been searching for a thicker chemise to wear to bed. Night had fallen, and the breeze stealing in around the closed shutters promised a heavy frost overnight.

After dining with Mary in the hall earlier, she'd been escorted back to her chamber where she'd spent the rest of the afternoon, torn between moments of utter boredom and terrible worry. After writing another entry in her journal, and finishing the wine left in her chamber, she'd decided to go to bed. A good night's sleep—if her thoughts would unravel enough to let her slumber—would do wonders for steadying her nerves. With luck, the more-than-usual amount of wine she'd imbibed would help her rest, too.

With the knock on the door, though, her plans for this evening might change. Mayhap she would be taken to Lady Brackendale's room again?

Not moving from the linen chest, Claire watched the door. She knew Tye stood outside, because she'd recognized his voice when he'd addressed the guards.

She waited for the door to swing open, for Tye to stride in with his usual swaggered arrogance.

The door didn't budge.

How curious. Last time, he hadn't waited for her acknowledgement before entering; he'd just done as he liked. Had Tye actually heeded what she'd told him about noble courtesy? What an astonishing development.

"Come in," she said.

The panel immediately swung inward, and Tye strode into her room. He wore a midnight blue wool tunic that draped to his knees, black hose, and black leather boots. With his hair tied back into a sleek queue, the sensual angles of his cheekbones were even more pronounced.

Holy Mother Mary, but he was magnificent. He stole her breath.

She was suddenly unsteady on her feet. With a strangled gasp, she pressed her right hand against her breastbone, where her pulse throbbed in loud beats.

"Did I frighten you, Kitten? You explained before that 'twas proper for a man to knock—"

"I did, and you did exactly the right thing. Thank you." As his grin broadened with pleasure, she wished she hadn't drunk so much wine. It did *not* help matters that she felt slightly giddy. "You did not frighten me. I was merely...catching my breath."

"I see." He studied the open linen chest. "Did you find what you were looking for?"

"Aye." She bent, reached under a pile of silk gowns, and drew a chemise from the chest. The lid dropped back into place with a resounding *bang*.

"Good. Then you are free to come with me."

"W-why?" She hadn't meant to reply so quickly, or sound so unsettled. There was no advantage in revealing that he intimidated her, not just with his demands, but with his raw sensuality that still made breathing more difficult than normal. No doubt the wine warming her innards was to blame for her intense reaction to him, too. If only she'd been more sensible.

Tye's lazy grin caused a fluttering sensation in her belly. "I only wish to talk. Surely there is no harm in that?"

"Not at all." *Talk.* She could do that. Of course she could, even if he *was* the most devastatingly handsome man she'd ever met—a rogue who'd kissed her with exquisite skill and implied he wanted more from her.

Mayhap tonight he will demand *more,* her conscience whispered. *Are you really willing to trust him? Do you dare?*

She crossed to the bed and dropped the chemise on it, glad her steady hand didn't reveal her anxiety. Then, she walked over to Tye. He motioned for her to quit the chamber, and she brushed past him and out into the hallway, doing her best to ignore his smoldering stare traveling over her.

"What do you wish to discuss?" she asked as he fell into step beside her.

"I will tell you when we reach the great hall."

The hall. A silent sigh of relief rippled through her. There would be plenty of other folk there. At least he was not taking her somewhere secluded, such as his solar.

They reached the landing, and with curious gallantry, he gestured for her to go ahead of him down the stairs to the hall. Most of the tables from the evening meal had been cleared back against the walls, allowing room for the servants to lay their straw pallets to sleep for the night. Three tables had been left standing near the dais, and mercenaries sat at them. Five thugs cast bets on a staring contest between two burly contestants. At another table, four men drank, talked, and laughed, not caring to caution their rough language or lower their voices.

As Claire's gaze skimmed the hall, she saw most of the reed torches along the far walls had been extinguished. Children were sleeping in the dark corner, several dogs lying alongside their pallets.

Tye motioned to the hearth. A fire blazed, its golden glow warm and inviting. Two high-backed chairs had been pushed up to the hearthside. A table nestled between them, set with a wine jug, two goblets, and a plate laden with two thick slices of cake.

"Please. Sit," Tye said.

She did, sitting close to the chair's edge. The faint scent of ginger wafted over the tang of wood smoke. Was that ginger cake on the plate? Cook's special treat, made from a recipe that had been passed down through the women in Cook's family? Claire's favorite? How had Tye managed that, and why would he have bothered?

You know why. Tonight, he will demand more, her conscience taunted.

Fighting a fresh wave of lightheadedness along with a tingle of dread—aye, 'twas surely dread, not excitement—Claire clasped her sweat-dampened hands on her lap. He might demand more, but she would refuse him. 'Twould take far more than a piece of cake to sway her.

Tye dropped into the other chair, leaned against the carved back, and propped his left booted foot sideways on his right knee—a posture that made him look both relaxed and controlled. The fingers of his left hand trailed over the smooth, polished arm of the chair; the small, deliberate caresses roused the image of him brushing his fingertips over her bare skin.

Claire stared straight ahead at the fire and tried to remember how many pairs of shoes were in her linen chest. Counting would help to rein in her wanton thoughts.

"You are ready to run, I see."

"Run?" She clasped her hands tighter. "Nay."

"As I said earlier, I wish only to talk. Anything more would require a far softer surface beneath you than a wooden chair."

Mercy. When Tye said things like *that*, counting shoes most certainly didn't help. "You speak very brazenly this evening, milord."

"Every evening, actually."

'Twas likely the truth. She smiled, while the scent of cake teased her. How shameful that her mouth watered with the remembered taste of the moist, spicy delicacy.

"Would you like some cake?"

Oh, indeed she would, but she mustn't be too eager. "What kind is it?"

His grin didn't waver, as if he knew exactly why she was delaying in taking her portion. "'Tis ginger cake, with plenty of raisins. The cook mentioned this is one of your favorites. I understand you also like apple tarts with custard and—"

"You were discussing me with Cook?"

"Not you in particular." He picked up the plate and offered it to her. Claire delayed one more moment, and then could fight the temptation no longer. She took the closest slice of cake. She bit into it, sighing as the spicy and sweet flavors tumbled into her mouth. Tye took the other piece, bit off a mouthful, and chewed. "Very good," he murmured.

"Mmm." Claire agreed. Out of the corner of her eye, she

watched him eat. He didn't cram the cake into his mouth and gobble it, but ate it a mouthful at a time, savoring it. When his tongue slid out to lick a crumb from the corner of his mouth, her mind immediately shot back to the day in her chamber when he'd licked the spoon, over and over in a most sinful manner. She fought to keep her thoughts under control. "You were saying?" she finally asked. "About Cook?"

"I visited the kitchens yesterday to see what kind of state they were in," Tye answered. "She went on and on about the leak in the thatched roof near the back wall, bemoaned her worn pots and pans, and pointed out the need for new pantry shelves. In her opinion, the kitchen is not to the standard it should be for a castle of this size and renown. She insisted she could make much finer fare with better cookware."

Fighting a pang of regret, Claire downed another mouthful of the cake. Cook had been asking Lady Brackendale for months to have the roof fixed and for new pots and pans. Her ladyship had promised to see to the matters, but caught up in her grief and despair, had done naught.

"I promised Cook that once Wode is formally awarded to me, I will fix the thatch and buy her whatever cooking implements she needs. I could see she was delighted, although she tried to continue the ruse of being indignant about my takeover here. Today, when I stopped by the kitchens, she presented me with the ginger cake. She barely smiled when she pushed the plate toward me, but I could see she wanted me to taste it." Finished eating his cake, he brushed crumbs from this tunic. "I did my best to sound appreciative of her talents. If I am lucky, she might surprise me with another treat tomorrow."

With a sigh, Claire finished the rest of her slice. "You are not only bold, but devious," she said, licking a bit of cake from her finger.

"Sometimes, 'tis necessary to be devious. It got me into Wode, and I am here to stay." Tye watched her tongue glide over her skin. His gaze darkened and filled with a hunger that made her quickly drop her hand back down into her lap.

"Tell me about Delwyn de Lysonne, Claire."

Her eyes widened. "How do you know about—?"

"He arrived at the castle gates earlier today. He brought a letter from your sister."

Claire could barely contain her joy. "Johanna is so good at sending letters. She must have realized, with the snowstorm, that I was still at Wode—"

"Still at Wode? Do you not live here as a ward of Lady Brackendale?"

"I do. However, I decided weeks ago, for…personal reasons, to leave Wode and go and live with my aunt. I was meant to travel to her keep, providing the weather was good, on the day of the siege."

"Lucky for me, then, that the snow fell and I chose that day to attack," Tye said with a wink.

Lucky? Goodness. Trying to ignore an inappropriate tingle of delight, Claire said, "I must write to Johanna. Once the situation at Wode is settled, of course."

Tye nodded, but the piercing heat of his stare didn't diminish. "You did not answer my question yet. Delwyn—"

"He is a friend, a squire at the keep where Johanna lives as a ward."

"He spoke fondly of you."

"I have known him since we were children. He has delivered every letter from my sister."

Tension suddenly seemed to define Tye's posture. "Is he courting you?"

Shocked laughter bubbled from Claire. "Nay."

"He seemed the perfect man to catch your eye. Young, comely, and of fine noble breeding."

In the flickering light and shadows of the fire, Tye's features appeared hewn from stone. If she didn't know better, she would think he was jealous. "If Delwyn is courting anyone," she said, "I hope 'tis Johanna."

Tye's gaze didn't waver. Not so much as a flicker of his eyelashes.

"I have always thought he and Johanna well suited. They are close to the same age. They share many friends. I have encouraged my sister to accept his advances, and I believe I have been successful."

"'Tis the truth?"

"If you have read my letters from Johanna, as you have claimed to have done, then you would *know* I am telling the truth."

The silence between them persisted, marked by the pops and hisses of the fire. Then, Tye smiled. His crooked grin held such devastating charm, Claire's head spun. She must still be feeling the effects of the wine she'd drunk a short while ago, or else Tye was entirely responsible for her giddiness. She grabbed hold of one arm of the chair to steady herself.

"I have read only a few of her letters," he finally said. "There has, as you know, been a great deal to accomplish in the last few days." Before Claire could say a word, he added quietly, "I am also a slow reader. It takes me a while to make out the words."

'Twas a rare admission from such a proud man. "If I may ask, who taught you to read? 'Tis not common for..." *a man of your ilk*, her thoughts continued. But, she didn't want to offend him. Not when she had such an ideal opportunity to learn more about him. Frowning, she tried to find the right words.

"For a rogue and a bastard, you mean?"

She bit down on her lip. "I did not mean—"

"If you must know, a wealthy French widow taught me. Her name was Georgette. I was her much younger lover, a role I greatly enjoyed and lived to the fullest."

Judging by his reckless grin and the teasing gleam in his eyes, Tye had hoped to shock her. He had. Yet, Claire couldn't ignore a pang of sadness, to know he'd been the plaything of a rich woman and subject to her whims. Had he let himself be used in such a way because he'd believed he had no other choice in life? Mayhap he'd desperately needed Georgette's generosity to eat and have a place to sleep. Claire shouldn't care to know his reasons, but she did.

"In the afternoons," he was saying, "after I had satisfied all of her desires, Georgette liked to sit in her bed, open to a page in a book, and teach me words. She had a small collection of leather-bound tomes that had become hers after her husband, a spice merchant, died. She told me that teaching me to read was her gift to me. She said her husband's ability to read had helped him in deals with less-than-honorable buyers, who had added clauses into contracts without telling him beforehand. He was able to point out the additions and correct the documents. Likewise, she insisted that being able to read would help me avoid unfavorable deals in my life. If I wished, I could become more than a mere sword for hire."

Georgette had obviously cared for Tye, otherwise she wouldn't have bothered to teach him. "How long ago was this?" Claire asked. "Do you still keep in contact with her?"

His smile tinged with regret. "She died. She caught a cough that worsened and would not go away, no matter how much she spent on visits from the local healer and foul-smelling poultices. In her last days, I simply held her, lying next to her in the bed, while she shivered and coughed. She died in my arms."

"I am sorry," Claire whispered.

"So am I. I will not soon forget her." He shook his head, as if to draw himself out of that sad moment. "Since her passing, I have not spent much time practicing my reading. 'Tis why I am still slow."

"Did you read Johanna's letter that arrived today?" Claire asked. She hadn't seen it yet. Mayhap he intended to keep it, along with the others he'd confiscated, rather than give it to her.

"Aye." He reached to his hip, lifted the edge of his tunic, and withdrew a rolled parchment tucked into the belt of his hose. He handed the letter to her.

Her fingers closed around the parchment, warmed by his body. The broken edge of the wax seal touched her palm. She shouldn't be angry that he'd read it first. After all—

"I had to be sure the letter was not a ruse," Tye answered, without a hint of apology. "Moreover, there might have been news in there of my father."

She set the letter on her lap. "Was there?"

"Nay."

"Then you read my personal correspondence for naught."

"I disagree, Kitten. I learned about the new gowns your sister purchased from a shop in the nearby village, and the four pairs of shoes that she bought to go with them."

Claire giggled. "She does like to shop."

Tye rolled his eyes. "And go on and on about the color

and design of her purchases." As Claire's laughter faded, he leaned forward, picked up the wine jug, and poured some of the dark red liquid into a goblet. He handed it to her.

"Thank you." She wouldn't drink much; she was lightheaded enough already. However, she'd linger as long as she could with Tye, for 'twas a welcome change from the solitude of her chamber. Through talking with him, she'd also glean fresh details about him to include in the journal.

She sipped from the goblet. The drink was not wine, as she'd expected, but a piquant, fruity liqueur.

"Good?" Tye asked, taking a sip as well.

"Delicious. What is it?"

"Blackberry liqueur. I found in the cellar."

She stilled, the goblet halfway to her lips. Her stomach knotted. Silently scolding herself for her obvious shock, she lifted the vessel to her mouth and drank. "The storage room below the keep?" she asked, proud that her voice didn't wobble.

Tye's dark brows rose. "There is another?"

She laughed, more brightly she'd intended. "There is only the one. However, if Lord Brackendale had been able to convince her ladyship otherwise, there would have been several. He loved his liqueurs. He purchased most of them from a monastery a few leagues from here. The monks use the fruit grown in their gardens and orchards to make wines and liqueurs, which they sell at a stall in the local market. His lordship had amassed quite a collection."

"Indeed, he had."

After swallowing another sip, Claire glanced down into the goblet. As her innards heated with the potent drink, sadness tugged at her, for she missed his lordship: his boisterous laugh, his kindness, and his wry sense of humor. She couldn't imagine him being very pleased that one of his prized and expensive liqueurs had been opened and enjoyed by a rogue who'd seized the castle.

Aware that Tye was watching her, she looked up, a little too fast. Her head whirled a moment before her vision cleared, but the knot in her belly remained. If he had been down to the cellar, he might have discovered the hidden door. She had to find out, and in a way that wouldn't alert him to the fact that the room was more than a place to store drink.

Tightening her grip on the goblet's stem, she asked, "What else did you find in the cellar?"

"Casks of ale. Barrels of wine." He shrugged. "Plenty of cobwebs as well."

He hadn't mentioned the secret door. Had he found it, or not? Claire scrambled to think of a way to continue her questioning and not make him suspicious.

"Why are you so curious about the storage room?" Tye asked.

Oh, God. Forcing a careless shrug, she said, "No particular reason. I have only been down there once. There are still some chambers in the keep that I have not visited."

"I have seen most of them." His tone hardened, as though in warning. Was he telling her that he knew about the cellar door and that if she hoped to escape through it, that such a plan wouldn't work?

Dizziness taunted her again. Whatever he was thinking, she must convince him otherwise. "A lord does need to know every chamber of his fortress. Likewise, he should know the history of his keep, all the way back to the day masons started building it."

Reaching over, Tye picked up the wine jug. "I know the history of Wode."

"You do?"

His lips thinned. "The parts that matter to me."

A cry for caution sifted through her. And yet, she could not stop the words from tumbling from her mouth. "Those parts, surely, mean more when considered as parts of the whole."

In the midst of pouring himself more liqueur, he paused. The wine goblet hovered, firelight glinting off the engraved silver surface.

"I see the history of this fortress as if 'tis a tapestry," she said. "If some of the threads are missing, or if there are holes in the fabric, the tapestry is incomplete."

He finished filling his goblet and offered more liqueur to her. She shook her head. He set the jug down, the tautness not leaving his features; his hand resting on the arm of his chair tightened into a fist.

"You speak of the history of this place as though every single year is significant," he said.

"Exactly right. Each year has contributed to making this fortress what it is today."

He sneered. "What matters to me—*all* that matters—is that Wode used to belong to my father. I conquered it. I won it through victory in battle. 'Tis mine now, and will remain mine. Do not believe there is more, Kitten, for there is not."

Her arms crossed, Veronique leaned against the wall in the inky shadows just inside the forebuilding, out of view of the folk in the hall. She watched Tye and the beauty sitting with regal poise near him, her hair shining like the purest gold in the firelight and her skin as pale as fresh snow.

Envy uncoiled within Veronique like a waking viper. She examined Claire's gown, noting every feminine curve and swell beneath the fine quality fabric. Once, years ago, Veronique's figure had been that remarkable, her breasts high and firm, her waist small, her hips generous—quite different to her aging body now that sagged, ached, and required extraordinary care with lotions, herbal potions, and ghastly tonics that made her vomit and left her mouth burning with the taste of rotten apples. But her beauty, aging or not, was the one thing Veronique would never let go, regardless of the cost. Any cost.

Veronique's mouth twisted as Tye smiled at Claire. Without doubt, he was wooing the little bitch, courting her with a civilized, indulgent drink by the fire, as if they had a lot in common, which they did not.

Tye was wise to have sent Braden to gather news of de Lanceau's whereabouts; such information was crucial to their victory and winning the spoils they all deserved. In the meantime, though, Tye should be plotting, scheming, reveling in his anger and the revenge soon to be his—not seducing a virgin. Such pursuit could cause Tye to become careless and weak. Veronique simply wouldn't allow it, not when she had invested so much, *sacrificed* so much, year after year to ensure that Tye would grow into the warrior to crush his sire.

Claire might shyly tilt her head and cast discreet glances at Tye's muscled body, but she would only look. She might secretly lust after him, but she'd not lie with him, not willingly. She'd not despoil her precious noble body, just as she'd not fornicate with the dumb louts who mucked out the stables.

A wicked laugh burgeoned within Veronique, for she could—and would—give Tye what he wanted. Tonight, he'd have his way with Claire. Then, instead of longing for her, he'd realize what he'd craved wasn't worth all of the effort. 'Twas a lesson that would bring him back under Veronique's control, focused once again upon the upcoming fight in which he'd destroy his father and claim all.

Veronique's fingers slid into the hem of her gown's sleeve. She lightly touched the dagger tucked there, as well as the small glass vial. The vial had worked its way close to the opening in her sleeve, and she made sure 'twas positioned where she wanted it before she strolled from the shadows.

With loose-hipped strides, Veronique walked to the hearth. In the glow of the fire, Tye's expression hardened. He clearly didn't like what Claire was saying. Smugness trailed through Veronique, for that anger was a good sign. She knew very well how a man's rage could be coaxed, manipulated, and with relentless patience, transformed into heated passion that required a lusty coupling to assuage it. Years ago, she'd used Geoffrey's desire for vengeance against Lord Arthur Brackendale to turn his fury into a fierce passion; the memory of that passion still had the power to make her womb clench and her breasts ache. Tonight, she'd turn Tye's fury into a powerful, undeniable lust.

Claire saw her first. Her blue eyes widened.

Was that fear in Claire's expression? She should be afraid.

Tye paused in the midst of what he was saying. "Mother."

"Tye." Veronique halted near the table. "You are enjoying a drink by the fire, I see."

"We are. What are you about this evening?"

If he only knew. "Actually, I was hoping to find you."

"Ah. And?"

Veronique's attention shifted to Claire, sitting as straight as a fence post. Her face was a bit flushed, but then, sitting in that ridiculous way would make any woman uncomfortable. "One of the mercenaries is sharpening my knives for me. I want to be sure I am ready for battle when your father arrives. Would you like me to see that your knives are sharpened, too?"

He studied her a moment and then nodded. "A wise idea."

"May I go into the solar and fetch your daggers? I assume they are still in your saddle bag, where you normally keep them?"

"Aye, you may go into the solar. And aye, the knives are there. The daggers are all that you may take from my chamber, though," he said, his words clearly a warning. He softened his threat with a smile. "I am still mulling my strategy for the battle ahead, and since I know where I have put the items I need, they should remain in their places."

In other words, Tye didn't want her meddling with any of his possessions, including what he'd taken from Claire's room. Damn him. He knew her too well, for those were exactly the items she'd love to borrow for a night and devour. They would no doubt be delightfully entertaining, considering what Veronique had read in Claire's journal.

"I understand," Veronique said, her tone polite despite her annoyance.

"Good."

His brusque reply proved he wanted to appear fully in control of the conversation, likely to impress Claire. Defiance kicked at Veronique's self-control, but she managed to keep her smile pleasant, her expression calm. Subtly shifting her fingers, she worked the vial out of her sleeve and into her palm.

"Your jug is almost empty," she noted. "Is that the bottle there?" She motioned to the earthenware flask sitting on the floor by the right rear table leg.

Tye eased up in his chair. "I will—"

"Do not trouble yourself. Allow me."

Tye looked about to protest. Refusing to let her smile slip, Veronique bent and drew the flask toward her. She swiftly pulled the stopper from the vial, poured in the liquid, and pushed the vial back into her sleeve, then rose to her feet with a stifled grunt of effort. She poured more of the crimson-colored drink into the jug resting on the table and then refilled both goblets.

"There," she said, her task complete.

"Thank you, Mother."

"I was glad to help." Indeed, she was delighted, for her plan had been far easier to execute than she'd expected. Neither he nor Claire could have seen her meddle with the drink; the table blocked their view. "You *are* the lord of this fortress. You should not have to pour your own drink. Such a chore is beneath you now." Catching Claire's gaze, Veronique grinned.

Claire dropped her gaze.

You should be afraid to hold my stare, bitch. Just you wait.

"Now," Veronique said, moving away, "I shall see to those knives."

Chapter Nineteen

R ubbing his thumb against the side of his goblet, Tye
watched his mother climb the stairs. She was scheming.
Of that, he was certain.

Whatever she was planning, he'd find out. She might
believe she had free reign here at Wode, but with his victory over
his father so near, the last thing he needed was for her to do
something unexpected.

"Have you ever talked to her about Lord de Lanceau,"
Claire asked, her voice cutting into his thoughts.

Tye wrested his gaze from his mother. "I have."

"All that you know of him has come from her?"

"Most of it. The rest I gleaned from legends and hearsay.
Why do you ask?"

"Is it possible…?" Claire hesitated, clearly choosing her
words carefully. His gaze riveted to her mouth, for he ached with
the desire to kiss her. She'd taste of liqueur, and cake, and a
hundred other sweet temptations. "What I mean is, she obviously
hates your sire."

"We both do."

"Could she…might she have lied to you about—?"

"*Lied?*" he growled.

Claire's throat moved with a hard swallow, but she held
his gaze and nodded.

"Lied about what?" The words broke from Tye's lips like
chips of ice. Most grown men would have immediately retreated
from their questioning, but his stubborn little Kitten merely lifted
her chin higher.

"Lied to you," she ventured on, "that your sire…never

wanted you. That he refused to accept you. You must admit, 'twas to her advantage—"

"He *did* refuse to accept me, in front of his own men."

"I see." She spoke so quietly, he almost didn't hear her over the fire. In the shifting light, her skin looked dewy, soft. He longed to touch her cheek, to feel her skin against his, to make her body melt against him in an impassioned kiss. He craved the feel of her in his arms.

"When did that refusal happen?" she asked.

Dragging his wayward thoughts back to their conversation, he said, "I was but a young boy. My mother had arranged a meeting with my father, to present me to him and make him acknowledge me. De Lanceau arrived in the field with a small army, determined to arrest my mother."

"Arrest her? There is more between your sire and Veronique than just a lord rejecting his former lover, then."

Tye shrugged. "De Lanceau barely escaped being poisoned years ago by my mother when he was recovering from a grave injury caused by a crossbow bolt. However, that is not relevant to him acknowledging me as his son."

"True. You can see, though, why he might be hesitant to believe her claims, especially one as important as you being his child."

God's bones, but she spoke so calmly, so rationally, as though she had every right to defend de Lanceau's damnable actions.

"Whatever lay between the two of them, my sire hoped to finish it on the day of the meeting. He intended to kill my mother. When he saw me, he realized he must eliminate me as well."

Claire sucked in a breath. "You cannot mean—"

Tye smiled coldly. "He wanted me dead."

"Never! Lord de Lanceau is known to adore children."

"But not his own," Tye sneered. "Not *me*, his bastard, born to the courtesan he cast aside."

"Listen to yourself! Do you really believe he meant to murder you? An innocent boy? A helpless child?" Claire's voice sharpened with revulsion.

"Why not? Then I would not grow up to be a threat to

him or his well-respected family."

Claire's eyes glistened in the firelight. "Is that what your mother told you?"

"She did."

"I thought so."

The dismissal in Claire's tone brought him forward on a surge of irritation, his arms braced on his knees. He cradled his goblet in his fingers as he said tightly, "I owe my mother my *life*."

"Tye—"

"*She* saved me from certain death that day. She refused to hand me over to de Lanceau or to let him take me from her by force. My mother protected me, fled England to keep me safe, raised me, and ensured I was trained to defend myself. I owe her everything."

"She did do all that you mentioned. But—"

"*But? She* made me who I am now. And now, I am ready to take what I am due."

Claire shook her head and stared down at her drink. The irritation simmering within Tye burned hotter.

"My sire will *not* have the pleasure of murdering me. He will find I am a far stronger opponent than he ever expected. I will slay him, and that day, I will rejoice. Each day that I conquer another of his estates, I will celebrate, until I have all that belonged to him."

Remorse touched Claire's gaze. "Have you seen Lord de Lanceau since your mother first presented you to him? That day was so long ago."

"Why do you ask?"

Claire's lips curved in a faint, hopeful smile. "People change. Mayhap if you could see him again, talk to him, just you and him…"

Talk? Like hell. Talking wouldn't bring about his sire's defeat. "I last saw my father when I was imprisoned months ago. Before that, I saw him at the battle at Waddesford Keep."

"That battle. 'Twas the first time he had seen you since that day long ago?"

"Aye." Tye would never forget the anticipation and anguish that had hounded him every moment of every day until he'd faced his sire at Waddesford Keep. Those same emotions lived within him now, only they had grown sharper, deeper, and far more painful.

"What happened at Waddesford Keep?"

He drew upon the intense hatred that flowed whenever he thought of his father. "I asked him to acknowledge me as his son. In front of witnesses, in front of his most trusted men and my mother, he refused."

Claire sighed, her expression troubled. "Did he give a reason why?"

"He claimed there is no proof that I am his child. I have been told, though, one has only to look at him and me side by side to see the resemblance."

"Still, you must surely understand his reluctance. He has only your mother's word, as well as a similarity in looks between you two, and that is not much to convince anyone that—"

With a furious growl, Tye slammed down his goblet and rose.

Claire hurriedly set down her goblet and huddled back in the chair, her eyes enormous. Spilled liqueur dripped from the table with a steady *pat-pat*.

Rage burned like white-hot flame in his veins. He caught the wary stares of the mercenaries at the nearby tables and glowered at them until they averted their gazes.

"Tell me this, if you can," he muttered, glaring at Claire. "If de Lanceau does not believe that I am his son, *why* did he try and save my life? Why bother?"

"Save your life?" Claire sounded astonished. "When?"

Tye flexed his hand, the one he'd used to cling to the side of the battlement. The memory of rough stone biting into his palm was as clear as if he were back at Waddesford Keep, in that dangerous, precarious moment. Fury and confusion whipped through him, and he faced the fire, its heat licking over him, as searing as his internal tempest.

"'Twas near the end of the battle," he said roughly. "I had nowhere left to go, except down."

"Down?"

"I fell over the edge of the battlement." Again, he heard

the shouts and clangs of fierce fighting, tasted death on the wind whipping around him. "At the last moment, I caught hold and hung there, with only air beneath my feet. The bailey was far below."

"Mercy!"

"Aye. *Mercy.*" Tye said between his teeth. He wondered if he'd ever be able to forget that moment of struggle, so fleeting yet so damned haunting. "As I fought to hold on, de Lanceau reached down his hand. He told me to grab hold, and he would pull me up."

"A kind gesture," Claire said. Her admiration for de Lanceau warmed her voice.

"Was it kind?" Anguish tore through Tye. All would have been so much simpler if de Lanceau had knocked away Tye's fingers gripping the stone, causing him to fall, or turned his back on Tye, withholding all compassion and leaving Tye to his fate. Instead, de Lanceau had knelt and offered his hand.

Why? *Why?*

Tye suddenly wanted to grab the jug of liqueur from the table and down it all at once. Drunken oblivion had to be better than this blistering pain.

"Of course 'twas kind," Claire said. "Your sire didn't have to offer you help."

"True. However, there were also many witnesses. No doubt he wanted to appear chivalrous in front of his men, by offering me his aid."

A disbelieving laugh broke from Claire. "He *is* a man of honor. He lives by the rules of chivalry. If you were his most bitter enemy, he would have offered the same."

"Ah. So 'twas not a gesture of kindness, then," Tye ground out. "'Twas a deception disguised as courtesy—"

"'Tis not what I—"

"—just as my mother said."

Silence answered him, a quietude measured only by the crackle of the fire and the hushed conversation of the mercenaries across the hall. He turned his back to the flames.

"Tye—"

"Do not try to convince me my father acted out of any

sense of *compassion*, for your own words have confirmed what I suspected. He did not offer to help me because of who I am, because I am his son. He did so because 'twas expected of him."

"Please, Tye. Whatever the reason, he still tried to save you. That should count for something."

"Should it?"

"Aye. When you see his lordship again, you must ask him about that moment. You should hear from his own lips why he wanted to save you."

"I do not care to hear his reasoning," Tye seethed, hauling a hand through his hair. Yet, a tiny part of his soul said he really *did* want to know. He did want to hear the truth. Indeed, he might ask—before he ran his sire through.

"You did not say what happened," Claire said. "While you struggled to hold on, did you take de Lanceau's hand?"

"I did not."

"You *fell?*"

"I let go."

She pressed her hand to her mouth. Horror and disbelief flickered across her features; the emotional torment inside him intensified.

"I let go," he repeated on a growl, "because I made a choice. I refused to yield to my sire. I would not willingly surrender and become his prisoner, his pawn."

"You are lucky to have survived such a fall," she said, lowering her hand to her lap. "You could have been mortally wounded."

"I was injured. I cracked the bones in my right leg. Regrettably, there was no hope of getting away, and my mother and I were taken captive. We were separated and imprisoned at different castles, but with Braden's help, we escaped."

"If I remember correctly, you saw Lord de Lanceau during your imprisonment."

"Aye. Once."

"Did you not have a chance then to discuss the fact you may be his son?"

Tye snorted. "He came to interrogate me about what happened at Waddesford Keep. When I would not cooperate, he left and never returned."

She trailed a slender finger over her bottom lip. He had the overwhelming urge to stride to her, grab her hand, and nibble on her fingers, before he claimed her mouth. 'Twould be so easy, to take her lips, press her back in the chair, her body soft beneath him…

"You must understand that 'twas your sire's duty to question you, as he would any man taken prisoner taken during a battle," she said. "Regardless whether or not he is your father, his duty had to take priority."

"As always," Tye muttered.

"As it had to be," she countered.

Tye chuckled, the sound harsh. She was so damned sure of de Lanceau's honor; naught Tye said would change her opinion. The frustration and bitterness within him could no longer be restrained.

"I do not know why I bothered to share my thoughts with you," he bit out.

"Why do you say that?"

"I should have known you would take my father's side." Tye grabbed his goblet from the table and drained the vessel.

Claire didn't answer. When he banged down the goblet and looked at her, a rosy flush stained her cheekbones. Her blue eyes glittered.

"Why the glare, Kitten?" he taunted.

"I have tried to help you."

"Really?"

"Really."

Admiration rippled through him, for she hadn't broken his stare. Had the drink made her so brave? He rather liked when she showed her little claws.

"*You*, however, have made it impossible for me to help you," she continued. "Your hatred is too deeply ingrained, and you are too stubborn to heed anyone but yourself."

"That surprises you?" Tye smirked. "I should have known you would not understand. You, the cosseted, sheltered, well-bred young lady who has never faced a difficult moment in her entire life."

Anguish flickered in her eyes, a pain that revealed she'd faced far greater turmoil than he'd imagined.

Regret weighed on his conscience. He hated that he'd caused her pain, even though he had every right to be angry. What, though, had happened to cause her such torment?

As though each action took immense self control, she picked up her sister's letter, placed her hands on the arms of the chair, and pushed to standing.

When he met her gaze again, all trace of her vulnerability was gone. She stared back with defiance and resolve.

"I do not need to have lived your life, Tye, to empathize with your situation. I, too, have had terrible things happen. I know what 'tis like to live with anguish in my heart."

"Anguish? Do you really think I *care* that de Lanceau doesn't acknowledge me? I hate him. You hear me? *Hate* him!"

She turned away. "Good night, Tye."

"Where do you think you are going?" he called as she started for the stairs. How dare she turn her back on him? He was lord here. He would tell her when she could leave the hall.

She didn't reply, just continued walking toward the stairs, her gown drifting at ankles. The mercenaries, watching from their table, muttered among themselves. Tye growled low in his throat, his fury and inner turmoil close to choking him. She'd not only disobeyed him, but she'd done so front of his hired men.

"I did not give you permission to leave," Tye roared.

Not the slightest slowing of her strides.

"You." He pointed to a mercenary. "Take the lady to her chamber." He sure as hell didn't trust himself to do it. Turning to the fire again, he cursed and hurled the goblet into the blaze, where it clanged against the back of the hearth and lay glinting amongst the flames.

Chapter Twenty

C laire struggled to hold back her tears. She held on until the door shut behind the mercenary, and then a sob wrenched from her lips. She set Johanna's letter on the trestle table to read later. Hugging her arms across her bosom, tears streaming down her face, she walked to the middle of her chamber, her steps unsteady.

Mercy, but her head whirled. Her stomach hurt from the strain of disagreeing with Tye. Her emotions hadn't been this sharply pitched in many weeks—the last time was when she'd learned of Lord Brackendale's death—but then again, she didn't usually drink so much wine, or such strong liqueur.

The intensity of Tye's hatred... 'Twas frightening and agonizing to see. That he could despise the man who was likely his father to such a soul-deep extent was very, very sad. He loathed his sire because of wrongs committed in the past that might or might not be true, as Tye had only his mother's word to go by.

Claire shuddered, remembering the gloating grin Veronique had cast her way before heading to the solar. That vile woman had only one interest: herself. Veronique had fed her own grievances against de Lanceau to Tye, year after year, until Tye's bitterness had become as keen as her own.

Wiping at the wetness stinging her face, Claire turned to the trestle table. She wavered, but steadied herself by grabbing hold of the edge of the table. Once her head had quit reeling so much, she snatched up a linen wash cloth to dry her eyes. A mug containing a greenish-yellow drink sat beside the bowl of water the maid had left for her nightly bathing, and as fresh tears brimmed, Claire smiled. A soothing herbal infusion had often been her nightly ritual before Tye had taken control of the castle. How thoughtful of the maid to have managed to bring her an infusion tonight.

The mug was barely warm against Claire's fingertips—the drink must have been made a while ago—but she brought it to her lips and sipped. The sweetness of honey swirled over her tongue, the flavor barely concealing the musty taste of the other ingredients. Frowning slightly, she sipped again. 'Twas not her usual infusion of chamomile, honey, and mint. But still, 'twas soothing.

She crossed to the window and opened the shutters. The frigid air soothed her hot face and she leaned into the embrasure while she gazed up at the star-sprinkled sky and drank her infusion. Mayhap the breeze would help to stop her head from spinning. 'Twas odd that she felt so giddy, but the liqueur she'd imbibed must have been more potent than she'd realized.

A man's voice carried from somewhere out in the night, likely a mercenary talking to one of his friends while patrolling the battlements. Claire's thoughts drifted to Tye. Was he still in the hall? He'd been angry, and yet, he'd seemed so alone.

How could Tye insist that she didn't understand his torment? She understood it all too well, having lost her parents, Lord Brackendale, and her beloved Henry. Henry's death especially had taught her the depths of pain.

With each of Tye's harsh words about his sire, she'd wept inside for the little boy who'd been so callously rejected, and for the grown man who'd become so embittered. She'd wanted to go to him, wrap her arms around him, and hold him tight.

Foolish thoughts. *Perilous* thoughts. And yet, even now, she longed to do what she'd imagined.

Her eyes drifted closed, for she longed very, *very* much to be in his arms. The craving coiled inside her, tantalizing and unrelenting, causing heaviness in her breasts and between her thighs...

Her eyes snapped open. Such feelings were not wise. Not wise at all.

But of all wickedness, she *burned* for him. She ached to taste his lips upon hers; to feel his broad, hard body pressed against her; to savor his touch upon her bare skin. . .

Her hand trembled as she raised the mug and drank again. She stepped back from the window, readying to close the shutters, and the room careened around her.

Frantic to catch herself before she fell, she grabbed hold of the window ledge. Her pulse was pounding at a frantic pace. Sweat beaded on her brow. Goodness, but she felt odd.

Disquiet raced through her, even as she shivered in a brisk gust of wind. She'd been tipsy before. Granted, only once, but she didn't recall having felt like this. Nay, the sluggishness of her thoughts, the dizzying heat racing through her, the feverish cravings taunting her... These were unusual.

Her fingers still gripping the ledge, she squinted down at the mug. *The infusion.* It also had been unusual.

Had she been drugged? Who would have dared to do such a thing, and why?

Anger burgeoned inside her. With careful, uneven steps, she made her way to the door and hammered on the panel.

"Settle down," a guard groused from outside.

"I want to speak to Tye," Claire called back.

"In the morning—"

"*Now!*" She hammered on the door again. *Thud, thud, thud.* "Did you hear me? Now!" *Thud, Thud—*

"Enough!" The man outside snapped. "Stop that noise."

"Please," Claire said. "I have to speak to him. 'Tis important."

Tye sprawled in the chair pulled up to the hearth in the solar, a goblet of red wine dangling from his left hand. With his right hand, he stroked the cat—Patch, he recalled—lying in his lap. Tye had asked servants about the feline and had learned his name from one of the stable hands. Patch dozed, enjoying the attention; his loud purr was akin to the rattle of an old cart wheel.

His touch gentle, Tye shifted his hand to Patch's head and then slid his palm down the cat's silken back, being careful not to brush the bandaged leg. It had taken some coaxing, and juicy chunks of chicken Tye had brought from the kitchen, but Patch had granted him a measure of trust tonight. Curling up on Tye, though, had been Patch's idea. The feline hadn't been deterred by his wounded leg, and had managed to get comfortable within moments of leaping onto Tye's lap.

A log in the fire popped loudly, and Patch startled, his eyes flaring wide—a look that, somehow, reminded Tye of Claire. With a steady hand, Tye soothed the feline. Patch's purring resumed, and his eyes closed again.

If only matters were as simple with Claire.

While he scratched the back of the cat's head, his fingers sinking into soft fur, Tye's gaze shifted to the hearth. He vividly remembered how, in the great hall, the fire glow had brushed Claire's curves and dips; he'd been almost drunk with desire for her.

Drunk. He sipped more wine. Aye, after the liqueur he'd consumed in the hall and what he'd imbibed in the solar, he might be a bit drunk now. However, that didn't entirely explain the heaviness in his head, the merciless ache in his loins, the way he wanted her with a need that defied all common sense.

He should be angry with her, not lusting after her. She'd turned her back on him, dismissed him as though he were naught but a hot-headed simpleton. And still, he wanted to—

A knock sounded on the solar door. Patch jolted awake.

Scowling, Tye called, "What is it?"

"Lady Sevalliere, milord," a mercenary called through the door. "She wants to speak with you."

Annoyance whipped through Tye, and then, smug satisfaction. Had she realized her mistake in departing the hall as she'd done earlier? Mayhap she intended to apologize.

If not, she'd better have a good reason for disturbing him.

Cursing as he straightened and his head spun, he lifted Patch from his lap and set him back in his bed. With a grumpy meow, the feline settled on his blanket.

Tye brushed the creases from his tunic and strode to the door. After shaking his head to try to clear the fog from his mind, he yanked open the door, sent the mercenary back to his post, and headed to Claire's chamber.

He knocked.

"Enter," she said, without a moment's delay.

He stepped inside. Claire stood by the window, one hand holding her hair up off her nape, as though to cool over-heated skin. Her face was pink, lightly misted with sweat, although the room was cold. He had a sudden, fierce yearning to know how the back of her neck tasted. When he pressed his lips to her nape, would her skin be like down? Would her skin taste sweet, like a ripe apple, or slightly salty?

Her expression turned wary, as if she was privy to his unruly thoughts. She dropped her tresses, and they tumbled in a wavy golden mass down her back. Then she squared her shoulders, although she seemed unsteady on her feet.

He pushed the door closed behind him. Whatever she had to say, his men outside didn't need to hear.

Claire inhaled a shaky breath. Her blue eyes blazed, glittering with accusation. She clearly wasn't going to apologize to him. Did she mean to continue their disagreement from earlier?

"You wished to speak to me?" he demanded.

"The infusion," she answered, gesturing to the mug on the trestle table. "Either that or the liqueur we drank earlier."

She didn't seem herself. Her mouth wobbled, as though she hovered at the edge of an emotional abyss, about to erupt in a thunderstorm of fury or burst into tears.

"What about the infusion?"

She blotted her forehead with her sleeve. "'Twas...not right."

"What do you mean? How was it not right?" He strode to the table and picked up the near empty mug of greenish brew.

"It does not usually taste so strongly of honey. I thought, at first, that could just be because of the way the infusion was brewed tonight, but—"

Suspicion scratched at the back of his mind. Fighting to control a fresh surge of rage, he asked quietly, "Who made the infusion for you?"

"I do not know. 'Twas on the table when I returned from the hall. The fire was tended and water left out for my wash, so I assumed the maidservant had left it for me—as she used to do before your conquest. I am certain, though, 'twas not any brew brought by the maidservant. Not the way I feel now."

Tye raised the mug to his nose and inhaled. There, underneath the pungent tang of mint: the murky essence he'd anticipated. The aphrodisiac his mother kept on hand for when her lovers, including Braden, needed some encouragement.

Damn her! How much had his mother poured into Claire's drink? The way his own lust raged, he wouldn't be surprised if she'd meddled with the liqueur and the wine in his solar, too.

Claire moved closer. "You do not believe me." She was near enough now that he caught her milk-and-honey scent. His whole body roused, acutely aware of her nearness and what he longed to *do* with her.

He set the mug down. Fury over his mother's actions mingled with his own frustration that he hadn't foreseen such a nasty ploy. "I do believe you. There is an essence I recognize in the infusion's scent: a strong aphrodisiac."

"Aphrodisiac!" Claire gasped and blushed scarlet. "You mean herbs that are meant to...to..."

She looked so appalled, he wanted to laugh. However, 'twas not a situation in which he wanted to find the slightest humor. "Aye."

Anger lit her eyes. "Who would do such a vile thing? Did you put it in my drink?"

"Of course not!"

"I thought mayhap 'twas why you had summoned me to the hall, so you could have the tainted infusion delivered to my chamber."

"I had no part in tainting your drink," he said firmly. "I promise you."

She pressed her lips together, as though deciding whether or not to believe him. "How long will I feel this way?"

"Once the potion has worn off, likely by morning, you will feel as usual."

"As usual." A strangled laugh broke from her. "Naught is as *usual* here. Not anymore."

The uncertainty in her voice, combined with a hint of despair, made him long to draw her into his arms and kiss her senseless. Fueled by the desire singing in his veins, the yearning became almost beyond his control. He drew in a slow, calming breath.

"You say you are familiar with the essence," she said. "How?"

"I know someone who has used it before."

"You have a good idea, then, who is responsible."

"I do."

"Tell me his or her name. I demand—"

"Demand all you like. I have no proof. I will not condemn someone who may have had naught to do with tonight's deception." While he doubted one of the servants had taken the aphrodisiac from his mother's belongings, 'twas not impossible. Once he was done here, he'd find his mother. If she was responsible, he'd expect an explanation.

Claire sighed harshly and wiped her flushed face with her hand. "Who would do such a thing to me? For what purpose?" Tears welled along her bottom lashes. "'Tis a vile trick, and I...I..."

Her eyelids fluttered. She wavered on her feet. Tye instinctively caught her elbow, and she sagged against him. His arm wrapped around her, and he inhaled the luscious, tantalizing scent of her.

She looked up at him, her face dangerously close to his. "The way I feel, right now—"

"How do you feel?" he whispered. He ached to kiss her, touch her, *have* her, no matter the consequences.

"Like my skin is on fire," she whispered back.

"On fire," he repeated softly. He knew exactly how she felt. His gaze dropped to the pink fullness of her lips.

"My heart is racing," she went on.

"Mmm." His own pulse slammed against his ribs. Could she hear it, where she leaned against him, with her fingers pressed into his tunic?

"My lips..." Shyness and craving touched her expression.

"Your lips," he coaxed, brushing his fingers down the side of her reddened cheek.

"They long to kiss you." Before he could say a word,

before he could begin to think about the possibilities ahead, she rose on tiptoes and pressed her mouth to his.

He kissed her back with all the longing and lust tormenting him. She tasted as he remembered: delicious and sweet.

"Claire." His greedy hands slid from her waist, moving down the sumptuous cloth of her gown until they settled on the rounded curves of her bottom. With a growl, he pulled her hips flush against his, showing her just how much she affected him.

She tensed, but didn't struggle to break free.

"I do not want to be alone, not feeling like this," she pleaded. "Tye, I want—"

"Want?" he urged and then slid his tongue against hers. She mimicked the teasing thrusts of his tongue, and his lust spiked to fever pitch.

"I want to…be with you."

He froze. Excitement whipped through him. A cry of caution sounded, too, but the roaring pleasure and desire inside him swiftly drowned out the protest. "I want to be with you, too," he whispered against her mouth. Kissing her deeply, he slid his arms under her, lifted her into his arms, and headed for the door.

Chapter Twenty-One

C laire lifted her head from the muscled pillow of Tye's shoulder as he strode into the solar. With a nudge of his booted foot, he shut the door.

Her head was still careening from the aphrodisiac in the infusion. And from *him*. Being in his arms, cradled against his hard body, made her yearnings even more intense. There was such pleasure in just being in his embrace, of feeling safe and protected and desired, if only for one night.

The quietude of the solar settled around them as Tye walked to the hearth. The fire was the solar's only source of illumination. None other was needed, though, for as her eyes adjusted to the dim light, she clearly saw the carved chair facing the blaze, the cat with a bandaged leg dozing by the hearth—Patch, from the stables—and the massive bed.

When her gaze skimmed the rumpled bedding, a tremor ran through her. She might be a virgin, but she knew what men and women did together in bed; she and Mary had talked about it several times when Claire had expected Henry to ask for her hand in marriage. Claire had no doubt why Tye had brought her here. She'd told him she wanted him, after all. 'Twas no lie; she *did* desire him. She ached for him, with a hunger that threatened to consume her if 'twas not quenched.

Part of her thrilled at the thought of lying with him, and yet...part of her was uneasy. She'd never expected to lie with anyone but Henry, once they were married. Now, she was going to lie with a man who had promised her naught, a rogue who'd had many lovers and who would most likely cast her aside in a few days.

Stop this foolishness while you still can, the voice of reason cried. *Tell Tye the potion made you speak unwisely. Go back to your chamber.*

That advice could have come from Lady Brackendale. Yet, Claire craved Tye, as she'd wanted no other man—truth be told, even Henry. The craving enticed her to stay, to seize this offered pleasure because she wanted it. Once she left Wode to live with her aunt, she'd forever be a spinster. Here, now, she had a chance to know what 'twas like to be a woman desired by a man.

Halting near the hearth, Tye turned his head and claimed her mouth in slow, thorough kisses that stirred a heated glow within her. He might be a rogue, but he made her heart soar with his kisses and his smile, and he'd brought excitement and wonder into her life.

Finally breaking the kiss, Tye set her down, releasing her slowly so that her body slid against his. She landed on her feet, glad of his arm around her waist, for she was still lightheaded. A sigh rattled in her throat, and his smoldering stare fixed on her lips, his expression stark with need.

A thrill chased through her, for that need was for her. That a man like him could want her...'Twas astonishing and wonderful.

"Kitten," he whispered, his voice ragged.

The raw emotion in his eyes touched her like a caress. She burned inside, burned only for him. His mouth descended upon hers, and she kissed him back, taking all of the passion he offered and asking for more.

Tye's kisses grew bolder, claiming her lips, conquering her tongue. She gasped, shuddered, her hands lifting to cradle his face, to touch him as their mouths suckled and nibbled and molded together. The fever inside her flared. She strained against him, yearning for something but not knowing quite what. Her skin felt taut, hot, and—

A groan broke from him, and his hands at her waist slid up. His wet mouth glided against hers, while his thumbs brushed the undersides of her breasts. The light touch sent a fiery jolt running through her. And then, his hands moved again, and his thumbs stroked over her hardened nipples.

"Oh, mercy," she moaned, pleasure spiraling straight to that secret, private place between her legs.

"Do you like that?" he murmured, his thumbs stroking again. He nuzzled her cheek and his breath fanned across her jaw.

She gasped, her eyes closing, the sensations almost too exquisite to bear. The rational voice inside her shrilled again, insisted she should step away and deny Tye, but the heat inside her licked hotter and hotter. The tiny voice was consumed by a flare of *wanting*.

She was vaguely aware of moving, of the back of her legs hitting the bed frame. His kisses fierce and deep, Tye eased her down, his broad body coaxing hers to sit on the coverlet and then move backward to lie on the bedding. The bed ropes squeaked as the mattress adjusted to their weight.

He pulled off his boots and crawled onto her. Shifting his weight to one elbow, he lowered himself to her right side, looked down into her face, and brushed stray strands of hair from her cheek with careful fingers.

"Kitten." The gentleness of his voice brought tears to her eyes.

"I need..." she began, but didn't know how to convey what she wanted. "I ache for..."

"I know," he whispered. His lips pressed to hers while his fingers glided from her cheek to her throat, and then spread wide upon her gown. Tingling fire skittered over her skin, following the path of his left hand as he slowly trailed it down to cover her left breast.

A mewl broke past her lips. Her hips tilted up, an instinctive response to his touch as he cupped her breast and teased, caressed. Her chemise and gown rubbing against her sensitized skin would surely drive her mad.

"Tye," she moaned, her head thrashing. An awful restlessness consumed her. She had to appease it. Now. With him.

His hand lifted from her breast. Missing the heat, desperate for his caress, she opened her eyes. His expression was a heart-wrenching blend of desire and tenderness.

Frustration churned inside her. "Why did you stop touching me?"

He kissed her again.

"Do you not want me?"

He laughed, the sound rough with disbelief. "I want you. More than I can ever say."

"Then—"

He pressed a finger to her lips. She gazed up at him, silenced but *wanting*.

Please, she silently cried. How desperately she wanted him to touch her, to show her what to do, to help her satisfy the overwhelming hunger. Naught else mattered, except easing the sensual ache.

He drew in a breath, as if he was going to speak. *Nay*. Talking wouldn't ease the fire within her. Parting her lips, she slicked her tongue over his finger. His skin tasted salty. Wonderful.

A hissed oath rushed between his teeth, and he rolled off her and sat up abruptly.

She blinked away tears. He sat with his back to her. She wanted to weep, for she had no idea why he'd drawn away. Her emotions felt bruised, volatile. As he swept his hand over his mouth, she rose up onto her knees behind him, wobbling on a rush of dizziness.

He'd said he wanted her. Mayhap, somehow, she hadn't proven to him how much she wanted him? A more experienced woman would have made her desires very clear.

She must show Tye that she wished to lie with him, bare skin to bare skin. Maidenly modesty would not achieve what she wanted.

Her hands shaking, Claire reached for the hems of her gown and chemise and tugged the garments up over her legs, thighs, and hips, and higher still. She slipped off her silken hose. Now wearing only firelight, she tossed her wadded clothing aside.

Tye glanced over his shoulder. "Claire—"

He stilled. His eyes widened and then narrowed in a purely predatory, appreciative stare. As his ravenous gaze raked down her naked body, triumph surged through her.

Ah, God, she was exquisite. From her flushed face to her elegant neck and high breasts with rosy-pink nipples, to the smooth flatness of her belly and the downy thatch between her thighs, Claire was even more exceptional than he'd imagined. Tye's desire became an inferno, raging and insistent.

She was his.

He would make her his, here, tonight.

An awed growl rumbled in his throat as he faced her and rose to his knees in front of her, towering over her. He buried a hand into her hair and kissed her upturned face. She sighed against his mouth, kissed him back with equal fervor, and yet, she shivered.

He lifted his lips from hers. "Are you cold, Kitten? This chamber can be drafty—"

"I am not cold."

She was nervous, then. He kissed her gently. "Do not be afraid."

"I am not."

"Why are you shivering, then?"

A shy laugh broke from her. "I do not know. I guess… Mayhap I am uncertain."

As he'd expected. She was an innocent. He would be her first lover.

The thought filled him with a powerful rush of pleasure. As she smiled up at him, though, so incredibly lovely, he couldn't dismiss a niggling sense of reluctance. His mind was muzzy from the liqueur and aphrodisiac, but he still had enough wits about him to know her passion was induced by the herbal potion. She wasn't her true self. If she were in full control of her senses, would she still be naked and begging him to couple with her?

Her hands slid under his tunic, drawing his full attention back to her. His fingers worked their way under his shirt, and he inhaled sharply at the touch of her bare skin on his. Laughing softly, she caught the hems of his garments and tugged them up and over his head.

Throwing the clothes aside, she stared at his naked chest. Despite his many scars, some of them jagged and furrowed, she didn't seem repulsed by what she saw. Thank God.

"Kiss me," she whispered, kissing his cheek and trailing little kisses down to his mouth.

"Kitten," he began, but she claimed his lips, swirled her tongue into his mouth with such uncanny skill, he forgot what he intended to say and kissed her back. Lost again to his hunger, he leaned into her and pressed her down onto her back, nudging her thighs apart so that he settled between them. His chest crushed against her plump, warm bosom. His manhood, as hard as rock and straining against his braies and hose, pressed into the dampness between her legs.

She gasped.

He groaned, his eyes squeezing shut.

He dipped his head to press his forehead to hers, flexed his hips again, the feel of her against his swollen flesh almost his undoing. As she moaned and shifted her hips, he shuddered. *Ah, God.* Too close.

"Tye," she whimpered. "Please."

He groaned again, his breath coming in harsh pants, for he ached to free himself from his clothes, to plunge into her hot, tight slickness. But she wasn't thinking clearly. In the morning, once the aphrodisiac had faded, she'd be ashamed of lying with him. She might never speak to him again, and he cared too much for her to lose her that way.

His head pounded with the intensity of his thoughts. Did he dare take her virginity, thereby ruining her chances of marrying a rich lord husband? What if she got with child this night? That babe would be a bastard, just like him.

Mayhap 'twas what his mother intended: for Claire to be ruined and to conceive his babe. No doubt his parent was already planning to further her ambitions through Claire's ruination—a thought that stirred his anger.

Pressing kisses to the side of Claire's damp neck, he fought a crushing sense of indecision. He wanted Claire, very much. But there was far more to consider than what he selfishly desired.

He met her gaze. Her glazed eyes shadowed with confusion. "What is wrong? What—?"

His body screaming at the injustice, he shifted to break

the intimate contact between them. "I cannot give you what you want," he said softly. "Not like this."

"Like this?"

"Under the spell of an aphrodisiac."

Dismay shone in her eyes.

"I am sorry," he added gently. "I may be a rogue and a bastard...but I will not ruin you."

"I was right, earlier. You do not want me." She sounded shaken, lost. She tried to squirm away, but he pushed up to sitting, locked his knees on either side of her thighs, and pinned her down.

"I have wanted you," he said against her mouth, "from the day you challenged me with the fire iron."

"But you said—"

"I know what I said." He grinned. "I will not couple with you, but I can still give you pleasure." He caressed her cheek. "There are ways, if you will let me."

"You will take away this unbearable craving?" she whispered.

He nodded.

"Will it...hurt? I have heard..."

"'Twill not hurt at all. I will make you cry out with pleasure."

"Then...aye."

His manhood throbbed, anticipation blazing within him like a freshly stoked fire. He kissed her lips and throat, coaxed her anew with his mouth and tongue until she writhed at his lightest touch. Then, moving down her body, he kissed a path between her breasts, down the smooth slope of her belly, until his head settled at the juncture of her thighs.

Rising up on her elbows, she frowned at him, her hair an endearing, tousled mess.

"What...?"

He dipped his head, lazily stroked his tongue over the bud of flesh cocooned in her downy fuzz. She gasped, her body flinching. He licked again and she collapsed back, her eyes closed, another gasp of wonder wrenching from her. He relished each sound. This night, she would know naught but sweet, shattering ecstasy. 'Twould be a night she'd never forget.

With his tongue and lips, he licked, suckled, and tormented. Her hands fisted into the bedding. Her head thrashed. Using her cries and gasps as his guide, he took her passion higher, higher.

He savored an intense, primal sense of satisfaction as her thrashing quickened. She panted, arched her back, and then tensed. She loosed a helpless, keening moan. He imagined himself buried inside her as she catapulted into pleasure, and a harsh breath tore from his lips.

"Tye! Oh—"

He licked again, swirled his tongue, and suckled. Dragging in a stunned breath, her hips lifted off the bed once more, her mouth open, her body convulsing on yet another peak of pleasure.

He slowed his tender assault, gentled his suckling, and drew away from her.

She lay sprawled on the bedding, breathing hard. How glorious she was in her naked, sated beauty. The desire inside him tightened to a breath away from release. He hadn't wanted a woman this much since…ever.

Her drowsy eyes opened, and she smiled up at him. Then, she frowned, and her gaze dropped to his swollen manhood, straining against his hose. "What about you?" She pushed up on her elbows again and extended her hand, readying to caress him.

"Nay." His fingers locked around her wrist. If she touched him, his fraying control would be lost.

"A-all right."

"Not tonight," he said, softening his denial with a kiss. When her eyes closed, he urged her to scoot up and rest her head on the pillows. She curled on her left side and he drew the bedding up about her shoulders. No doubt within a few moments she'd be asleep.

"Tye?" she murmured.

"Aye?"

"Thank you."

A proud smile curved his lips. "Sleep now, Kitten."

He crossed to the fire, where Patch opened his eyes a fraction but did not stir, unwilling to move from his cozy box. The blankets on the bed rustled, and Tye glanced over his shoulder to see Claire nestled deeper into the bedding, her eyes shut, her hair streaming across the pillow. *His* pillow.

She sighed, sounding thoroughly contented.

Tye turned back to the fire and smiled. *He* had brought her to that contentment. *He* had pleasured her as no other man ever had.

The relentless ache in his loins reminded him that he hadn't slaked his own desire. He fought the hunger. He could satisfy the carnal need himself with a few skilled strokes of his hand, but that notion held little appeal; mayhap 'twas his penance to suffer this eve. He pulled his fingers through his sweat-dampened hair that at some point had come loose from its leather binding and laughed softly. The drink and the potion had definitely addled his mind.

The potion.

Fury flared anew, warring with Tye's lust. That his mother would deceive him so, *use* him so, without concern for his wishes or feelings, left an ashy taste in his mouth.

He moved to the trestle table and poured more wine. Then, realizing 'twas likely tainted, he tossed what was in his mug as well as the jug into the fire. The flames hissed and smoked as he set the vessels aside and sank into the chair by the hearth.

"Damnation," he muttered. At least the anger was defeating his lust. His flesh was no longer rock hard, but the desire would never vanish completely. He wanted Claire. He wanted her more than anything.

Except finally slaying his sire.

He rubbed the heel of his hand against his brow. A dull pain had settled in his forehead, likely caused by the aphrodisiac. 'Twould be best to sleep it off, but no way in hellfire was he going to lie next to Claire now, not until his blood had cooled.

His focus shifted to the letters and the journal he'd taken from Claire's chamber. He'd read some of the letters, but not all. With a brisk tug, he took one from the stack of correspondence she'd received from her young lover. Tye's grip instinctively tightened on the crisp, cured skin, for the lad had used fine-quality parchment; eager Henry had obviously intended to impress Claire with this proof of his wealth.

Bitter jealousy coiled through Tye. From all he'd seen and heard of Henry, the lad had been a good match for Claire; if he hadn't died, he'd have given her a life of luxury and respectability—all the things Tye couldn't offer her. Not now, at least. Not until his right to rule Wode had been validated by the King.

How very much Tye wanted Claire to be *his*, not just tonight, but forever.

His finger brushed the broken wax seal as he flipped the parchment page open and squinted at the lines of black ink. He silently sounded out each word, as Georgette had so patiently taught him.

My dearest Claire...

Claire woke with a start. She rubbed sleep from her eyes while assessing her shadowy surroundings. Her mind, groggy and sluggish from a brutal headache, recognized that the mattress beneath her was plumper than the one in her chamber, the sheets were softer, and the play of firelight across the stone wall ahead of her was different.

As she inhaled the scent of air-dried linens mingled with a faint, earthy male essence, recollections rushed into her mind: the potion; Tye coming to her chamber; Tye lifting her into his arms and carrying her to his bed.

She was still in his bed. Naked. Moreover, she still felt wonderfully languid from the incredible sensations he'd drawn from her willing flesh.

What he'd done to her... It had been most sinful, and even more so since she'd enjoyed it.

Claire rolled over onto her back and flung an arm over her face, fighting both dread and wicked excitement. Rolling over caused intense pain to focus at her brow. Groaning, she rubbed her forehead.

Across the chamber, a chair creaked.

"Kitten?" Tye neared the bedside, his bold presence softened by the golden glow of firelight. He still wore his hose, although he'd drawn on a black woolen robe. The front edges of the robe gaped where it tied at his waist, revealing the scars on the well-defined curve of his chest, the ripple of taut muscles across his stomach.

Tousled and partly naked, he was the most striking man she'd ever seen. Yet, she couldn't quell a stirring of unease.

"How do you feel?" he asked.

Her head hurt so much, she could barely think. "Terrible," she whispered.

He sighed, and the bed dipped as he sat beside her. "Let me guess. Your head aches as if a blacksmith is making horseshoes out of your skull, and your stomach is ready to throw up yesterday's fare."

A grudging smile tugged at her mouth. "How do you know?"

"'Tis the aftereffects of the potion. I feel that way myself."

The genuine concern in his eyes made her throat tighten. She shouldn't be lying in his bed, speaking to him so freely, or care how he felt or what he thought. He was the enemy. Part of her, though, refused to believe that any longer.

Not after what they'd shared.

He rose, crossed the chamber, and returned with a goblet. He offered it to her. "'Tis fresh wine. I promise it does not contain any aphrodisiac."

She pushed herself up to sitting. He sat beside her again, his attention dropping to her hand clutching the blankets to her bosom.

She took the vessel and drank.

"How do you feel otherwise?" he asked softly.

His rumbled words brushed over her, stirring a fresh wave of sinful longing. "All right," she said.

"Just all right?" He shook his head, clearly disappointed. He was *pretending* to be disappointed, at least.

She couldn't hold back a smile. "In truth, more than all right. What we did...*you* did..."

When she said no more, his brows rose, a clear request for her to continue.

She stared down into the wine. Their earlier intimacy was

a most awkward and delicate subject, and yet she found herself distinctly curious. "Is the experience always that pleasurable?"

He grinned. "In most instances, aye."

"I see. So there is some truth to what I have overheard when the maidservants think I am not listening."

Tye chuckled. "What, pray tell, have you overheard?"

"Well, that if a man has skill at...um...his role in the... undertaking, then the act can be quite wonderful. However, if a man is drunk or is not...um...well-endowed..." She scowled. Judging from Tye's crude snort, he was trying very hard to choke down laughter. "Now you are laughing at me."

He threw up a hand. "Nay, Kitten—"

"You *are* laughing at me." She glared, doing her best to appear outraged. "I cannot help that I have little experience in such matters. In fact—"

"In fact," he cut in, grinning, "I find it quite charming."

"You do?"

"Mmm." He leaned in toward her. She didn't dare move, for with the mattress shifting, she feared she'd spill wine all over the bed.

The scent of him, purely male, filled her senses, sent heat licking down to her toes as he nuzzled her cheek and pressed a kiss close to her ear. Her eyes fluttered shut. "Tye—"

"Fear not," he murmured against her skin, while he kissed along her cheekbone. "I know you are unwell. I will not do any more than kiss you."

She fought disappointment.

How very shameful, surely.

He eased away from her and took the goblet. After setting the vessel on the bedside table, he took her free hand in his, linking his callused fingers through hers in a gentle grasp. "Did the wine help any with the headache?"

"A little." Fatigue now taunted her, making her eyelids heavy. She longed to curl up beneath the blankets again. Should she return to her own chamber? 'Twould be best, but she found herself reluctant to leave him.

She forced out the words: "I should go back to my own room."

"Why?"

"'Tis not…proper that I am here."

Annoyance glinted in his eyes. "Ah. Now that the passion induced by the potion has waned, you realize I am not worthy of pleasuring you."

"'Tis not what I meant."

"Then what did you mean?"

Claire tried to make sense of the feelings knotting up inside her. "I am not entirely certain myself. I do not regret what happened between us. Yet, if the servants should find me here…"

"You worry what the loose-tongued folk will say."

"I cannot help it," she said miserably. "As a lady, I have been taught to protect my reputation. 'Tis not possible to simply ignore what I have been taught since I was a child. 'Tis part of who I am."

Tye's mouth flattened. "I am lord here," he said between clenched teeth. "I do not care what others think or say. You will stay."

Claire held his glittering stare, refusing to yield to his fury. "You took great pains not to ruin me," she said quietly. "Therein is proof that indeed, you *do* care. There is some honor in your soul, Tye."

"I am no gallant hero. Do not delude yourself, Kitten. I will not deny you were in my bed, especially not when my mother schemed to bring it about."

Claire swallowed hard, anguish settling in her breast. "You mean to gloat to your mother, then, that she was successful? That her scheme got me to lie with you?"

He looked down at their joined hands, his tangled, silky hair partially hiding his features from her. "I do not intend to gloat, but I will not deny we lay together, Kitten. 'Tis not entirely a matter of male pride."

"Nay?" She arched her brows.

"Nay. 'Tis also a matter of protecting you. If my mother learns that her plan didn't work—that I didn't take your maidenhood—she will concoct another deception to make it happen. Or, she will…ensure that you are no longer a temptation for me."

No longer a temptation. So much went unsaid in those few words.

Tye pressed her hand. "Do not worry. I will deal with my mother." After a pause, he added, "I will also see you returned to your chamber before the servants begin their daily duties."

Relief washed through her. "I would like that. Thank you."

He nodded. Raising his head, he met her eyes, his expression grim. "I apologize for the potion. That my mother would dare to do such a thing…" He scowled. "I will be sure she understands my displeasure."

"At least neither of us was hurt."

His expression turned puzzled. "Are you not angry?"

"Indeed I am. I am very angry at your mother. However, we cannot change what has happened this night. We can only move onward."

"Bravely spoken, Kitten."

"In truth, what other choice do we have?"

He swept his thumb over her knuckles in a tender caress. "At least, despite my mother's meddling, you are still a virgin. You do not have to worry that you conceived a babe this night, or that you are ruined for the nobleman who wishes to make you his wife. If there is ever any question about your innocence, you can go to a physician to be examined. He will confirm you are untouched."

Tye spoke so solemnly, as though while she'd slept, he'd been mulling what had transpired between them; 'twas even more proof that he did care about her. Claire's heart warmed, even as her head pounded in its relentless torment.

"Come, now," he said, freeing his fingers from hers. "You should get some rest." He urged her to lie back against the pillow and tucked the bedding up around her shoulders.

"Are you not going to sleep?" she asked, staring up at him.

He winked. "Turn onto your side."

"Why?"

"You will see."

Sighing, she obeyed.

He walked around to the other side of the bed and

stretched out behind her, lying atop the coverlet. Curving his arm around her waist, he drew her snugly against him, and kissed the back of her neck bared by the spill of her hair. How she loved the feel of his lips on her skin.

"Mmm," she murmured. "I like sleeping this way."

He kissed her hair. "So do I."

A sense of contentment filled her. Smiling against the pillow, Claire closed her eyes.

How curious, that here in Tye's arms, she felt as though she was right where she was meant to be.

Long moments later, Tye eased himself from Claire's embrace. Sleep had eluded him. Her scent, her warmth curled against him, and her breath upon his arm had conspired to make him acutely aware of every single place their bodies touched. He couldn't settle down to rest when his loins throbbed.

She stirred as he drew away, and then her breathing steadied again in the rhythm of slumber. Standing beside the bed, he gazed down at her, beautiful even while she slept, the wonder of her being in his bed still warming his soul. Now that he'd lain beside her, his bed would feel empty without her.

How he wanted her to be *his*, not just now, but forever. Once he'd killed his father, and King John acknowledged his right to rule Wode, would she see him as worthy suitor, even a lord she wanted to wed? Tye would, after all, be her social equal. Or, would she loathe him for having murdered de Lanceau, whom she considered a man of great honor? Once de Lanceau was dead, Tye might never see her again; she could refuse any contact with him, abandon him as his sire and others had done.

Tye's heart clenched, for he couldn't bear to think of his life without Claire. He'd never imagined taking a wife; until now, he hadn't lived in one place long enough to establish a home. Moreover, he'd never considered himself worthy of being any woman's husband, especially a titled lady's. Yet, if he could spend the rest of his life with Claire, he would do anything—*anything*—to make it possible. He'd cherish her, enjoy to the fullest each day spent with her, learn all there was to know about her. He'd be as good a husband to her as Henry would have been; better, even.

There was only one thing in which he wouldn't yield: his goal to kill his sire. The slaying, though, was exactly what Claire opposed. Regrettably, that likely meant Tye's wish to be with Claire forever was *im*possible.

Restless from his thoughts, he crossed to the hearth, stretching his arms over his head and then rolling tension from his shoulders while he walked. Tye sat and reached for another letter, the last one in the stack from Henry. A good dose of jealous fury should help to sap his lingering lust.

Beloved Claire, I write to you this day with tremendous excitement.

Tye rolled his eyes and read on.

I have been sent to Branton Keep. 'Tis a great honor indeed that I have been assigned to serve his lordship Geoffrey de Lanceau.

Misgiving scratched at the back of Tye's mind, and not just because the lad had worked for de Lanceau. Something in the words, the situation…was vitally important. Something he didn't yet comprehend.

Branton Keep…

His conscience buzzing a warning, Tye slowly read on. The memory of a defiant young man, a fool trying to be a damned hero, rose from the shadows of Tye's thoughts.

Nay. Surely not—

I have been ordered to guard the prisoners in the dungeon.

Chapter Twenty-Two

C laire woke to a rustling sound. Lying on her side, the pillow soft against her cheek, she kept her eyes closed and savored the lazy warmth coursing through her. 'Twas a wickedly delicious sensation.

Almost as wickedly delicious as what Tye had done to her last night.

Hot-cold tingles danced over her skin. Sleeping together had been wonderful, too.

She missed him lying next to her. She vaguely recalled him easing away from her during the night, the jostling of the mattress as he'd left the bed, but she'd quickly fallen asleep again.

Another rustle came from across the chamber. The noise sounded like unfolding parchment.

"Tye?" she murmured, her voice throaty from sleep, while she pushed tumbled hair from her face.

"Tye," Veronique mocked. "Bleating for him to fornicate with you again, are you?"

Oh, God. A nasty chill raced through Claire. She sat up, hugging the sheets to her naked body.

A smile curving her painted red lips, the older woman met Claire's gaze. With her red hair pinned into a braided coil around her head, her embroidered crimson wool gown skimming her figure, Veronique looked polished and composed, as if she considered herself the lady of the keep. Her assessing stare traveled slowly, thoroughly, over Claire's mussed hair and bare shoulders.

Claire fought the urge to cringe, instead drawing strength from her anger. Not only was Veronique holding Henry's letters, but she'd conspired for Claire to end up in Tye's bed. Veronique had drugged them both, a ruthless act Claire would not forgive.

Her fingers tightening on the bedding, Claire asked, "Where is Tye?"

"He is off attending to his duties," Veronique said. "There are matters far more important than *you*."

Claire tried to ignore the bite in the older woman's words, but they were sharply spoken and stung like bits of chipped stone.

Glaring at Veronique, Claire said, "You have no right to read those letters in your hand."

"Of course I do."

"Nay, you do not. I did not give you permission—"

"I did not ask for it," the older woman leered. "Why should I, when I have no need of it?"

Shock raced through Claire. "Tye gave you permission, then?"

Veronique's eyes glinted. "Not exactly. However, he is this castle's lord, and he is also my son. Since I have helped him win what he is due, he will understand why I wish to know the contents of these letters, especially if there is information of use to us."

Information of use, as if Claire's private correspondence was as inconsequential as a map or a list of goods to buy in the village market. Claire stifled a disgusted cry. Did Veronique have no compassion at all? No respect for another's personal possessions?

"I will tell Tye that you read my letters," Claire said.

"I care not." Veronique tossed the parchments onto the table. "Tell him I have read them all. I have, you know. I came by earlier, to return Tye's sharpened knives, only to find you fast asleep."

Oh, mercy. Nothing good would come of Veronique discovering Claire in Tye's bed, even if the wretched woman had planned for it to happen.

"What a surprise that was, to find you curled up under the bedding, so exhausted, you did not even stir when I walked in. I left the knives and took the letters back to my own chamber to read. Of course, it did not take much to guess what had happened between you and Tye last night."

"You put potion into the wine," Claire muttered, "as well as my infusion."

Veronique's eyes widened with mock innocence. "Did I?"

"Aye. Tye recognized the potion's scent."

"Clever boy." The older woman grinned, an unpleasant twist of her mouth. "I should have known he would figure out what I had done."

"You drugged him too," Claire continued, her words taut with fury. "You plotted for us to lie together, so in truth, 'twas no surprise to you at all to find me here."

Veronique's hand fluttered in a dismissive wave. "Well—"

"Tye was not pleased, either, that you had tricked him. 'Twas a foul deception you played upon us both."

For a fleeting moment, Veronique seemed astonished by Claire's boldness. Then, her expression darkened with menace. "Beware, Lady Sevalliere. I am not the only one who has resorted to deception."

"I know not what you mean."

"Is that so?" Veronique picked up a leather-bound tome: the journal Claire had kept hidden in her chamber.

"Recognize it?" Veronique drawled, opening the book with its spine pressed against her torso so the pages of writing in black ink were visible to Claire.

Oh, God.

"I found pages and pages about the siege, including detailed descriptions of the mercenaries who took part and the daily developments. There are also fascinating insights from you. What you wrote about Tye is, shall we say, highly entertaining and pathetically romantic?"

Claire's cheeks burned. She could simply perish from embarrassment. Humiliating her, though, was just what Veronique intended.

"What did you say about Tye?" Veronique tapped her chin with a crooked finger. "I remember now. You said he was misguided, manipulated by me into committing terrible deeds."

Fine hairs prickled on Claire's nape, for she had indeed written such words. Judging by the older woman's punishing stare, she wanted to crush Claire emotionally, to beat her down until she collapsed into tears. That could only happen, though, if Claire allowed it. She'd rather *die* than yield in any way to this woman.

Gathering her courage around her like a shield, Claire refused to let her stare waver. "'Tis true. I did write such words."

"*Tsk, tsk.* What dangerous sentiments for a hostage whose life may be at risk." Veronique smiled in a manner that made Claire feel ill with foreboding.

"'Tis what I believe," Claire said, less defiantly than she'd hoped. "Neither you nor Tye nor anyone else told me that I was forbidden to write down my thoughts on what was happening at this keep."

With an irritated sniff, Veronique shut the journal. Crossing her arms, she held it against her bosom. "It does not matter whether you had permission to write such words or not. Tye will have this journal, and he will decide what to do with it." She giggled. "And, what to do with *you.*"

Claire's knuckles whitened as her hold tightened on the bedding. She'd never intended for Tye to read her private writings about him. She'd been critical in some instances, sympathetic in others. Mayhap she could get hold of the journal and hide it again before he had a chance to read it?

Even as her desperate mind clung to that thought, one of the solar doors opened. Tye walked in. He was fully dressed in a heavy gray tunic draping to his knees and black hose, with his sword belted at his waist. Stubble darkened his jaw.

A flush warmed her as she recalled him half naked and gilded by fire glow, his bronzed skin gleaming while he dipped his head between her thighs. A dull ache spread through her, an ache she now recognized as sensual hunger.

Veronique clapped her hands together. "We were just talking about you, Tye."

His gaze settled on Claire, and her pulse fluttered wildly. She smiled—she couldn't help it after their night spent together— but the smile froze before it had fully formed on her lips.

Something was wrong.

Tye seemed uneasy, his feelings tightly guarded—far from the lighthearted lover she'd known last night.

Why? What had happened while she slept? Fear snuffed

the yearning inside her and left her chilled.

Tye broke their gaze, his hands clenching at his sides. Restless fury flickered over his features as he shut the door and halted near Veronique. "Mother."

"Tye." She patted his cheek.

He stepped sideways, out of her reach. "What are you doing here? The servants are not even awake yet."

"I returned your sharpened knives, as I promised."

Hands on his hips, he scowled.

"Earlier," Veronique went on, "I also borrowed Claire's letters. I just returned them. What fascinating reading they were."

"God's blood! I told you not to touch them. Why—?"

"*Why?*" Veronique laughed, a harsh sound. "We have yet to win our battle against your sire. The letters might have contained details that would help us defeat him."

Claire stifled an indignant cry. Surely Tye wouldn't accept that justification for what his mother had done.

"Do not look so hostile, Tye." Veronique held out Claire's journal. "Did you know she has been keeping a written account of the takeover and all involved? There are fascinating sections about you."

Tye's gaze slid to Claire. She sucked in a breath at the weight of his anguished stare; the vulnerability vanished on a blink, was replaced by fury. "Is this true?"

There was no sense denying it. His mother held the proof in her hands. Claire nodded.

Tye took the journal from his parent.

"You did not know about this journal, then?" Veronique asked gleefully.

"Not until now," Tye said.

Veronique clucked her tongue as if Claire had committed the gravest of crimes. "How deceitful, Claire, to keep secrets from the lord of the castle."

Claire choked down a shriek of frustration. "As I told you—"

"Tye has secrets of his own, though," Veronique went on, drowning out Claire's words. "*Dark* secrets. Aye?"

He looked haunted, unsettled right down to his very soul.

225

"Mother."

"The last letter from Claire's beloved Henry is especially enlightening."

Tye's visage had turned so fearsome, Claire shuddered. "*Enough!*" he roared.

Veronique smiled at Claire. "Did you know that Tye killed Henry?"

Chapter Twenty-Three

Y *ou* killed Henry?" Claire's words emerged on the barest breath of sound. She gaped at Tye, while horror washed through her in a flood of numbing shock. Her heart became a leaden weight struggling to beat in her breast.

Tye's face was a mask of outrage. His blazing gaze shifted to his mother before returning to her. "I did," he finally said. He spoke without the faintest remorse.

The coldness inside Claire settled into her bones. Tears stung her eyes. Unable to control her trembling, she turned her head to stare at the opposite wall and pressed a hand to her lips. *Oh, God. Oh, merciful God.* She had never expected to hear such a terrible admission from Tye. Yet, days ago, he'd told her he had escaped captivity in Branton Keep, where Henry had been working for de Lanceau.

She should have pressed Tye for more information about his escape, gleaned as much detail as possible. Instead, she'd let the bastard seduce her.

Through her weakness, she'd dishonored Henry.

The fault was not entirely hers, though. By withholding the truth until now, Tye had dishonored her, each and every time he'd wooed her, and most of all last night.

He had betrayed her in the worst possible way.

Never would she forgive him for that. *Never.*

She stared down at the coverlet on the bed. "How...?" The rest of her words failed her. Guilt and loathing surged, for she'd kissed the villain who had murdered Henry. She'd lain in the same bed as Tye and done so *willingly.* She'd let him caress her, pleasure her...

Vomit scalded the back of her mouth. She forced it down.

"Such a pitiful expression." Veronique cackled. "She looks as though you just stabbed her in the heart."

"Be quiet," Tye growled.

Claire drew in a shuddered breath, barely holding back her sobs. She refused to cry in front of Veronique or Tye. Never would she allow herself to appear so defeated. Yet, the numbness inside her was melting into an agonizing pain.

Forcing herself to meet Tye's stare, she asked, "Why did you not tell me before?" She sounded as if she'd lost everything she'd loved; in many ways, she had.

A glimmer of regret touched his eyes, but was gone in an instant. "I did not know he was the man I had killed. Not until I read your last letter from him a short while ago."

Was that the truth, or had Tye hoped Claire would never find out what he'd done?

Fury boiled inside her. "I hate you, Tye. I *hate* you for all that you have done!"

"*Tsk, tsk*," Veronique clucked. She seemed delighted by the unfolding drama.

"Leave her be," Tye snapped at his mother. His attention again settled on Claire, and she averted her gaze, tears streaming down her face. "I never intended for you to find out in this way," he said.

A hollow laugh broke from Claire. "Did you intend to tell me at all?"

He didn't reply. 'Twas answer enough.

Holding the bedding against her bosom, she leaned over and grabbed for her clothes, still lying on the coverlet. As she struggled to straighten the garments to put them on, Tye walked to the bedside. He set a gentle hand upon her bare shoulder.

Claire recoiled. "Do not touch me!"

"I was going to tell you," he said quietly, his hand falling away. "Once I knew how."

His words held a raw pain that touched upon the wound inside her. He almost sounded kind—a new emotional challenge she couldn't bear. Her mouth crumpled on a sob.

He made a small, strangled sound. "You must believe

me."

Why did he care whether she believed him or not? She didn't want to care either, but she did. Her torment gouged deep.

"Poor Claire, reduced to tears," Veronique cooed, her tone undeniably gloating. "She has endured such a lot tonight."

Claire's head reeled on a swift surge of anger and despair. Soothing oblivion hovered at the edges of her mind.

As Tye growled a reply to Veronique, a buzzing noise rang in Claire's ears. It grew louder and louder, like an insect readying to bite. The blackness beckoned.

She closed her eyes, and the darkness rushed in and took her.

His jaw taut, Tye stared at Claire collapsed on her side on the bed, her eyes shut, her hair spilling around her. Her body curled inward, as though she instinctively tried to protect her broken heart from further attack. A crushing ache spread through his chest for he'd never wanted to hurt her in such a way. He leaned over her, drew up the bedding that had fallen away, and covered her exposed breasts.

His mother walked up behind him. "She fainted?"

"Aye, thanks to you," he ground out. Knowing his mother, she'd wanted to see Claire devastated by grief; his mother enjoyed such sport.

"You blame me?" Veronique snorted. "I did not kill Henry."

"You did not have to tell her in such a careless manner, either." Tye faced his parent, bitter words crowding up within him, his fury a wild, dangerous beast clawing up inside him to get free. She'd hurt Claire, his captivating, lovely, beautiful Kitten.

Such fierce protectiveness roiled inside him. He struggled with the intensity of his feelings, while part of him admitted Claire would soon have found out about Henry anyway. He *had* intended to tell her. After reading the letter, and grappling with his conscience, he'd decided he must tell her the truth. Even though 'twould be difficult, 'twas the right thing to do. A matter, of all ironies, of honor.

"Why are you so angry?" his mother asked.

"Why not?" he snarled. "You disobeyed my orders regarding the letters. You—"

"I was trying to help you," she cut in. "Before you berate me for the potion in your drink, *that* was meant to help you as well."

He suppressed a stunned laugh. "Help me?"

"Once you had taken her, she would no longer be such a temptation. Your lust slaked, you would be able to focus again on the challenge ahead: the reason why you conquered this fortress in the first place." Her eyes widened, softened with a plea. "Do not be upset. I *want* you to succeed. I am proud of the man, the leader, you have become. Surely you understand that I must do all that I can to ensure your victory? 'Tis a victory you *deserve*."

Tye shook his head. *Damn her.* His mother didn't offer praise very often. When she did, it meant a great deal to him, as it did now.

Rage still seethed inside him, though, warring with the pleasure of his mother's words. He had a right to be furious. Claire wasn't a strumpet for him to use and cast aside. Neither was he a dim-witted boy who needed a parent to assert firm control over his decisions and actions. "I am well aware of what I aim to achieve, Mother."

"Then all is settled."

"Nay, 'tis not. I appreciate your confidence in me. However, what you did to Claire was unjust."

"*Unjust?* Why, I—"

"Do not drug me again. Do not tamper with Claire's wine or infusions, either."

A disappointed gasp broke from his parent. "You...you feel sorry for her?"

He looked back at Claire's motionless form, and a sickening anguish filled his gut. He did feel sorry for her, and so much more. Indeed, more than he'd ever felt for any woman in his entire miserable life.

"Tye, tell me the truth. Do you care for her?" His mother sounded merely curious, but he discerned a darker intent behind the question.

He wouldn't admit to caring. He'd never reveal that he wanted Claire to be his wife. He couldn't, for her life could be in terrible and immediate danger. Forcing an indolent shrug, he said, "I made last night enjoyable for her, if 'tis what you are asking."

Glee lit his mother's features.

"What you planned, with the potion in the drink, came to pass," he added, ensuring his parent learned what she wanted to know. "Claire will no longer be a distraction."

"Good." His mother chuckled. "Was fornicating with her—?"

"Do not ask me anymore about last eve." He retrieved Claire's chemise, as silken soft as her fair skin, and shook out the wrinkles. "Now, I must ask you to leave. There is much to do this day if I am soon to defeat my sire."

"Claire."

Mary's voice filtered into Claire's slumbering thoughts. Then, she felt a nudge on her shoulder.

"Come on. Wake up."

Claire blinked her eyes open. Recollections of all that had happened in the solar rushed into her mind, making her eyes burn anew. She groaned against the pillowcase.

"At last you are awake." Mary flopped down on the edge of the bed. "I shall start calling you the Queen of Day Long Slumber."

Swallowing hard, her throat parched, Claire lifted her head. She was in her own chamber, under the blankets in her own bed, wearing the chemise she'd worn last night. Her gown was lying in a heap on the trestle table.

Tye must have left it there after carrying her back to her chamber before the servants had started their morning chores, as he'd promised. No doubt he'd also dressed her in her chemise. She knew instinctively Tye had done so, not Veronique; the older woman wouldn't have bothered. A shiver rippled through Claire, for he'd put the garment on her naked body after she'd fainted, as if she were a living doll. How awful, simply unforgivable, that she'd swooned; yet, she hadn't been able to help it.

Her stinging gaze returned to Mary. Her dear friend looked concerned. "Are you unwell? You have not said one word, and you look awful."

"I…" Words vanished. Claire fought the pressure of a sob welling within her. How did she begin to tell Mary what had happened last night?

"Tye came to fetch me from the great hall, you know," Mary said, folding her hands in her lap. "I spent last night in Lady Brackendale's chamber, and then was escorted down to the hall to break my fast. 'Twas quite unexpected, not to be immediately returned to my chamber, but I was glad of a chance to stretch my legs and enjoy some of the day in the hall. 'Tis where Tye found me. He said you were still slumbering, although 'twas late morning. He asked me to look in on you. He seemed, I dare say, worried."

"Worried," Claire echoed with a small laugh. She dropped her head back onto the pillow and, despite her best efforts to hold them back, tears brimmed in her eyes.

Mary gently ran her hand down Claire's loose hair. "Claire? Please. What is wrong?"

Sniffling, Claire pushed up to sitting. She wiped tears from her face with shaking fingers.

"Whatever is weighing on your heart," Mary said solemnly, "I can tell 'tis a matter of great consequence. You must tell me. I will perish from not knowing."

"I will tell you," Claire said, sniffling again. "I have to. 'Tis too much for me to bear alone."

"Did something happen last night?"

"A-aye."

Impatience glimmered in Mary's eyes, but she sat quietly, waiting for Claire to continue.

"Tye…" Claire forced down an anguished cry. "He killed Henry."

"Oh, God!" Mary whispered. "How?"

"In the escape from…Branton Keep." Claire's words trailed off on a despairing moan, and then Mary's arms were around her, holding her tight, as she wept.

While Claire cried on Mary's shoulder, she told Mary all that had happened, right up until the moment she'd fainted. When there was no more to tell, Claire simply cried, wrenched by sobs that drained every last drop of her sorrow and left her shuddering and exhausted. Through it all, Mary murmured comforting words and never once let her go.

At last, Mary eased away from Claire and fetched a handkerchief. "You had quite an adventure last night," she said, handing over the folded square of linen. "Did you speak true that Tye did not hurt you?"

"I did. He was gentle with me and, in truth, most gallant. 'Tis what makes all of what I told you so much worse." Claire dried her eyes. She could only imagine what a mess she looked, her face red and blotchy, her tresses an unruly tangle. As her breathing steadied, misery set in. She was no longer an unspoiled maiden. She hadn't lost her virginity, but that seemed insignificant next to the realization that she'd found pleasure in the bed of the man who'd murdered her betrothed.

Fresh tears threatened. Mary might be so shocked by what she'd heard, she wouldn't want to be best friends any more.

Mary's gown rustled as she turned away from the bed.

"Please," Claire whispered. "Do not go."

With an impatient little huff, Mary said, "Of course I will not go! What kind of best friend do you think I am?"

Hope warmed Claire. "I am glad. I could not bear…to lose your friendship."

"Nor I yours," Mary said with a tender smile. "I am pacing because, well, I think better on my feet. We must follow the examples of our favorite *chanson* heroines. We must figure out what to do next."

Claire sighed. "We still have not managed to get to the storage cellar and unlock the door, as Lady Brackendale suggested."

"We must make that our priority," Mary said.

Claire nodded and dried the last of her tears. "De Lanceau must have learned of the siege at Wode by now. Indeed, the sooner we get that door unlocked, the better."

Chapter Twenty-Four

A steady hum of noise filled Wode's great hall. Mercenaries at tables near the entrance to the forebuilding shoved food into their mouths as they talked, chortled, and belched their way through the vegetable pottage, cheese, and bread served for the evening meal. Sitting at a quiet table with Mary on the other side of the hall, Claire took small mouthfuls of the fare and kept a discreet watch on all who entered and left.

Lady Brackendale hadn't joined them for the meal; she'd likely not been allowed. Veronique and Tye also hadn't appeared. Claire had expected at least him to dine at the lord's table, if only to show his authority, but either his duties had kept him from partaking or he'd chosen to stay away.

Whatever the reason, Claire was glad. She didn't want to have to face him. Not right now. Not until she had a firm grip once again on her emotions.

Especially when she was preparing to slip down to the wine cellar.

Seated at the table opposite them, along with a group of servants, Witt picked at a chunk of bread. The lad had been more than willing to help with their plan, quickly explained to him while the mercenaries greeted one another and grabbed places at the benches alongside the tables.

Witt lifted his head, nodded slightly to her, and returned to his meal.

Claire's gaze moved on, as if the silent communication hadn't been significant, but she couldn't suppress a flare of apprehension. When the moment came to act, she and Witt would both be ready. So, hopefully, would Mary.

Mary set her spoon down beside her bowl of pottage. "I simply cannot eat another bite. My stomach is churning."

"So is mine," Claire admitted. They'd reviewed the plan several times before the mercenaries had escorted them down to the hall to eat. However, so much depended on Mary fainting and doing it brilliantly. What if, despite her best intentions, she couldn't succumb at the right moment? 'Twould be catastrophic.

Claire sipped her wine. In hushed tones, she said, "At least we do not have to worry about Tye keeping watch on us."

Mary gnawed at her lip. "I promise to do what you need me to do. Just tell me when."

Claire studied the tables of mercenaries. Most of the thugs had finished eating. Many were red-faced from plenty of ale. Soon they would be heading back to their posts.

Claire drew in a shaky breath. "All right. Let us begin." She downed one last mouthful of wine for good luck and then stood.

A shrill sound, akin to an anxious squeak, burst from Mary. She rose from the table, her lips moving on a fervent prayer.

Witt set aside his bread. After a quick word to the servants seated either side of him, he rose, tugging down the grubby sleeves of his tunic. He strolled to the end of the table.

"Good luck," Claire said softly to Mary.

"You too." Her head held high, Mary walked toward the mercenaries.

As Claire made her way to Witt, several maidservants caught her gaze and discreetly nodded. Excitement rippled through Claire, for the clever boy had clearly managed to recruit more helpers for their distraction.

Mary reached the mercenaries. The men eyed her with suspicion and amusement.

"You." Mary pointed to the thug who had searched under her garments for weapons the day the castle was besieged. "I want a word with you."

His arms resting on the table, the man squinted at her, his grin revealing stained teeth. "What do you want with me, milady?"

Curious servants crowded in closer to watch the unfolding drama.

Just as Claire had hoped.

She resisted the urge to hurry. *Slow, steady steps.* Only a little farther and she'd reach Witt's side.

"*You* did me a grave disservice," Mary said, clearly indignant.

"Did I?" The lout's grin broadened. His fellow mercenaries, enjoying the spectacle, laughed and elbowed one another.

Claire reached Witt, and he fell in beside her. Carefully, they moved back toward the small room off the great hall.

"You had your filthy hand up my gown," Mary said.

Shocked cries rippled through the hall.

"A violation!" one woman cried.

"How awful," another shrilled.

After grabbing a burning torch from the nearest wall bracket, Claire hurried into the shadowed side chamber, Witt right behind her. He followed her to the arched door at the room's far end.

Her hand on the iron door handle, she glanced back over her shoulder. "We must go quietly," she whispered. "There may be guards below."

"Aye, milady," Witt whispered back. He withdrew an object tucked into the waistband of his hose: a slingshot made from flax. He patted the cloth bag stowed there as well.

She smiled. "Well done."

"I am a good shot," he said, grinning. "You will see."

Claire opened the door. Faint light flickered farther down the curving stairwell, indicating torches had been lit; even more reason to be cautious.

She descended the uneven stone stairs, her right hand pressed to the wall, her left hand gripping the torch. Her gown rustled with each of her steps, and her shoes rasped softly on the stone, but she couldn't help those sounds. Witt was but one step behind, his movements almost silent, his slingshot at the ready.

The steps ended at a wide corridor. To the left was the way to the armory. To the right, the storage rooms. Peering around the wall of the stairwell, she searched for guards.

A tall, armed thug stood outside the armory. However,

instead of watching the corridor, he was picking at a scabbed-over cut on his left cheek. An earthenware pot, similar to the ones the local healers used for ointment, rested on a waist-high stack of crates beside him.

She sensed Witt peering around her.

Before she could say a word, he whispered, "I can take care of him."

The boy stepped out of stairwell, ran for the opposite wall, and crouched; the stack of crates blocked him from the thug's view. With silent, cautious strides, Witt moved toward the armory.

The guard, still oblivious, continued to pick at his wound.

Claire didn't want to watch what was going to happen, but she also couldn't look away. She would never forgive herself if Witt came to harm.

Halfway to the mercenary, Witt halted and reached into the cloth bag. He must have made a slight sound, for the thug frowned, set his hand on his sword hilt, and stepped away from the crates.

Witt raced out into the passageway. Raising his right arm high, he spun the slingshot, causing a hissing noise. A small rock flew from the weapon and hit the mercenary in the forehead, and he winced and stumbled back. As he tried to draw his sword, Witt fired another rock. The man hit the wall, his head knocked against the stonework, and he collapsed, unconscious.

"Well done!" Claire breathed.

Witt returned to her. "I have plenty more rocks if we need them."

"Good. Now, let us hurry, in case he is not the only guard down here."

Together, they made their way to the wine storage chamber. Claire set the burning torch into the wall bracket inside the room. Light flickered over the large, iron-bound wooden barrels, three rows deep and two high, some coated with thick dust, that were stacked against faded tapestries on her left. On the right were tall shelves bearing smaller casks and jugs along with several reed torches and coils of rope.

"I will keep watch, milady," Witt said, "while you find the

hidden door."

"All right." With a pang of dread, Claire hoped the door wasn't behind the barrels. If they were full of ale or wine, she and Witt wouldn't be able to move them.

Pausing beside the shelves, she ran her finger down one of the jugs with a cork stopper. Her gaze slid back to the tapestries, both depicting battle scenes. One portrayed a victorious crusader holding a beast's severed head. The weaving was so long it spread onto the floor beneath the back row of barrels. She remembered Lady Brackendale saying she didn't like looking at such a gruesome sight while eating, and had thus ordered that tapestry put into storage. Why, then, was it hanging in the cellar?

Claire examined the tapestry as she walked in front of the rows of barrels to the back wall. She could see naught out of order, but a secret door was intended to stay secret except to those who knew 'twas there.

"Witt, come and help me. We must move these barrels aside."

Doubt touched the lad's gaze, but he came to help. Together, they grabbed hold of a top barrel perched at the end of the front row near the back wall. They gave it a good shove. While heavy, the barrel was definitely not full. With a dull *thud*, it toppled onto the floor and rolled away, liquid sloshing inside.

"Easier than I thought," Witt said.

Claire glanced toward the chamber entrance. The falling barrel had made a loud noise. She hurried to the corridor, listened for any approaching footfalls, but all remained quiet. Still, they must hurry.

"Now this barrel," Claire said, catching hold of the one that had been underneath the barrel they'd just moved. With strong pushes, they managed to move it to the opposite wall.

They moved four more barrels. Now the right half of the tapestry was freed. She pulled the dusty tapestry away from the wall.

Beyond was a rectangular wooden door tall enough for a crouched man to step through.

"There," she whispered.

Witt reached out and pushed at the door. It didn't budge.

"'Tis locked."

"Lady Brackendale said the key is under a flagstone." Dropping to her hands and knees, Claire felt around the stones by her feet. If the key was under a flagstone beneath one of the full barrels, 'twould be hard to get to it. However, the partially-filled barrels in front of the tapestry suggested someone in the keep knew of the door and had left it fairly easy to access if necessary. That meant the key should be in an accessible place, too.

Claire methodically pushed on each stone on the floor in front of her, searching for any that wobbled or shifted while she made her way to the back wall. On his hands and knees beside her, Witt tested the stones in front of him. Biting her lip, Claire pressed and crawled. Nothing.

Just before her hand brushed the back wall, she pushed down on a stone with a dip near one corner. With a gritty rasping sound, the stone shifted up a fraction.

"You found it!" Witt said.

"I hope so." Again, she pressed down on the corner with the indent. The stone moved up at the opposite end, but not enough for her to get her hand around to lift it.

"Try standing on it, milady."

Scrambling to her feet, Claire did as he'd suggested. The stone rose on Witt's side. Moving so that he faced the rising edge, he took hold of the flagstone and pulled up with a grimace. The heavy stone came loose.

With an elated laugh, Claire dropped down by Witt again. Together, they shifted the stone aside to reveal a shadowed cavity.

Before she gathered the courage to reach into the recess, Witt put his hand in, felt around, and pulled up a key dangling on a thin leather cord. "Shall I unlock the door, milady?"

Such eagerness lit his face. Claire smiled, for she sensed 'twas important to him that he be the one to fulfill that important task. Once de Lanceau had regained control of the keep, the lad could boast that he'd opened the door so that his lordship's men could secretly enter the fortress. One day, the lad might even be lauded in a *chanson*.

And why not? He was a courageous young man. He deserved the honor.

"Go on, then," Claire said. Before the words had left her lips, he dashed over to the door.

The key slid into the lock with a muffled grating noise. Then, as he turned the key, a *click*.

The boy pulled the door open. A gust of frigid, dank air wafted out of the opening, as if a long-forgotten spirit had reached out icy arms to haul him inside.

Looking into the darkness, he shivered. "It smells musty in there."

Peering in beside him, Claire said, "That passage has likely not been used for years."

"I should go inside and make sure 'tis clear. "If 'tis all right with you, milady?"

Witt was as brave and noble as his grandfather. "All right. Hold on a moment." Claire fetched one of the reeds from the shelves, lit it using the torch in the wall bracket, and handed it to him.

With a grateful nod, the boy took the light and stepped into the tunnel. The flame crackled, illuminating cobwebs drifting down from the low ceiling. As he moved farther into the narrow corridor, the torchlight shifted on the rough stone walls. The light grew dimmer. His footsteps became no more than muffled scrapes.

Hugging herself, Claire stayed very still, listening not only for sounds from the secret tunnel but the main corridor. The thug that Witt had rendered senseless would wake soon, or one of his comrades would find him and sound the alarm.

Hurry, Witt. Hurry.

As the silence continued, a nagging sense of regret weighed upon her. Tye would be furious if he discovered the unlocked hidden door; she was, after all, doing what she could to help his sire enter and retake Wode. Tye might even be wounded or killed in the battle. While she hated that Tye had murdered Henry, she couldn't honestly say she wanted him dead.

You have a right to loath him. He deceived you, another little voice inside her said. *Have you forgotten?*

Nay. She hadn't and never would. Gathering her resolve, she forced the regret aside.

A scrabbling noise came from inside the tunnel. The light grew stronger again. Witt clambered out, his clothes coated with dust and cobwebs, his eyes huge.

"T-there is something in there," he said, shuddering.

"Rats?"

He shuddered again. "I do not know. I did not see it, but it moved away from the range of the light."

"The tunnel is clear, though?" Claire asked, taking the torch from him.

"As far as I saw. Please, milady, do not make me go back in there."

'Twould be best if the whole tunnel were checked for blockages, but she knew they'd been lucky not to have been discovered yet. "We have done what we came to do." She pushed the door closed, extinguished the reed and set it aside, then pulled the tapestry back into place. "Now, let us move these barrels so they are not so obviously out of order."

They maneuvered the barrels to the front of the rows. Just as they finished moving the last one, shouts carried from down the corridor. Witt made a strangled sound and lunged for the dislodged flagstone. He tossed the key into the cavity and pushed the stone back into the floor.

The voices grew louder. "Find them!" Veronique snapped.

Oh, God. Oh, God!

"Milady!" the boy gasped. He frantically brushed the grime from his garments.

There was no way to run past Veronique and her men who'd be heavily armed. Rocks and a slingshot also were no match for trained mercenaries when there was no element of surprise.

Grabbing Witt's arm, Claire pulled him toward the shelves of wine and liqueurs. "Play along," she murmured.

Looking terrified, he nodded.

"Let me see," she said thoughtfully, not caring to lower her voice. She picked up one of the earthenware jugs. "This one might work. Or—"

Veronique rushed into the cellar, four grim-faced mercenaries close behind. "There they are!" the older woman screeched.

Claire fought the thundering of her pulse. Feigning surprise, she glanced at Veronique. "Is something wrong?"

The woman's eyes narrowed to glittering slits. "You know very well."

Fear lashed through Claire, but she held Veronique's accusing gaze and said calmly, "We were looking for wine to help heal Witt's grandfather's wounds."

"Nay, you were not. Tell me what you were *really* doing."

"As I said, Witt wanted wine to bathe his grandfather's injuries. We did not think 'twould cause any trouble."

Veronique's stare was as cold as her disbelieving laugh. "You are lying."

"Mayhap *you*—"

"Quiet," the older woman ordered.

"Please. No harm has been done. Let us return to the hall—"

"*Quiet!*" Veronique slapped Claire hard across the face. Claire reeled back into the shelving, and the earthenware jug slipped from her grasp. The pottery shattered on the floor, splashing red wine on her gown and across the flagstones.

"Milady," Witt cried. "Are you all right?"

Her hand pressed to her smarting cheek, Claire straightened. Never had she been hit before. Oh, how she wanted to scratch that conceited smile off Veronique's face.

"You." Veronique pointed at a mercenary. "Search this room. Find out what they were doing. The rest of you, take these prisoners to the hall. If either of them says a word, hit them. Hard."

Two mercenaries crowded in and took hold of Claire's arms. Witt shook as the third mercenary took his slingshot and bag of rocks, tossed them onto a shelf, and then grabbed him by the back of his tunic, but remained silent.

Claire and Witt were shoved out into the main corridor, where the mercenary from the armory stood, red welts on his forehead.

"The lad had a slingshot," one of the thugs said from behind Claire.

"No wonder my head hurts like hellfire," the mercenary

from the armory said. His lips pulled back from his teeth as he took a step toward Witt.

Veronique intercepted the man and placed her left hand upon his chest. "A pity he was able to best you." She smiled up at him.

Shame, tinged with fear, touched the thug's features. "'Twill not happen again. I swear it."

"You are right. 'Twill not." Veronique raised her right hand, revealing a thin dagger, and plunged it into the man's neck.

Witt screamed and cringed.

A frightened cry welled within Claire, but she forced it down. She didn't dare risk Veronique's wrath; she must do all she could to protect Witt. The mercenaries behind her shifted restlessly, as if shocked by the stabbing, but afraid to speak out.

Blood flowed down the wounded thug's tunic. A gurgling noise broke from him. His eyes rolled back into his head and, after falling to his knees, he fell facedown onto the floor.

Veronique stepped over his twitching body and strode for the stairwell. "Bring them."

Chapter Twenty-Five

"Kneel," Veronique snarled.

Her breath gusting between her teeth, Claire was shoved down to her knees in the great hall, her wine-soaked gown pooling around her on the rushes. Witt was forced to kneel beside her.

The mercenaries stood close behind, watching, waiting for either of them to resist in any way. A cruel excitement hovered around the thugs. They seemed eager for a fight, and Claire forced herself to stay very still.

The hall, buzzing with noise moments ago, had fallen deathly silent. Claire felt the weight of many stares, from mercenaries and servants to the children who cowered behind their mothers' skirts. Mary lay on her side on the floor, her eyes closed, near where she'd confronted the mercenary. The maidservants tending her had frozen where they crouched; their expressions filled with shock as they stared at Claire and Witt.

Intense worry swirled inside Claire. Was Mary all right? She desperately hoped her dear friend hadn't come to harm.

Witt, also, must be saved from maltreatment. She'd drawn him into the plan. She'd do all she could to spare him from punishment.

"Find Tye," Veronique said. "He was searching the upper level."

One of the men behind Claire hurried away.

An awful, sick feeling settled in the pit of her stomach. She didn't want to face Tye. Yet, she must. In memory of Henry, she must.

Veronique strolled into Claire's line of view. "Those of

you in this hall," she said, loudly enough for all to hear. "You will witness what happens to those who try and deceive us."

Witt whimpered softly.

Claire yearned to slide her hand into his, to offer him comfort, but she didn't dare tempt the mercenaries behind them.

The tense silence continued, each of her breaths more excruciating. Claire stared out at the fearful faces watching. The mercenaries in the hall had moved to stand at all four sides of the room, ready to act if ordered.

Oh, God. Oh, God.

Brisk footfalls echoed on the landing and then the stairs descending to the hall. *Tye.* She knew the exact moment he saw her, for awareness seared through her.

Fight, Claire. For Henry. For the gallant man you lost.

She stiffened her spine against the piercing weight of Tye's stare and refused to let her proud posture slip. Despite her trembling, she stared straight ahead and counted his steps. Nine. Ten…

The crunch of rushes warned he'd reached the hall floor.

He crossed to her. Memories of lying naked in his bed taunted her. Shame and unwanted desire tormented her, and she bit down on her lip, waiting for him to halt in front of her. Instead, he kept walking and moved in behind her and Witt. The muscles in her shoulders and lower back tightened. Her entire body was pitched to an acute state of waiting.

She strained to hear his next movement. The faint *creak* of his leather boots reached her, just as his fingers caught a length of her hair and gently pulled it back over her shoulder. She flinched. Even worse, her flesh responded, recalling every tender touch of his fingers upon her and making her traitorous heart ache.

Mortification lanced through her, for she hadn't meant to flinch. She should have been stronger than to instinctively react in that way. Yet, with the touch upon her hair, he'd shown her more than she'd ever expected: that he had a form of control over her, whether she wanted it or not.

"What were you doing in the cellar, Claire?" He spoke quietly, but with an authority that carried his voice through the hall. As he spoke, he resumed walking.

She bit down harder on her lip, welcoming the pain, drawing upon the rage that simmered in her breast. If she kept silent, she couldn't condemn herself or Witt; neither would she cause the mercenaries or Veronique to harm the boy. Hadn't Veronique ordered her to be quiet?

Tye came into her view and stopped in front of her. Her eyes were level with his groin, and she refused to stare at him or the sheathed sword secured to his belt. When Claire glanced at the onlookers, she saw Mary was sitting up, watching, her face ashen.

"I will ask you but once more, Claire. What were you doing in the cellar?"

She was on the verge of collapse, but she couldn't fold now. She also couldn't remain silent. She must save Witt. "Witt and I were getting wine, so he could bathe Sutton's wounds."

"A *lie*," Veronique said.

"'Twas my idea, to go to the storage room," Claire added, "not Witt's. I take full responsibility."

Tye's garments whispered as his left hand caught her chin. Slowly, patiently, he exerted enough pressure that she was forced to look up at him. She refused to meet his stare, but then, he cursed. Fury blazed in his eyes as his fingers lightly brushed her cheek where Veronique had struck her.

"Who hit her?" His voice was a furious growl.

"I did," Veronique said. "She refused my order to be quiet."

"How unwise of you."

"She was disrespectful. Lady or not, she has to obey those in command."

"Now she is reluctant to speak."

Veronique tsked. "Shall I convince her to talk? I can start cutting the boy—"

Gasps rippled through the onlookers in the hall.

"Leave the boy. Claire will tell me what I want to know."

She shivered, hating that he'd feel her shaking. She'd rather bite off his fingers than offer one word that would lead him to the secret door. His touch, though, was warm, coaxing, wreaking havoc on her with the press of flesh upon flesh.

The sound of approaching footfalls reached Claire. She

prayed 'twas not the mercenary returning from searching the cellar.

"What did you find?" Veronique demanded.

"A door. 'Tis hidden behind one of the tapestries."

Claire closed her eyes. *All that she and Witt had done had been for naught.*

"Ah." Veronique tittered. "This door. Where does it lead?"

"I did not investigate. I thought you would want to know right away."

"'Tis unlocked?"

"Aye," the mercenary said. "I would have locked it, but I could not find a key."

"Claire likely knows the whereabouts of that key," Veronique said. "Whether she will tell us or not…"

Tye's hand fell away from Claire's face, and she opened her eyes. How she wished she could simply vanish from the uncertain situation she faced now.

"Tell me about the door," Tye demanded. "Where does it lead, Claire? Where is the key?"

She pressed her lips together. *Stay strong.*

But poor Witt—

"Do not tell him, milady!" Witt cried. "Do not."

Her lips quivered.

"If you will not talk, Claire, you leave me no choice. Chain the boy in the dungeon," Tye ordered, turning his back to her. Over the worried mutters of the servants, he said, "Take Lady Sevalliere to my solar."

Tye stood on the windswept battlement, looking down at the dark bailey, where torches lit the shadowed forms of mercenaries keeping watch. More of his hired thugs walked the battlement opposite, their words to one another snatched by the wind and reaching Tye in unrecognizable fragments of sound. Beyond the fortress walls, he could see no more than inky black, the village beyond and the countryside smothered in the blanket of night. All seemed to be in order, but as he well knew, the darkness was good at concealing danger. Out there, somewhere, his father lurked.

The wind wailed past the stone merlons and slipped through the crenels to pull at his hair and garments. He caught his breath at the iciness, for he hadn't stopped to put on his cloak. When the mercenaries had hauled Claire to her feet, he'd walked away, unwilling to give her a glimpse of the turmoil churning inside him, a ruthless pressure fueled by disappointment and anger. He curled his hands against the boiling fury that urged him to slam his fist into the stone wall, to hit it again and again and curse until his hand bled and his mouth was bone dry.

Months ago, he might have given in to the relief in those urges. Now, he resisted. He needed his hand to wield his sword. He needed his voice to command his men. So close to conquering his sire, he needed every resource he had. That did not make the agony inside him any easier, though.

Claire. He gave in to a rough groan. He'd hated to see her so terrified, and finding the swollen mark on her face had pitched his mercurial emotions to a lethal fervor. He should loathe her. She'd betrayed him, opened a secret door his father no doubt knew about in order to help his sire broach the keep. Yet, when Tye thought of what she'd done, admiration kindled within him. She was a warrior, his fierce little Kitten. Clever, too. He'd seen Mary collapsed on the floor and guessed that the shy friend had been coaxed into providing a distraction in the hall, while Claire accomplished her task below.

The night breeze tangled hair into his eyes and he shoved it back with cold fingers, remembering, of all things, how soft Claire's hair had felt against his skin. He'd loved running his fingers through its silkiness, loved the scent of it against his face while he'd dozed with her lying in his arms. His heart constricted with a sensation he could remember feeling only a few instances before—and never this intensely.

What did it mean, this feeling? Why did every thought, every decision, seem more complicated, because of Claire? The thought of her despising him, never wanting to lie with him again, left him empty inside, for with her, he'd finally felt that he'd *belonged.*

"Tye?"

Hellfire. His every muscle tightened at his mother's voice.

"You forgot your cloak." She walked up beside him, enrobed in her heavy, fur-trimmed mantle. "Do you want to catch a chill?"

"I am not a child." If she intended to scold him about how he'd handled the situation in the hall, he'd storm away.

Her gloved hand swept over his back in a caress, stirring up a snarl of conflicting emotions within him. "I am worried about you, 'tis all," she said.

"Worried." He practically bit out the word.

In the flickering light cast by a wall torch, she appeared shocked. "You are my son. 'Tis a mother's right to worry about her child."

He studied her, seeking a hint as to her purpose. Was she silently mocking him?

"Why are you so furious?" she asked, her expression now deceptively guileless.

"You hit Claire."

"She betrayed you. She acted to undermine you—"

"—and I will deal with her in my own way. You should not have struck her."

His mother snorted, a sound of indignation.

"With that very noticeable injury to her cheek, you have proven us to be impetuous and cruel," he said, glaring at her. "I thought I had made it clear that none of the women were to be harmed, *especially* the ladies."

His mother's mouth pursed in disapproval, and then she shrugged. "The mark will heal."

"In a couple of sennights. In the meantime, she wears proof for everyone in the castle to see that we are unprincipled ruffians."

A wry smile curved his mother's lips. "Well, we are."

"We may appear to have control over this keep, but I vow there are many folk here who are still loyal to Lady Brackendale. Can you not see that Claire's wound will garner support for her ladyship and bolster resentment for me?"

"You have armed men, indeed some of the best

mercenaries in England, to quell any resistance." His mother frowned. "Why are you so fixed on Claire's injury? 'Tis a minor wound and not worth such concern."

"Is it not? I may be a bastard-born knave, but I have never hit a woman, especially a highborn lady. I would not under any circumstance."

"How bloody noble of you," his mother sneered. "You may have forgotten, but Claire is a captive. She is the enemy in this takeover that will bring us victory over your sire. Compared to our end goal, she is insignificant."

He struggled not to raise his voice. "Claire was not—"

"Claire," his mother mocked. "Always Claire!"

He thought he heard anguish in her voice. "What do you mean by that?"

Anger glinted in his parent's eyes. "Are you really so foolish as to ask me such a question?"

He glowered. "I am no fool."

"You are with her."

Tye's rage flared. "Beware, Mother."

"I will not! *She* threatens all. I tried to help you by using the potion. Yet, you still—"

"You are overly bold," he growled, baring his teeth.

"And you are a disappointment."

The words were akin to a brutal slap. Tye's eyes burned, for even worse than the fury roused by those words was the angst. What a rotten thing for her to say. He'd always done what she'd asked, worked hard to become the man she'd wanted him to be. Now he was a disappointment to her?

The urge to slam his hand into the stone wall rose again, even stronger than before.

"Tye, I did not mean to be unkind. I am just...concerned."

He bit back his reply.

His mother's features softened. "I love you. As I have said before, I want what is best for you."

"Of course you do," he said, steeling all emotion from his voice. The frozen night air seeped into his skin, and he was suddenly chilled, right to his soul.

His mother slid her arms around his waist and embraced him, resting her head against his chest. He wrapped his arms loosely around her and savored the embrace for the briefest moment, for his mother didn't hug him often.

Moreover, whatever he said or did tonight, he didn't want to put Claire in further peril.

At last, his mother drew away. "You should go inside," she said. "You need to warm up by the fire."

He nodded. "At dawn, we will review our plans one more time. I want to be sure we have covered every eventuality." Resentment gnawed, but he tamped it down. He'd said what she'd wanted him to say, what she'd expect him to say. His words wouldn't disappoint.

His mother smiled. "A wise idea. In the morning then."

As Tye walked away, the annoying ache filled Veronique's breast again, along with the sense of loss. 'Twas akin to someone slowly pressing a knife into her breast to bleed out her heart. Most unpleasant.

Why could Tye not just do as she told him, as he'd done just weeks ago? He'd been such an obedient boy once. Why did he have to be so damned obstinate when now, more than ever, they needed to work together?

If only Braden were here, but he was still away on the mission for Tye. Through sweaty, impassioned lovemaking, Braden would have helped her purge her feelings and regain a clear mind. Also, she had her answer to the question he'd posed. When he returned to Wode, she'd make him pay for each day he was away from their bed, and then she would say aye: She would indeed marry him. But for now, she must find a way to handle the situation with Tye herself.

Tonight, she must consult her rune stones again. They would guide her through this troubling time.

Veronique pressed her hand against the closest merlon and leaned into the gap beside it, letting the icy wind snarl her hair and buffet her face. She welcomed the coldness. It took her focus from the agony within her; it brought piercing clarity.

Claire. She'd become a far greater problem than anticipated.

A problem that must be eliminated before the pivotal battle began.

The potion hadn't sated Tye's lust for her. Claire still had a firm hold on him. Had she possibly even won his love?

Opening her eyes to the brutal breeze, Veronique grinned, a merciless curving of her lips. Before she met with Tye in the morning, she'd deal with Claire.

Once and for all.

Chapter Twenty-Six

Bound to the chair in Tye's solar, Claire waited. Her cheek hurt, and she wished she could gently rub it to ease the discomfort, but her bound wrists, lashed to the rear sides of the chair, prevented such movement. Her ankles were also tied together and secured to the chair.

While her body was forced to remain still, her mind raced, taunting her with imaginings of what would happen once Tye strode in. Memories tormented her too, of last night in this very room, when they'd lain in each other's arms. Those precious recollections pained her far more than she'd ever believed possible.

If only she and Tye weren't enemies.

If only circumstances were different.

If only.

It seemed an eternity ago that Tye had turned his back on her, and she'd been brought to the solar. Mayhap his rage had cooled somewhat since then. Or, it might have grown into a violent tempest ready to be unleashed.

Claire shivered despite the heat rising off the fire to her right. The mercenaries had turned the chair so that it faced the door, making it easier for them to look in and ensure she was where they'd left her. They'd tied her tightly, and the rough ropes cut into her flesh, most of all at her wrists.

Wincing, she wiggled her hands and feet as best she could, trying to ward off the numbness settling in her fingers and toes. Patch, watching her from his box by the hearth, got to his feet, stretched lazily, and lay down again, his eyes drifting closed.

What she would give to be able to stand up and stretch like Patch had just done.

Voices reached her through the closed solar doors. She tensed as the right panel opened, and Tye walked in.

His face was a carefully controlled mask. So very different from the way he'd appeared last night, with tenderness softening his eyes and his mouth quick to form a grin. Sadness swept through her, for last eve, she'd thought him the most charming man she'd ever met. Now, he might as well be a stranger.

Tye pushed the door closed behind him. Hands on his hips, he studied her for a long, strained moment before he strode to the table where her journals and letters were still stacked.

Should she speak first? Would that help, or only make matters worse? If only she knew.

He took an object out of his saddlebag, lying at the end of the table, and faced her.

"What happened earlier," she said, her words rushing out.

He raised a hand, silencing her, while he crossed to stand in front of her. His unique scent, of frosty winter air, leather, and soap made her insides twist with longing and regret. She stared blindly at his hands—what was he holding?—even as she heard the *pop* of a cork stopper being released and inhaled the brisk scent of herbs.

Tye's gaze settled on her cheek.

"The pot...holds ointment?" An idiotic question. Yet, she couldn't imagine he'd want to help her in any way, not after what she'd done.

"Aye, 'tis ointment. 'Twill help bring down the swelling." He dipped his finger into the pot, then brushed the greenish unguent over her cheek, his touch far kinder than she'd expected.

"T-thank you."

A muscle in his jaw ticked. He applied more of the pungent smelling ointment and then stepped back to set the pot on the table. As he moved, his tunic stretched over his broad shoulders, outlining bunching muscles beneath, and yearning spiraled through her. Fighting the unwelcome desire, she curled her fingers against the back of the chair.

"I know you are angry with me," she said.

Tye faced her, tension in his posture, as though he prepared to battle an armed opponent. "I am."

"You must understand—"

"I do understand your reasons."

"As I said in the hall, *I* am entirely to blame for what happened." His brows rose as she spoke, but she forged on. "I organized the deception. 'Tis no one else's fault. Only mine."

Eyes narrowed, he studied her and then nodded.

"If I am to be punished—"

A ragged sigh broke from him. He claimed the distance between them so fast, she gasped and lurched back against the chair, causing the joints to squeak. There was no escaping him, though. He cupped her face with his hand, his thumb hovering over her injury. "This," he said tightly, "proves we are far beyond mere punishment."

Oh, the feel of his skin against hers! She quivered inside, but fought the forbidden hunger. She needed to understand his words.

"W-what...?"

"We must get you out of this keep, away from my mother. 'Tis the only choice now."

Confusion muddled her thoughts. "But—"

"Listen." He let go of her face and set his hands on the chair's carved arm rests. "I was angry about today, aye. However, you are a brave and intelligent woman. I expected you to try and escape."

"You did?"

"What I did not ever expect..." He hung his head, his silky hair close to her mouth. Sighing, he raised his head to meet her wary stare. "I did not expect to feel as I do...about you."

His voice had softened, and his words had held a slight tremor. What she'd heard wasn't anger. Far from it.

Astonishment rippled through her, swiftly followed by shock and an onslaught of other intense feelings that all jumbled together. "Tye—"

"Just...*listen!*" His growl was akin to a wounded beast, and as his gaze bored into hers, she slowly nodded. "I must say it now, for 'tis not easy, and I...may not have the chance again." He hesitated, clearly searching for his words. "I...never intended to kill Henry. I did not want to slay anyone that night, only escape."

A hard lump lodged in her throat. She dreaded what Tye was going to say next, but had no choice but to listen.

"Henry was overpowered and wounded by my mother's men. When she said she was going to geld him—"

"*Geld* him?" Claire choked out.

"Aye. A terrible fate for a young man. To stop my mother, I knocked Henry down to the floor. I hoped he'd be senseless long enough for us to get away. However, he woke. Instead of staying down, where he was safe, he...attacked me." Tye shook his head. "'Twas a senseless, foolhardy act."

"Henry was *not* a fool!"

"He was, Claire. He obviously wanted to be a hero, even though he had no hope of succeeding."

"De Lanceau praised Henry as a gallant, chivalrous warrior." Claire's tone roughened with anguish. "His lordship honored Henry in a special ceremony—"

"My father was nowhere near the dungeon that night. He never saw what happened."

"Surely, there were other witnesses who gave accounts."

"The only other guard in the dungeon was killed early on by Braden. While a few other prisoners might have seen what took place, we set them all free that night. Even if some were recaptured, my sire would not trust the accounts of convicted criminals. No matter what they said, my sire would consider me a ruthless murderer."

"But—"

"My mother was there that eve, and Braden, and the men they had hired to broach the dungeon. They might tell you the truth, but I doubt you or anyone else would believe it."

Indeed, she wouldn't. Claire couldn't bear the thought of facing Veronique again, especially to ask about Henry's demise.

"Believe me, Henry was a fool." Tye's words ground between his teeth. "He threw his life away."

"He did not! He did his duty, and—"

"If that were me, if I had been betrothed to you... If I had been honored with the love of a woman of such loveliness, grace, and compassion..." Tye paused, and the drumming of her heart rang in her ears. "I would have done anything—*anything*—to stay alive, so we could be together."

Tears filled her eyes. She struggled to sustain the rage she'd drawn upon for inner strength, but 'twas becoming more and more difficult.

"When I realized the Henry from your letters was the guard from Branton Keep's dungeon, I tried to think of how best to tell you about his death. You spoke so highly of him. I did not want to hurt you, even though I…knew I must."

"The truth is always the wisest path," she said as if by rote. Lady Brackendale had told her that long ago. Claire had clung to those words for comfort in her darkest moments of despair.

"'Tis what I decided, too. It made me angry, though, having to hurt you," Tye said. "I cannot forget how Henry selfishly thought only of himself, and not of you."

Tears slipped down her cheeks. She stared into Tye's eyes, searched his expression for the barest hint of guile, but found none. Indeed, his eyes were damp, as though what he'd just told her had been difficult.

Did she dare to believe him? Could his account of what had happened that night be the truth? It seemed impossible.

He straightened and stepped away, letting his hands fall to his sides.

"How do I know that what you have just told me is true?" she asked quietly.

"I swear it, upon my honor." His mouth ticked up in a despondent grin. "What little I have."

Her beautiful eyes revealed all: her heart longed to believe him, but her rational mind told her not to heed one word. He'd told her the truth about Henry's killing, though. At least he'd managed to say that much before he was to lose her forever.

Fighting an overwhelming sense of regret, Tye strode past the chair. Claire's head turned to the right as she tried to follow his movement, and her shimmering tresses, the lower portion trapped between her back and the chair, gathered at her shoulder. How he yearned to touch her, to slide his fingers into her hair and pull it aside to press a kiss to her sweet-scented skin. He'd wanted to touch her from the moment he'd walked into the solar, but he mustn't. After his confession about Henry, she'd be more likely to spit in his face than accept his caresses.

Halting directly behind her, he looked down at her hands, tied to either side of the chair. Her fingers clasped the wood. As he stared, they tightened their grip, a sure sign that he was making her uneasy.

He dropped to a crouch and drew the knife from inside his boot.

"W-what are you doing?"

The dagger rasped from its sheath. "I am cutting your bonds." The sharp knife sliced easily through the ropes and they fell to the floor.

With a groan of relief, Claire drew her hands into her lap and rolled her shoulders, easing knotted muscles.

After sheathing the knife and returning it to his boot, he walked back in front of her and knelt, catching hold of her hands. Turning them to the right and left, he examined the angry red marks encircling her wrists. She'd have unsightly bruises. Had his mother ordered Claire to be bound so tightly? Frowning, he reached behind him for the ointment pot.

"Nay," Claire said quickly. "Thank you, but I think I will be all right."

Tye fought disappointment. She didn't want him touching her again. With a terse nod, he released her hands, letting her fingers fall back into her lap.

He remained on his knees. His conscience told him to move away, but when her gaze locked with his and held it, he couldn't. Her eyes held him captive, as if he were manacled to the floor.

He could lose his soul in those expressive eyes. Regret welled up inside him, for he could never admit it to her, but he was going to miss her when she was gone.

In the firelight, the ointment on her cheek glistened.

"How does your cheek feel now?" he asked.

"Better than before."

"I am glad." If only he could slide his arms around her

waist, lean in, and kiss her, prove with his lips and tongue that he was still the man she'd loved so selflessly last night. Knowing he had no right to act on that impulse, he sat back on his heels, giving her some distance. "There is a matter we need to discuss, as soon as you feel able."

"Not Henry." Her bosom rose and fell on a ragged breath. "Please. No more. I cannot bear—"

"'Tis not about Henry. 'Tis about you."

Her shoulders lowered in obvious relief. "Go on."

"We must get you out of Wode. You are no longer safe here. If I could send you away *right now*, I would. However, 'tis perilous for anyone, above all a young lady, to travel the roads at night."

"What has happened—?"

"The fact that my mother hit you, when I told her you were not to be harmed… She considers you a threat. I know her. I know exactly what she is capable of if she believes it necessary."

Claire's face had paled. Again, he battled with the desire to reach for her, to comfort her.

"Before dawn, I will take you to the cellar. You will get into the hidden passageway and stay there, until the battle with my sire begins. Any day now, he will arrive with his army."

"But—"

"Run to my sire's men. They will get you out of the castle walls and keep you safe."

Claire looked uncertain. Was she going to refuse her chance at freedom? At safety? He wouldn't allow it.

He drew the sheathed dagger from his boot and pressed it into her hands. "Hide this under your garments. If anyone tries to stop you from escaping, use it."

"You trust me with a knife?"

"I know you are not foolish enough to try stabbing me."

The barest smile touched her lips, an acknowledgement of his wry humor. "Thank you. However, I will not leave without Mary."

"Claire!"

"Lady Brackendale as well. She—"

"She is an old woman. She would never manage the

tunnel," Tye said. "She would only be a hindrance to you."

"I cannot just leave her!"

"You must. I will do my best to protect her." Unable to restrain himself any longer, he rose up on his knees and gently set his hands upon both of hers that were clutching the knife. "Please. Mary can go with you, but you must do as I say."

Claire nodded, finally. A sigh rushed from his lips, before her right hand slid over his, her touch so unexpected, his eyes burned.

"Come with us. Ask to meet with your father. I will help—"

"Never," Tye ground out. He hoped the word conveyed the full extent of his loathing for his sire.

"You just said that you cannot trust your mother," Claire rushed on. "How can you be sure that all she has told you about your father is true?"

A sickening pang of foreboding rolled through Tye. He fought it down with a curse. "He rejected me."

"Are you certain?"

"Aye."

"What if you are wrong? What if—?"

"Enough," he growled. "We have discussed this already."

She glared back. "You owe it to yourself to learn the truth."

"I already *know* the truth." Tye laughed bitterly. "I am bastard-born. I have lived by my sword. I have slept in filthy stables, killed knights, stolen food so I wouldn't starve—"

"Stop it." Her eyes shone with tears.

"I have done far worse things too. I am not a good man, Claire. Far from it."

"Tye."

"I am—"

"Compassionate," she whispered, squeezing his hand. "Honorable."

"God's teeth!" Shame smothered a momentary flare of astonishment. She was speaking madness. He was not at all the man she was describing. Nowhere near.

"A man who does not see the goodness within him, even

though 'tis there."

Tye shook his head. "Listen to what you are saying!"

"I know exactly what I am saying." Conviction blazed in her damp eyes. "You have a choice, Tye. The most difficult choice you may ever make, but a choice all the same."

"Why do I want any other choice than to slay my sire?" he sneered.

Her gaze filled with grudging resignation. Tears trailed down her face. "Mayhap you should consider the answer to that question."

He yanked his hands free from hers and stood. Anger and confusion churned within him as he stared into the fire. Heat rolled off the blaze, as intense as the inferno seething within him.

Claire rose from the chair and touched his arm. He stiffened, aflame with anguish and the soul-deep need to take her in his arms. "Tye—"

"You can have the bed," he said. "Get some sleep. I will post additional guards at the door tonight, and I will wake you before dawn."

Chapter Twenty-Seven

"Lord Delwyn de Lysonne is waiting outside the gatehouse, milord."

Holding the solar door open a crack, Tye rubbed his neck to relieve a cramp from lying on the floor by the hearth. "*Now?* 'Tis not yet dawn."

"His horse is drawing a small cart. He said he has a delivery of goods for the castle. He also asked after Lady Sevalliere."

Tye scowled. Disquiet wove through him, along with a hot spark of jealousy that the lad had asked about Claire.

Tye glanced at her, sitting in the chair by the fire as though she was still bound, as he'd ordered when the knock had rattled the door. Judging by her expression, she was equally surprised by Delwyn's visit.

As he faced the mercenary outside again, one of the four men he'd ordered to guard the solar until he could get Claire to the cellar, Tye's scowl deepened. Delwyn's arrival could be naught of consequence. Or it could be a trap, part of a greater plan of de Lanceau's to gain entry to the keep.

"I will be down in a moment," Tye said. "Wake the rest of the mercenaries."

The man bowed and strode away.

As soon as the door shut, Claire leapt to her feet. "What is Delwyn doing here again?"

"I do not know. I was about to ask you that question."

"Why would I know? Mayhap he has another letter from my sister?"

Fresh jealousy gnawed at Tye as he crossed the chamber,

snatched up his chain mail, and pulled it on over the clothes he'd slept in.

"You are readying for battle. Do you suspect Delwyn is trying to trick you?"

"I do not know yet what to expect. I will not be caught unawares."

Tye donned his cloak, gloves, and sword belt. She watched, her gaze akin to her hand trailing over his bare skin, making him acutely aware of her on a basic physical level. He heard the shallow rasp of her breathing, smelled the honeyed fragrance clinging to her skin, turned and saw her fingers fluttering at her throat.

She hadn't slept much last night; as he'd lain by the fire, trying to slumber, he'd heard her restless sighs and frequent turning. He couldn't help but wonder: Had she worried for herself, or for him?

Tye gathered the rest of his knives and shoved them into a leather bag. As he secured the bag to his sword belt, he saw the bee in amber glinting on the trestle table. Hellfire, he felt just like that bee, trapped by his life, never able to break free. He snatched up the amber and shoved it into the bag.

"Delwyn is a fine young man," Claire said. "I am certain he has a good reason for his visit this morn."

Tye bit back a less-than-admirable retort. How he longed to walk over to her, pull her into his arms, and to kiss her for good luck. To kiss her just because he wanted to. To kiss her because...he couldn't imagine living without her. He wanted her. He *needed* her. She'd brought light into his miserable, worthless life, and he never wanted their days together to end.

During the night, he'd thought of many things he wanted to say to her, words he'd never said to any other woman. *I love you, Claire. I will always love you, my beautiful warrior Kitten.*

Yet, to say such things when he was letting her go would be unfair.

"Stay here," he told her. "The guards will not let anyone in. I will fetch you as soon as I can."

"All right." In her voice, he heard understanding of all they'd discussed last night. When he came to get her, 'twould be to take her and Mary to the secret tunnel. "Be careful," she added softly, as he strode to the doors.

Be careful. His hand on the door handle, he paused. It seemed she did care for him, at least somewhat. Yet, he still had no right to hold her to him.

He quit the chamber and made his way to the bailey, where servants had begun their morning duties. A hard frost coated the ground. Snow still lingered in places; some of the higher mounds of it hadn't completely melted and were crusted with ice. He strode to the outside stairs leading up to the battlements above the gatehouse. A group of mercenaries had congregated there, their breaths emerging as white puffs in the air.

"Milord," they said in greeting.

Tye looked down at the opposite bank. Delwyn sat on his horse that was harnessed to a wooden cart. Tye recognized the style of wagon; one of the local woodworkers made them for transporting goods from the market.

"Good morn," Delwyn called up to him.

"Good morn," Tye answered. While small, the canvas-covered cart was big enough to conceal two men. "What brings you here today?"

The lad gestured to the cart. "I am honored to bring you fresh herbs, potent herbal tonics, and healing goods from my lord's own supply. When I told him of the sickness at Wode, he insisted that I bring these to you as soon as possible. He wishes dear Lady Brackendale a swift recovery."

"'Tis kind of your lord," Tye said, "but—"

"Is the sickness waning, or is it still spreading?"

"'Tis contained. For now."

"Is Lady Sevalliere all right?"

"Aye," Tye bit out.

Relief touched the lad's features. "I am glad. The goods I bring will help ease the discomfort of those who are unwell. Of course, Lord Geoffrey de Lanceau has been informed of the situation."

The mercenaries muttered to one another.

"De Lanceau?" A jolt rippled through Tye. At last, word of his sire. Braden hadn't returned to Wode yet—whatever was delaying him?—and Tye needed current news of his father's whereabouts.

"My lord is a close ally of de Lanceau's," Delwyn went on. "When my lord heard about the sickness, he immediately sent a missive to de Lanceau. His lordship said to do whatever was needed to help Lady Brackendale, since she belongs to his family."

Tye nodded, acknowledging the lad's explanation. While Delwyn told a good tale, Tye sensed there was far more that the lad wasn't revealing. Moving closer to the edge of the battlement, he forced a genial smile and said, "You seem well informed about Lord de Lanceau."

Delwyn grinned proudly. "He is a great man. I have met him on several occasions. 'Tis an honor to…"

As the lad chattered on, Tye mulled his options. While there was a risk in opening the gates to Delwyn, the cart could only hold two men at most. If indeed Delwyn was trying to deceive Tye, his mercenaries could easily subdue a pair of unwanted guests.

Moreover, the lad could be useful. The better informed Tye was, the better prepared he'd be for his sire's assault. Once Delwyn ran out of information to divulge, he could be held for ransom; he obviously belonged to a wealthy family and was valued by his lord, so there was an excellent chance of earning a sizable ransom payment.

The lad's horse snorted and stamped a front hoof, as if sensing his master's impatience. "Well? Will you let me in?" Delwyn's face reddened with irritation. "I cannot return to my lord with a full cart. Not when these supplies were sent as a gesture of good will."

"Lower the drawbridge," Tye called to the men in the gatehouse.

With the metallic squeal of chains, the massive platform began to lower over the moat.

Tye summoned over two of the mercenaries. "You and I will meet him. He is to go no farther than the drawbridge until we have seen what is in the cart. If he does not bring herbs and potions, you will take him captive and escort him to the great hall, to await my questioning."

"Aye, milord."

Tye hurried down the stairs to the bailey, the hired thugs close behind.

In the shadows of the gatehouse, Tye waited until the drawbridge hit ground level. The portcullis slowly rose. Delwyn nudged his horse forward and the cart rumbled onto the platform.

Striding ahead of Tye, the two thugs drew their swords. Once the portcullis had risen to waist level, they ducked underneath and approached the cart.

At the mercenaries' approach, Delwyn halted his mount. "What is the meaning of—?"

"Forgive my men," Tye said. "'Tis merely a precaution, but they must check the cart."

Delwyn hesitated, but then said, "Of course."

One of the thugs reached for the edge of the canvas.

The tarp flew up, falling over to cover the mercenaries' heads as two men in chain mail armor jumped up in the back of the cart. Shock whipped through Tye, for he recognized them instantly: his half-brother, Edouard, his sire's son and heir; and Aldwin, one of his father's most loyal warriors and the finest crossbowman in the land.

Ah, God, he'd been tricked. Tricked!

Cursing, Tye drew his sword. "Kill them! Lower the portcullis!" he bellowed. His voice was drowned by the cries from the battlements above.

Tipping his blond head back, Aldwin put a horn to his lips and blew a single, loud note.

An answering blast sounded from a short distance away.

Arrows flew down from the battlements above, several embedding in the side of the cart with a *thud, thud, thud.* Still entangled in the tarp, the two mercenaries staggered backward. Leaping down from the wagon, Edouard shoved the mercenaries, propelling them off the drawbridge. They splashed into the icy moat.

"Attack! Attack," men screamed from the ramparts. "We are under attack."

Tye froze where he stood; the thunderous rumbling he'd barely heard over the men's shouts was growing louder. Scores of riders galloped down the road toward the castle. To the right of the road, foot soldiers streamed out of the trees.

Hellfire!

"Raise the drawbridge," Tye yelled again, his throat burning. "Lower the portcullis!" Shouting the orders, he hurried toward the bailey, but before he had taken three steps, a crossbow bolt slammed into the gatehouse wall beside him, spraying chunks of mortar.

Tye spun. Behind the cart, Aldwin reloaded his crossbow.

Aldwin was an excellent shot; he never missed. Why, then, had the bolt not killed Tye? Had de Lanceau had ordered his knights to spare Tye until he could fight him face-to-face?

Aldwin readied to fire. The crossbowman might not be allowed to kill Tye, but could wound him, weakening him for the confrontation with his father.

Aldwin wasn't the only threat. Sword raised, Edouard walked under the teeth of the portcullis toward Tye. In the hard angles of his face, his steely gaze, his muscular stature, Tye saw the image of his sire.

Tye raised his sword, ready to fight, noting, with a flare of rage, that Aldwin had already killed two of the mercenaries on the parapets. Their corpses lay on the drawbridge. As he watched, frustration clawing at his innards, Delwyn coaxed his horse forward and positioned the cart directly under the portcullis. Not only did it provide a defensive shield for Aldwin, but it prevented the barrier from lowering all the way to the ground. There was no way of keeping out his sire's men now.

Damnation. *Damnation!* His sire would die for this deception, along with all of the others!

Edouard neared, his smile grim. "Good day, Brother."

"Go to hell," Tye spat. Loathing for his half-brother made his blood burn. He'd almost killed Edouard at Waddesford Keep; mayhap today he'd finally have the pleasure of slaying him.

"Surrender," Edouard commanded.

"Never."

The words had barely left Tye's lips when Edouard lunged. Their swords clanged, the sound echoing in the enclosed area beneath the gatehouse. Edouard was strong, his assault skilled and powerful, and the ferocity of the strikes jarred down Tye's arms. Again and again the swords clashed, metal flashing in the dull light.

Tye growled, pivoted, lashed out once more, his blade skidding across the front of Edouard's mail hauberk. Edouard jumped back and then retaliated, bringing his blade arcing down, but the toe of his boot caught on a raised stone. He twisted to avoid falling forward, and Tye seized the advantage. He raced at his brother, and with a vicious thrust, propelled him backward. With a grunt of pain, Edouard slammed into the wall. His head hit the stone and he went still, his eyes rolling.

Breathing hard, Tye lifted his sword, readying to shove it against his brother's neck. Taking Edouard hostage would give him leverage against his sire—

Tye caught the whistle of a crossbow bolt an instant before it flew past his head. The bolt bounced off the stone and clattered on the ground. Again, Aldwin had missed. That shot, though, had been closer than the other; a warning, meant to protect Edouard.

Stepping away, Tye dared a glance at Aldwin. The blond warrior took a fresh quiver of bolts from Delwyn and began reloading his weapon. Edouard groaned and straightened on his feet, his grip tightening on his sword.

Shouts from the bailey drew Tye's attention, reminded him of the greater fight yet to be won. This day, he would confront and kill his sire. 'Twas far better to save his strength for that fight than waste it sparring with his brother.

Moreover, he had to get Claire to the hidden tunnel. She was waiting for him; he wouldn't forsake his promise to get her away from the bloodshed.

Sensing his brother rallying for another attack, Tye raced for the bailey washed in weak morning light. Ahead, arrows flew down from the battlements. Mercenaries were battling a crowd of bedraggled men. With a fresh jolt of shock, Tye recognized the fighters: prisoners who'd been chained in the dungeon.

How had they escaped? They had weapons, too. Tye's men guarding the dungeon last night should have quelled any beginnings of an uprising. Fury knotted inside Tye and he vowed to punish the mercenaries himself once the battle was won.

Sweat slicked his brow as he dodged a mercenary and prisoner engaged in a knife fight and headed for the forebuilding. Out of the corner of his eye, he caught movement near the stables. Sutton, his face ashen, peered out from behind a wagon.

A hard object smacked into Tye's forehead. Stinging pain spread across his brow. Grimacing, he looked down at the ground. A small rock rolled across the dirt by his right boot.

He dodged an arrow fired from the battlements, then cursed as another rock smacked into his head. He scowled, for Sutton wasn't the only one hiding behind the wagon. Witt darted out, his slingshot whirling. Meeting Tye's lethal glower, the boy stuck out his tongue and aimed the makeshift weapon.

Tye spun away and loped for the keep, ignoring the *thump* of a rock hitting the back of his cloak. A dying mercenary, staggering backward with an arrow through his neck, bumped into Tye; he shoved the lout into one of the men from the dungeon, who had charged at Tye with a sword. With a roar of frustration, the man careened to the ground, the mercenary collapsing on top of him.

Tye yanked open the door to the forebuilding and thundered up the stairwell to the great hall. Women and children huddled behind a barricade of stacked trestle tables. Many of the maidservants glared at him. Some smiled gleefully, clearly believing he was doomed.

He glowered at them as he raced past and up the stairs to the solar.

As he reached the upper level corridor, his strides slowed. A sickening fear crawled up inside him. The mercenaries he had set to guard the solar lay in the passageway, dead.

Claire! Oh, God, nay. Kitten—

Skirting the bloody corpses, Tye shoved open the right solar door and hurried in. The chamber was warm, quiet, and illuminated by fire glow. And empty, apart from Patch hiding under the bed.

A knife lay by the hearth: the dagger he'd given Claire.

Chapter Twenty-Eight

T he moment Tye left the solar, anticipation raced through Claire, chilling her like a scattering of icy snowflakes. She rubbed her arms, trying to chase the unpleasant sensation away.

Longing for Tye spread through her, along with concern. She sensed something was going to happen this day. Something momentous and far more crucial than her and Mary escaping through the hidden tunnel in the cellar.

Cold sweat dampened her palms as she tugged on the clean gown, chemise, cloak, gloves, and boots Tye had fetched from her chamber last night. She was eager to get away from Wode as quickly as possible; Veronique was a ruthless, frightening, and unpredictable woman. Claire never wanted to be subjected to Veronique's cruelty again.

Yet, as she straightened her gloves on her fingers, part of her whispered that by retreating into the tunnel, she was abandoning Tye. He had no one to speak for him; his mother thought only of her own ambitions, and Tye was blinded by the torment Veronique had fed him since birth.

Claire stooped and patted Patch, who nuzzled her hand. A heady warmth filled her, the sensation strongest in her heart. She shouldn't run; for Tye, she must stay. She must try to find a way to resolve the enmity between him and his father. At the very least, Tye deserved the chance to ask his sire about the past.

There *had* to be a way to stop that deadly fight. Somehow.

De Lanceau wasn't a man to yield the castle. That meant Tye would be slain.

Agony shot through her at the thought of Tye dying. Tye

was right; he wasn't of the same social class as Henry had been. Yet, Tye's life still had value. He'd survived so much, endured so much, especially through his mother's manipulations.

He deserved to know that life could be very different to what he'd experienced. He deserved to be respected, to be able to live his life the way he wanted, not the way his mother demanded.

Tye deserved to be...loved.

She doubted he'd ever experienced true, unwavering, and unconditional love. A tragic thought.

Claire paced before the hearth. Patch watched her with half-closed eyes. Aye, she was right to remain at Wode. Freedom could wait; saving Tye's life, though, could not, for the meeting between Tye and his sire drew ever closer.

When Claire turned to pace again, one of the solar doors opened. It could only be Tye, since the guards would not let anyone else pass. "Tye—"

Veronique strolled in, garbed in her fur-trimmed cloak, bringing with her the scent of rosewater. "Not Tye."

Oh, God. Oh, God.

Two mercenaries followed; they also wore outdoor garments and wielded swords glistening with fresh blood. One of them carried a length of coiled rope.

Through the open doorway, Claire saw men lying on the ground, their clothes slashed and bloodstained. Veronique and her thugs had killed the guards.

Claire reached for the dagger she'd tucked into the snug sleeve of her gown. A weight suddenly brushed against her legs: Patch, limping his way over to the bed to cower underneath.

"Were you planning to leave?" Veronique's brows arched as her gaze traveled over Claire's fastened cloak, right down to her boots. "How strange, when you are a captive. One who only yesterday plotted against the lord of the castle."

Venom sharpened the woman's words, and Claire shivered. She pointed the dagger at the three intruders. She wouldn't answer Veronique. She'd never betray Tye to his mother.

She had to get past Veronique and her thugs and *run!*

A harsh cackle broke from Veronique. "Do you really hope to deter me with that knife?"

"Stay away from me," Claire said firmly.

"I am afraid not. You see, you are quite important for what is to come."

Wielding the dagger, Claire took a nervous step sideways, toward the door. "W-what do you mean?"

"Tie her," Veronique said.

Claire dashed for the door, while lashing out with the knife. A mercenary caught her arm, knocked the dagger from her hand, and pinned her arms. She shrieked, struggled, but the men swiftly subdued her and tied her hands behind her back, heedless of the sore marks on her wrists.

Her garments rustling, Veronique approached Claire. The older woman grabbed Claire's chin, and her bent, aged fingers dug into Claire's skin until she gasped with pain. "Whatever secrets you are holding, I will get them out of you."

"Never," Claire shot back.

"Today, I will also have the pleasure of killing you."

Fear lashed through Claire, but she refused to yield to Veronique's cruel glare.

Smiling as if she had secrets of her own, Veronique lowered her punishing hand. "Did you know an army draws near?"

Claire's frantic thoughts shifted to Tye. Was he aware of the approaching army? His mercenaries must have alerted him. That meant, though, that Delwyn was working with de Lanceau. The deadly battle had begun.

"Ah. I see from your expression that you *now* realize what will take place today." Veronique tittered. "'Tis why I need you."

"Me?" Claire said, her mind reeling.

"*No one* will keep Tye from doing what is expected of him. *Especially* you."

"You will use me to force Tye to kill his sire?"

"See, you do understand."

Revulsion broke through the panic churning within Claire. "Do you care about Tye at all?"

"How dare—?"

"Do you love him as your child? Or from the day he was born, did you view him only as a means to destroy de Lanceau?" Claire shook as she spoke, but she meant every word. Given the chance, she had far more she wanted to say to this horrible woman.

Veronique's head lifted as she sucked in a sharp breath. Fury flashed in her eyes. Her gnarled hand slid toward her cloak, as though to draw a dagger, but before her fingers touched the garment, she seemed to change her mind. She turned away. "Bring her."

Claire fought, but the men hauled her across the planks. Following Veronique, they dragged Claire down passageways and into a cramped stairwell. The iron-bound wooden door at the top opened onto the battlements. The men shoved her into the dawn light.

The bitterly cold morning breeze snatched the air from Claire's lungs. Shouts, the clash of weaponry, and screams of wounded men echoed up from the bailey, while a short distance along the parapet, mercenaries scrutinized the landscape below, fired arrows, nocked more arrows to their longbows, and fired again.

The men holding Claire pulled her to the middle of the battlement where Veronique stood. Mounded snow remained on some parts of the wall walk; where the snow had melted but then frozen overnight, slick black ice glinted.

The thugs halted. One man either side of Claire, they held her firm. Through the gap between the squared stone merlons, she saw that on the frost-laden ground outside the castle, foot soldiers with crossbows and longbows were engaged in a full-scale assault. A few warriors were throwing grappling hooks with ropes to try and scale the fortress walls. Mounted knights circled farther back, issuing orders. Without doubt, Tye's forces were outnumbered.

Over the din in the bailey, she heard a shout. Was that Tye's voice? She looked down into the bailey, to see him running from the shadows of the gatehouse. He ducked, barely missing an arrow, while he wove through the throng of men fighting by the entrance to the dungeons. Tye was heading for the forebuilding. Was he on his way to the solar, to take her to the cellar?

Oh, Tye, she silently cried. *Beware.*

Her heart ached, for when he found her missing, his mercenaries dead, he'd know his mother had betrayed him.

A brown-haired man down by the well, who'd just slain a hired thug, saw Tye and started toward him. Claire didn't recognize the man, but by his authoritative stride and fine cloak, he appeared to be someone of importance. He stayed far enough behind that Tye wouldn't sense he was being followed.

Veronique brushed past Claire, her sharpened gaze also on the man. "Dominic." She spat the name like a curse.

"Dominic?" Claire asked.

"De Lanceau's closest friend." She sneered. "Arrogant bastard. He thought I could not escape from his dungeon after the battle at Waddesford Keep. How wrong he was."

"He will be glad to recapture you, then," Claire said. Veronique belonged in an isolated cell where she could no longer wreak harm upon anyone, including Tye.

Veronique dismissed Claire's words with a disgusted snort. "Dominic will never succeed, that I promise you. Yet, if Dominic is here, that means Geoffrey is as well." She studied the warriors in the bailey with obvious eagerness.

Claire discreetly twisted her bound hands. The mercenaries had tied her tightly, and the ropes cut into her sore flesh. Still, there must be a way to get free. She'd just have to find it.

As Veronique leaned farther over the battlement, searching below for de Lanceau, the door they'd used crashed open. The *clang* of swords rang from the stairwell's shadows.

Moving backward, his sword poised to strike again, Tye emerged from the stairs. After him came two knights wearing chain mail beneath their mantles.

In the lead by a few steps was the man named Dominic. Close behind was a tall, broad-shouldered warrior whose brown hair was streaked with gray. His silk surcoat, worn over his chain mail, bore the embroidered image of a flying hawk.

Claire immediately recognized him: Lord Geoffrey de Lanceau.

Sweat ran down the back of Tye's neck and trickled down

his temples as he faced Dominic and his sire. He'd come upon them in the upstairs corridor. They'd just broken through the locked door of the chamber where Lady Brackendale and Mary had been huddled together.

"Do not worry," de Lanceau had been saying. "Wode is ours. Tye's conquest is finished."

Upon seeing him, his sire's face had contorted with fury. The two men had raised weapons and rushed at him. Tye had fought them both, but they were excellent swordsmen. Changing his strategy, Tye had lured them into the stairwell, along the torch lit corridors, and up to the battlement.

As Tye deflected another strike from Dominic, this one perilously close to slashing his forearm, he realized others were close by and watching the confrontation.

He snatched the quickest of glances. *Hellfire!* Claire was on the battlement, near his mother. Sickening panic clenched his gut, for he guessed why his parent had brought Claire to the fight; by holding her hostage, his mother ensured Tye killed his sire.

"'Tis not as we agreed," he snapped to his Mother.

"I changed the plan."

His anger became a blazing hot tempest. He wanted to round on his mother, demand that she let Claire go, but he didn't dare take his gaze from the men before him. If he didn't give this fight his full attention, he'd die.

"I see you have brought your father. What a pleasure to see you again, Geoffrey."

"'Tis no pleasure for me, Veronique," de Lanceau muttered. Baring his teeth, he lunged at Tye, his attack a swift onslaught that forced Tye to stumble backward to avoid being wounded.

As Tye regained his balance, he stole another glance at Claire, pinned between the mercenaries. Her arms were behind her back; her hands had been bound. Rage warred with a ghastly sense of helplessness, for he had no means to help or protect her.

Once he'd slain his sire, his mother would probably kill Claire—just as she'd taken away the kitten in his childhood and everything else he'd ever cared about.

He'd failed Claire; he'd never meant to, but he had.

Somehow, he was going to have to get her away from the danger.

As Tye waited, calculating his next move in the brief standoff, he became aware his father was studying him, not a cursory glance-over, but an intense assessment. Was he realizing how much Tye had changed from the battered man he'd held in his dungeon months ago? Was he seeking a strategic advantage, a weakness, so he could win this fight? Tye glowered, challenging his sire with all his saved-up years of hatred.

De Lanceau wouldn't find weakness; he'd find death.

His lordship's stare hardened, and he shifted the angle of his sword. Dominic edged to Tye's right. They were going to strike together.

"You two," Veronique said to the mercenaries. "Go help Tye. I can watch over Claire."

The thugs approached.

With a flash of steel, de Lanceau lunged. Tye met the blow and turned sharply to counter a strike from Dominic. Then the meeting of steel became a constant ringing sound as the mercenaries joined the skirmish.

Tye struck, retreated, struck again. Beneath his chain mail, his tunic stuck to his skin, despite the frigid morning. His arms burned with the strain, his shoulders ached, but he ignored the discomfort and fought on, making his way back to Claire.

With an agonized cry, one of the mercenaries stumbled, blood oozing from a slash across his neck. He collapsed, falling in a heap against the side of the battlement.

"Now the odds are a little better," Dominic said, wiping his sweaty brow on his cloak sleeve.

The remaining mercenary glanced over at his dead comrade, roared with fury, and lunged. As his sword whipped down toward Dominic, his boot slid on a patch of ice. The mercenary wobbled and fell with the *crunch* of bone onto one knee. With a swift thrust of de Lanceau's sword, the man toppled over, dead.

Tye took several steps back, bringing him closer to Claire. He *had* to get her away from his mother. Somehow.

His mother's eyes gleamed in the sunshine. "Kill your sire.

Kill him now, as you have wanted since you were a boy."

Tye inhaled the metallic scent of blood: the smell of battle. Anticipation whipped through him, and his grip tightened on his sword.

"Go on! Kill him!"

Chapter Twenty-Nine

H er fingers working at the rope binding her hands, Claire shivered in the wind blowing across the battlements. How she feared for Tye, feared so intensely, she wanted to scream.

"Kill him!" Veronique shrieked again, standing barely a step away from Claire. "Slay the man who denied you all."

Tye's shoulders tensed, a prelude to an attack, and Claire's heart ached with the agony of watching him, his movements controlled like a skilled predator's. He was stunning in his own raw, untamed way. If he died on this battlement, 'twould be a loss from which she'd never recover.

How foolish that she cared for the man who'd murdered Henry. Yet, if she were honest with herself, she'd never really known Henry at all; not the way she knew Tye, as if he was part of her soul.

She loved Tye. She *loved* him. He was flawed, his soul badly damaged, but he wasn't beyond redemption.

"Tye!" she cried.

His body jerked as if she'd struck him. He lifted his head, and hope flared within her. She must try to reach him, to sway him from his deadly purpose. "Please. Stop this fight."

"Silence," Veronique hissed. She grabbed a fistful of Claire's hair and yanked, wrenching her head back. Claire gasped, but then shouted, "He is your sire!"

"Who has refused to acknowledge me," Tye snarled. "A man who wishes I never existed."

"God's teeth," de Lanceau growled.

As Claire twisted her head sideways, ignoring the

punishing pain at her scalp to see the confrontation, Tye lunged, his sword meeting his sire's with an ear-splitting *clang*. De Lanceau retaliated, his blade arcing down with a lethal glint. The weapons collided and clashed again and again.

Tye jumped back, swiping a hand over his sweaty face. "Admit it, *Father*. You want me *dead*."

De Lanceau smiled grimly. "'Tis the only choice, unless you surrender."

"Never." Tye lunged again, his sword catching de Lanceau's left arm and slicing through the fine mantle. The older lord winced, but jerked back before Tye could repeat the strike, and advanced with powerful blows that drove Tye back several paces.

Claire pulled against Veronique's hold. The wretched woman didn't let go, only twisted Claire's hair tighter around her hand. Hatred boiled within Claire, but she didn't dare look away from the fight.

"Surrender," de Lanceau commanded, breathing hard, "Or I *will* kill you."

"Because you hate me?" Tye goaded.

Claire swallowed a moan. *Oh, Tye!*

"Must I list the reasons why you should die? You are a criminal. You escaped my dungeon, and then had the bollocks to seize Wode—"

"*Our* family's keep."

"Well done, Tye," Veronique murmured.

"*My* family's keep," de Lanceau roared, eyes flashing. "A fortress the de Lanceaus earned through loyalty and honor."

Claire trembled at the violence about to be unleashed. *Oh, God.* Soon, there would be no hope of resolution.

"I will never return to your dungeon," Tye spat.

"'Tis where a man like you belongs. Unless you are dead."

"A man like me. *You*, Father, made me into the man I am now."

Dominic whistled.

"Me?" De Lanceau swore.

"You cast me aside when I was a boy. Do you dare to deny it?"

A disbelieving laugh broke from Dominic. "Do you mean the meeting years ago in the meadow?"

"Aye, it took place in a meadow," Tye said.

"I was there. I witnessed all that happened. As I remember—"

"I cast you aside, did I?" De Lanceau's narrowed gaze slid to Veronique, then back to Tye. "Did your mother also tell you I asked her to hand you over to me, but she refused?"

Tears stung Claire's eyes. De Lanceau *had* wanted to care for Tye, just as she'd thought.

"Did she also tell you she held a knife at your throat, threatening to kill you, so she could escape?"

Claire gasped in horror.

"A knife…" Tye sounded uncertain.

"He lies," Veronique shrilled. "Do not believe him!"

"His lordship does not lie," Dominic said, casting Veronique a foul look.

"What kind of mother would hold a dagger at her child's throat?" de Lanceau bit out. "Think about that."

Tye's fingers flexed on his sword. Claire sensed him struggling to make sense of what he'd just learned.

"Tye!" Claire cried. "Please! Listen to him."

"Silence!" Veronique snapped. A dagger flashed and then cold metal pressed against Claire's neck. "One more word from you, and I will slit your throat."

Claire stilled, her head still twisted back at an odd angle from Veronique's punishing hand in her hair.

"Deception is your mother's game, *not* mine," de Lanceau ground out, sweat glistening on his brow.

"If you wanted me," Tye shot back, "you would have gone after her. Captured her."

"I tried—"

"Another lie!" Tye yelled.

"I sent men-at-arms to search my lands. I searched for sennights. I followed every lead, every possible sighting of you. When your mother fled with you to France… There was little I could do."

De Lanceau's voice caught, a betrayal of suppressed

emotion. He *had* cared about Tye. It seemed he *still* cared, even now.

Tye's lip curled. "You are telling me this to make me surrender."

"I am telling you the *truth*," de Lanceau said. "Whether you believe it or not is up to you."

Tye, believe what he says. Ask what lies deepest in your heart, and you will finally know—

Behind de Lanceau, the door to the battlement flew open again. A dark-haired man with a bloodied sword ran out, followed by a blond-haired warrior with a crossbow.

"Edouard. Aldwin," Veronique called. "How good of you to join us."

Tye glared at his brother who cast him a ruthless smirk and strode in behind his sire. Aldwin moved to stand beside Dominic.

Tye silently cursed. One against four. Hellish odds, and he still had to save Claire. His mother now had knife against her neck.

"Would you like me to step in for a bit, Father?" Edouard asked, rolling his shoulders. "I can wear Tye down for you."

"Nay," de Lanceau snapped. "No one fights this battle for me."

"I meant no offense, Father."

"I know. This fight is not just to determine who rightfully rules Wode," de Lanceau said. "It has been a long time coming between me and Tye."

Tye kept his gaze upon his opponents, while he struggled with the conflicting emotions warring inside him. His sire claimed he hadn't abandoned Tye. False words. They had to be.

Otherwise, all that his mother had told him about his childhood was a lie, as Claire had insisted. As de Lanceau himself had said.

Ah, God! What was the truth? Fury and torment whipped through Tye. From that maelstrom rose the question that had kept him awake too many nights to count. "Tell me this, *Father.* Why did you save my life at Waddesford Keep?"

An odd emotion flickered in de Lanceau's gray eyes, an emotion Tye couldn't define.

"'Twould have been easier to let me fall from the battlement," Tye pressed. "Yet, you reached down your hand to save me."

"So I did," his lordship muttered.

"Why?"

"Men have died from such falls. You were lucky you only fractured your leg—"

"You were concerned I would die? You believed my life was worth saving?" How idiotic that he wanted his sire to say that Tye's life *did* matter.

A thin smile tilted de Lanceau's mouth. "For the information you could have provided, aye."

"I told you," Veronique sneered. "He offered help only because of what you could tell him. *Not* because you are his son."

"'Twas only a matter of honor between enemies then?" Tye said, "Naught more?"

De Lanceau looked unsettled. He drew in a breath to answer, but Tye knew what that answer would be. His sire would never admit that Tye was his flesh and blood. He'd had opportunities before.

Bellowing, Tye lunged. De Lanceau met his advance, retaliated, his sword grazing Tye's cloak and slashing open the bag tied to his sword belt. Sheathed knives fell on the stone, along with the amber. The resin bounced, cracked, and broke into two uneven pieces, partially freeing the bee.

Squinting down at the amber, Aldwin said, "You still have that?"

Tye frowned. "What do you mean?"

"I gave that to you. You were just a boy..." For an instant, Tye saw a flicker of compassion in the crossbowman's eyes. "I was once that bee, fighting to break free of my circumstances. I did. You can too, if you wish."

Tye choked down a cry. How did Aldwin know exactly how he felt?

How did he escape? How?

"Yield!" his sire commanded, striking out again. Tye met the assault, his blade ringing off his sire's once, twice. Three powerful strikes in, his lordship stepped on black ice. He wavered, scrambled to find his foothold, and lashed out with a belly-level strike that forced Tye to jump back and turn so that their bodies were parallel to the battlement walls.

Their swords crashed together. Step by step, they edged closer to Claire and Veronique.

De Lanceau kept up a steady onslaught. Yet, he was tiring.

"Kill him!" Veronique screamed.

De Lanceau hit more black ice. He staggered. Pitching forward, he slid toward Veronique.

Frantic cries erupted from Edouard and Dominic.

A knife glinted. Veronique raced toward de Lanceau. Raising her dagger, she readied to plunge the knife into the side of his neck.

"Nay!" Claire rushed at Veronique.

Tye raised his sword. Lunged.

As his mother's knife flashed in its downward arc, Claire careened into her. Veronique screamed, struggled, struck out with the blade. At the last moment, Tye adjusted the fall of his weapon. Metal collided with a *clank*.

With a pained cry, his mother dropped the dagger. It hit a merlon and clattered across the stones to stop against a mound of snow behind her.

Eyes glittering with fury, she gaped at Tye.

Silence carried across the battlement, broken only by the scrape of his lordship's boots as he straightened. With tremendous relief, Tye saw Claire was unharmed. She also was no longer within his mother's reach; she'd run behind him to Edouard and Aldwin. She was safe. Thank God.

"Lady Sevalliere, are you all right?" Edouard was saying.

"I am."

"I have a knife, milady. Let me free your hands."

Tye felt the punishing heat of his mother's glare. Rubbing her hand, she asked, "What madness was that?"

"As Father said, this fight is between him and me."

"Stupid boy! I could have gravely wounded him so you

could slay him."

"And have the outcome of this fight questioned from this day on?" Tye shook his head. "I will win this fight fairly. I will be lord of Wode because 'tis my *right*."

Veronique moved toward her dagger. "After all the years I protected you? Raised you? After Braden risked so much to help me free you from Branton Keep?"

"Braden," de Lanceau echoed, and Aldwin, Edouard, and Dominic exchanged glances. They clearly knew what had happened to the man—and why he hadn't returned to Wode.

"What do you know of Braden?" Veronique demanded.

"We captured him yesterday." When Veronique gasped, de Lanceau added, "Dominic suspected the interrogator had used his influence to free you and Tye from imprisonment. One of Dominic's men-at-arms recognized Braden in a nearby village, and we arrested him."

"I do not believe you!" Veronique sneered.

De Lanceau reached inside his cloak. A gold skull ring flashed in the sunshine: Braden's ring.

"He..." Veronique choked out.

"He died trying to escape last night," de Lanceau said.

Never had Tye seen such a tortured expression on his mother's face. If he didn't know better, he'd swear she had loved Braden. A keening moan broke from her, swiftly replaced by a shriek of fury.

"Braden is dead because of *you*, Tye," she screeched. "You!"

"That is not true, Mother."

"See what kind of man your sire is? You betray *me* this day to save *him*?"

Keeping a watchful eye on his sire, standing silent but poised to fight, Tye said, "Mother—"

"Why should I heed one word you say?" She bent to pick up the dagger. Black ice gleamed amongst the snow by her foot.

"Beware!" Tye cried.

Her hand closed on the knife, just as she slipped. She fought to regain her balance.

Fear wrenched through Tye. His mother was too close to

the battlement's edge. Aye, he was furious with her, but he didn't want her to fall.

His sword raised to fend off an attack, he darted toward her, slipping on a patch of ice concealed by the mottled color of the stone.

Screeching, she grabbed for the closest merlon. Her gnarled fingers caught hold, but her lower body continued to slide. Her heel knocked the stone, she twisted, and then, with a shrill cry, she tumbled through the gap between the merlons.

"*Mother!*"

"God's blood!" De Lanceau muttered.

Tye skidded over to the wall where she'd fallen. On his knees, his breath so tight in his ribs he could barely breathe, he peered over. She clung to the edge of the wall by her left hand, her knuckles as white as bone. She was still clutching the knife, little good 'twould do her now.

"Drop the dagger. Let me help you." Tye couldn't let her fall. She'd never survive.

He was vaguely aware of shouts behind him and others running to the wall walk. His mind numb with horror, he reached down to grab his mother's arm. A memory flashed through his mind, of his sire reaching down to him months ago on another windswept battlement.

His eyes stinging, Tye shoved the memory aside. His fingers closed around her wrist. "Drop the knife," he called down to her. "Grab onto me. I will pull you up."

"You betrayed me." Her eyes, blazing with fury, also glistened with tears.

Tye fought for calm. "Please. I do not want you to fall."

"You chose *him*. You chose your sire over me. How could you?"

"'Tis over, Mother—"

"I should have killed you long ago!"

"*Mother!*" Anguish lanced through Tye, even as the knife in her hand winked with deadly purpose. The blade slashed across her left wrist. Blood spurted. Crimson spattered her luxurious cloak and the wall.

"Oh, God," Claire whispered somewhere behind him.

"Nay," Tye whispered hoarsely.

His mother's red lips parted on a laugh as her head tilted back. He fought to keep hold of her, but the knife flashed again and cut his hand.

At the stinging pain, he instinctively loosened his grip.

Her wrist slipped free of his fingers.

"*Mother!*"

She fell backward into the icy water of the moat. A ragged cry seared Tye's throat as he watched her broken, bleeding body submerge.

Tye straightened away from the wall. His vision blurred. His mind reeled.

Over the eerie whistling of the wind, he heard his sire approaching.

Fight, his senses screamed. *Fight!* Yet, he had no desire to raise his sword.

A solid object slammed into the back of his head.

Chapter Thirty

"Tye!" Claire screamed.

He'd collapsed on the parapet, the right side of his face against the stone, his arms and legs splayed, his cloak tangled beneath him. His sword hit the battlement wall by its leather-wrapped handle and fell onto the snowy drift beside him.

His expression grave, de Lanceau stepped away and lowered his blade that had subdued Tye with one calculated blow.

Edouard brushed past. Cautiously, he knelt beside Tye and put his fingers to the side of his half-brother's neck. "He is still alive."

"As I intended," de Lanceau said. "I want him to answer for his crimes."

As Edouard pushed to his feet and joined his father, leaving Tye where he lay on the wind-scoured stone, despair swirled up inside Claire. Standing against the battlement wall which provided a solid, supporting weight behind her, she pressed a shaking hand to her mouth. Tye had lost the battle. He'd lost his mother, a vile woman, but the only parent he'd known. Soon, he might well lose his life. 'Twould be a tragic end for a man whose gallant heart proved he could have accomplished wondrous things, if only he'd been raised in a life of honor instead of vengeance.

His lordship's steel-gray gaze met hers, then those of the other knights. "Let it be known to all that Tye lost the fight. Wode is once again mine."

Aldwin stepped to the side of the battlement, put his horn to his lips, and blew. At the three crisp notes, clearly a signal for victory among de Lanceau's warriors, cheers rose from the bailey and the grounds surrounding the fortress. Then, obviously seeing an opportunity in the fray, Aldwin primed his crossbow and fired into bailey, before nocking another bolt and firing again.

"Well done," Dominic said, clapping his lordship on the shoulder.

De Lanceau smiled. The two men began talking in hushed tones.

His lordship and his men rejoiced, but Claire's stomach churned with worry and revulsion. Shoving away from the wall, she hurried to Tye, heedless of Edouard trying to intercept her. She dropped to her knees and gently swept back the sweaty, tangled hair that had fallen over Tye's face. His eyes were closed, his jaw slack, his lips parted. His eyelids didn't flicker, nor was there any other sign that he knew she was near.

Was he dead? Had he perished in the moments since Edouard confirmed that he was alive? Nay. *Nay!*

She placed her hand near Tye's nose and mouth. With relief, she found he still breathed.

"Tye," she whispered, stroking his cheek. "Wake. Please."

No faint stirring. Not even the barest trace of a response.

Oh, Tye. I cannot lose you. I will not, because I love you. A sob broke past her lips as she trailed her fingers over his brow and cheek. "Tye," she whispered.

Edouard crouched beside her, his smile kind. "Fret not, milady. Your ordeal is over now. The bastard got what he deserved."

"Did he? Forgive me, milord, but I do not share your hostility toward your brother."

Edouard's eyes widened with surprise. "He took you hostage. I was his prisoner months ago at Waddesford Keep, and I know how you and many others will have suffered at his hand."

Suffered. She forced down frantic laughter. What Tye had done to her, *shown* her, could never be deemed suffering. Far from it. "I assure you, my relationship with Tye was far from unpleasant."

Astonishment now defined the young lord's face. He glanced up at his father, who was still speaking with Dominic, and then back at her. "Well."

Claire almost laughed, except that Tye remained unresponsive on the cold, hard stone. Anger stirred within her that no one—not even his lordship—had bothered to check how badly Tye was hurt.

Rage propelled her to her feet. She met de Lanceau's curious stare.

"I will do as you bade, milord," Dominic said, stepping away. "Aldwin, we are to retrieve Veronique's body and then help secure the bailey."

With a bow to de Lanceau, the blond crossbowman fell into stride alongside Dominic, and the two hurried into the castle.

Claire became excruciatingly aware of his lordship's scrutiny. There was no mistaking that this man was Tye's sire; the resemblance was undeniable. Tye had the same gray eyes. He also clenched his jaw and slightly pursed his lips in exactly the same way.

"I regret Veronique drew you into today's conflict, milady," his lordship said. "Are you all right?"

"Forgive me, milord, but I am not all right. I am far from it."

His lordship's brows rose, a mannerism that again reminded her of Tye.

"With respect, I am worried about Tye. We must get him off this battlement to a place where he will be warm and comfortable. His wound needs to be tended."

"You sound as though you care what happens to him."

"I do."

After a moment, De Lanceau's free hand moved in a silent command, and Edouard once again dropped down beside Tye, parted the hair at the back of his head, and examined the wound.

"Why do you care?" his lordship asked.

Because I love him. Because he has lost all. For those reasons, I will fight for him, fight to be with him, until my very last breath. "He..." She struggled to find the right words. "He proved to me that his life is worth saving."

Still on his knees, Edouard snorted, a sound of utter disbelief.

"Forgive *me*, milady, but I find that hard to believe," de

Lanceau said, frowning down at Tye.

"In his days as lord here, Tye showed me…that there was far more in his heart than a desire to kill and conquer."

Concern shadowed de Lanceau's eyes. "I regret having to ask such an indelicate question of you, milady, especially after all you have endured over the past few days. Yet, as the lord responsible for this keep and all folk within its walls, I must. You seem to hold Tye in high regard—"

"I do."

"Did he…seduce you? Make you—"

"He did not force me or, to my knowledge, any other woman at this keep to couple with him. What I did, what Tye and I shared…was by my own choice." Her face burned. However, she would not dishonor the memories of the pleasures she and Tye had enjoyed by denying the truth.

"God's bones," Edouard muttered.

"Indeed." De Lanceau scratched his jaw with his gloved fingers. He looked uneasy. "If I may be so bold, are you are saying you and Tye lay together?"

Her face must be scarlet, but she clung to her vow not to look away. "In a certain manner, aye."

"A certain manner?" De Lanceau's gaze flickered with understanding. "Ah. Forgive me again, milady, for having to ask such a question. You are still a maiden?"

She nodded. "Veronique drugged both of us and tried to make him…take me, but Tye…resisted. He did not want to ruin me. That, surely, proves he has some honor?"

De Lanceau and Edouard exchanged glances again, while a nervous sweat beaded on her brow. Such discussion was most uncomfortable and unseemly, but she must persevere. No one else would champion Tye.

Edouard pushed to his feet, wiping his bloody fingers on his mantle. "Father, he has a large welt at the back of his skull. However, the injury is not life-threatening."

De Lanceau nodded.

Claire breathed a sigh of relief.

"You continue to think favorably of Tye, Lady Sevalliere," his lordship said. "Are you aware that he killed your betrothed,

Henry?"

"I am. Tye told me what happened that night in the dungeon."

"Really?" Edouard shook his head. "'Twould have been to his advantage, especially if he was trying to seduce you, to keep that a secret."

"He wanted me to know the truth," she said firmly. "He said he did not want to kill Henry, that he tried to render him senseless so he could escape, but Henry...refused to stay down. Henry insisted on being a hero, and forced Tye into a situation in which he had no choice but to kill him."

De Lanceau seemed surprised by what she'd said.

"Why do you look at me that way, milord?" Claire asked.

"Several other prisoners who escaped that night, who were recaptured, gave a similar account. I did not believe them, of course."

Hope warmed Claire, a feeling akin to being caught in a flood of summer sunshine. "Tye's trying not to kill Henry... That proves even further there is honor within him, does it not?"

De Lanceau exhaled a heavy breath. "Milady—"

"Surely, his gallantry is even more remarkable, considering he was raised by a mother who manipulated his every thought and deed. She loved him only for the vengeance he would exact upon you when she believed him ready."

"That much is true." Sadness stole into his lordship's features. He suddenly seemed weary, as if haunted by the past. "How I wish I could have stopped her long ago. Regrettably, I was not able to."

The hope within Claire grew brighter. "Tye became the man he is now because he believed you did not care about him."

De Lanceau growled.

"Please. You must tell him you did care about him. That you still do."

"Milady." His lordship scowled. "He is no chivalrous hero. He is a dangerous, trained killer—"

"So he may be. Does that not describe every knight in this realm?"

"He is also a traitor to the crown."

"Respectfully, milord, so are you, if recent rumors are true. Are you not recruiting fellow lords to your cause: a Great Charter soon to be presented to King John, which will limit the ruling powers of the crown?"

A ruddy flush darkened his lordship's cheekbones. He clearly didn't like to be challenged in such a manner. "We are not discussing my character, but Tye's."

"If I may, I suggest asking other folk around the keep about the days when Tye ruled here. He ensured we were all warm and fed. The wounded were cared for, and he stopped his mother from stabbing Lady Brackendale—"

"That may be so. He still seized this keep, though, and in the past year, committed other crimes. He is also a rogue, an unapologetic seducer of women."

Claire couldn't help but smile. "Were you not a rogue in your younger days, milord? I recall a famous Moydenshire *chanson* that tells how you kidnapped Elizabeth Brackendale and held her for ransom to win back Wode. In doing so, you won both the castle and her love."

A muscle ticked in de Lanceau's cheek. "True, but—"

"*Why* are you so determined to condemn Tye? He *is* your son. He may not have unquestionable proof to offer you, but there can be no doubt, for he looks just like you."

His lordship's gaze flickered, but he said naught.

De Lanceau was as stubborn as Tye! For Tye's sake, though, she had to reach his lordship, to break through the years of enmity between the two men. "Tye also saved you from Veronique's attack earlier," Claire insisted. "Tye risked harm to himself to ensure his mother didn't kill you. He wanted the fight to remain fair."

"He did indeed," Edouard murmured. "'Twas quite unexpected."

"Not unexpected. Not for the Tye I know," Claire said fiercely, holding de Lanceau's gaze. "You cannot deny 'twas a selfless, honorable act. It should at least earn Tye some measure of respect."

His lordship muttered a word under his breath that sounded like "women." He glanced at Edouard, who shrugged.

"You know how much I hate Tye, Father. Yet, in this instance, I have to agree with Claire. He did save your life."

De Lanceau sighed, and his attention shifted to the bailey, where the battle was winding down. "I will consider all that you have said, milady. As you suggested, I will speak with others about the keep. In the meantime, Edouard, take Tye to the dungeon. Once Wode is secured to my satisfaction, I will decide his fate."

Chapter Thirty-One

T ye jerked awake at the slamming of a door. Opening his eyes to shadows, he blinked several times to clear his vision. His mind was sluggish, groggy, as if he surfaced from a deep lake.

Slowly, he became aware that he lay on his right side on a dirt floor that smelled of mold, rot, and blood. *His* blood. He vaguely remembered the stunning blow that had rendered him senseless.

De Lanceau had won the battle.

His sire had reclaimed Wode.

His mother had betrayed and rejected him.

Tye had lost all.

Claire's image drifted into his mind, and his eyes burned as he remembered the last moment he'd seen her on the battlement. He hoped she was all right.

Tye flexed his hands and feet. His injured hand felt stiff; the cut had scabbed over. Metal bit into his wrists and ankles. His boots were gone; his bare feet were so cold he could no longer feel his toes.

Carefully, he flattened his palms to the dirt and pushed himself up to sitting, wincing at the *clank* of the chains attached to iron rings in the stone wall behind him. His head swam.

He stayed motionless until the reeling sensation subsided and then swept aside the hair stuck to his face, so he could see where he was imprisoned. With that simple movement, pain shot through his skull and neck. The agony… He was going to vomit.

Tye heaved in breaths to calm his queasiness. His strength gave out and he slumped back against the wall. His head lolled.

In his quick study of his surroundings, he'd recognized the dungeon at Wode. He must be at the back of the belowground chamber.

Tye swallowed hard, his mouth parched, a foul taste clinging to his tongue. Darkness beckoned him, urged him to close his eyes and succumb to nothingness, but he fought for consciousness with the last tattered threads of his willpower. He *had* to stay awake. There were things he had to say—*must* say— before he died.

He heard men approaching. His sire's lackeys were coming for him. They were going to kill him; of that he had no doubt. He'd lost the crucial fight, lost all that he'd so arrogantly tried to claim. He'd perish this day forced to acknowledge his sire as the victor, with Edouard, Aldwin, and Dominic there to witness his surrender and his slaying.

Why wouldn't his sire kill him? He deserved to die.

Bile rose in Tye's throat again, but he forced it down, determined not to retch in front of the other men. 'Twas senseless, mayhap, to cling to such vanity, especially when he was as good as dead, but he'd prefer to die with some dignity.

He was going to die.

A terrible emptiness filled him, for he had lost far more than he'd won.

The only parent he'd ever known had spurned him and was dead.

His sire had not acknowledged him as his child.

Moreover, the truth was now painfully clear: Tye's whole life had been built upon lies. With his sire's revelations, all Tye believed about his childhood had been shattered, the very foundation of who and what he was broken into inconsequential pieces that would swiftly turn to dust.

How had he been so stupid to believe he deserved acknowledgement from a lord like de Lanceau? Tye was naught. No one would miss him once he'd died, except mayhap Claire.

Tye shut his eyes as Claire's loveliness filled his thoughts: her beautiful smile; the sparkle of her eyes when she knew he was going to kiss her; the shimmer of firelight on her hair. He'd been a fool, an arrogant, selfish *fool*. If only he'd heeded Claire that night in the great hall. She'd tried to make him question what his mother had told him, but he'd been too proud to listen.

Claire. Sweet, precious Claire. My dark soul was seduced by the purity of your light.

How he yearned to sink his hands into her tresses one last time. How he wanted to kiss her, to touch her, to tell her how much she meant to him… But those wishes were no more than fragile dreams now.

As he drew his last breaths, as the world around him faded to eternal blackness, he'd hold her image in his mind. She'd been the best part of his life. He'd leave this earth treasuring all that she'd given him so selflessly.

The *jangle* of keys warned Tye that his sire's men drew near. Soul-deep sadness pressed upon him. He couldn't lift his head. Hell, he didn't want to. When they stopped in front of him, he didn't bother to look up.

"Not so fearsome now, is he?" Edouard said.

"We cannot underestimate him." Aldwin's voice. "Your sire will not be pleased if he tricks us and escapes again."

Edouard laughed roughly. "He'd never get past the guards outside. He will not escape us."

Tye remained still, head down, as a strong hand grabbed his left wrist and the weight of a key brushed against his skin. A *click*, and his left wrist fell free. A moment later, his right one.

"On your feet," Edouard ordered.

Tye struggled to stand. The men grabbed his arms, hauled him up, his toes scraping on the floor before he could maneuver his feet into position. His head careened, and he groaned at the renewed dizziness and pain.

One of them shoved his feet into his boots. Then, the men hauled him along at a brisk pace. He stumbled as he was propelled up the dungeon stairs, into the daylight, and then into the dank, torch lit confines of the forebuilding.

More steps, and he reached the great hall. His weakened body wobbled, but his senses were sharp enough to recognize the scents of dried straw, crushed herbs, and ashy smoke from the freshly stoked fire. His heart twisted in his chest, for there was another note too, the hint of Claire's milk-and-honey fragrance.

Mayhap he only imagined that scent, because he so desperately wanted to see her one final time.

The hall, drenched in sunshine, was silent, but he sensed a number of people watching him. Edouard and Aldwin propelled him forward and shoved him to his knees in front of the dais. He landed hard, his breath expelling on a grunt of agony. He pitched forward, his hair falling over his face, his forehead almost touching the rushes. With his last failing reserves of strength, he forced himself to straighten.

De Lanceau stepped down from the dais, the embroidered hawk on his surcoat glinting in the sunlight. Rushes crunched as he strode toward Tye.

Emptiness welled again inside Tye. For so many years he'd loathed this man he *knew* was his father—all because of his mother's lies.

If Tye's life had been different, he'd have been acknowledged as a de Lanceau—not as a criminal whose death would be reason for his sire to celebrate.

If his life had been different, he'd have been spending the rest of it with Claire, days filled with joy, contentment, and love.

So much love.

He loved her, without question. He loved her fiercely, completely. His life might have been built on bitter lies, but this he knew without the slightest doubt: his love for Claire was true.

"Tye," his sire said, his voice loud in the hall.

"Father," he answered.

"For all those who bear witness here this day, do you understand why you have been brought before me?"

"I besieged Wode," he said quietly. "You won the battle to take it back. Now, I will die."

Silence stretched.

"Capturing Wode is only one of the offenses for which you are condemned. Among the most recent are the siege of Waddesford Keep and the murder of Lord Henry Ridgeway."

The emptiness inside Tye deepened. "I know."

"Do you acknowledge your crimes, this day, before witnesses?"

He would not deny all that he'd done. Here, now, he'd

take responsibility for his miserable life. At least he might die with a shred of honor. "I do acknowledge my crimes," he said.

"Do you acknowledge my right, as lord of Moydenshire, to mete out punishment worthy of the gravity of your crimes?"

He was going to die. Yet, death must be better than living as he did now, with all, including Claire, lost to him. "I do," he answered.

"Is there aught you wish to say, before I deliver your fate?"

Fighting the pain in his skull, Tye raised his head, forced his aching shoulders back. He must say what lay in his heart. In these final moments, he'd try to be the man Claire always claimed was within him. Meeting his father's gaze, he said, "I acknowledge I have committed crimes that are worthy of your punishment. I take full responsibility for what I have done. For all the anguish I have caused, I am..." His voice hitched. "I am sorry."

His sire's brows rose. "Sorry?"

Tye nodded. Tears slid down his face, but he didn't bother to wipe them away. "I wish I could begin again. I wish I could be..." He thought of the way Claire made him feel, and he fought a sob. "True." In his mind, he saw her smiling, and his heart soared with love for her. "Gallant. Honorable. A man worthy of your respect." All that he would never be.

"Bold words." An odd note rang in his sire's voice.

"Do not heed him. He is not repentant," Edouard muttered.

"Quiet," his lordship commanded.

"Father, he is trying to trick you, because he lost the battle."

"No trickery, I swear." What Tye must say—had to say—burned bright and clear in his soul. "Please, tell Claire that I loved her. I ask...for all I have done, I hope you will...forgive me," he whispered.

The silence in the hall seemed to stretch as taut as a hangman's rope.

"What did you say?" his sire demanded.

More firmly, Tye said, "Forgive me. I beg you." He fell back to sit on his heels, his head bowed. It no longer mattered if he was too weak to remain upright; he was going to die. With Claire no longer in his life, it wasn't worth living anyway.

"Beg?" Edouard said. "That does not sound like the Tye I know."

Tye shut his eyes. He prayed his death was swift. Merciful.

The piquant scent of rosemary rose from the floor as his sire took another step toward him. Tye waited for the *rasp* of steel as his sire drew his sword; the whisper of garments as his sire lifted the weapon to bring it slashing down—

A hand settled on Tye's shoulder. "Those words," de Lanceau said quietly, "are what I would expect from my son."

Tye froze. He mustn't have heard correctly. Slowly, his mind spinning, he forced his head up.

His sire's damp gaze burned with emotion. His face held the same expression as when he'd tried to save Tye from falling from Waddesford Keep's battlement months ago.

"*Son?*" Tye rasped. Confusion whipped through him, chased by the tiniest, thinnest glimmer of hope.

His sire nodded. A faint smile ticked up his mouth. "'Tis only right that I finally accept you are my flesh and blood."

Tye gasped. *Son. Ah, God.* He wanted to speak, to honor this incredible gift from his sire, but words failed him.

"Claire gave me a full account of what happened before our battle," his sire went on. "She showed me her journal documenting the siege and the days following. She was most insistent that I understand how nobly you had acted toward her and others here, despite your mother's interference. The other folk I spoke to confirmed what she told me." His lordship's gaze narrowed. "Tye, are you willing to swear an oath to me this day, pledging your allegiance to me, vowing to obey me without question for the rest of your living days?"

Shock pounded through Tye. 'Twas a generous offer, far more than he deserved. "I am."

"Good."

He was indeed willing to take the vow, but there was no point if he was going to be slain. "Am I...to be killed?"

"Not this day."

Relief raced through him, so intense, he almost fainted.

"Claire," Tye choked out. He *had* to see her. "Please. Is she——?"

His sire stepped away and motioned to someone behind Tye. "Let her in."

Tye heard the *creak* of a door, followed by running footsteps.

"Tye," Claire sobbed. "Oh, Tye." She dropped to her knees, her gown spreading across the rushes. Catching his face in her hands, she kissed him over and over while she wept. He laughed against her mouth, slid his arms around her, and buried his face in her neck, as he, too, sobbed.

"Well," Dominic murmured from close by. "'Tis not what I expected to happen this day."

"Nor I," Edouard muttered.

"Nor I," Aldwin said with a smile.

His face wet with tears, Tye looked up at his sire. "Thank you." Joy filled the empty void within him. He'd been given a second chance; he wouldn't waste a single moment. "I promise, Father, with my very soul, I——"

"Indeed, you will," his sire said. "There is still a great deal for us to discuss and resolve. The coming days will not be easy. Now, though, you will say the oath pledging allegiance to me in front of these witnesses. Then we will tend to your head wound, before you collapse on the hall floor."

Chapter Thirty-Two

S eated at the lord's table on the raised dais, finishing her meal of vegetable pottage, sharp white cheese, and grain bread, Claire couldn't help but smile, for the hall was *alive* again. It hadn't felt this way for many, many days, even before Tye's conquest.

Candles flickered on the rows of trestle tables filling the hall and cast the faces of the castle folk in a wash of gold while they ate. Reed torches burned in the brackets along the walls, chasing away the shadows lingering at the timber beams overhead. Knights, seated together at the tables close to the dais, laughed and jested as they discussed the day's battle and de Lanceau's victory. By the hearth, two men plucked their lutes. The vibrant melody wove into the swell of sound, while behind them, a great blaze burned in the hearth.

Mary was seated to Claire's right. Light from the nearby centerpiece of beeswax candles made Mary's blue silk gown shimmer. "Does the hall not look beautiful tonight?" she said with a happy sigh.

"It certainly does," Claire agreed.

"The pottage is much tastier than usual, too," Mary added with a grin, "no doubt because his lordship is dining here this eve."

Claire could easily imagine the red-faced cook flying about the kitchen, shouting for more chopped vegetables and throwing handfuls of spices and dried herbs into the bubbling cauldron to get the pottage into a fit state to serve to Moydenshire's great lord and his men.

As she sipped her wine, Claire felt some of the tension of the day slip away. Not all of it, though. There were still matters left

301

unresolved, including what would happen to her and Tye now that he'd yielded to his sire. She hadn't been able to speak to him after the reconciliation in the hall, for de Lanceau had taken him away to have his wounds treated. Then, according to what Claire and Mary had gleaned from the servants, his lordship and Tye had talked for most of the afternoon, while Dominic, Aldwin, and Edouard completed other assigned duties. How she wished she knew what Tye and his lordship had discussed.

Setting down her goblet, she glanced to her left, where Lady Brackendale was having a lively discussion with Lord de Lanceau and Dominic. Rings once again gleamed on Lady Brackendale's fingers, and Claire smiled, glad to see that Tye had returned what he'd confiscated from her ladyship, as he'd returned what he'd taken from Claire.

Her attention slid to the table directly below the dais, where he sat between Aldwin and Edouard. Several more of de Lanceau's trusted men were seated there as well, keeping watch on him. Tye's head injury must be paining him. Yet, in his posture, the proud tilt of his head, she sensed resilience. Admiration warmed her, for while de Lanceau's men were clearly reluctant to accept him among their ranks, he was determined to endure. And she knew he was doing it, in part, for her.

As he spooned pottage into his mouth, he glanced up at her, and their gazes locked. He smiled, and she smiled back, so very grateful that he was alive and that he'd reconciled with his sire. He and his father still had years of enmity to overcome, years of Veronique's manipulations to undo, but they would, one day at a time. Together.

Lady Brackendale set down her goblet with a sigh and dabbed her lips with a linen napkin.

"You are well, milady?" Claire asked.

"Very well, now that Tye no longer rules my keep." Her cheeks were flushed, and her eyes sparkled. "'Tis a tremendous honor to have Lord de Lanceau back in my hall, eating at my table." Leaning closer, she whispered, "He is such an intelligent, handsome man."

Claire smothered a laugh.

"How pleased dear Arthur would be, too, to see this castle

returned to the way it should be."

"A place free of mercenaries," Mary added with a shudder. "I heard that those who survived the battle are chained in the dungeon, until his lordship can take them away for punishment."

"I am relieved we are finally free of Veronique," her ladyship said with a disdainful sniff. "Falling from the battlements is a terrible way to die, but I am not sorry she is gone."

Regret tugged at Claire as her focus again shifted to Tye. She couldn't imagine the anguish of being rejected by one's own mother and then watching her die. Claire hadn't witnessed her parents' deaths, but she had some idea what Tye was feeling now. She'd do all she could to support him, help him as he grieved.

"'Twill be interesting to see what happens with his lordship and the son he has just acknowledged," her ladyship murmured.

Claire sipped more wine.

"I am also most curious as to what will become of you and Tye," Lady Brackendale added with a meaningful smile.

The wine stuck halfway down Claire's throat. With those few words, Claire sensed her ladyship had been very well informed of all that had transpired during the days following the siege. Blushing, Claire forced herself to swallow and then coughed into her hand, while Mary giggled and patted her on the back.

"Whatever comes to pass between Claire and Tye," Mary said, "their romance will be recorded in the account of the conquest."

"Oh, God," Claire spluttered.

"We *do* have an obligation to finish our account," Mary added, "and not just for our own satisfaction. We must consider folk of de Lanceau ancestry who are born years from now, who want to know the details of this castle's vivid history."

"You are right." Sighing, Claire toyed with a piece of cheese. "Even I do not know how my relationship with Tye will turn out. His life has changed. He will have other commitments and greater opportunities. As a de Lanceau, he can have any woman he wants."

Mary tsked. "Claire, do not be so dramatic."

"I am only speaking the truth."

Mary rolled her eyes and then glanced past Claire. "Tye is rising from the table."

Goose bumps raced down Claire's arms. 'Twas ridiculous to feel so anxious, but a lot had changed for all of them this day.

Tye walked to the dais and stepped up onto the platform to stand before his father. He bowed. Silence settled across the hall.

"Milord," Tye said, his tone perfectly polite.

"Aye?" his sire asked.

"With your permission, I would like to speak with Lady Sevalliere. In private."

His lordship's gaze slid to Claire. A secretive grin touched his lips before he said, "Of course."

Claire's pulse fluttered. She rose a little too quickly, almost knocking over her wine.

De Lanceau waved Tye on. Tye strode down the front of the table, nodding respectfully to Lady Brackendale as he passed, then matched Claire's pace, until they both reached the end of the table. He took her arm and helped her step down from the dais.

The chatter and music resumed, but Claire sensed many folk watching them, including Edouard, who walked several paces behind; he was obviously following Tye.

"My father's orders, I am afraid," Tye said close to her ear as he led her to the stairs up to the landing. "Edouard is to be my shadow until Father is sure he can trust me."

Claire squeezed Tye's arm. "Edouard will not be your shadow for long, then."

"Why him, though?" Tye scowled as they climbed the stairs. "Why not Dominic or Aldwin?"

"Edouard is part of your new family. You will have plenty of opportunity to get to know him well."

"If we do not end up killing each other first," Tye muttered.

Claire managed a mock frown. "That would be very silly of both of you."

Mischief gleamed in Tye's eyes. "You must keep me on the path of virtue then, Kitten. If I spend my days with you, I will not be tempted to fight with my brother."

She leaned in close, savoring the familiar, earthy scent of Tye. "You might be tempted to do something else?" she asked. She was being very coy, but with Tye, such lively banter felt right.

"Most certainly, I would be tempted." Tye's lustful wink sent delicious, hot-cold sparks dancing through her. On the keep's upper level, he paused outside her chamber door. "Fetch your cloak. I do not want you to catch a chill."

Once she'd donned her cloak, Tye took her through more smoke-hazed passageways and up to the battlement, shadowed in twilight. A short distance down the parapet, he'd been defeated by his sire. His mother had perished there, too. Claire ached at the thought that he'd returned to the place that held such anguish for him.

"Why here?" Claire asked softly.

Tye halted and took both of her hands in his. The feel of his rough, warm skin sent heat spiraling into her lower belly. "Here," he said softly, "is where I finally understood what I'd truly wanted—what I'd been searching for—all of my life."

Behind Tye, Edouard leaned against a merlon and gazed down into the bailey lit by torches. He was far enough away to give them some measure of privacy, although the breeze no doubt carried their conversation to him.

Meeting Tye's solemn gaze, Claire asked, "What were you searching for?"

"Not vengeance," he said earnestly, "not riches or power." He gently pressed her hands. "You."

Claire sucked in a breath. "Me?"

"Aye. The days I spent with you... They made me feel complete. *Wanted*. I never again wish to feel as I did before I met you. I do not want to be that man anymore."

Tears brimmed in Claire's eyes.

"I love you, Claire."

"I love you too, Tye," she whispered. "More and more each day."

He smiled, as though her words meant a great deal to him. Then, despite the cold breeze, he dropped to one knee on the stone and took her right hand in his.

"Tye—"

"Will you marry me, Claire?"

A sob broke past her lips.

"I have no castle or fortune to offer you. I do not even have a betrothal ring yet. However, when my sire and I spoke today, and I told him my intentions toward you, he said to ask you anyway."

"Tye—"

"Please. I want you to have a ring you love. I want you to choose it and every time you look upon it, to feel joy. And I am not asking you to wed me just because we…lay together. I know I am not the perfect man, not a fine and noble lord. Yet, I promise here and now, I will provide for you and, God willing, our children. I will be a devoted husband. I will be all you want me to be—"

With her free hand, she touched his cheek, coaxing him to tilt up his face. "Tye," she said gently.

His eyes filled with the agony of awaiting her answer.

"I will be honored to marry you."

Tye shot to his feet. "Truly?"

"Truly." Before he could say another word, she threw herself into his arms, kissing him deeply, showing him how much love and happiness brimmed inside her.

With a groan, Tye kissed her back. His arms closed around her, holding her tightly against him.

A chuckle came from behind them. "Well," Edouard said. "This day just gets more and more interesting."

After slowing the kiss, Tye lifted his mouth from Claire's. "Edouard, do you have to interrupt while we are kissing?"

"When you are kissing a beautiful woman and I am missing my wife back home?" Edouard groused. "Aye, I do."

Claire laughed.

Grinning down at her, Tye said, "Shall we go and tell the others the good news, Kitten?"

"I think 'tis a splendid idea."

Epilogue

Branton Keep, Moydenshire, England
Early April, 1215

Sunshine glinted off the chain mail armor of the scores of knights gathered in Branton Keep's bailey. A sense of excitement carried through the throng as the men tied weapons and saddle bags to their bridled horses and readied to ride to London at Geoffrey de Lanceau's command.

"Where are you, Tye?" Shading her eyes with her hand, Claire searched for him in the crowd. A little over a week after de Lanceau had retaken Wode, she and Tye had married on the portico of the small church near Branton Keep, on a mild day at the beginning of February. Branton Keep's bailey had been just as crowded then. Lady Elizabeth, Lord de Lanceau's wife, had invited many influential guests; some, including Aunt Malvina and Johanna, accompanied by Delwyn, had traveled for leagues to attend the ceremony and the lavish feast afterward at the castle.

Claire smiled at the memory, for it had been a grand celebration, a day she'd never forget. Afterward, she and Tye had continued to live with the de Lanceaus while he'd worked alongside his sire every day to build the trust and loyalty between them that both men clearly wanted. Mary still lived with Lady Brackendale, but visited often. Patch, who'd moved with Claire and Tye to Branton Keep, slept on their bed every night and had grown very attached to Tye.

Soon, Claire, Tye, and Patch would be moving into their new home: a riverside castle with rich lands his lordship had granted to Tye just last week. How proud Tye had been, that his sire entrusted him with an estate. She was incredibly proud of Tye, too, for he was indeed a changed man from the one who'd besieged Wode months ago.

Today, though, Tye would leave with his father and army as Lord de Lanceau journeyed toward London, gathering support from noblemen along the route who hadn't yet committed to the Great Charter, the Magna Carta, that was now in the hands of King John. The King had promised to give an answer to the proposed charter on the twenty-sixth day of April, but de Lanceau had received word from his peers that the sovereign was planning to reject it—a refusal his lordship wasn't willing to accept.

Months ago, in great detail, Tye had divulged how he and Veronique had spied on de Lanceau in a clandestine agreement with the King. De Lanceau had gathered proof that the sovereign had acted upon that information to subvert progress on the Great Charter, and planned to use what he'd discovered to persuade the King to ratify the document.

An anxious sigh broke past Claire's lips, for she *must* find Tye. While her husband had promised to stay goodbye, she couldn't wait a moment longer to tell him what she'd intended to say earlier that morning; however, he'd risen and left their chamber early, likely to help his father with final preparations. Mary, who was visiting for a sennight, had been the first one to hear Claire's news. They'd clung to each other and wept.

As tall as he was, Tye was usually easy to spot. The scents of sun-warmed stone and horses reached her as Claire rose on tiptoes and strained to see as the crowd parted.

"Mayhap he is in the stables?" Mary said, standing beside Claire.

Claire squinted against the bright sunshine. "Mayhap. Or… Wait. There he is, to the right of that wagon. He is talking with his father. Lady Elizabeth, Aldwin, Edouard, and Dominic are there too."

She made her way toward the group, Mary close behind. Tye still wore his hair long and tied back with a strip of leather, and he was still not entirely comfortable around his brother, but in other ways he'd changed so much since she'd first met him that fateful, snowy January day. He'd kept his promise to live an honorable life. She had no doubt he'd continue to do so.

As though sensing her approach, he glanced in her direction and found her in the crowd. He grinned.

Tye spoke to his father and then wove through the throng to reach her.

"Kitten." He kissed her cheek. "You are well this day?"

"Very well."

Mary smothered a giggle behind her hand.

Tye looked at Mary, then back at Claire. "Why do I see mischief in Mary's eyes?"

Claire laughed, such excitement bubbling up within her, she could barely contain it. "Mary knows my secret. 'Tis one I must share with you before you ride away."

"A secret?" Tye winked. "I am intrigued."

"Good, because I cannot keep the news to myself any longer."

"News? What kind of news?" His gaze skimmed over her, while concern touched his features. "Are you all right, Kitten? Is something wrong?"

Mary giggled again.

Not saying a word, Claire reached out, caught Tye's hand, and placed his palm on the gentle curve of her belly.

His widening gaze locked with hers. "You are with child?" he whispered.

"Aye," Claire murmured.

Tye pulled her into his arms and kissed her, thoroughly, splendidly. "God's bones," he said, drawing back to arm's length. Joy and awe shone in his eyes. "I am to be a father."

"I am very happy for you both," Mary said.

Tye swallowed hard. "Whether 'tis a son or a daughter, this child will be greatly loved, each and every day."

"It will," Claire agreed, touching his cheek. "Of that I have no doubt."

Tye kissed her again, and joy filled Claire's heart and soul, for she knew, right here and now, she'd never been more content.

Never had she been more grateful for Tye, her husband, her gallant hero.

Dance of Desire

By Catherine Kean

She risked everything in one seductive dance . . .

Disguised as a veiled courtesan, Lady Rexana Villeaux dances for Fane Linford, the new High Sheriff of Warringham. Desperate to distract him while her servant steals the missive that condemns her brother as a traitor to the Crown, she entices Fane with all the passion in her soul--and he is tempted.

A hero of the crusades, Fane has been granted an English bride by the king. Fane wants only one woman: the exquisite dancer. When he discovers she's actually a highborn lady, and that her rebellious brother is imprisoned in his dungeon, he will have no other wife but her.

Rexana doesn't want to become the sheriff's bride, but it may be the only way to save her brother. Yet as she learns more about her brooding husband tormented by barbaric secrets, she finds it harder and harder to deny his love or their dance of desire.

ISBN-10: 1479342890
ISBN-13: 978-1479342891

Also available in eBook.

My Lady's Treasure

By Catherine Kean

The moment widowed Lady Faye Rivellaux sees the tall, commanding warrior riding toward her, she senses the danger in him— a powerful sensuality that she has never experienced before, especially not in her marriage bed. Fighting her unexpected desire, she clings to her promise to rescue the kidnapped child she loves as her own. When he demands a ransom she cannot meet, she offers her one last hope: a gold cup.

Former crusading knight Brant Meslarches never expected the widow he was ordered to meet to be a tempting beauty. Nor did he expect to see such a chalice. Worth a small fortune, it's proof that a lost treasure of the legendary Celtic King Arthur does exist—as Brant's murdered brother believed. Of all things, the lady has offered Brant the one means to redeem his terrible past.

He makes her a deal: he will help her find the little girl, if she will help him locate the treasure. Faye is uneasy about an alliance with the handsome, scarred rogue, especially when he stirs up strong yearnings within her. Yet, she has no other way to find the child. Risking all, Faye joins Brant's quest, and as the passion they've both denied flares between them, they find a treasure worth more than gold.

ISBN-10: 1479389412
ISBN-13: 978-1479389414

Also available in eBook.

About Catherine Kean

Award-winning author Catherine Kean's love of history began with visits to England during summer vacations, when she was in her early teens. Her British father took her to crumbling medieval castles, dusty museums filled with fascinating artifacts, and historic churches, and her love of the awe-inspiring past stuck with her as she completed a B.A. (Double Major, First Class) in English and History. She went on to complete a year-long Post Graduate course with Sotheby's auctioneers in London, England, and worked for several years in Canada as an antiques and fine art appraiser.

After she married a tall, handsome, and charming Brit and moved to Florida, she started writing novels, her lifelong dream. She wrote her first medieval romance, *A Knight's Vengeance*, while her baby daughter was napping. Catherine's books were originally published in paperback and several were released in Czech, German, and Thai foreign editions. She has won numerous awards for her stories, including the Gayle Wilson Award of Excellence. Her novels also finaled in the Next Generation Indie Book Awards and the National Readers' Choice Awards.

When not working on her next book, Catherine enjoys cooking, baking, browsing antique shops, shopping with her daughter, and gardening. She lives in Florida with her husband, teenage daughter, and two spoiled rescue cats.

www.catherinekean.com

Made in the USA
Charleston, SC
03 July 2015